Annette Broadrick
weaves indelible stories that resonate with heart and
passion. A bestselling author of over forty books, Annette's
heroes and heroines spring to life on every page.
Enter the world of the *Daughters of Texas* and
laugh, hope and fall in love right along with them!

MEGAN'S MARRIAGE
Heartbreaker Travis Kane needs reluctant Megan O'Brien to
be his partner so he can save his ranch. The hitch: Megan
has to say, "I do"! Question is—just how long will it take
this "business-only" marriage to turn into a lifetime love
affair?

INSTANT MOMMY
Widowed rancher Deke Crandall knew horses and cattle—
and not one whit about newborn baby girls. But Deke
desperately needed a mother for his daughter, so
Mollie O'Brien accepted his "convenient" proposal. After
all, for years Mollie had secretly loved Deke from afar....

THE GROOM, I PRESUME?
Maribeth O'Brien had everything a bride-to-be could want—
except the runaway groom. Until best man Chris Cochran
stepped up and volunteered for the job. Was Maribeth crazy
to say yes to his sudden proposal? Or was she ready to fall in
love with the *real* husband of her heart?

ANNETTE BROADRICK

believes in romance and the magic of life. Since 1984, when her first book was published, Annette has shared her view of life and love with readers all over the world. In addition to being nominated by *Romantic Times Magazine* as one of the Best New Authors of that year, she has also won the *Romantic Times Magazine* Reviewers' Choice Award for Best in its Series for *Heat of the Night, Mystery Lover* and *Irresistible;* the *Romantic Times Magazine* W.I.S.H. award for her heroes in *Strange Enchantment, Marriage Texas Style!* and *Impromptu Bride;* and the *Romantic Times Magazine* Lifetime Achievement Awards for Series Romance and Series Romantic Fantasy.

ANNETTE BROADRICK

DAUGHTERS OF TEXAS

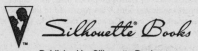

Silhouette Books

Published by Silhouette Books
America's Publisher of Contemporary Romance

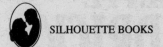 SILHOUETTE BOOKS

ISBN 0-373-20170-2

by Request

DAUGHTERS OF TEXAS

Copyright © 2000 by Harlequin Books S.A.

The publisher acknowledges the copyright holder
of the individual works as follows:

MEGAN'S MARRIAGE
Copyright © 1996 by Annette Broadrick

INSTANT MOMMY
Copyright © 1996 by Annette Broadrick

THE GROOM, I PRESUME?
Copyright © 1996 by Annette Broadrick

Visit us at www.romance.net

Printed in U.S.A.

CONTENTS

Dear Reader,

Once upon a time on a ranch in the hill country of Texas there lived the three O'Brien sisters—Mary Margaret, Mary Katherine and Mary Elizabeth, also known as Megan, Mollie and Maribeth.

Orphaned when the oldest was still a teenager, the young girls formed a deep family bond that would see them through the darkest times.

Megan, being the oldest, fights to preserve their legacy— the O'Brien Ranch—despite numerous financial setbacks.

Mollie is the natural homemaker of the trio. She loves nothing better than baking, sewing and caring for the household and her sisters.

Maribeth is the tomboy of the trio, who spends most of her time with her two best friends, Bobby—whom she vows to marry when she grows up—and Chris, their best friend.

Life is never predictable and takes many twists and turns unplanned by the O'Brien sisters. Nevertheless, each of them finds her heart's desire, sometimes in the most unexpected ways.

I hope you enjoy getting to know these three daughters of Texas.

Sincerely,

Annette Broadrick

MEGAN'S MARRIAGE

One

"**W**hat in the hell do you think you're doing?"

The sudden sound of a voice when she thought she was alone startled Megan O'Brien, causing her to sway. She grabbed the wooden frame of the windmill she was repairing to regain her balance before she looked down the fifty feet or so to the ground.

A late model pickup truck sat several hundred feet away. The relentless wind bringing spring to the central hills of Texas must have muffled the sound of the engine. Otherwise, Megan would have had some warning that she was no longer alone on that part of the family ranch.

However, no warning could have effectively prepared her for the sudden sight of the man standing directly below her, his Stetson shoved to the back of his head, his hands braced against his slim hips.

Travis Kane was the last person she wanted to find glaring up at her while she clung precariously to the outdated relic that provided water—*when* it worked— to the cattle pastured on this section of the Circle B Ranch.

She stared at him with a sense of dread and frustrated dismay, wondering what Travis Kane was doing on the ranch. What could he possibly want with her?

"You got something against living to see your next birthday, woman?"

Anger at his high-handed, arrogant and demanding attitude shot through her. Who did he think he was, anyway, criticizing her, yelling at her? She rested her forehead against a crossbar, fighting to control the strong surge of emotion.

What more could happen for her to have to deal with? She sighed in disgust. For the past several weeks she'd been battling first one calamity, then another. She felt like a punch-drunk fighter, reeling from one disaster to another, unable to successfully cope with any of them.

The frozen gears of the windmill had been one more thing that had to be faced. When she'd discovered there was no water in the holding tank, she'd wondered just how many more things could happen. Well, now she knew. Travis Kane could show up.

Megan couldn't think of anyone she'd less rather see than the neighbor who'd spent most of their lives delighting in making *her* life miserable. Well, he didn't need to worry. Trying to run the ranch on her own had certainly added to her woes over the years, all without his help. She didn't need any more aggravations, thank you very much.

She glanced back at the rusted gears. The piece was shot—past being repaired. Somehow, she'd have to scrape up the money to buy a replacement part. The cattle had to have water out there, no question about it.

With a shrug at the silent question of where she might find some spare change for the part, she gave up her task for the moment. Concentrating on her footing, Megan began the long climb down the side of the wooden structure to the man whom she'd thought a scourge during her childhood.

"Couldn't you find an easier way to kill yourself than breaking your blasted neck?" he growled near her ear once she was within range. He wrapped his hands around her waist and swung her to the ground.

As soon as her booted feet touched the ground, she pulled away and turned to face him. From this position, she had to look up at the tall, dark-haired male who had spent their childhood causing her nothing but grief and frustration. She'd known him all her life—twenty-four years. Their families operated neighboring ranches.

The unexpected presence of Travis Kane was all she needed to complete a perfectly rotten day, that capped off a worse month and an abysmal year. She hadn't seen him in over two years. *Twenty* years would have been even better.

"What are you doing here? What do you want?" she asked, lifting her straw hat from her head and running her fingers through her short blond hair.

Although it was only April, the hot Texas sun was already causing her to perspire, despite the brisk breeze. She could feel a trickle of moisture slide down the valley between her small breasts.

Megan resettled her hat and watched him through narrowed eyes, waiting for some answers. She didn't have any time to waste on the man.

Despite his obvious irritation, Travis responded with a reluctant lopsided smile and shook his head. He tilted his hat forward so that it now sat low on his forehead, drawing her reluctant attention to his unforgettable eyes. They shone from beneath the shadowed brim with a resilient and mocking good humor, their deep purplish blue color reminiscent of the bluebonnets that covered Texas during a moist spring. Unfortunately Texas hadn't seen enough moisture in much too long.

"Well, howdy to you, too, sweetheart," he drawled, eyeing her grimy coveralls and worn shirt with the torn-out sleeves. "It plumb touches my heart to witness your excitement and enthusiasm at seein' me after all this time." He leaned against the windmill and propped a booted foot against one of the upright supports. "Can't you drum up a little neighborly affection for an ol' friend, honey?"

Megan peeled off her work gloves and shoved them into a back pocket of her coveralls. "You always were a pain in the posterior, Kane. I can't see where much has changed since the last time I saw you."

He gave her a level-eyed stare, his smile fading. "You know, I thought you had more sense than to clamber around like that out here by yourself. If you were to slip and fall nobody would know about it.''

She turned away from him and started toward Daisy, who she'd left nibbling on a patch of sun-dried grass.

''You don't need to concern yourself about me.'' When she saw that he was following her, she added, ''If I were you, I'd worry about my own neck. I hear you're still working the rodeo circuit. Not exactly a safe occupation to have.''

''Those are calculated risks, Megan, whereas what you do is—'' He waved his hand, as though at a loss to understand her.

She gathered up her horse's reins. ''Look, Kane. I don't have the time or the energy to chat. I've got work to do.''

''Damn it, Megan. I'm trying to talk some sense into your head. Will you listen?''

''I don't have time for you, Kane,'' she muttered.

He grasped her arm and turned her so that she was facing him. ''You never do. As far back as I can remember you've brushed me off, treated me like I'm invisible. Well, fine, maybe I was a pest when we were kids. I'll give you that. I used to enjoy getting a reaction from you. You always were fun to tease.'' He waved his hand at the windmill. ''But this is serious stuff, Megan. You have no business being out here by yourself, risking your neck that way. If nobody else will tell you, then I certainly will!''

His eyes glittered with suppressed feeling.

Megan glanced away from him before saying, ''I'm deeply touched by your concern for my safety. Thank you for your no doubt well-meant advice on how I manage the ranch, Kane. I'll be sure to file it along with other words of wisdom that have come my way over the years.''

She spun away from his grip and vaulted up in the saddle.

"Hold on for a minute, will ya?" he said, laying his hand across both of hers where they held the reins. "Don't be in such a hurry. I came lookin' for you because there's something I want to talk to you about."

Enough was enough! She didn't like to be man-handled and this was the third time he'd touched her since he'd shown up, uninvited, for this little social call.

She glared at his hand and fastidiously lifted it away from hers as though it were a snake. "Really? Well, I do appreciate the effort you've made to in-dulge in a neighborly visit, but I'm afraid I'm busy. Sorry, Travis. Maybe some other time," she added, thinking about the possibility of hell freezing over.

"What's wrong with the windmill?" he asked, ig-noring everything she'd just said to him. He'd stuck his thumbs into the back pockets of his snug-fitting jeans, nodding over his shoulder.

She didn't have to follow his gaze. "It's worn-out, like everything else on the place. I'm going to have to order a new part."

"Why didn't you have Butch check it for you? Isn't that why you have a hired man, to do some of the more physical work around here?"

Megan wanted to scream at him, but she didn't.

She held on to her temper, which wasn't easy, but she had learned long ago that losing her temper gave the other person the edge. She needed all the advantages possible around Travis. He had an unerring ability to get under her skin.

In a carefully even tone, she said, "It's not your business, but I'll tell you anyway. I was up there because the ranch is my responsibility. If there are any risks to be taken, I'll take them. Besides, Butch is too old to be climbing around up there."

Travis returned his gaze to her. "Better not let Butch hear you say that. He doesn't think there's anything he can't do."

Megan knew that he was right. Butch was one tough bird. "Maybe so, but I happen to know that his rheumatism has been acting up. He has no business taking chances."

"Neither do you."

So, they were back to that. She turned Daisy's head and started back down the track toward the barn. "Somebody has to do it."

"Damn it, Megan, will you wait up for a moment? I'm serious. I want to talk—"

She pulled on the reins. "You? Serious? Don't make me laugh. You've never been serious about anything a day in your life."

She gave her horse a nudge in her ribs and leaned forward, a signal that she was ready to move. Daisy, like the sweetly trained animal she was, responded beautifully, leaving Travis behind in a cloud of dust.

It was all Megan could do not to laugh out loud,

especially after she heard his muttered remarks between the sounds of his coughing.

However, the urge to laugh was quickly gone.
There was no reason to be taking her bad mood out
on Travis, despite her dislike of him. It wasn't his
fault that she felt like such a failure.

She couldn't shake the sense of impending doom
that was with her from the time she opened her eyes
each morning until she fell asleep exhausted each
night.

Whether she liked it or not, she and her sisters were
going to lose the ranch. It was only a matter of a few
weeks now before the mortgage was due. Despite all
her efforts, she would have to tell the bank manager
that she couldn't make this year's payment. The
O'Briens of Agua Verde County, Texas, were going
to lose the Circle B after the ranch had been in the
family for four generations.

Megan had been in charge of the place for the past
eight years. She'd done everything she could to pull
them through this bad patch, but it was more than a
patch. For the past three years everything had been
going from bad to worse.

She'd done everything she could, but it wasn't
enough. It was never enough.

Butch was waiting for her when she arrived at the
barn. "Did your company find ya?" he asked when
she got off the horse. "I wasn't sure what to tell him
other than you'd taken off to the hills somewhere.
Where ya been?"

"Yeah, he found me. I was checking the southeast
pasture and discovered there was no water in the

holding tank. The windmill's frozen up. There's no way to fix it without ordering a new part for it.''

"You want me to crawl up there and check it out, just in case something can be done?"

She shook her head. "I already did. The whole thing is worn-out. I need to replace the entire rig, but I can't. A new part will get us through the worst of the heat. Maybe by fall I can—'' She stopped because there was no use talking about the fall. By then, the ranch would no longer be theirs...unless she could somehow produce a miracle.

A sense of futility swept over her.

They both turned at the sound of an engine and watched as a late-model pickup with Travis behind the wheel appeared. He made a sweeping turn and stopped in front of the house.

"Somebody mentioned to me yesterday that Travis was back in town for a few days," Butch said, rolling a handmade cigarette. "It kinda surprised me when he showed up, asking for you. I didn't think the two of you were exactly on good speaking terms.''

She turned away from the house and led Daisy into the barn. Butch followed her, placing the newly formed cigarette behind his ear. "We're not," she said, leading Daisy into her stall, "but you know how Travis is. He just naturally thinks he's God's gift to us all and that we should feel honored that he decides to visit.''

Butch uncinched the saddle and lifted it off the horse while Megan wiped her down. "So what did he want?''

She shrugged without looking around. "He said he

wanted to talk to me about something. I can't imagine what.''

"Maybe he got wind of the trouble you've been having. You reckon he might want to buy this place from you?''

She poured some grain into the feed trough of the stall. "He's not that stupid. Why would he want a place like this? He's never home. Besides, the Kanes already own a large portion of the county. Why would Travis take on another spread?''

"'Cause his pappy's young enough and healthy enough to be running their place for a long time, yet. Travis never was one to want to answer to anybody, not even his dad.'' Butch grinned at the thought. "Most especially his dad, if you want to know the truth.'' He stepped out of the stall and held the door open for her.

She motioned to the nearly empty feed storage bin as they retraced their steps to the barn door. "Did you remember to pick up the grain at the feed store today?'' she asked, ignoring the fact that Travis now was leaning against the front fender of his pickup truck, watching, and making no effort to join them.

Butch took his time lighting his cigarette, then he removed his hat and carefully smoothed down his sparse and receding hair before replacing his battered hat. "Yeah, I got the feed. It's still in the back end of my truck. Ol' man Brogan said that unless you pay something on the account, he can't give you any more credit after this.'' He recited the message without inflection, studying the horizon.

"So what else is new?''

"It isn't just you, you've got to know that. Everybody in the county's been hit hard by this drought. It's been rough. They're all having to supplement the feed to keep the stock fed."

"I know."

"Ranching's never been a way to get rich, missy. It's a hard life."

"You aren't telling me anything I don't already know, Butch." Megan rubbed the back of her neck. "However, the ranch is my life. It's the only one I know. It's Mollie's and Maribeth's home."

He awkwardly patted her shoulder. "You've done a fine job, missy. A fine job. You took on way too much responsibility trying to look after the girls and run this place all by yourself, but you showed everybody you could do it. Don't feel bad if you have to give up now."

She stiffened at the mention of her sisters. "We've done just fine so far on our own. You just said it's nobody's fault the drought's lasted so long. Well, it isn't my fault that all our equipment seems to be breaking down at once, or that the blasted well for the house ran dry last month and we had to drill another one."

"I never said it was anybody's fault. Don't start gettin' so prickly. All I'm sayin' is that a young gal like you shouldn't have to be shoulderin' such a heavy burden. You should be out enjoying life with friends of your own."

She gave an unladylike snort. "My friends are mostly married and busy raising families. At least

Mollie and Maribeth are old enough to look after themselves.''

He nodded toward Travis. ''So when are you goin' over to find out why he's hanging around here? He don't look like he's plannin' on going anywhere anytime soon, so ignorin' him isn't going to help ya none.''

Once again she looked over to where Travis waited—his long legs crossed at the ankles, his arms folded across his chest—still leaning against his truck.

She glanced to the west before she spoke again. ''I don't suppose this day could get any worse than it already has. I'll go see what it's going to take to get rid of him.''

''I wish I had the money you needed. I'd sure give it to you if I did have it,'' Butch said in a gruff voice.

She patted his arm and smiled. ''I know, Butch.''

''I watched you girls grow up. I seen every one of you in diapers, following your folks around, playing with one another. Rory and June were always so proud of their girls. They wanted the very best for you. Always.''

''I know. Sometimes life just works out different from what we plan...what we want.'' Straightening her shoulders, Megan turned away from Butch and headed toward the house, where Travis stood waiting.

Megan was aware of Travis watching her as she crossed between the barn and the house. She was well aware of what he saw—a skinny blond with a mop haircut, a plain face with a mouth too wide and, from the feel of it, a glowing, sunburned nose covered with a smattering of freckles.

Her coveralls were old, faded and wearing thin in some places, while her work boots were too scuffed to be able to tell their original color.

A regular fashion plate, that's what she was. She was also exhausted and totally out of sorts.

"So what are you hanging around for?" she demanded as she approached him. "What do you want?"

He slowly straightened in his lazy, loose-limbed way. "I told you. I want to talk to you."

She fought to control her impatience. She couldn't think of anything that this man could say to her that she would want to hear, unless he planned to announce that he was moving away from Agua Verde County and determined never to return.

Megan came to a stop a couple of feet in front of him and folded her arms across her chest. "What about?"

He glanced toward the house. "Couldn't we go inside and talk? This may take a while."

She didn't want to invite him inside. She didn't want Travis Kane anywhere around her, the house, or the ranch. Unfortunately, at the moment, she couldn't think of a single reason he would accept for asking him to leave.

There was no help for it. She'd just have to put up with him and the uncomfortable, itchy way she always felt whenever she had to be around him.

Megan stepped around him and led the way up the steps to the wide porch that led into the kitchen. "C'mon in. Mollie's probably got some tea made."

She walked into the large room that was the heart

of the house. The kitchen doubled for the family conference room, the homework room, the problem-solving room, or for whatever reason the three O'Brien sisters needed to gain help and support from each other.

The place looked worn and frayed, now that she was looking at it through the eyes of a visitor. Any spare cash she managed to accumulate went back into the running of the ranch, unless it provided necessities for a sixteen-and eighteen-year-old to finish their high school educations.

She found the pitcher of tea, filled two glasses full of ice, poured the tea, then set the glasses on the round table situated in the middle of the room.

Megan waited until Travis sat down before she picked a chair across the table from him and carefully lowered herself. Lordy, Lordy, but she was tired. Not only was she not sleeping well at night, but she was also pushing herself harder with each passing day as though through sheer force of will she could turn the ranch's fortunes around.

Her body ached with every movement. She longed for a long soak in the tub and promised herself that particular reward for tonight in exchange for having to deal with Travis now.

Travis Kane had always caused problems in her life since she was a kid riding on the school bus. Why should anything be different now?

"So when did you get into town?" she asked, not really caring, but determined to curb her impatience and make a stab at being polite.

"Wednesday night."

"Mmm," she responded as noncommittally as possible. She picked up her glass and took a long, refreshing swallow of iced tea.

Travis waited until she looked at him before he leaned forward, his weight on his forearms resting on the table, and said, "I happened to run into Maribeth at the post office this morning."

She eyed him for a moment, waiting for him to continue. When he didn't, she prompted him with, "Did you?"

"She said y'all are having some problems."

She made a mental note to have a long discussion with her youngest sister about not discussing private family matters with outsiders. Striving for nonchalance, Megan shrugged and studied the ice cubes floating in the amber liquid. "No more than anyone else around these parts. Looks like the drought's about to do the whole county in."

Megan made herself look at Travis, only then noticing that he'd removed his hat. Up close, his unusual eyes were even more noticeable, if possible, what with the stark contrast between their bright color and his tanned face.

"Megan—" he began, then paused, as though searching for words.

Megan knew that Travis had always had a way with words, so his hesitation surprised her. "What?" she finally asked.

"Maribeth says that since the new management took over at the bank, you don't think they're going to be willing to work with you on the mortgage payments anymore."

She could feel her jaw tighten at more evidence of her sister's loose-lipped ways. She took another drink of her tea before responding. "Maribeth has a big mouth," she finally muttered through clenched teeth.

He placed his glass between his palms and rotated it around and around in a circle. "Megan, I know you have no use for me. I'm not certain why, exactly. I mean, I know I used to give you a bad time when we were kids, but that was all part of growing up. I never meant anything bad by my teasing. I always thought of us as friends, even if we haven't seen much of each other in the past few years. I always thought that, if you ever needed anything, you'd know that I'd help you out in any way I could."

She shot out of her chair, knocking it over on the floor. "Is that why you're here? You think we're some kind of neighborhood charity case? Is that it? Well, you couldn't be—"

"Whoa, whoa, whoa!" he said, coming to his feet, his hands held out in front of him. "Damn, woman, do you have to go off like that over every little thing? What's the matter with you, anyway? Why would you take offense at an honest offer of help?"

She could feel her face flaming, which didn't help her temper in the slightest. "We don't need your help. We're doing just fine," she muttered, picking up her chair and replacing it on its legs. She sank into the chair and grabbed her glass with both hands.

"C'mon, Megan, it's me you're talking to. Needing help isn't anything to be ashamed of. We all need help at one time or the other."

She looked up at him and knew she was making a

complete fool of herself. Why didn't that surprise her? She had never learned to act naturally around this man, not even when they were kids. "I'm sorry," she muttered. "I'm just tired, that's all. I didn't mean to take it out on you."

He sat down once again. "I know this is a tough time for you. I think you've done a hell of a job holding this family together. I just want you to know that I'm here to help you, if you'll let me. I've got money just sitting in the bank, drawing interest. I figure you could use it to help get over this bump in the road. Let's face it, we're bound to get some rain sometime. Cattle prices will be coming up. I figure you could be using the money since I don't need it right away."

Megan couldn't sit there any longer, facing him. She got up from the table and walked over to the counter, her back to him. Never had her temper made her so ashamed. It didn't matter what Travis had done in the past, or how uncomfortable she felt around him. He had driven all the way out here to offer her a helping hand. And what had she done? Ignored him, left him standing in her dust, been rude and unsociable for no good reason.

It wasn't his fault that his good looks had seemed to make his life so much easier, that his irresistible grin had made all the girls carry on about him in school, or that she had received a great deal of teasing because they lived near each other.

It wasn't his fault that she didn't like him.

She picked up the iced tea pitcher and brought it back to the table, filling both their glasses. "I'm sorry for being so rude," she said, sitting down again. "It's really very kind of you to offer to help." Megan couldn't make herself look into those eyes. Hadn't they haunted enough of her dreams over the years without her being confronted with them now?

Travis leaned back in his chair and smiled at her in silent acknowledgment. "Dad tells me this new bank management team seems to be more concerned about their asset and liability reports than they are about the welfare of the people in the county. So you may be right about them," he said.

"Can you blame them? With some of the banks in the state going under, it's no wonder they're concerned."

"Have you spoken to them at all?"

She nodded.

"Did you offer to make interest only payments?"

"They aren't willing to do anything but accept full payment of all money due or to foreclose. Those are my options."

He muttered something under his breath that she couldn't understand, which was probably just as well.

Megan straightened in her chair. "Why do you care?" she finally voiced the nagging question that had been gnawing at her throughout the conversation. "Travis, you know as well as I do that we aren't friends. We've never been friends. It seems to me you probably expected me to fail. You never had a very good opinion of me, either, as I recall."

He rubbed his jaw. "I guess you're right. As far back as I can remember you've treated me like some piece of trash that was cluttering up your immediate area. I should be gloating about now that the high-and-mighty princess is taking a nosedive.''

''Exactly.''

They looked at each other for a long time without speaking. After several minutes of silence, Travis sighed. ''I guess I deserved your haughty treatment, though, didn't I? I used to treat you pretty badly—pulling your hair, grabbing your books, making fun of your friends....''

''You made it clear what you thought of me, that's for sure.''

''Would it help to remind you that I've grown up a little since then?''

He gave her that heart-melting smile of his that had gotten him out of all kinds of trouble as a kid.

''No,'' she said baldly.

''Oh.'' He looked around the kitchen before meeting her steady gaze. ''The thing is, I was really shaken when Maribeth told me what was happening with y'all. I'd lost touch with you since high school. I mean, all that stuff I did to you was years ago. I've been on the road for the past eight years.''

She knew that. He'd been two years ahead of her in school. She'd been sixteen the year he graduated. He'd been president of the student body, captain of the football team, homecoming king. By the time he'd graduated, he'd been driving to school for two years. So they were talking about behavior of more than ten years ago...almost half a lifetime.

''Will you let me help you, Megan? Please? Then I'll know you've forgiven me for all that childish stuff I used to pull. I can't stand by and watch you lose this place, not when I could help you. Surely you can understand that.''

She couldn't believe she was having this conversation. Especially with Travis Kane, of all people. Of course she wasn't going to accept his offer, but the very fact that he'd made it blew her away.

Her silence seemed to spur him on. ''You've done a hell of a job, Megan...keeping everything going. You were just a kid when you took over here. The girls were still in grade school back then, weren't they?''

''Yes.'' She looked away, absently drawing designs in the moisture collecting on her glass.

''When is the mortgage due?''

She glanced back at him, grateful that he had changed the subject. ''The first.''

''It's paid annually?''

''Yeah.''

''It's no time to try to sell stock.''

''Not at the current prices. Who knows if they're ever coming up. Nobody seems to be eating beef these days, according to present market indicators. I've been hanging on, hoping the drop is only temporary. If I sold at today's prices I'd lose everything I've invested in this herd.''

''So will you let me loan you the money?''

''I appreciate the offer, Travis. I mean that. It was kind of you to hang around today when I was being so—rude. But, in the long run, borrowing the money from you isn't going to help. I would just owe another debt I couldn't pay.'' She rubbed her forehead where a headache was forming. ''I've thought and thought about it. There's just no way out of it, no reason to prolong any of this.'' She forced herself to smile. ''You know, it's kinda funny when you think about it. Paddy O'Brien won this place in a card game more than a hundred years ago, closer to a hundred thirty-five.'' She wondered if he knew that. ''My illustrious ancestor was a riverboat gambler at the time. Didn't know a thing about ranching.''

He didn't seem particularly surprised, but then few families in the county had histories that weren't known by all their neighbors.

''You've always been a gambler, too, Megan,'' Travis said in a tone more gentle than she'd ever heard from him. ''Don't forget that. You're a fighter. A survivor. You never give up.''

An unexpected lump formed in her throat. ''Is that how you see me?''

''Of course. Why are you so surprised?''

''I always thought—'' She decided not to tell him what she'd thought his opinion of her was. ''Never mind. It doesn't matter.''

He hitched his chair closer to the table and leaned toward her. ''Look, if you don't want to owe me money, then I have a suggestion on how you could buy yourself some time—so that you could pay this year's mortgage payment, wait on the market to sell your cattle, maybe investigate other stock you might choose to bring in. It would give you some breathing room.''

She eyed him warily. ''What do you suggest I do, win the lottery?''

''Nope. Marry me.''

Two

Megan realized that her jaw must have dropped because she suddenly became aware of the fact that her mouth was dry. She groped for the glass in front of her, draining it while her thoughts raced around in her head like a rioting crowd of protesters.

Travis Kane was suggesting that she marry him? *Travis Kane?* How could he be sitting there watching her so calmly?

"Marry you?" she finally repeated weakly.

"I know you think I'm crazy," he replied hurriedly, as though afraid she was going to demand that he leave, "but listen to me for a minute. Just hear me out. It won't be considered a loan that way. I'll be making an investment that may or may not work out, but whatever happens, you'll have the money you need, plus some left over. You'll have enough to repair that blasted windmill and whatever else's broken down. You'll have the money to hire extra help, which I'm sure you could use. We'll treat it like a business arrangement, like a partnership contract, or something. We'll set a time limit—say one year. Twelve months. At the end of that time we'll review the situation, decide if we want to continue the partnership. If we don't, well—who knows what will have happened by then?'' He flashed that smile of his and she could feel herself succumbing. ''I mean, the drought can't last forever. Things are bound to pick up and you won't have to be worried all the time about—''

''What's in all of this for you?''

He'd been talking rapidly but he stopped at her question as though a hand had been clamped over his mouth. He swallowed, eyeing her cautiously. ''For me?'' he repeated, as though puzzled by the question.

''Uh-huh. Why are you willing to be so generous? If you want the ranch, why don't you just make me an offer on the place and we can talk about it?''

''Megan, there's no way you'd ever sell this place and we both know it. This is your home. I don't want it. Ranching doesn't fit in with my life-style. You know that. Besides, if you sold the place, where would you and the girls live?''

She couldn't believe she was sitting there at the kitchen table having this conversation, and with Travis Kane, of all people. ''If we were to sell the ranch, we would have the money to move anywhere. If the bank forecloses, I'm not sure where we'll go,'' she admitted. "But we'd find a place somewhere. We certainly wouldn't starve."

"This way you could stay here and still have the money you need to make repairs and—"

"You didn't answer my question. Why would you make such an offer? What do you expect to get out of this?"

The look he gave her was definitely wary. "A wife?" he offered a little hesitantly.

"C'mon, Travis. The last thing you could possibly want is to get married. You need a wife like you need another hole in your head. And even if you've suddenly decided that marriage appeals to you, you certainly don't want to be married to me, of all people!"

He fidgeted. There was no other word for it. He pulled his earlobe, scratched his nose, fussed with his collar, then shoved his hair off his forehead. Finally he muttered, "Don't underestimate yourself, Megan."

Seeing his nervousness gave her some comfort, but not much. "Are you saying you're in love with me?"

He straightened in his chair. "Umm—well, would you believe me if I told you I was?"

"Absolutely not," she immediately responded.

He flexed his shoulders in another restless movement. "Then I'm not in love with you."

She gave him an approving nod. "Well, at least you're being honest."

He cleared his throat and took a long drink from his glass without meeting her gaze.

She studied him for several minutes in silence. "You can't be serious," she finally said.

"I am," he argued. "Try me."

"Try you?" she repeated suspiciously. "Would you care to explain what you mean by that remark?"

"It's just a figure of speech and you know it. I'm willing to prove to you that I'm serious, that I'm making an offer in good faith. I want to help you. That's what friends are for—to help each other."

"You make it sound like some kind of a game!" She leaned back in her chair and deliberately deepened her voice. "Hey, there's not much going on in my life these days. Maybe I should get married!" In her normal voice she added, "Life is always a joke to you. Admit it!"

"Well, what about you? You always look at life so blasted seriously all the time. Can't you lighten up a little, once in a while, have some fun?"

"Of course you would see things that way. Life's always been easy for you. You've never had to be responsible about anything or for anyone. You've never been serious about anything in your entire life."

"A few things," he murmured.

"Such as?"

"I've taken my rodeoing serious. I've won some good prize money. I take that serious enough. It's the money I'm willing to offer to you, money that I've worked hard to earn. You don't hear me joking about that, do you?"

Grudgingly she said, "Okay, I'll go along with that one."

"I take my friendships seriously, as well. I know I haven't been home much these past few years but whenever I'm in town, I've always made a point of checking on you, to make sure you and the girls were okay. As I recall, a couple of years ago I actually asked you to go to the movies with me. As also I recall, you were quick enough about turning me down.''

''Going to a movie would have meant an hour's drive to the next town.''

''Is that why you turned me down?''

She stared at him. ''I get up early. I can't stay out late at night. I didn't figure you meant it, anyway. You were just trying to get a reaction out of me, like always. You've always been the biggest tease I've ever known, Travis, bar none.''

''You don't date at all, do you?''

She looked down at her shirt and coveralls, then at him. ''Of course I do. Why, I've got men lined up outside the door, impatiently waiting their turn to take me out. A stunning creature like me has to fight 'em off.''

Travis frowned. ''Don't, Megan.''

''Don't what?''

''Don't make fun of yourself that way. You're a very attractive woman. Just as important, you're a very warm and loving woman, protective of your family, willing to do whatever it takes to keep everyone safe.''

She narrowed her eyes and peered at him. ''Did you by any chance get kicked in the head by one of those bulls you ride or something, Travis? I can't believe what I'm hearing coming out of your mouth. Are you sure you don't have me confused with someone else?''

"What I think is that we haven't spent much time together in the past several years and that there's a lot you don't know about me. Obviously what you do know doesn't impress you much. So how about giving me a chance to prove to you that I can make a good husband?"

A shiver ran over her at the word *husband*. Travis Kane? She would have to be out of her mind to consider marrying *him*, of all people. For any reason.

Even if it means saving the ranch? a little voice whispered inside her head.

For the first time in her life she finally understood what the preacher was talking about when he chose the subject of temptation for his Sunday sermons.

Temptation was a mighty insidious thing. It teased and tantalized, making all her beliefs dance and jump around, stand on tiptoe and fall over.

Travis Kane had been a pest as a kid, and his constant need to tease her had come close to breaking her heart in high school. Of course he'd never known the crush she'd developed on him back then. She had no intention of ever letting him know.

What would the star-struck girl back then have done if she'd known that someday in the future the ever-popular Travis Kane would actually come to her and propose marriage.

As a friend.

He didn't love her, of course. Hadn't he just said so?

But then, she didn't love him, either. She knew better.

So. It would be a business deal, that's all. It would have an expiration date.

"A year, you said?"

"It can be longer, if you want."

"Oh, no. A year would be fine. It would give me some breathing space, like you said. I'd have some time to make plans, decide whether I should try to sell the place. After that, I could—" She paused, her thoughts finally leading her to ask, "I, uh—I guess you'd expect to live here, then?" She laughed nervously and answered her own question. "Well, of course you would. We'd be married and it would look strange to everybody if you continued to live at home with your folks." She knew she sounded rattled because she was. This was the most bizarre thing that had ever happened to her. Even more bizarre was the fact that she was actually considering accepting his outlandish offer...because the alternative was too painful for her to face. She'd been praying for a miracle, hadn't she? She just hadn't realized before God's strange sense of humor.

"I'm not home all that much, anyway, Megan," Travis was saying, quietly. "I'm still following the rodeo circuit."

"Oh, that's right!" she replied, unable to hide her obvious relief. "Well, that would work out okay." She went on, hopping up from the table. She began to pace. "I mean, we've got plenty of room," she said with an expansive wave of her arm. "Why, this old house rambles in all directions. There's several bedrooms..." She came to an abrupt halt, her voice trailing off. She eyed him uncertainly. "Would you expect to share my room?"

He took a deep breath and held it, his gaze never leaving hers. When he finally exhaled, he gave her a lopsided smile. "Whatever you're comfortable with, Megan."

"Oh." She thought about the idea of sharing a bedroom with Travis Kane and shivered. "Well, I'm certainly not comfortable with the thought of sharing my room with you...or anybody...really."

"I see."

She began to pace once again. "Well, I mean, the whole idea takes some getting used to, you've got to admit. I never expected to get married so I've never given it much thought."

"Why?"

She'd reached the window and was looking outside, wondering when the girls would be getting back from town, wondering how she could possibly explain to them what she was thinking about doing. She whirled around to face him, vaguely recalling his question. "Why what?" she repeated. "Why give it much thought? Because I've had other more important things to think about."

Travis stretched his long legs out straight, then tipped his chair back and crossed his ankles. "No, I want to know why you never thought you'd get married."

She threw her arms wide and grinned. "Who would be interested in marrying somebody like me who's trying to keep a run-down ranch going as well as raise a couple of sisters? Nobody in his right mind is going to be interested in getting involved in a situation like that.'' She eyed him speculatively.

"I am," he said mildly.

She continued to study him. Had she found the fly in this particular ointment? Had he fallen off a bull onto his head one too many times and scattered his brain cells? He appeared rational enough, but his suggestion had all the earmarks of a crazy man. However, he'd been smart enough to place a time condition on the agreement. She smiled at him as she reminded him. "Yes, but only for a year. Believe me, after a year you'll be more than ready to get away from this place." She nodded, seeing more and more advantages to his wild suggestion. "By that time Mollie will have graduated from high school. Who knows? Maybe both of them will want to move into town. Or maybe to Austin or San Antonio."

Suddenly feeling more lighthearted than she'd felt in weeks—no, more like months—Megan realized that she was starved. She went over to the refrigerator and opened the door. "Speaking of the girls, both of them stayed in town last night with friends. I don't know when they'll get home tonight, but I don't intend to hold supper for them. I'm hungry." She peered over her shoulder at him. "Do you want to stay and eat with me?"

He smiled and in a gentle voice, said, "I'd like that, Megan."

She began to rummage around inside the refrigerator. "It won't be anything fancy. Mollie's the real cook around here. I just throw together some of the basics and—"

She straightened and backed away from the refrigerator with her hands full, then turned to find Travis immediately behind her. He took the dishes out of her hands and placed them on the nearby counter, then reached behind her and closed the refrigerator door.

"I think we should seal the bargain, don't you?" he murmured, trapping her between him and the refrigerator.

Megan couldn't remember ever having been caught so off guard. Before she could think, his lips were pressing against hers. A bolt of electrical shock went through her. Travis was kissing her. Travis Kane. Kissing her. Her...Megan O'Brien...tomboy...the girl who...

Her thoughts scattered as her senses took over. She became aware of the woodsy scent of his after-shave, the minty flavor of his mouth, the muscled wall of his chest as it pressed against hers, his uneven breathing as he tilted his head to another angle, teasing her with his tongue. Her eyes drifted closed, savoring all the new and glorious sensations that were sweeping over her.

She'd never been kissed by a man before, a man whose hands were tracing her spine, shaping her buttocks and pulling her closer so that she could feel— could feel...

Megan's eyes flew open and she gave him a sudden shove. Caught off guard, he took a couple of quick steps back before regaining his balance.

They stared at each other, both of them breathing unevenly. Her heart felt as though it were going to leap out of her chest.

"It was just a kiss, Megan. That's all," he said quietly.

"Yeah, and Carlsbad Caverns is just a hole in the ground. That's all," she said, mimicking him.

"That's true," he replied, smiling.

She spun away and began to busy herself with making some sandwiches, doing her best to forget how she'd felt when Travis kissed her.

"I take it you don't want me to kiss you," he finally said in the silence that stretched between them.

She bit down on her lower lip, knowing that she couldn't lie to him, but not knowing exactly what the truth was. Continuing to keep busy with their meal, she said, "It isn't that. I— It's just that— I mean, I don't have a lot of experience in these things, and..." She couldn't think of how to continue.

He kept his distance from her when he said, "And you think that I mind? Just because you're innocent doesn't mean—"

She turned and glared at him. "I'm not innocent!" She closed her eyes and swallowed. Now she was *really* giving him the wrong idea about her! She opened her eyes and tried again. "I mean— What I *meant* was that anyone raised on a ranch knows all about reproduction and sex and— Well, you know what I mean. It's just that—" She waved her hand helplessly, not knowing how to explain how confused she was feeling at the moment.

He watched her intently. "Yeah, you've told me. You haven't done much dating. I understand."

She turned back to the counter, picked up the plate of sandwiches she'd prepared and carried it to the table. After refilling their glasses she motioned for him to sit down. "I don't know what you expect from me, that's all," she finally muttered, sitting down across from him and looking everywhere but at him.

He reached for a sandwich and put it on his plate. "I don't expect anything you don't want to give," he said in a careful tone of voice. "I realize that what I'm suggesting isn't the usual way of doing things."

"It's crazy, that's what it is. Who's going to believe it? It doesn't make any sense. I can't believe I'm actually considering it!" She took a big bite out of her sandwich, concentrating on eating and trying to distance herself from the familiar stranger across the table from her. How could she know somebody so well and yet not know him at all? How could she hate him—well, resent him anyway—for not noticing her when he was the big man on campus and she had so wanted him to see her as a young woman, and not the tomboy he'd pestered on the bus for years. She'd been invisible to him then. So why now? Why was this happening all these years later?

"I have a suggestion," he said, after finishing one of the sandwiches and reaching for another.

"What?" she asked suspiciously.

"I think we should keep the arrangement we've made just between the two of us. I think we'll both be more comfortable that way. Why don't we tell our families that we suddenly discovered our true feelings for each other and—"

"Nobody's going to believe that! Everybody knows that I— That is, that we—uh—"

"Yes?"

"What I mean is, we've never even been seen together."

"So maybe I've been writing you."

"The girls know better."

"Maybe I finally got up the nerve to confront you and admit how I feel about you."

She covered her mouth and began to laugh, shaking her head. "Oh, no. The girls would see right through that!"

"Not if you helped me."

"How?"

He watched her, his distinctive eyes glowing. "By pretending a little that you care for me, that we both want this."

"Your folks will—"

"I'll take care of my folks. You don't need to worry about them."

"Oh." She looked at the forgotten sandwich on her plate. She realized that although her stomach had been growling she was no longer hungry.

"When do you want to get married?"

She jerked her head up. "I—uh—"

"If you want to wait a while and let everyone get used to the idea, that's fine with me. An engagement would look more normal, anyway."

"You wouldn't mind?"

"I want you to be comfortable with the idea."

Her thoughts raced in all directions at once. "Well, if I'm going to make the mortgage payment on time—"

"You don't have to marry me before you get the money. I'll write you a check tonight that should cover it, plus whatever else you're going to need for a while.''

"But I don't want you to think—''

"Don't worry about my thoughts, okay? Or my feelings. This is a straightforward business deal. I'm going to be going back out on the circuit next week and will be gone several weeks.'' He paused, thinking. "Maybe we should announce our engagement now. I'll get you a ring to wear, and we can start to plan the wedding. I assume you want to be married in the church.''

"The church?'' she squeaked. "But isn't that—I mean, for a business arrangement isn't that being a little—'' She waved her hand helplessly.

"It's going to be a real marriage, Megan. Don't you think it needs to start out in the church?''

This must be the way Alice felt when she fell down the rabbit hole. "But knowing it's only going to be for a year makes it seem like a sham, somehow. I mean, if everybody's there to see us get married, aren't they going to wonder later why we decide to part?''

He washed the last bite of his third sandwich down with a long swallow of tea before replying. "In the first place, it's none of their business. In the second place, the way things are these days, more marriages than not end up that way.''

She thought about that for a moment. "I suppose,'' she acknowledged.

"This way you'll have time to find a dress and decide what your sisters will wear.''

All of this was coming too fast and furious for her.

Her head was swimming. "A dress! Travis, I haven't worn a dress since my high school graduation!"

He grinned. "Well, maybe you can make an exception this one time. Of course if you feel more comfortable wearing your boots beneath it, go ahead."

Megan forced herself to eat her sandwich while Travis chatted on as though he planned weddings on a regular basis and there wasn't anything difficult about it. When she finished eating, he helped her clean up their dishes.

"Do you want me to be here when you tell the girls?" he asked, folding the dish towel he'd used and carefully hanging it on the rack.

"Uh, no," she said quickly, jolted by the mere thought. "No, I can tell them. I've just got to decide how to bring it up."

He folded his arms across his chest and leaned against the kitchen counter. "We could go to town tomorrow and look at rings."

She hid her hands behind her back. "Do you really think that's necessary?"

"Rings?" he asked, lifting his brow slightly. "Yes, I do."

"I mean, if we go into Agua Verde to look for rings, everybody in town will know about it within the hour."

He grinned, reminding her of the mischievous boy he'd once been. Not a good omen at all, in her mind. "Well, that's one way of getting the news out."

She dropped her gaze to the floor, feeling horribly out of her element. She had no problem discussing anything at all about the ranch or the girls, but rings?

Weddings? Marriage? She'd never given them a thought.

"Or…we could drive into Austin, if you like. We could make a day of it, maybe see a show. You know, make an occasion of it. Surely you can stay out late for one night."

She looked up and caught his intent gaze. "Why are you doing this, Travis? I don't understand. Why are you willing to tie yourself up in such a fashion? Surely you've met women during your travels that—"

"None that I'd marry."

"But still—"

"I always intended to marry a hometown girl, didn't you know?" he said, grinning once again.

"Then why didn't you marry Carrie Schwarz? You dated her most of your senior year."

He looked startled. "Carrie? Isn't she married?"

"She is now, but she waited for you for years."

He laughed. "I doubt that."

"No. She did. She went away to college, but came home as often as she could, hoping to find you here. She found out during the Christmas holidays that first year that you were seeing Trish Kronig whenever you were in town."

"You sure have a memory for names. I'd forgotten both of those girls."

She walked back to the window and looked outside. It was dark. The yard light near the barn gave off a faint glow. "I'm sure they haven't forgotten you," she said quietly, reminding herself how easily a heart could be broken. Hadn't she congratulated herself for not being pretty enough to get his attention back then? Hadn't she considered herself lucky that she'd never gone through what those girls had? Where was her sane, sensible self *now,* when she really needed her?

He picked up his hat. "All that was years ago, Megan. I was just a kid back then."

She turned to face him. "But now you're all grown-up, huh?"

He flashed his devastating smile, his eyes sparkling. "God! I hope so, since I'm making plans to get married and settle down."

"But you aren't giving up the rodeo," she said pointedly.

"Well, no, not yet. I only have a few years to ride. The rodeo makes an old man out of you real quick."

"Or kills you."

He settled his hat on his head. "Not me. I'm too mean and too tough to die." He opened the screen door and stepped out onto the porch. "I'll pick you up right after lunch tomorrow, if that's okay with you?"

She paused for a moment. Now was the time to back out, if she was going to. Unfortunately she had a sinking feeling in her stomach that she was actually going to go through with this completely insane idea. Her options were limited. She'd prayed for a way to save the ranch and she'd been given one. The irony of her situation flooded over her.

She crossed her arms, hugging them against her. "All right, Travis. I'll be ready," she finally replied, silently acknowledging to herself that in all of her life she'd never made such a frightening decision. She and the girls wouldn't lose the ranch, but marrying Travis Kane could end up costing her even more than her home in the long run.

Keeping her distance from him had protected her as a young girl. What could she use as protection now?

Three

Megan took a long, soaking bath after Travis left, trying to come to terms with what she had agreed to do. Eventually she got out and dried off, putting on her faded nightshirt and worn bathrobe, but she was too restless to go to sleep. Instead she curled up on the couch to watch television and wait for the girls to come home.

She was still on the couch, dozing, when she heard the family pickup truck coming up the lane. The thing rattled and roared, sounding more like a threshing machine than a vehicle for transportation.

She'd let Mollie take it into town last night, since both Mollie and Maribeth had wanted to spend the night with friends. They never complained about living twenty-five miles from town, but were always eager to go into town to visit their friends, or hang out at the local hamburger haven.

The girls didn't complain about anything. She'd fought so hard to keep them when the county officials first suggested they might be placed in foster homes. She'd insisted that she could look after them and that with Butch's help she could also run the ranch. After all, she'd been following her daddy around that ranch from the time she could walk. He'd have her sitting in the saddle in front of him on the back of his favorite mount or riding next to him in that old pickup.

She should have been a boy, but her dad never seemed to mind that he had girls. She remembered how he used to laugh when the other ranchers in the coffee shop would mention his harem.

There were times, like today, when the ache of missing her mom and dad was so painful she thought she might die from it. Maybe according to the calendar she was twenty-four years old, but she didn't feel as if she'd ever gotten past sixteen when it came to knowing about men and how to socialize. In a few short hours her youthful teenage years had abruptly ended with the news that both parents had been killed in a fiery car crash outside of Fort Worth. Practically overnight she'd had to become both mom and dad to Mollie and Maribeth, as well as in charge of the Circle B Ranch. She'd had to become an adult in order to deal with all the officials who'd tried to separate the three of them. She'd fought hard to keep them all together—and she'd won. Tonight she'd made another decision to ensure her sisters' continued well-being. Her peace of mind was a very small sacrifice to make to protect them.

The kitchen screen door squeaked as one of the girls opened it. Megan could hear Maribeth chattering away. She smiled. Maribeth was such a live wire. Whatever thought crossed her mind popped out of her mouth. She seemed to run through life with her arms flung open wide, ready to embrace the world and everything in it.

She wore her bright red hair streaming over her shoulders and down her back, pulled away from her face by a large hair clip. Her wide brown eyes were her most expressive feature, mirroring her every thought.

Maribeth had been eight when their parents had died.

Although Mollie was two years older than Maribeth, Megan thought of Mollie as being almost as old as she was. Maybe it was because she was the quiet one in the family. She'd always been close to Mama. After Mama died, Mollie seemed to become less talkative than ever.

She was good in the house, keeping the place clean, cooking their meals while she still kept up her schoolwork.

Mollie was so bright. She deserved the chance to go on to college. Megan had tried so hard to put money away for Mollie's education but there had never been enough to stretch. Mollie would be graduating from high school in a few short weeks. She'd already found a job clerking in one of the stores in town, but Mollie deserved so much more in life.

She was the real beauty in the family, with her creamy white skin and dark, auburn hair. Her eyes looked too blue to be real, as if she wore tinted contacts. She never seemed to be aware of her looks and was the only one in town who was surprised when she'd been named homecoming queen the previous fall.

"Hi, Megan!" Maribeth said, bouncing into the room. "What are you doing up? You're usually sacked out in bed by this time of night." Maribeth threw herself into the big overstuffed chair across from Megan.

Megan made a face and grinned. "You make me sound like an ol' grandma. I've been known to stay up past nine o'clock on occasions."

Mollie paused in the doorway. "You want something to drink? I bought a six-pack of soda."

She glanced around, still smiling. "Mmm. Sounds good."

"You'll never guess who I saw in town today!" Maribeth announced dramatically, her eyes wide.

"Probably not," Megan drawled. "So why don't you tell me?"

"Travis Kane! I couldn't believe it. Me and Bobby and Chris went to the post office for Bobby's mom, and who should be walking out of the post office but Travis Kane, himself. You should have seen Bobby! He's always dreamed of being able to ride wild bulls as well as Travis, not to mention his skill with calf roping. He was practically stuttering when Travis spoke to us."

Mollie walked back in with three large glasses

filled with ice cubes and soda. She offered one to Megan, who took one, then Mollie handed another to Maribeth.

"I know. Travis came out here today."

Mollie looked around at her in surprise. "Travis Kane came out here? What in the world for?"

Instead of answering her, Megan looked at Maribeth. "Just what did you tell Travis about us, Maribeth?"

At least her youngest sister had the decency to blush. "Well, nothing, really. He was just asking about you and all and I told him— Well, I guess I may have mentioned that you were making yourself sick worrying about us maybe going to lose the ranch."

Mollie sank down at the other end of the couch and stared at Maribeth. "Maribeth! You didn't! You can't go around telling everybody our business like that!"

"I wasn't. Everybody already knows everything about us, anyway. It's no secret that we're probably going to lose the ranch. So what's the big deal?"

Mollie shook her head in disgust. "Well, you don't go around blabbing everything you know," she replied.

Megan dropped her head back against the couch. "Oh, yes she does!" she said with a sigh.

"Well, he was asking about you and I was just trying to be polite and—"

"More than likely, you were trying to hold his attention just a little longer," Mollie said. "You and Bobby would be charter members of his fan club if he had one."

Maribeth swung her legs over the side of the chair. "Hey! That's a great idea. Maybe we can start—"

"I was just joking," Mollie said hastily. "Travis Kane certainly doesn't need a fan club! His ego's already big enough as it is."

"You can say that again," Megan muttered.

Maribeth stuck her bottom lip out. "I don't know why y'all have to be so hateful about Travis. What has he ever done to make you both sneer at him so much?"

Megan shifted, pulling her knees up and resting her chin on them. She wasn't comfortable with the turn in the conversation but she couldn't think of any way to change the subject that wouldn't be too obvious.

She was surprised when Mollie answered. She had seldom heard Mollie so vocal. "Because he thinks he's God's gift to women, that's why. Always swaggering around in those tight jeans he wears, with his hat brim pulled down low over those fancy mirror sunglasses of his, giving all the girls that drop-dead gorgeous smile so they'll swoon at his feet. I think he's perfectly disgusting."

Megan's heart seemed to sink in her chest. "I had no idea you disliked him so," Megan said quietly.

Mollie glanced around at her in surprise. "Well, you've never had much good to say about him, yourself! I remember when you were both in school, you used to come home complaining about him and calling him all kinds of names. Mama used to laugh at how mad you got at him, remember?"

"I was just a kid. He used to delight in teasing me on the school bus to and from school. Since it was almost an hour to get to town, he had plenty of time to think of ways to torment me.''

"Well," Mollie replied, her cheeks flushed with color, "my friend Betsy told me about how he flirted with her older sister, carrying on until her sister fell in love with him, then he just dropped her like that, like she was nothing to him. He's broken a lot of hearts in this county. I think he should go away and stay away!''

"Well, *I* think he's definitely hunk-of-the-month material, myself," Maribeth announced. "Just because you two don't ever have any boyfriends doesn't mean you shouldn't appreciate a good-looking specimen like Travis when you get the chance. Bobby says—''

Megan just shook her head. "Here we go again. If Bobby says it, it must be gospel, right?''

"Well, he knows rodeos. He and his dad are always going to them. He's seen Travis compete and says he's totally awesome. That's why he was named World Champion last year.''

Megan uncurled herself from the couch and stood. "Well, I think I'm going to take myself off to bed. You're really making me feel my years, Maribeth," she said, ruffling her sister's long wavy hair. "I take it you had a good time in town.''

"Oh, yeah. Rita's a lot of fun. Her mom said to tell you that anytime I want to spend the night in town, that I can stay with them.''

"Well, I'm glad to hear you didn't totally wear out your welcome.''

She glanced at Mollie, caught her eye and nodded toward the hallway. "I'll see y'all in the morning."

Megan climbed the stairs to her bedroom. She hoped Mollie recognized her signal. She wasn't going to be able to sleep tonight until she talked to her and tried to explain.

She hadn't realized Mollie's feelings toward Travis were so strong or so negative. Megan knew that she had herself to blame for some of that. She'd never kept her disdain for Travis hidden from Mollie or anyone else around home. Now she was going to be forced to provide some kind of explanation for the change in her attitude—without giving the real one. If Travis preferred people not to know the truth, she owed him that much.

She slipped out of her robe and sank onto the side of her bed. What a mess. It had all seemed so logical and businesslike when Travis first made his suggestion. A year's marriage; a limited partnership agreement. A business deal. She would be his wife in exchange for help with the ranch. Wasn't that reasonable enough?

She doubted that Mollie would see it that way. As protective as Mollie was, she'd probably think that Megan was in love with him or something. She'd probably think she was having her heart broken when that wouldn't be the case, at all.

Megan heard a soft tap on her door. She smiled and softly said, "Come on in."

Mollie opened the door and slipped inside. "You wanted to see me?"

"Yeah." She patted the bed and Mollie sat down

beside her. "There's something I need to talk to you about that I would just as soon not discuss in front of Maribeth. At least, not yet."

"I can certainly understand that. Telling Maribeth anything is like putting it on the six o'clock news!"

"I need to ask a favor of you."

"Sure. Anything."

Megan smiled and shook her head in amusement. "You don't know what the favor is."

"Doesn't matter."

Impulsively Megan leaned over and hugged Mollie. "Have I ever told you how much I love and appreciate you? I couldn't have made it this far without you."

Mollie's cheeks pinkened. "Don't be silly. You make it sound like you're on your deathbed or something. So...what gives? What's the favor?"

Megan took a deep breath, feeling very uncomfortable. She let the air out of her lungs in a gusty sigh. "I was wondering if I could borrow one of your dresses tomorrow."

Mollie stared at her in shock, as though unable to credit what she was hearing. "A dress?" she repeated. "You want to borrow one of my dresses?"

"Isn't that just what I said?"

"I was sure my hearing had suddenly gone on the blink. You never wear dresses. Why do you need one now?"

"It's a long story."

Mollie slid up further on the bed and folded her legs, lotus-fashion. "Well, I don't care how long it is, this is one story I've gotta hear!"

Megan scooted back on the bed as well, leaning against the headboard, resigned to facing Mollie's reaction. "I'm going with Travis Kane to Austin tomorrow."

"You mean, on a date?"

"Um-hmm."

"But you never date."

"I know."

"You haven't dated anyone since high school."

"I know."

"You never wear dresses."

"You've already pointed that out, Mollie! I know I never wear them, which is why I'm asking to borrow one of yours. We're close to the same size. I'm probably no more than an inch shorter than you. It won't really matter what it looks like on me." She shoved her hand through her hair. "I know I'll look silly, but I wanted to appear more—" she waved her hand in a circle "—you know, more feminine."

Mollie's smile was filled with amused affection. "You couldn't help looking feminine if you tried, Megan."

"Huh! You've got to be kidding. With my bobbed hair and in my coveralls more than one stranger has thought I was a boy!"

"Only if the stranger was blind. You have a very feminine face, a long slender—almost regal looking—neck, a graceful way of moving, and a beautifully shaped body."

"Now I know you're crazy! Me? I'm too skinny. I'm—"

"You're small-boned and delicate looking...not

skinny. I think we could maybe trim your hair a little, find one of my dresses that you'd like as well as be comfortable in, and perhaps try a little makeup on you.''

''I've never worn makeup in my life.''

''So? If you're going to change your habits by wearing a dress, you might as well go whole hog and do it all.''

Megan hesitantly touched her hair. ''I don't know what to do with it. I just whack it off when it starts getting in my eyes. You've always been the one who trims the back for me.''

''Teresa at the beauty shop in town has been teaching me how to cut hair when she didn't have any customers. It's not all that hard. She gave me some scissors and things. I think I could do something really cute with your hair.'' She, too, ran her fingers through Megan's hair. ''It's so thick and curly.''

Megan scowled. ''Looks like a mop.''

Mollie grinned. ''Once it's shaped, I think it'll look fine.''

''Whatever you think,'' Megan replied, sighing. ''I'm going to put myself in your hands on this one.''

Mollie slipped off the bed. ''Okay, we'll look through my closet in the morning, and I'll do your hair. It shouldn't take long. When is he coming?''

''About one o'clock.''

Mollie paused in the doorway of the bedroom and said, ''I don't understand. Why, after years of not dating, would you suddenly decide to accept a date with Travis Kane, of all people?''

Megan tried to think of something to say that

would prepare Mollie for what was going to happen, but her mind remained blank. After a moment, she shrugged and lamely offered, "He isn't that bad, Mollie."

Mollie snorted. "Hah! He's arrogant, he's egotistical, and he's irresponsible. And that, my dear sister, is a direct quote from you the last time he happened to be mentioned in a conversation. Exactly when did he redeem himself in your estimation?"

Megan clasped her hands in her lap, carefully studying them. "He's offered to help us out until we can get back on our feet. He doesn't want us to lose the ranch."

Mollie leaned against the doorjamb, folding her arms. "I find that a little hard to believe. What's in it for him?"

Megan avoided Mollie's gaze. "He says he just wants to help, since we've known each other for so long and we're neighbors and all."

"Uh-huh. And then he asks you for a date. What exactly is the catch here? There's got to be a few strings attached. I'm sure Maribeth fed him all the details about our situation. No doubt he knows there's no way we have the money to pay back any loan he might make to us."

So there it was. There was no way she could avoid telling Mollie the truth. She clasped her hands tightly in her lap and looked up at Mollie, who continued to steadily watch her from across the room. "He asked me to marry him."

"*What?*" Mollie shouted, leaping away from the

doorway and over to the bed as if she'd been shot out
of a cannon.

"*Shhhh!* Don't let Maribeth hear you."

Mollie clasped both hands over her mouth and began to pace jerkily up and down the room. Megan
closed her eyes. This wasn't going well at all, but
then, what had she expected, given the circumstances
and the long-standing feud she'd carried on—albeit a
trifle one-sided—with Travis.

Mollie finally paused long enough beside Megan to
hiss, "The nerve of the man! Thinking that you would
even consider selling yourself like some—"

"Mollie, I told him I would," Megan said quietly.

Mollie looked as though she'd been slapped across
the face. She'd been leaning over the bed when Megan gave her the news of what she'd done. Mollie's
blue eyes slowly widened, larger and larger, as though
she was seeing a specter slowly rising from the grave.
"Oh, Megan, no," she whispered, scarcely breathing.
"Please no. You mustn't do this. I know you've been
worrying about what's going to happen to us, but
nothing is worth your sacrificing your happiness like
this." Tears began to fill her eyes.

Megan scrambled off the bed and threw her arms
around her sister. "Oh, Mollie...it's okay. Really it
is. We're treating it like a business arrangement. He
won't even be around all that much. He's going to be
on the rodeo circuit, traveling for most of the year.
You know the circuit runs from January to December
and he has to enter as many as he can to get the points
he needs. Why, we'll seldom see him."

She leaned back so that she could see Mollie's

stricken face. She grabbed a handful of tissues and patted Mollie's cheeks. "I couldn't accept a loan from him, Mollie. I didn't want to be obligated to him."

"Megan! What in the world do you consider marriage to be, if it isn't an obligation?"

"A partnership," she hastily replied. "That's what we're forming...a partnership. He says it's time for him to settle down. He says he wants a home. He says—"

"Oh, Megan, honey," Mollie said, shaking her head. "Travis Kane is going to break your heart."

Megan tilted her chin slightly. "Not unless I let him."

"You may not have a choice."

Megan dropped her arms and moved away from the bed and her sister. She walked over to her dresser and picked up a comb. Absently playing with it, she said, "We always have choices, Mollie. Remember that. Both Travis and I know and understand what we're doing and why we're doing it. It'll be okay, I promise. Please don't worry about me. I'm a big girl now." *I would do this—and more—to take care of you and Maribeth,* she added silently.

Mollie just shook her head. "I know. You've been like a parent to us for so long," she replied, as though reading Megan's thoughts. "But in some ways you're still so young and so naive. I swear, if that bastard ever tries to—"

"Mollie! I've never known you to use such language." Megan stared at her in disbelief.

"I've never watched my sister sell herself to the highest bidder, either," she blurted out before Megan's shocked look registered. Mollie hurried over to her, hugging her older sister. "I'm sorry, Megan! I'm so sorry. I didn't really mean that. It's just that you've made so many sacrifices for us already that it breaks my heart to see you throwing yourself away on someone who isn't worth it."

Megan hugged her back before she said, "You know, Mollie, I think that maybe we've both been too quick to judge Travis. Let's face it, if he was really as irresponsible as we think, he would never have made such an offer in the first place. Besides, look at it this way. I'm twenty-four years old. I've never dated anyone. I've never socialized. I never—ever— thought that I might get married someday. And now, all of that is going to change. Maybe, for the very first time in my life, I've got the chance to have what other women take for granted—a man who cares about me, who's willing to help me with my responsibilities. It's not as if we're total strangers, after all. Our families have been friends and neighbors for years and years." She went back to the bed and sat down. "I want to give him a chance, Mollie. I think I owe him that much, just for his willingness to help us out. I also want the ranch to have a chance to survive as the Circle B. Please trust me to know what I'm doing. Please?"

Mollie walked over and gave her a quick kiss on the cheek. "You're worn-out, Megan. I should have seen that before. Get some sleep now. Just because he made the offer doesn't mean you have to take him up on it. Let's just treat tomorrow as a chance for you to go out and have some fun for a change." She turned off the lamp beside the bed. "We'll work on getting you dolled up in the morning. Ol' Travis won't know what hit him when he gets a look at you all fixed up. He won't believe his good luck at getting the chance to take you out for the day!" She turned and left the room, quietly closing the door behind her.

Megan sat there in the darkened room, staring toward the door for a long time before she got into bed. She pulled the covers up around her shoulders and stared at the ceiling, wishing she knew if she was doing the right thing. Mollie's arguments were valid and she knew it. Megan knew she was way over her head on this one. What if she was wrong? She'd sounded so sure of herself, asking Mollie to trust her judgment. What a fraud she was.

She had no idea if she was doing the right thing. The only thing she knew was that she had to try to save the family's legacy. She had to do whatever she could, no matter how painful or uncertain the future appeared.

Marrying Travis Kane seemed to be the only answer.

Four

Travis turned off the county road onto the lane leading to the ranch buildings of the Circle B. His dad's ranch entrance was a little over five miles down the road from here. The O'Brien house could be seen from the road, sitting on a rise overlooking the surrounding countryside. The two-story building had an old-world grace reminiscent of a much earlier era, its stone walls decorated with wooden filigree and curlicues around the veranda, which circled the lower floor and provided shade from the hot Texas sunshine.

The house where he'd grown up didn't look all that different. Many of the ranches in this area had been established more than a hundred years ago, handed down from one generation to the next in keeping with family tradition.

The closer he got, the more he could see the signs

of neglect and decay around the aging dwelling. One of the front porch steps looked rotted through and would probably be a hazard to anyone unsuspecting enough to approach the often ignored front entrance of the house.

Nobody living in these parts used front doors to a house, anyway, which was probably why Megan hadn't attempted to make an unessential repair.

His knowledgeable gaze noted that all the fences he could see were in good working order, as were all the outbuildings such as the barn and shed located a short distance from the house. Like most ranchers, Megan had neglected the house in favor of keeping the ranch property itself in repair.

Travis pulled up beside the low stone fence that separated the house and its neglected lawn from the rest of the ranch yard. From the corner of his eye he caught the slight flutter of a curtain in one of the upstairs windows. Somebody knew he'd arrived.

He'd been awake since before dawn this morning, thinking about the day ahead. He more than half expected Megan to greet him with the news that she'd changed her mind about going to Austin with him, much less marrying him.

If she wasn't the most unworldly person he knew, she was certainly high on the list.

Did she honestly believe that the only reason he had offered to marry her was so that she would accept his help to save the ranch? Could she possibly be so blind to her many wonderful qualities, to her attractiveness, to her adorable traits that she didn't recognize the way he felt about her, the way he had always felt about her?

Travis couldn't remember how old he'd been when he first faced the realization that he loved Megan O'Brien, but it must have been while they were still in grade school. He'd been a typical show-off male back then, vying for her attention by dropping pebbles down the back of her shirt, grabbing her pigtails and treating them like reins of a horse, and teasing her unmercifully at every opportunity.

Hadn't she known, even then, that little boys signal their devotion in such a way? He sighed. She sure didn't know much about the male animal, that's for sure. Everybody else in the county had known what his behavior meant. He'd gotten a lot of teasing, which was why he'd backed off by the time he reached high school. She'd had little use for him by then and made her opinion of him quite clear, snubbing him, ignoring him. His adolescent ego had taken a real beating and he hadn't wanted to place himself in a position to be rejected by her back then.

Instead he'd gone out of his way to excel in sports and in the classroom in hopes of impressing her with his abilities. Even his rodeoing had been an attempt to show her what he could do.

As soon as Maribeth had told him what a struggle she was having, he'd immediately wanted to leap upon his dazzling white charger and come dashing to her rescue. His concern had been enough to overcome her last rejection of him when he'd come home a couple of years ago, flush with success, and had dared to invite her out on a date. She'd turned him down.

Well, now he had that date…finally…after all these years.

He'd scarcely slept the night before, his mind racing with thoughts about today. They were going to spend several hours together for the very first time as adults. He was no longer that silly kid with a crush. He was now a grown man with a deep abiding love for a woman who could barely tolerate him. However, she had agreed to marry him. Wasn't that a start?

The hardest part for him was to remember not to show too much interest in her. He kept reminding himself that he had to remain casual and offhand toward her. The family friend role, that's what he had to concentrate on. Man oh man, that was going to take some real concentration on his part. He'd spent most of his life comparing every girl he met—then all the women he'd met—to Megan O'Brien. None of them had been able to measure up.

He'd never forget that time back when he'd been a senior in high school and captain of the football team. The team was doing great that fall and he'd been looking really good on the playing field. All of that had finally given him enough confidence… finally…to get up the nerve to ask her to the homecoming dance.

At sixteen, she wasn't dating anyone. He'd made it his business to find out for sure. Her folks had always been very strict with her, and he hadn't been sure exactly how to go about asking—whether or not to discuss it with her father first in order to convince him that she would be perfectly safe going out with him and that he would treat her with respect and care.

Before he could get up his nerve for that particular hurdle to his hopeful plans, her parents had been killed in that god-awful car crash. She'd missed several weeks of school after that and, even when she'd returned, he'd known she wouldn't be interested in anything he could say to her.

All of that was years ago, though. They'd both grown up. They'd both survived. Now, here he was once again determined to win his fair lady, even if she thought it was merely a business offer.

He had a year to convince her to make it a permanent merger.

He glanced up at that window again, trying not to think too much about the possibility that she might have already changed her mind.

Travis slowly opened the truck door and stepped out of the truck cab, tugging his hat low over his sunshades.

"Howdy, Travis," Butch called from where he stood between the wide opening of the barn. "You lost or somethin'? What brings you back out here today?"

Travis briefly glanced at the house before sauntering over to where Butch stood watching him. Facing Megan once again would come soon enough. He wasn't in any hurry if she had bad news to tell him. If the news was good, she'd be spending the rest of the day with him, anyway.

"It's nice to see you again, Butch. How're things going with you?" he offered, holding out his hand. The men shook hands.

"Can't complain. I been hearin' some good things

about you, son. You been winnin' some pretty fancy titles on the circuit, I hear.''

"Yeah." Travis grinned. "It's been a hoot, all right.''

"Kinda dangerous profession, though. I mean, it's okay to go to some of these regional affairs, but doing it all the time can get kinda rough, can't it?''

Travis nodded. "Yeah. It's definitely a young man's sport. I figure I'll have to quit by the time I'm thirty or so. That gives me another three or four years."

"When are you going out on the road again?''

Travis glanced at the house before answering. "Probably next week.''

"So what brings you out here today?''

"I'm taking Megan to Austin for the afternoon and evening.''

Butch shoved his hat to the back of his head and scratched his temple. "The hell you are! Did she agree to go?''

"Um, yes," Travis mumbled, looking down at the pointed toes of his boots. "Yes, she did.''

Butch grinned broadly. "Well, I'll be hornswoggled. That's good news. That girl never does get away from this place. You know, now that you mention it, she didn't come outside this morning. I didn't give it much thought...figured she'd finally decided to rest up a little. Looks to me like she decided to take the whole day off.''

Travis glanced toward the house. "Guess I'd better go see if she's ready.''

"Well, y'all have fun today."

"Thanks, Butch. See you later."

From her position behind the sheer curtains of her bedroom, Megan watched Travis walk away from Butch in his loose-limbed saunter toward the back entrance of the house. She shivered. What had caused her to toss out all her long-held beliefs about this man and decide to accept his unorthodox offer of marriage?

Travis Kane was a law unto himself. She was the first to admit that he'd always made her jumpy and nervous. What if she couldn't get over the way she reacted around him?

Mollie's blunt comments last night had shaken her more than she had expected. Mollie was right. Megan had never had anything good to say about him. Her decision to marry him made no sense whatsoever.

She'd lain awake last night, thinking about refusing him. She could do that. Nobody was forcing her into anything. She could go to the bank, tell the banker she couldn't make the payment. She could let them foreclose on the ranch. And sometime in the future, after they'd lost everything, she could remind herself that if she'd just had a little more courage, she might have made a different choice. She might have found herself married and still living on the family ranch.

Travis suddenly glanced up at her window and she hastily took a step backward, not wanting him to know that she was still lurking in her room, uncomfortable about going downstairs and facing her world dressed the way she was.

Megan turned nervously toward the oval mirror in

the corner and stared at her image. She was forced to admit that the dress she wore fit her surprisingly well…as did the sandals with the tiny stacked heels. The problem was that she didn't look like herself. Peering more closely into the mirror, she studied her face and hair.

She was still amazed at how successfully Mollie had trimmed her thick hair. She had thinned and shaped it around her face and ears, calling attention to her eyes. She didn't remember them ever looking quite so large or so blue. She always thought of them as blueish gray, but now they sparkled like blue topaz.

Megan wasn't used to seeing herself in makeup. Mollie had darkened her lashes and brows slightly, added touches of color around her eyes and across her cheekbones, and finished with a soft pink lipstick that made her mouth look slightly pouty.

"Megan," Mollie called from downstairs. "Travis's here."

The cool tone made Megan wince. She knew she'd better hurry down before Mollie made her dislike toward him obvious. For a quiet person, Mollie certainly had strong opinions and, for some reason these past two days, she wasn't having any difficulty expressing them.

Travis had already noticed a definite chill in the air as soon as Mollie came to the door in response to his light tap on the screen. Without a word she opened the door, then turned away and called out to Megan without greeting him.

"How've you been, Mollie? I haven't seen you in quite a while."

Mollie went back to mixing and stirring something on the counter. From the looks and smell of things, she was in the midst of some heavy-duty, mouth-watering baking.

Without looking around at him, she said, "Fine," in a short tone of voice.

He glanced around the large kitchen, recognizing the place as the hub of the home. He looked back at her, but she was studiously ignoring him. He slowly removed his hat and held the brim in both hands, turning it.

"Have you finished school yet?"

"This is my last year."

"Where do you intend to go to college?"

Her glance held a hint of contempt. "We don't have the money for college."

"Did you try for any scholarships?"

"No. Megan needs me here."

There was a slight sound at the doorway into the hall and he looked around. He froze at the sight of Megan standing there, her manner more hesitant than he'd ever seen her.

She wore a lemon-colored sundress that lovingly cupped her breasts and waist, then flared into a full skirt that ended at her knees. He caught himself staring at her curving calves and slender ankles before his gaze ended on her pink-painted toenails in strappy sandals.

He swallowed hard, his gaze bouncing back over the unfamiliar sight of her bare legs and shoulders. Shoestring-size straps were the only things holding the dress in place.

When his eyes finally met hers Travis forced himself to nod. His throat felt dry. He couldn't get over the change from the coverall-covered woman of the day before. Even her face looked different. Softer, somehow. Her eyes were definitely wary. Even her hair looked smoother, silkier, somehow.

Travis could feel his heart racing and he battled for control, determined not to reveal his stunned reaction to this new look Megan had chosen.

"Hi, Megan," he said, his voice sounding gruff and raspy to his own ears. He cleared his throat. "You look very nice."

She came toward him, only her eyes betraying her unease. "Thank you." She looked past him and he turned. Mollie was watching them, her displeasure obvious. "I don't know when I'll be home," Megan was saying, "so don't worry if it's late."

Mollie gave her a brief nod and returned her attention to her dough. "Be careful" was all she said.

Megan hurried past him, pausing on the porch to wait for him to join her. It didn't take a rocket scientist to figure out there was something obviously wrong between the two sisters, Travis thought, as he followed Megan outside.

She kept at least two arm's length distance between them as she ran down the steps.

"Well, look-ee here," Butch hollered, striding across the open space between the barn and the house. "I almost didn't recognize you, missy."

Travis thought he heard a sound suspiciously like a groan from Megan.

"I'd look a little foolish working around here in a

getup like this, now, wouldn't I?'' she replied a little tartly.

Butch laughed. ''That's for sure. I'm so used to seeing you in those shapeless coveralls I'd almost forgot what a good-lookin' gal you are,'' he said, his admiration evident. ''Those sure are show-girl legs hidin' beneath all the denim.''

''Butch!'' Her face had turned as rosy as her nail polish. ''Cut it out!''

Travis laughed. He couldn't help enjoying the interplay between the two of them. Stepping around her, he opened the passenger side of the truck and helped her inside. He was able to enjoy the flash of exposed legs as she took the step up into the cab. He closed the door, then turned around and winked at the older man. ''Never underestimate the O'Brien women, Butch,'' he warned. ''They're just full of surprises.''

''You take good care of her now, you hear?'' Butch said, straightening to his full height. ''Just because she doesn't have no daddy to look after her doesn't mean—''

''I know, Butch. I promise to take very good care of her and not let her come to any harm.''

Megan rested her arm on the open window and leaned out. ''I'll probably be late getting back home since we're going to Austin, Butch. I don't want you waiting up with your shotgun, you hear me?'' she warned.

Butch looked sheepish and nodded.

''I'm a grown woman and I can take care of myself,'' she added for good measure.

"You're no bigger'n a minute and you know it," he muttered, half under his breath.

Travis clapped him on the back and in a low voice said, "I'll keep her safe. Count on it."

They drove away from the house and down the lane. Megan leaned forward and looked out the side mirror. "I can't figure out what's got into Butch today. He's acting like you've kidnapped me and plan to sell me into white slavery."

"Can't say that I blame him," he drawled, glancing at her out of the corner of his eye. "You're looking mighty good…pretty near irresistible, if you ask me." He had the pleasure of watching her turn rosy once again.

"I should have worn jeans, I suppose. I never dreamed that putting on a dress would cause such a stir," she muttered half under her breath.

"I'm sorry, Megan," he said, reaching over and taking her hand. She stiffened, but didn't try to pull away. "I find it too easy to tease you, I suppose," he admitted. "I guess it's because you respond so easy to teasing."

Encouraged by the fact that she hadn't jerked her hand back and socked him—which he knew she was perfectly capable of doing—he slipped his fingers between hers and rested their clasped hands on his thigh.

"I take it from her attitude that you told Mollie about our plans and that she's a tad less than thrilled to have me as a brother-in-law."

He could feel her body tense all the way to her fingertips. "She just doesn't want me hurt."

He glanced at her in surprise. "And she thinks I would hurt you in some way?"

She smoothed her skirt with her free hand. "She's just a little protective, that's all. We've always been close, especially since the folks died."

"What's Mollie got against me, if I may ask?"

She sighed. "Your reputation, mostly."

He frowned. "I wasn't aware I had one."

He could feel her gaze on him. "C'mon, Travis. This is me you're talking to. Don't be so modest."

"I don't know what you're talking about."

She shook her head. "I suppose you're going to deny that you're known as a heartbreaker around these parts—that love 'em and leave 'em seems to be your personal creed?"

"What?!" The truck swerved and he let go of her hand to place both hands on the wheel. He hadn't wanted his reaction to her words to show, but he knew he was too late to hide it.

"What did you expect would be said about you when you've stopped seeing everyone you ever dated the minute she got serious about you?"

He rubbed the frown that had formed over the bridge of his nose. "What was I supposed to do? Anytime somebody started talking about the future or an engagement or about having a family I knew it was time to stop seeing her."

"Exactly."

He gave her a quick glance of surprise. "And that was wrong? Since I had no intention of marrying anyone it seems to me I did the honorable thing. I never led anyone on, or promised them anything. I never took advantage of anyone...."

"Just walked away and left them with their hearts broken. Yes, I know."

He gripped the steering wheel a little tighter. "But this is crazy, Megan. How can I be responsible for how somebody else feels? I don't have any control over that."

"I know."

"I dated women whose company I enjoyed. We had fun together. I liked them, but I never told a one of them that I loved them."

"So?"

"Lying would have—"

"Nobody's talking about lying." She didn't say anything else for several minutes and he was too astonished to think of anything more to add to the conversation. When she finally spoke again, she said, "I suppose Mollie's concerned about your motive. Why would anybody believe that Travis Kane—the guy who's run from any kind of commitment for all these years—would suddenly show up out of the blue and offer to marry me, even if it's only a business arrangement? Mollie's concerns make perfect sense to me. Of course, the way I look at it, marriage can work for your benefit, too. I mean, if you don't want to be hounded all the time by women wanting to marry you, then marrying me is a solution of sorts." She glanced over at him. "At least it'll give you a few months' breathing space."

"I'm not believin' this conversation," he muttered under his breath.

''What did you say?''

''I was just wondering if you're gettin' hungry. I skipped lunch today—'' there was no use admitting he'd been too nervous to eat ''—so I thought I might stop somewhere along the way and get something.''

''Okay by me.''

He glanced at her out of the corner of his eye. ''You hungry?''

''Not particularly.''

''Then we can wait until we get to Austin.''

''Don't be silly! I can always have something to drink while you have a hamburger or something. What's the matter with you today?'' She leaned forward so she could see more of his face. ''You've been acting kind of strange.''

''I'm feeling kind of strange,'' he admitted, hoping that eating would be a cure of sorts.

They passed into the outside limits of a small town and Travis saw a fast-food place up ahead. He pulled in and gave them an order that included a drink for each of them.

They were pulling back onto the highway when Megan asked, ''So, are you going to tell me what's bothering you?'' She unwrapped his burger and handed it to him, then scooted closer to him and held out his fries so that he could reach them.

Rather than answer her, he took a big bite of the burger and thoughtfully chewed, deciding what he was going to say to her. After taking a drink, he cleared his throat and said, ''I thought maybe that you'd change your mind.'' There. He'd admitted it out loud.

"I thought about it."

He continued to eat his meal in the silence of the truck's cab. "And?" he asked when she didn't say anything more.

She gave a tiny shrug and sighed. "I decided that since you were willing to help us out by going to such an extreme as to marry me, I would accept your offer in the spirit you meant it. At least you didn't talk a lot of nonsense about being in love with me or actually *wanting* to be married to me or anything silly like that. I figured that as long as we're honest and totally up-front with each other, everything should work out all right."

"I see," he said, suddenly feeling his hamburger weighing heavily in his stomach. "We're treating this as a business deal," he repeated in a hollow voice. He took a long drink to relieve his suddenly very dry throat.

"Exactly. Of course we don't need to tell anybody else the truth. We'll just let all the family and friends think we're madly in love with each other." She chuckled. "That will be a shock to lots of 'em, I'm sure...Travis Kane finally falling for somebody and wanting to settle down after all this time. I guess the joke will be on them."

Travis felt as though he'd just seen the door slam shut on a trap of his own making. How could he ever admit to Megan now that he did love her without her immediately doubting him and his motives? The irony of the situation didn't escape him. She could accept that he might be willing to help her as a friend, but obviously would never believe he might be in love with her.

Wow! He'd really done it this time, hadn't he? He'd set up a situation where he was going to be walking a very thin line pretending they were no more than buddies and pals. After all this time, he'd managed to get stuck with an undeserved reputation for being a heartbreaker. In the end, *he* could very well be the one with a broken heart.

If so, he'd only have himself to blame…for not telling her the truth about his feelings years ago. His lack of courage back then could cost him plenty. His only hope was that somehow, someway, she would end up falling in love with him, too.

Five

Travis pulled into one of the shopping malls near the highway they'd followed into Austin. They hadn't talked much after their stop for food. He'd asked a few questions about the ranch, and she had answered easily enough. He guessed she'd come to terms with her reasons for marrying him and was now dealing with the consequences of her decision.

He hadn't realized just how difficult being with her and covering his true feelings was going to be.

Travis reached for her hand and they crossed the huge parking lot and entered the air-conditioned mall, taking their time looking at all the window displays and watching the other shoppers.

He discovered, to his surprise, that he was enjoying just being with her. She'd never pulled her hand away from his and he reveled in the slight contact. He could

scarcely hide his need to laugh out loud at this en-
actment of all his adolescent dreams.

Megan O'Brien had agreed to marry him. Why, it
was all he could do not to throw his hat in the air
and let out a big yahoo! of a yell.

Eventually in their wanderings, they came upon a
jewelry store. Travis paused in front of it, then looked
down at her. "Well…we found what we were lookin'
for, right?" She seemed to hesitate so he gave her
hand a little tug and they walked inside the store.

"Good afternoon," the smiling clerk said by way
of greeting. "How may I help you?"

With all the aplomb he could muster, Travis said,
"We want to look at matching wedding rings," he
said.

"Certainly, sir. They're over at the far counter. I'll
be right with you."

Travis led the way to the back of the store to where
the clerk had pointed.

"Do you mean you intend to wear a ring, as well?"
she asked.

He eyed her a little cautiously, trying to figure out
her mood. "You have a problem with that?" he finally asked.

"Oh! Of course not. I guess I'm just surprised. I
thought the ring was going to be for show, to make
all of this more convincing."

He nodded. "The engagement ring will be. It
leaves no doubt about our intentions." He glanced
down at the sets of rings on display. "Do you see
anything you like?"

She laughed nervously. "I don't know anything about rings, Travis. I've never owned one."

"Not even a high school ring?"

She shook her head. "I figured it was a waste of money we could better use elsewhere."

He shook his head, feeling his dismay wash over him. "I wish I'd realized what you and the girls were going through back then. I guess I was too young to fully understand."

"Why should you? None of it had anything to do with you."

He stepped back from the counter so that he could see her face, since she was seemingly concentrating on the rings beneath the glass. He'd heard a peculiar tone in her voice, but could tell nothing from her expression.

"Now, then," the clerk said, arriving behind the counter. "What would you like to see?"

Travis studied the display for several minutes before he pointed out a set. The clerk placed the rings on top of the counter. "What do you think?" Travis asked Megan.

"Aren't they too expensive?" she whispered.

"No. Do you want to try one on?"

The clerk said, "You can have it sized to fit your finger, of course."

When she hesitated, Travis took the engagement ring and slid it on her finger. It fit as though it had been made for her. "I like it," he said in a matter-of-fact voice. "Do you?"

"It's beautiful," she said, her voice unsteady.

He nodded to the clerk. "Fine. We'll take the set."

The clerk measured his finger, then explained they would have to have his sized. "No problem." Travis took out his checkbook and wrote a check. "That's my address. Have it mailed to me. Meanwhile, we'll take hers with us."

When they walked out of the store, Travis looked at Megan and said, "You're sure quiet. Is something wrong?"

"I didn't know how quickly we could do that." She glanced down at her ring. "It's truly beautiful." When she looked up at him, her eyes were shining. "Thank you, Travis."

He took her hand and guided her into an alcove off the mall. Placing his hands around her face, he leaned down and kissed her softly. "You're quite welcome," he murmured when he finally raised his head.

She was staring up at him in surprise. "I—uh—"

"You might as well get used to me going around kissing you. It's all part of the window dressing. When we get back home, we're going to be convincing lots of people that this is something we've both wanted for a long time, but this was the first time I was able to offer you anything."

"People will wonder why you'd take on a whole family."

"Who cares what they think? Besides, I've got an older brother and a baby sister of my own. You'll be taking them on, as well."

She kept her gaze on their linked fingers and the sparkling ring on hers. "Not really. They won't be living with us like Mollie and Maribeth."

"Living with us," he repeated, grinning. "I like

the sound of that. I think I'm going to enjoy living with you very much."

She jerked her head up to meet his gaze. "You know what I meant, Travis. We'll be sharing the same house and all."

"Is that what we'll be doing?" he teased, watching her blush.

"Of course."

He draped his arm around her shoulders and casually suggested, "Let's look around here some more then, after we get tired of window shopping, I know this great place to get some delicious barbecued ribs. After that, there's a band I want you to hear. I first heard 'em a few years back when I was in Dallas. I think they're really good, and I'd like to know your opinion."

He was greatly encouraged by the new light that seemed to be shining from her eyes. It was as bright as the sparkling ring she wore on her finger. His ring. His brand-new fiancée. Hot damn, but he felt good.

Travis gave her a quick hug before leading her back into the main part of the mall to continue their browsing. He no longer tried to hide his beaming grin.

It was past midnight when Travis turned into Megan's driveway. She'd dozed most of the way home, her head resting against his shoulder. With the change in speed and the turn, however, Megan lifted her head away and slowly straightened.

"I'm sorry. I didn't mean to fall asleep," she said, smothering a yawn.

"It's okay," he replied gruffly. "I know I've kept you out past your bedtime."

He parked next to the back gate. The yard light, positioned near the barn, gave off enough illumination for him to see her face. She looked pleasantly rumpled, sleepy and utterly adorable. His breath caught in his throat at the notion that this woman would soon be married to him and he wouldn't have to leave her and go to bed alone.

Travis turned in his seat and draped his arm over her shoulders, pulling her against him. "I guess I should let you go inside, huh?" he said, knowing his reluctance was obvious.

She drooped her head on his chest. "Um, I guess. I doubt I'll be able to walk tomorrow," she said with a chuckle. "My calf muscles are already complaining. I told you I wasn't used to dancing."

He slid his fingers through her hair and slowly massaged her scalp in a kneading, soothing motion. "You did fine, honey. Just fine. I was proud of you."

She tilted her head back slightly in order to see his face. Her eyes glowed in the light. "You were? I felt so awkward. And there were so many women there who knew all the steps and were watching you. It's obvious you're used to going out dancing."

He shrugged. "There's not much else to do after a rodeo lets out, unless you want to sit around the bars all night and drink. Since I'm not much of a drinker, I learned to do some of the line dances. They're kinda fun."

"Yes. Today's been such an eye-opener for me. I had no idea there were so many things to do and see.

I can't remember when I've had such good tastin' ribs or so many! They just kept bringing 'em. It was surprising to find so many dance bands and clubs in the Austin area.''

"I think it's time you started havin' some fun in your life, Miss Megan. You definitely deserve it." He picked up her left hand and brought it to his lips, placing a kiss on her knuckles, near the engagement ring.

She sighed and snuggled against his chest like a sleepy kitten. Did she have any idea what kind of effect she was having on him? His tight jeans were rapidly becoming tighter and more uncomfortable. He shifted and reached for the door handle.

"Thank you for showing me such a nice day," Megan murmured, slowly straightening so that her mouth was only a few inches from his. "You're really a very nice man, Travis Kane."

"No matter what anybody says, right?" he added with a grin. He was fighting his impulse to grab her and kiss her, reminding himself that his mama had raised him to be a gentleman, but it was a damn tough proposition to remember when the woman he loved was draped across him like this.

He quickly turned the handle and opened the door, then eased his leg down to rest on the ground. Instead of waiting until he walked around to the other door, Megan followed him out his side of the truck cab, so that he found himself wrapping his hands around her waist and swinging her off the running board to stand beside him.

She gave a breathless whisper of a chuckle before

she slid her arms around his shoulders, went up on
her tiptoes and kissed him.

He had to let go of her. He knew that. He knew
that he needed to step back, fast, before she became
aware of how strongly he was reacting to her, but the
yearning he was feeling compelled him to deepen the
kiss, instead, and he ended up pulling her even more
snugly against his overheated body.

Megan knew that she must be dreaming. This wan-
ton woman in Travis's arms couldn't possibly be her!
She was shy around men. Shy and awkward. How
could she be so comfortable being pressed against his
hard muscled body, content to allow him to tease her
lips with his tongue, nudging them open so that he
could explore the depths of her mouth.

His thrusts seemed to be causing his hips to sway
slightly forward with every rhythmic movement of his
tongue. She could feel the taut ridge of his jeans zipper rubbing sensuously against her stomach, creating
the most unexpected tingling responses deep within
her. She shifted restlessly, mimicking the movements
he made with both his tongue and hips, her grip tightening around his neck.

"My God, Megan," he managed to pant after several heated moments. "We've got...to stop this...
now...or else—"

He didn't say what else. Instead he gripped her
arms and stepped back from her, his eyes blazing with
heat and his features taut.

Already relaxed and half asleep when she climbed
out of the truck, Megan wasn't certain her legs were

going to be able to support her. Her knees gave way and she sank down to the running board of the truck.

Travis knelt beside her, his expression worried. "Are you all right?" he asked, his breathing a little more even.

"I'm not sure," she admitted, rubbing her hand across her face. "What's happening here, anyway? I feel so—so strange. I've never felt like this before. It's weird."

He touched her face lightly with his fingertips and traced the line of her brow, cheek and chin. "I'm sorry. I didn't mean to come on so strong."

"It isn't that," she replied. "I mean, you weren't doing anything I wasn't encouraging. I just didn't realize—" She shook her head. "Wow!" she said once again.

"I guess that's what happens when our hormones start kicking up," he said with a lopsided smile.

"Powerful stuff," she admitted.

"Yep."

After a couple of moments of silence she added, "Of course it doesn't really mean anything. It's like some kind of chemistry or something." She didn't want it to mean anything. She was afraid of what it could mean. The last thing she needed in her life was to fall for Travis Kane!

He didn't actually move, and his expression didn't really change, but he seemed to withdraw from her in some indefinable way. "It means that we're compatible, wouldn't you say?" he finally offered by way of explanation.

She leaned her head against the seat behind her and sighed, her eyelids drooping. "I suppose."

"It seems to me that a couple planning to get married would want that in their relationship," he said after a moment.

She forced her eyes open and focused on his. "Well, of course, if it was a real marriage."

Still kneeling, he clasped her hands between his much larger ones. "Believe me, Megan, this is going to be a real marriage."

She frowned, her mind still muddled with sleep. "But not a permanent one. That makes a big difference."

"I said that it doesn't have to be permanent. Your choice. I'm willing to make it as permanent as you like."

Something in his serious tone jump-started her heart, causing it to race. She swallowed. "You are?"

He held her gaze for a long moment before answering her. "Yeah."

"Why?" she asked, baldly, suddenly needing to understand what was happening between them.

"What kind of question is that?"

She shook her head in an effort to clear her fuzzy thoughts. "It doesn't make sense, Travis. I watched you tonight. There wasn't a female in the place who wasn't keeping an eye on you and wishing she was the one with you."

"You're crazy."

"No, I'm not. I know you weren't paying any attention to them, but I was. It was the same thing when we were in high school. All the girls wanted to date you. You must have run into the same thing during the years you've been on the road.''

His frown had been steadily growing while she talked. ''Is there some point you're trying to make here?''

''Yes! There is. I'm trying to understand what's going on here. Why me, Travis? Why, of all the women you know, are you willing to tie yourself down to me?''

He didn't answer her right away. He shifted his weight, still in a kneeling position in front of her. He cleared his throat and finally asked, ''Are you going to believe me if I tell you that I love you?''

''Of course not!'' she replied immediately with more than a hint of irritation. ''That's ridiculous. I'm nobody special. I don't have anything to offer somebody like you.''

He recaptured her hands. ''Megan, don't sell yourself short. Listen to me, okay? Yeah, I've met a lot of women, women who saw me as some kind of trophy to win. Don't you understand? Once you're in any kind of limelight, there's always goin' to be people who are attracted to the idea of who you are, but they really don't see you, the person.'' He shifted once again, this time sitting alongside her. ''But with you, it's different. You know me, the *real* me. The one you don't particularly care for that was always giving you such a bad time. But you see? We've known each other all our lives. Why wouldn't I want to be married to you? Look at it from my point of view. You're honest and dependable and extremely loyal. You're willing to accept being married to me without making any conditions.''

She eyed him a little warily. ''Such as?''

''Well, you know how important the rodeo circuit is to me, and how much I enjoy participating in the events, even though they're dangerous and I've been hurt a few times. You see, I've dated women in the past who insisted that I give it up because they worried too much about my getting hurt and because I traveled too much. But you're willing to accept me for who I am and for what I do without trying to change any of that. You can't possibly know how important that is to me.''

She took a deep breath and held it for a moment before finally letting it go in a gusty sigh. ''And if I decided after a year that I don't want to be married to you anymore?''

''The bargain would still stand,'' he replied promptly. ''I'm not going to carry any unreal expectations about a future between us. I'll just take it each day as it comes and let whatever happens happen. At least I'll know I helped you out at a time when you needed it.''

Her expression was earnest when she said, ''You know I'll pay you back as soon as I have the money, don't you?''

''You don't have to do that, Megan. This isn't a loan. It was never meant to be. Remember that.''

''I don't guess I'll ever really understand. It looks to me like I'm the one getting all the benefit out of this.''

He turned so that he could kiss her very softly once

again, without passion. Unfortunately for Megan her heart and body didn't notice the difference. Her heart began to race and her body seemed to turn into mush.

When he pulled away from her she couldn't look at him.

"I'm going to be leaving tomorrow," he said. "I'll be gone for three weeks. Do you think you can plan a wedding in that length of time?"

She shrugged. "What's to plan? Don't we just go to the courthouse, get the license and make an appointment with the pastor?"

"Yeah, and maybe invite a few friends and have a reception and—"

She nodded slowly. "I suppose that's going to be part of it, too."

"Our families wouldn't forgive us if we did it any other way. You know that. I'll be the first one in our family to be getting married. The same in yours."

"Maybe so," she reluctantly agreed. "It just seems to be a whole lot of trouble to go through for something that only takes a few minutes," she grumbled. She was sleepy and aroused and feeling a frustration she'd never before experienced.

Travis's deep laugh caused her body to quiver. "There aren't any other women like you, honey. You're definitely one of a kind." He tugged on her hand. "Let's get you inside before you fall asleep sitting right here."

Her leg muscles protested and she groaned. She reached down and took her shoes off. "Remind me to never wear these kind of shoes again."

"They aren't any higher than your boots."

"It's the straps. My feet keep sliding around. At least the boots hug my foot."

"Whatever you say, darlin'. But you looked really good today in your pretty dress and sandals—like a glowing sunbeam."

She paused when she reached the back door and turned toward him. "Thank you for a wonderful day."

He took a step toward her, then stopped, jamming his fingers into his back pockets. "I'll give you a call tomorrow before I leave...and I'll call you while I'm gone, so you can let me know what's happening around here."

She nodded.

"I forgot to give you a check yesterday so I'll mail it to you on my way out of town. That way you can make the mortgage payment and not be worrying about it."

"Oh, but you don't—"

"Oh, but I do. Let's not argue about the money. It's not that important."

"Not important! Why, that's not so. That's the whole reason we're getting married, Travis Kane, and you know it. How can you—"

"Do you always have to go off like a short-fused firecracker? All I'm saying is that I want you to have it now and not have to wait until after we're married. Since the bank's being so hard-nosed about all this, let's not give 'em reason to refuse the payment, okay?"

Megan felt foolish, listening to his reasonable tone and rational explanation. She felt jumpy and on edge.

She wanted him to leave and she wanted to throw herself around his neck and kiss the holy fire out of him. She couldn't remember a time when she'd felt so restless and confused.

She watched Travis take another step backward. He could hardly wait to leave, she could tell. "Good night, Travis. Take care." She opened the door and slipped inside the darkened kitchen.

She watched him through the window as he walked back to the truck. She didn't turn away until he swung the truck into a wide circle and headed back down the lane to the county road. Only then did she tiptoe barefoot upstairs and down the hallway to her bedroom.

Once inside her room she absently unzipped her dress and stepped out of it, dropping it on the floor. She walked over to the window and looked outside. Nothing was stirring. Even Butch's rooms there at one end of the barn were dark. Everybody was sleeping and now that Travis was gone, she was wide-awake.

She slipped off her strapless bra and half-slip, put on her shortie pajamas, then went down the hallway to the bathroom.

In a few short weeks Travis would be living here with them, having his meals with them, making a place for himself within their family circle. While she brushed her teeth she wondered what her mama and dad would think about her decision to marry in order to save the ranch.

Would they think she was wrong? Would they want her to sell it?

She rinsed her mouth, turned off the light and returned to her room. After getting into bed she lay there staring sightlessly at the room she'd had all her life. Everything about her life was changing. It was a scary feeling.

Just as the way she'd felt in Travis's arms tonight was scary. Something was happening to her. It felt as if her body was waking up to all kinds of things she hadn't known about. She wished she had somebody to talk to about all of this, but she didn't. She was the one the girls came to with their questions.

It was times such as now when Megan felt the most alone.

Six

"Hey, Megan!" Maribeth said, bounding into the room the next morning. "You planning to sleep all day? I need to know if it's all right with you if I go with Bobby and a bunch of the kids to Brady this afternoon. I forgot to ask yesterday before you left, and Bobby's already called to see— Megan? Hey, Megan, are you awake?"

Megan groaned and pulled her head out from under the pillow. "I am now," she grumbled. "I swear, Maribeth, you could wake the dead." She rolled over and glared at her little sister.

Maribeth wore her long hair in a single plait this morning. A smattering of freckles decorated her nose and cheeks. It was hard to believe that her baby sister was sixteen years old. She'd always been a tomboy,

racing around with Bobby and his friends, determined
not to be left out just because she was a girl.

Megan's eyes drifted closed. She knew she should
have been training Maribeth more for household
skills, but she'd left that up to Mollie. She didn't
know much more than Maribeth about how to keep a
house running smoothly.

Unfortunately she wasn't showing her much about
how to keep a ranch running, either. Instead she had
wanted her to enjoy her childhood and not be weighed
down with too many responsibilities.

It was difficult to believe that Maribeth was the
same age now as Megan had been when their parents
had been killed. Megan couldn't ever remember being
as young as Maribeth.

"Megan?"

Maribeth's voice sounded funny. Megan forced
herself to open her eyes to see what was wrong. Maribeth had thrown herself onto the side of the bed.
When Megan had turned over she'd let her arms fall
across the bed in a sprawl. Now Maribeth was staring
at her left hand, her eyes wide.

Oh, no. I forgot about the ring.

"What is it?" she asked, knowing full well what
had drawn Maribeth's attention.

"I've never seen you wearing a ring before. Not
ever. Even though we kept all of Mama's jewelry, I
know Mama never had anything that looked like
this." She touched the diamond setting as though she
thought it might explode at any moment.

"You're right. It isn't Mama's."

"Then where did you get it? I never noticed it before."

"Travis Kane gave it to me yesterday."

Maribeth's eyes grew even larger, if that was possible. She stared at Megan as though she'd never seen her before. "Travis Kane gave *you* a ring? Why?"

"For the usual reasons, I guess." She hesitated, searching for the right way to tell her sister about the decision she'd made.

"Well, it looks way too expensive to be considered a friendship ring. The only other reason I can think of for him to give you such an expensive ring is because you're engaged to marry him," Maribeth said, obviously teasing her.

"That's right," Megan replied quietly.

Maribeth let out a shriek, then yelled, "Mollie! You've got to come quick and look at this!"

Megan scrambled to sit up. "For Pete's sake, Maribeth, calm down. There's no reason to carry on like—"

"What's wrong! What's the matter!" Mollie raced into the room, out of breath, then skidded to a halt beside the bed where the two sisters were lying. She stared at them as though looking for physical injury or some sign of impending annihilation. "Maribeth! What's wrong with you? How many times have I told you not to carry on like that? I thought somebody was trying to kill you!"

"The thought did occur to me," Megan muttered under her breath as she sat up and propped her pillow against the headboard and straightened the covers over her.

Maribeth ignored both of them. She was too caught up with her astounding discovery. "Megan and Travis Kane are getting married! Did you know that? Did she tell you? I can't believe she didn't say a word to anybody. She just—"

Mollie looked at Megan, her eyes filled with horror. "Megan? But I thought that we'd talked about—"

"Show her your ring," Maribeth demanded, bouncing on the bed. "Go ahead. Show her."

Megan slowly removed her hand from beneath the protective covers and reluctantly extended her arm toward Mollie. Mollie came around the bed and sat down on the other side, watching Megan's hand as though it were a rattlesnake.

"Megan?" she whispered, her voice shaking. In a stronger voice, she asked, "Oh, Megan, I thought you'd at least wait a while, give yourself some time to think it through. I didn't think you'd actually— Oh, Megan, what have you done?"

Megan reminded herself to stay calm. She'd already told her sister her intentions. It wasn't her fault if she hadn't believed she'd actually go through with it. At least she had a few weeks to talk to her, to convince her that she knew what she was doing.

"I agreed to marry him, Mollie. It's going to be okay. I promise. Everything is going to be all right."

Tears filled Mollie's eyes. "Oh, Megan."

"Come on, Mollie. You're supposed to be happy for me, didn't you know? I'm actually getting married! Me, Megan O'Brien...a bride!"

"Happy? That you've been hypnotized into believing Travis Kane is serious about getting married, to you or anybody else?'' Mollie said, her eyes flashing. She stared at the ring but refused to touch her hand. "Did he give you the ring to make you think that—'' She paused, taking a deep breath. "Did he try to seduce you last night? Did he? Please tell me he didn't.''

Megan scrambled out of bed and stared at her sister in disgust. "Oh course he didn't seduce me, you idiot! Travis isn't like that. He was a perfect gentleman.''

Mollie shook her head. "He's just using you, Megan, for his own mysterious purpose. Don't you see? He's softening you up so you'll trust him and believe in him. Then he'll walk away from you like he did all those other girls he used to date.''

Megan was getting angry. This was her life she was talking about, after all. And her decision. She could understand that Mollie felt protective of her and her feelings, but enough was enough.

"He told me he never wanted to marry those other girls.''

Mollie just looked at her. "But he wants to marry you.''

Megan nodded sharply. "Yes.''

"Oh, Megan.''

"You don't believe me?''

"Of course I believe you. It's him I don't believe…or trust.''

"Well, you better get used to the idea because he's going to be your brother-in-law in a few weeks.''

"Weeks! What are you talking about? Surely you're going to wait a while and see if you get along, see if he's going to treat you right. Did he promise to stop rodeoing?''

''Of course not. I would never ask him to.''

''Is he going to stay here at all and help you run the ranch?''

''I'm sure he'll help all he can when he's here.''

''I doubt that very much. Since he's paying good money to buy a—a wife and a ranch, he probably figures he's done all that's necessary.''

''Mary Katherine O'Brien, how *dare* you say something like that to me! I am your sister and I deserve your respect. How could you think—''

Mollie threw herself into Megan's arms, sobbing. ''I'm sorry, Megan, so sorry. I didn't mean it, I didn't mean it,'' she cried.

Megan began to cry as well. It wasn't long before tears streamed down Maribeth's face, too, as she patted first one sister, then the other. Eventually Megan blotted her eyes with a corner of the bed sheet, then did the same for Mollie and Maribeth.

''Would you look at us? Between the three of us we could end the drought we've been having! C'mon. That's enough sobbing and wailing. Butch has probably heard us and thinks we're holding a wake in here.''

''Aren't you happy for her, Mollie?'' Maribeth asked, looking wounded. ''I thought you'd be glad that Megan has fallen in love with somebody. Why, she hasn't even dated anyone before.'' She looked at Megan. ''Not even Travis! So why the sudden engagement?''

''Because it's what we both want,'' she managed

to say. "He says he's ready to settle down and that he wants to marry me. He knows I won't try to change him and he knows better'n to try to change me. I think we'll get along just fine." She took her sisters' hands in each one of hers. "Please be all right with this. It's going to be hard for me to adjust to the idea, too. It's all happened so suddenly. But it's what I want. What he wants. Can't you both just accept that?"

"Of course we can!" Maribeth said heartily. She glanced at Mollie. "Can't we?" she asked hesitantly.

Mollie studied Megan for a long time before she spoke. "I just want you to be sure that you know what you're doing, Megan."

"I am sure."

Mollie patted her hand and stood. "In the long run, that's what counts." She scrubbed her face with her hand and forced herself to smile at them. "If I don't get back downstairs, the biscuits are going to burn. Come on down and get something to eat and tell us about your trip to Austin." She glanced at the ring, then quickly away. "It must have been quite a date."

Mollie hurried out of the room.

Megan turned to her baby sister. "Now, tell me again what it is you and Bobby plan to do today?"

"I'm really happy for you," Maribeth said. "I think Travis Kane is the handsomest thing. If I wasn't already planning to marry Bobby, he'd be the one I'd want to marry, myself."

Megan stiffened. "What did you say?" she asked faintly, feeling the shock of Maribeth's blithe statement hit her in the stomach. "You and Bobby are—"

"Oh, not for years yet, don't worry," she replied airily. "We've already planned it all out. We're going to college together—Texas A & M—and as soon as we graduate we'll come home and get married and live on his dad's ranch. His dad has already told Bobby that he'd build him a house on the place. After all, Bobby's an only child, so eventually the ranch will be his. In the meantime, he and his dad will run it and we'll get married and have lots and lots of children and—"

"Lots and lots—?" Now it was Megan's turn to question a sister's decision.

Maribeth laughed. "Oh, well. Maybe we don't have every single thing planned out yet, but we've still got plenty of time."

"I should say so. At least another six years."

Maribeth stood and stretched. "We aren't in any hurry. We've been best friends for years, ever since the first grade. I don't mind that you're getting married first. It makes sense, since you're the oldest."

Megan looked at her in disbelief. "I'm so glad you approve."

Accepting the comment at face value, Maribeth nodded. "So it's okay with you if Bobby picks me up to go over to Brady?"

"Since when is Bobby driving?"

"Oh, he's been driving for ages, but he finally got his driver's license a few weeks ago. He's a really safe driver."

Megan closed her eyes and sighed. She hated these judgment calls. She'd gone through it with Mollie and now it was Maribeth's turn. Of course, Mollie had never been one to run around with a bunch of friends. She'd been content to stay home most of the time and try out new recipes, and practice sewing, and baking and—

"Just be careful," she muttered, looking for some clothes to wear.

"Thanks, Megan," Maribeth said, giving her a hug. "I think it's great about you and Travis. He's going to be a terrific addition to the family." She darted out of the room and Megan listened to her noisy progress down the hallway and into her room. She shook her head.

In the morning sunlight she looked at her ring once again. If it wasn't for the tangible evidence, she could easily believe that she'd dreamed everything that had happened yesterday—shopping for rings, dinner and dancing. Was this what being married was going to do to her life?

She hugged herself before hurrying into the bathroom for a quick shower.

Much later that day, Megan was going over the accounts once again, this time making a list of what had to be paid, when Mollie poked her head into the office. "Can I interrupt you for a minute?"

Megan leaned back in her chair and stretched, smiling. "Please do. I need a break. I've been looking down my nose so long I'm getting cross-eyed."

Mollie came in and sat down across the desk from her. She was quiet for a moment before she finally said, "I owe you an apology for my behavior, not only for all those things I said this morning, but also for the way I acted toward Travis when he was here yesterday. I was rude to both of you. I guess I figured that if I told you not to consider his offer, that you'd see things my way. It was a shock to see you wearing his ring so soon." She shook her head. "It's really none of my business if this is what you want, and I had no right to say any of those things to you."

"Of course you did. You had every right to say whatever you want to me. You're my sister. We share whatever we're feeling about things, even if we don't happen to agree. We always have. You know that."

Mollie looked at her, her eyes damp. "The truth is, I guess I was afraid."

"Afraid? Of what?"

"Of losing you. You've been everything to me these past eight years—both mother and father—and I've gotten spoiled thinking that I would always have you in my life."

Megan leaned forward, resting her elbows on the desk. "You aren't going to lose me, Mollie. I'm not going anywhere."

Mollie shook her head. "I can't believe I could be so selfish. You've sacrificed the past eight years of your life for us, struggling to keep everything going, and now here you have a chance for happiness and I throw a tantrum." She reached over the desk. "Will you forgive me?"

"There's nothing to forgive. I understand. All of this is a shock for me, too. Believe me. I'm still wondering if I could have made it all up. I keep looking at the ring to make sure it's real."

"The thing is, I want you to be happy, Megan. You deserve it more than anyone I know."

"I'll be just fine. You'll see."

"Is Travis going to be able to help with any of those?" She nodded toward the stack of bills Megan had been sorting through.

"He's offered to, yes."

"I hope you aren't going to be too stiff-necked to accept his offer."

"I can't afford to be, Mollie. Like it or not, we need all the help we can get right now."

"Will he be coming over today?"

"No. He's leaving town today but he said he'd call before he left. He's heading back out on the road."

"Will you tell him how sorry I am for behaving the way I did?"

"Sure."

The silence that fell between them was a companionable one. Mollie finally broke the silence. "There's one more thing I wanted to say."

"Okay."

"About your wedding dress."

Megan smiled. "Oh, I'm not going to worry about that. I'm sure I can find something suitable that—"

"That's what I want to talk to you about. I remember Mama once said that she never had a wedding dress since she and Daddy eloped because he was going into the army. I was thinking that it might be fun if us three girls find a pattern we might all like and I could make a gown that each of us could wear when we get married. I would love to do that for you, if you'd let me. I promise to do my very best and if

I get into any difficulty I'm sure Mrs. Schulz, my Home Ec teacher would help me with it.''

"Oh, Mollie, what a marvelous idea!''

"You think so?''

"Oh, yes. We just can't let it give Maribeth any ideas.''

"What do you mean?''

"She said this morning that she and Bobby are already planning their wedding for after they graduate from college. I just want to be sure she doesn't move the date up any because there's an available dress to wear.''

Mollie's mouth twitched, and Megan snickered, then they both burst into laughter. When they finally calmed down, Mollie said, "Maribeth has been talking about marrying Bobby since she was eight years old. I really don't think we have to worry about their making any sudden plans.''

"You know, I don't know where I've been all this time, but I didn't realize she felt that way about him.''

"Oh, Megan, she's still such a child in so many ways.''

"She's only two years younger than you are.''

"I know, but I'm not all that sure she sees herself as anything other than one of the guys. She takes no interest in how she dresses or what she looks like. She's still as tomboyish as she ever was. A lot of her talk is habit more than anything. A carryover from childhood.''

"Then you don't think I need to worry about her that much?''

"No, I don't. I rarely see them alone together anyway. Bobby's friend, Chris, is usually with them wherever they go.''

"Now that you mention it, I think Maribeth did mention a group of kids was going to Brady with them today."

"That's what I mean. They're all buddies. I don't think that's going to change anytime soon."

The phone rang and Megan picked it up.

"H'lo?"

"Megan?"

"Oh. Hi, Travis."

Mollie slipped out of the room with a quick wave and shut the door behind her.

"How's your day going?"

"Fine."

"So how did your sisters take the news?"

"Maribeth was ecstatic. As for Mollie, well, she asked me to tell you how sorry she was for the way she behaved toward you yesterday. She admitted that she was a little jealous that her big sister was developing a life of her own."

"Oh!" His laugh sounded relieved. "Then it didn't have anything to do with me, did it? That's good to know."

Megan crossed her fingers. "Of course not. She would have reacted the same way toward anyone. At least she recognized what she was doing and why. In fact, she was just now mentioning that she would like to make me a wedding dress."

"Wow, that *is* a change of heart!"

"Yes. Yes, it is."

"Well, I'll leave here feeling a little better about

things. Did you figure out how much money you need until I get back?''

She looked down at her list. "Yes, but you don't need to give it all to me now.''

"Just tell me, okay, and I'll drop it at the post office on my way out of town. You'll have it by tomorrow. I'd bring it by your place today, but then I'd have a hard time leaving. I'm going to miss you, Megan. That probably sounds silly to you, under the circumstances.''

"No. It doesn't sound silly at all,'' she replied, feeling shy. Somewhere between Travis's first kiss outside the jewelry store and the last one that had turned her bones to putty, she'd lost track of the purpose of this new business partnership.

She shook her head to clear it. "All right. Here's the total," she said, as though she'd been hunting for the figures. She read off the amount to him and said, "Is that going to be too much?''

"Not at all. So. When do you think we can get married?''

She chuckled. "You sound like an eager bridegroom.''

"What's wrong with that?''

"Nothing, I suppose. I thought I'd go into town in the morning for the mail and stop by to speak to the pastor.''

"I should be home by the fifth. Could we be married that Saturday? The eighth?''

"That's a lot of pressure to put on Mollie's skills as a seamstress.''

"Well, why don't I give you a call in a few days,

and in the meantime you can find out what she says, what the pastor says, and then we'll make more definite plans.''

''Okay.''

''Megan?''

''Mmm?''

''It's all going to work out just fine. Stop worrying.''

''That's going to be a hard habit to break.''

''That's understandable. Just try to remember that you aren't doing this all alone now. I'm going to be there for you. Maybe you can start off by letting me worry about things, okay?''

''Such as?''

''Where I'm going to sleep once we're married, maybe?''

''Travis!''

''Well, you never said.''

''You'll have your choice. We have two empty bedrooms that we've been using for storage. One is the largest bedroom in the house, the one our folks used. None of us wanted to move out of our own rooms so we left it empty.''

''Ah. A bedroom that's big enough for two. Now that sounds promising.''

''Travis, please don't get any ideas about—''

''Too late. The ideas have already arrived.''

''I'm not at all sure about that part of our relationship. I think it's just going to complicate an already complicated situation.''

''Not if we don't let it.''

''But we don't know each other well enough to—''

"Good Lord, woman, how many more years do we need to know each other before—"

"But we haven't gotten to know each other as adults, don't you understand? We haven't even seen each other in the past few years, or talked, or dated or…" Her voice trailed off.

"Or kissed? Or necked? Or petted?"

"You know what I mean."

"Okay," he said, chuckling. "Guess you win again. I promise not to badger you about sharing a room, or a bed. How's that?"

She was glad he wasn't there to see her face. She could feel it flaming. "Fine."

"I don't promise that I'm not going to be dreaming about you, though," he said in a husky voice. "I'm not responsible for what we do in my dreams. I'll be talking with you, Miss Megan. Bye now."

Seven

"**C**an't you stand still for just another moment?" Mollie muttered as she pinned the veiled cap to Megan's head.

"I'll just be glad to have all of this over. I can't believe the fuss everybody's been making."

Mollie stepped back and looked at her sister, standing there in one of the anterooms of the Aqua Verde church. "You look beautiful, Megan," she said softly. "Just beautiful."

Megan grabbed handfuls of the satin skirt and walked over to the full-length mirror Mollie had set up earlier. She stared at her image in surprise.

Once again Mollie had pulled off a miracle. The creamy satin gown hugged her breasts, ribs and waist, then flared over the hips into an ever larger swirl to the floor. The neckline dipped across her chest and hung just off her shoulders. The sleeves were long, ending in a point over the back of her hands.

The veil covered her face, but she could still see her face. She looked flushed, which wasn't surprising. She'd been rushing around all morning.

She turned back to Mollie who watched her with a smile. Mollie had not only made her wedding gown but with the help of friends had made her own maid-of-honor gown and Maribeth's bridesmaid dress. Mollie was in pale yellow; Maribeth in soft green.

Someone tapped on the door. Before either of them could answer Maribeth opened the door and slipped inside. She was holding a cluster of flowers. "Thank God your flowers arrived. Aren't they gorgeous?" Not waiting for a response she went on, "The church is almost full. I can't believe so many people turned out for the wedding."

Megan sighed. "I don't know why you're surprised. I think the whole county was invited."

"Well, the Kanes are telling everybody to come on out to their place for the barbecue reception. It's going to be great."

Travis's father, Frank, had offered to escort Megan down the aisle. Travis's brother, Zack, was his best man. The Kanes had been a godsend these past few months, helping with all the preparations.

She and Travis had been naive to think they could marry in three weeks. It was now the end of June, almost three months since he'd given her the ring. He'd been home only twice in that time, but during both visits he'd worked with her and Butch organizing needed repairs around the place.

He'd hired two more ranch hands to live on the place, which meant they'd had to build a bunkhouse near the barn to house them.

The extra help had been another blessing for both her and Butch. She'd overseen the repair of the windmill, and she and the girls had looked at paint samples to choose the color for the trim and the porch area of the house.

Everyone knew that Travis was paying for the improvements but nobody said anything. The townspeople and the surrounding ranch people appeared pleased that the O'Brien women finally had some needed assistance around the place.

Since everyone else seemed to accept the situation, Megan had worked hard to overcome her resistance to all the changes. Travis had assured her that he wouldn't try to run the ranch for her. He'd made it clear to the new hands that she was the one giving the orders, which appeased her somewhat.

However, when he showed up the second time with his arm in a sling and three cracked ribs, she'd suddenly come face-to-face with a brand-new fear—fear for Travis's safety.

However, he'd showed up at the church yesterday in time for the wedding rehearsal looking fit, taking the ribbing from all the participants, and wearing a cheerful grin. He was congratulated for having made it home in time to get married with no discernible injuries.

She hadn't seen him today. Mollie and Maribeth had smuggled her and her wedding clothes into the church before anyone else had arrived. All three of them had changed there.

There was another tap on the door. "Megan?"

It was Frank Kane, Travis's father.

Maribeth hurried to the door and opened it.

"It's time to get this show on the road," he said, looking around at each of them. "My, my, my. I can't remember the last time I saw such a dazzling bunch of ladies gathered in one small room. Y'all look smashing."

They could hear the organist playing in the chapel.

Mollie quickly knelt and rearranged the train to Megan's gown. When she straightened, she quickly wiped the corner of one eye. After a quick, silent hug, she went out the door, motioning to Maribeth.

Frank took Megan's hand and tucked it around his forearm. He patted her fingers. "I guess you know that you're making my boy a very happy man today."

She swallowed. "I hope so."

He smiled. "That young'un has carried a torch for you for years. I'd 'bout given up on him actually doing something about it."

His comments puzzled her for a moment until she remembered that Travis had told her he wanted everyone to think this was a love match. There was no telling what stories he'd made up to convince his family.

The music had paused moments before and now with a new melody, Maribeth was going down the aisle. As Frank had so aptly put it, it was time to get this show on the road. It couldn't be over soon enough for Megan. She'd never been cut out for all these fancy skirts and delicate veils. She'd take her jeans and boots over this stuff any day of the week.

She was halfway down the aisle when she saw Travis standing beside his brother. They both wore Western-cut suits—no sissy ruffles and tuxedos for them. As far as the men were concerned, women could get all dolled up to their heart's content, but wearing a suit instead of their jeans was as fancy as they intended to get.

In all the years she'd known him, Megan had never seen Travis wearing anything other than jeans. Now, in the black suit and the glossy black boots that showed beneath the flared boot-leg pants, he looked devastatingly handsome. His blinding white shirt emphasized his deep tan. He wore a Western bolo tie and his hair had been freshly trimmed.

For a moment Megan forgot to breathe. Here was the man she was about to marry, the man upon whom almost every female in the county had, at one time or another, had a crush. She'd been so busy planning for this day that she had lost sight of what today represented. In a few short minutes she would become the wife of Travis Kane...Megan O'Brien Kane. He would be her husband.

She lost the beat of her measured steps. Thank goodness they were close enough to the altar that it didn't really matter.

Megan turned her gaze toward Travis. He gave her his lopsided smile and a slow wink, then took her hand, rubbing his thumb over her knuckles.

The ceremonial words went by in a blur. Brief moments stood out clearly to her. Both Mollie and Zack produced the rings at the proper moments. Bemused, Megan stared at the glint of gold on Travis's bronzed hand. After a moment her eyes rose to search his. His face was solemn now, almost austere.

The next thing she knew Travis was lifting her veil and carefully draping it back over her head. "Hello, Mrs. Kane," he whispered before kissing her tenderly on her mouth. The pressure lasted only briefly before he raised his head. They turned to face the congregation. The pastor introduced them and the organ joyously released the refrains that accompanied them as they returned up the aisle together, Travis's arm wrapped securely around her waist.

Megan felt dizzy and disoriented by the time they paused on the steps of the church. Well-wishers poured out of the church behind them, quickly surrounding them, all laughing and talking.

"Are you okay?" Travis murmured.

"I don't think so," she whispered back, wondering if she was going to make a complete fool of herself by fainting for the very first time in her life.

To her astonishment Travis whisked her up into his arms, accompanied by more laughter and catcalls, and strode across the carefully manicured lawn to where his father's late-model sedan waited for them.

"Travis," she protested. "Put me down. I can at least walk to the—"

"Of course you can. Indulge me a little, okay? This is the first time I've had my arms around you in a while. Let me enjoy it while I can." His eyes were filled with amusement and his engaging grin tugged at her heart.

''What about the bouquet?'' somebody yelled from the crowd who were following them across the lawn.

Megan glanced down at the flowers she still clutched in her hand. Without looking, she tossed it up and over her head amid cheers and whistles. She glanced around in time to see the look of shock on Mollie's face when the bouquet fell in her hands. Frank opened one of the rear doors and Travis placed Megan on the seat. He laughingly stuffed yards of satin in behind her, then closed the door.

Megan allowed her head to drop back and rest against the seat of the car while she listened to the buzz of conversation, laughter and jokes nearby. Someone was teasing Travis about his devastating effect on women. She could hear Maribeth's excited voice in the midst of the babble. Megan opened her eyes in time to see Maribeth push through to the side of the car.

''What happened? Are you all right?'' she demanded, her eyes round.

Her little sister looked so grown-up in her dress. Bobby was standing a few feet away, excitedly talking to Travis...she caught enough words to recognize that rodeo was still his most avid topic of conversation. Mollie stood to the side, still holding the bouquet, her smile a little dazed.

How could so much change in such a short time? Megan had brushed away thoughts of the ceremony whenever it crossed her mind since April. It was just a necessary ritual to her. And yet...today she had felt the holiness, the commitment of what she was doing and she felt like the worst kind of sneak and liar.

Because he had wanted it that way, she had gone along with Travis's suggestion to let people think this was a culmination of a long-standing romance. People tended to believe what they wanted to, anyway. She'd never been the romantic type. She hadn't had time. Instead she'd put all her time and energy into hanging on to the ranch.

As a result of their marriage, the ranch was safe, which was what she had wanted, of course.

The door on the other side suddenly opened and Travis slid onto the seat beside her. Frank and Mona, Travis's mother, were getting into the front seat. They would now be driving out to the barbecue that was already cooking at the Kane ranch.

"Come on, Travis," somebody yelled. "You gotta kiss the blushing bride for us. We need to get a picture of this!" A camera was stuck in the open window.

Travis pulled her closer and laughingly kissed her with a loud smack.

"No, no! You gotta show some feeling here, man!"

"Not in front of the entire county, I don't," he retorted, making those who heard him laugh. "Let's get out of here," he muttered to his dad, who obliged him by pulling away from the curb with a honk and a wave. People started running for their cars, ready to follow them out to the ranch for the party-reception that had been planned.

Mona turned in the seat and said, "What a beautiful wedding, Megan. You and your sisters did a wonderful job of decorating the church…and your gowns are absolutely stunning.''

Megan felt her lips quivering. She was determined not to cry. Where had all these blasted emotions come from, anyway?

''I really didn't have that much to do with it. Mollie, Maribeth and several of their friends did all the work.'' She glanced down at her hands. ''I'm not really good at that sort of thing.''

''Your talent lies in other areas,'' Travis murmured, causing her to stiffen and stare at him in dismay. ''You know as much if not more than I do about raising cattle, managing property, keeping up with the accounting—'' He broke off with his list and grinned. ''What did you think I meant, honey?''

''Now, Travis,'' his mother admonished. ''Don't tease her. I swear you're the worst tease I've ever known.''

''He is, isn't he?'' Megan said, grateful for his mother's comment. ''He used to delight in making my life miserable when we were kids.''

Mona nodded. ''Oh, I remember. Your mama used to call and tell me about the times you'd get off the bus in tears, vowing vengeance on that rascal.'' She shook her head. ''I'd get on him about it, but it never did a lick o' good.'' She smiled at Megan. ''I was sitting there during the wedding thinking about how proud your parents would have been of you if they could have witnessed what happened today.''

''I like to think that they were there today,'' Megan replied softly. ''If we never die—if our spirits live on—then I know that they were there today.''

Travis squeezed her hand. He still had his other arm around her. "You scared me earlier. You were as white as a sheet. I thought you were going to faint."

"I was thinking the same thing. I don't know what came over me—maybe the crowd, the sudden heat after being in the air-conditioned church, or a mixture of it all."

"At least we don't have to worry about the possibility you might be pregnant."

"Travis!" Mona and Megan said in unison, their expressions of outrage almost identical.

He grinned unrepentantly. "Well? It's true, isn't it? Why are you shocked? Mom, I could see you being shocked if we'd announced that Megan *was* pregnant, but—"

"That's quite enough, Travis Franklin Kane," his mother admonished.

Travis and his father laughed. Mona turned so that she could see Megan and just shook her head. "I can't say I'm sorry to see him setting up his home somewhere else, but I must say, you have my sympathy, Megan, dear."

Thankfully, Megan didn't have to respond as they were pulling up at the Kane home where several people were already milling around setting up long trestle tables and tending to the meat being barbecued.

"I was going to change clothes but I forgot to get my bag at the church," she said, looking down at her dress. "I don't want to get it soiled, not after all the work Mollie went to making it."

"No problem," Frank said, stepping out of the car.

"Travis can run you home. That's one nice thing about being neighbors."

Mona got out and waved at them while Travis slid under the wheel. "No use fighting all your slips and skirts for the short ride over there," he said, resting his arm on the back of the seat and glancing at her as he backed up and turned the car around. "I'll play your chauffeur, madame."

Just like that, they were alone. The car seemed to be filled with a silence that was almost tangible. Megan searched her mind for something to say, but her thoughts had scattered.

She was relieved when they pulled up in the deserted yard of the Circle B. Travis walked around the car and held the door open, offering her his hand.

Feeling ridiculously shy, Megan accepted his help and stepped out of the car. She picked up the front of her multilayered skirts and as naturally as though he was used to helping a bride, Travis took the train and draped it over his arm and followed her up the back steps.

The kitchen seemed to echo with emptiness. Together they walked up the steps and down the hallway to her room. She paused in the open doorway and looked up at him, feeling ill at ease.

"You're going to need some help with those buttons," he said quietly. "Mollie must have thought she'd be here to get you out of that dress."

Megan groaned. "Oh, I forgot all about them. I don't know why she didn't just put in a zipper."

He led her into the room and turned her back toward the window, where there was more light. "I can do it."

She fought to control her reaction to his touch as his fingers moved at an excruciatingly slow pace down her spine, from her neck to her lower back.

When he was finished he nonchalantly walked around to face her and without meeting her gaze, took the end of the sleeve of each arm, one at a time, and allowed her to pull her arms out. Holding the dress, he said, "Step out."

Most of the underskirt was sewn to the dress so that Megan now wore her strapless lace bra and a matching pair of bikini panties beneath a sheer half-slip.

She hastily took a step toward her bed to pick up her housecoat when he caught her hand. "Please don't," he said, his voice sounding husky.

She knew her cheeks were fiery red when she looked up at him. His gaze moved over her body, his expression wistful. "You are so beautiful, Megan."

Now that was a lie, and she knew it. "You don't have to say things like that to me, Travis. Remember? We're going to be honest with each other. I'm too skinny, my breasts are too small, my hips too narrow, my—"

"Hush," he said, pulling her into his arms and placing his finger across her lips. "You are a beautiful woman, inside and out. And you aren't too skinny. You're just right." His arms locked around her. "You're an exact perfect armful. What more could anyone possibly want?"

He replaced his hand with his lips, kissing her, nipping at her bottom lip, then soothing it with his tongue. He kissed and caressed her, his hands roaming restlessly up and down her spine.

She couldn't think when he kissed her that way. She knew that they needed to get back to the party. They were the guests of honor. They had wedding gifts to open and— Her mind began to reel, doing cartwheels in her head until she clung to Travis for balance.

His kiss intensified, his mouth hot, his tongue thrusting between her lips in a hypnotic rhythm. Megan felt a heated response from somewhere deep inside of her. She was having those restless sensations again that seemed to occur whenever he kissed her. She leaned into him and only then realized that sometime in the past few moments Travis had unfastened her bra. Now her bare breasts were pressed against his coat jacket. Feverishly she fumbled to unfasten the buttons on his shirt, loosened his bolo tie and with a soft sigh rubbed her breasts against his hair-roughened chest.

Travis continued to kiss and caress her mouth and face with his lips while he picked her up and placed her on the bed. He pushed the half-slip down, and stroked his hand along her hip and thigh, sliding over to her inner thigh then up until it rested on her curly mound.

Her eyes flew open and she let go of him, staring up at him in shock. "What are you doing?" she asked, her voice unsteady with the need for air. She realized that she was lying there with her slip around her ankles, wearing only her lacy thigh-high hose and her bikini panties.

Travis sank onto the bed beside her and ran his hand through his hair in disgust. "Losing my mind, that's obvious," he muttered, giving his head a hard shake.

She scrambled to sit up against the headboard and grabbed one of the pillows, hugging it tightly against her.

"I don't suppose it would do any good to say that I didn't mean for that to happen." He stood and walked away from her toward the windows. He kept his back to her.

She stared at the wide expanse of his shoulders beneath the coat. "I believe you," she finally admitted. "I didn't mean to unbutton your shirt and— Well, I don't know why I—"

He turned and looked at her, his shirt hanging open, pulled out of his pants. "We seem to catch on fire like a spark in dry tinder every time I touch you. I swear, all I wanted to do was help you with the dress. And then when I saw you standing there, I couldn't resist. I needed to touch you and taste you— I'm not trying to force you into anything. I want you to know that."

"Please, Travis. It's okay. Really. It's nobody's fault. It's like you said. Whenever we kiss we just kind of go—I don't know—crazy somehow. At least we know that's what happens. So we can avoid kissing from now—"

"Now, wait a minute! We don't have to go to that extreme, darlin'," he drawled. "I think I can control myself enough to be able to kiss and hold you without coming completely undone.''

''Well, maybe *you* can,'' she replied with more than a little exasperation, ''but I can't seem to keep my hands off you. It's so silly. I mean, I've known you forever and spent most of my life detesting you, and yet—and yet—''

''Yes?'' he said, silently stalking back to the bed and leaning over her.

She pulled back closer to the headboard. ''Travis, we don't have time to discuss this right now. We've got to get back to the party before everybody else gets there.''

''The folks will tell them where we've gone.''

''But still, it doesn't take all that long to change clothes. They'll wonder what's taking so much time!''

Travis straightened, his hands resting on his hips, and laughed without restraint. ''Oh, honey,'' he finally managed to say, ''they'll know exactly what's going on. We're newlyweds, have you forgotten?''

She slid off the bed, still holding her pillow as a shield and hurried to her dresser drawers. Opening one of them, she grabbed a pair of faded jeans and, with her back to Travis, dropped the pillow and hastily stepped into them, tugging them up to her waist. She filled them out quite nicely, Travis noted, still grinning.

Opening another drawer, she took out a plain white cotton bra and put it on, fastening it on the way to her closet. She pulled a Western-style shirt off a hanger, grabbed a pair of boots and walked over to the chair.

"Is that what you're wearing to the party?" he said, making no effort to hide his amusement.

She stood, stamping her feet into the boots and looked at him belligerently. "This is me, Travis. This is who I am. I don't own fancy clothes. I had to borrow the dress I wore the first time you took me out. If this—" She looked down at what she was wearing. "If *I'm* going to be an embarrassment to you—"

"No way, Megan. You could never be an embarrassment to me."

He held out his hand. "C'mon, sweetheart. Let's go enjoy our party. It isn't every day a person gets married. Let's make the most of it!"

Eight

Travis leaned against one of the stately live oak trees
that surrounded the grounds of the home where he'd
spent his life and watched his friends and family celebrate his wedding.

Somewhere in that throng was his bride, laughing
at the jokes, blushing at the innuendoes, gamely going
through the pantomime the day called for.

He'd really messed up earlier. He'd been moments
away from taking her as if he were some undisci-
plined lout staking his claim, making her his wife in
fact as well as name. He'd lost his head in the inti-
macy of the moment. That was no way to start out
their relationship, not if he intended to convince her
that they belonged together.

He was going to have to cool it, somehow, which
was going to be much more difficult than he'd imag-

ined during his long weeks away. Hadn't he planned how he would carefully woo and win her? Hadn't he thought all of it through, coaxing her to become used to his presence in her life?

At least now they would be sharing living quarters, another step in the process of establishing a permanent relationship with her. Didn't it help to know that she was as easily aroused as he was? He'd discovered today that she would be as passionate a lover as she was passionate in her zest for life. He had to make certain that he didn't scare her off by rushing her. One step at a time, remember that, he reminded himself.

"Travis? Why are you lurking here under the trees?"

He glanced around at the sound of his brother's voice. "Just thinking about things, I guess. It's probably not all that unusual, considering that today represents a traditional milestone in anybody's life."

Zack shook his head and grinned. "Better you than me, but then, you've had it bad for a long, long time. Megan hasn't a clue how you feel about her, does she?"

Travis smiled at his tone. "You noticed, huh?"

"Why haven't you told her?"

Trust his brother to get to the point.

"Because she wouldn't have married me."

Zack narrowed his eyes. "Care to run that past me one more time?"

Travis leaned his head against the tree. "Megan agreed to marry me in exchange for my help in running the ranch. She didn't want me to pretend any feelings for her and I realized if I told her the truth, she'd run in the opposite direction. So, I convinced her I could and would help her as a friend and neighbor and for no other reason. Lucky for me she had pretty much exhausted all her other options and she rather reluctantly accepted my offer.'' He threw his hands wide and said, ''I'm her last resort. That's always good for a man's ego.''

''Oh, I don't think we have to worry about the condition of your ego, bro. I'd say it's alive and well.''

Travis shrugged. ''I convinced her that we needed to pretend we were getting married for all the usual reasons.''

Zack laughed. ''Then I think Dad may have blown your cover. He told me earlier that he mentioned to her the fact that you'd been carrying a torch for her for years.''

''When did he tell her that?''

''Just before he walked her down the aisle. He said she looked a little shocked for a moment. I can see why.''

''Then she no doubt convinced herself that Dad didn't know the truth. She's determined to think of herself as incapable of attracting anyone. I decided to wait until the deed was done before I set out to convince her that my feelings are considerably more than friendly.''

''How did you convince her to make such a commitment to you?''

''By telling her that she can end it in twelve months.''

Zack shook his head. "Well, bro, I think you've been thrown off those bulls onto your head once too often. I'm afraid there's a real good chance you're going to end up with a busted heart as well as a busted skull if you aren't careful."

"To be honest, I fully expected for her to back out before the ceremony. That's one reason I hired the two guys to go to work over there. I gave her the money to pay the mortgage. I did everything I could to insure that she wouldn't renege on her end of the bargain."

"Why, you're like one of those dumb animals who not only knows it's headed for slaughter but actually races to get there. You amaze me, little brother, plumb amaze me."

Travis grinned. "Well, the way I look at it, I've got a year to convince her that I'm the greatest thing that ever happened to her and that she wouldn't be happy without me. I figure if I work it right the odds have to be in my favor."

Zack laughed and slapped him on the back. "Like I said, that ego of yours is alive and kicking, all right. C'mon, Dad sent me over here to tell you that it's time to get the music going for some dancing. And that means you've gotta lead that wife of yours out first."

Travis pushed away from the trunk of the tree and sauntered across the lawn to the swirling mass of people. "I can only try to make this marriage work, Zack. You know me. Stubborn as a mule. I'm determined to give it all I've got."

* * *

Megan felt a distinct tingling between her shoulder blades. She turned, wondering what had caused it. That's when she spotted Travis and Zack coming across the wide expanse of lawn toward the gathering that still lingered in the vicinity of the food.

Travis had removed his suit coat earlier in the afternoon, as well as his tie. He'd unbuttoned the top three buttons of his shirt and rolled up the sleeves above his elbows.

The trousers to the suit looked tailor-made for his lean, long-legged body, the slight flare below the knee to accommodate the boots adding to the graceful line of his muscular length.

She wondered where the two men had been. The only thing in that direction were the trees and the wooden fence of one of the horses' pens. Who knows? Maybe they'd slipped off to have a heart-to-heart talk. She smiled at the idea. She had a hunch there was very little that Travis hadn't already figured out about male-female relationships.

Travis walked up to her and hugged her. For the obvious benefit of the onlooking crowd he gave her another smacking kiss and said, "Hi there! Did you miss me?"

She grinned. "Desperately," she said, playing along with his mood.

"Now that's what I like to hear," he said, this time as though it was meant for her ears only. She gave him a puzzled glance. "Zack says it's time to begin the music...and we're expected to start off the dancing."

"Who made up all these rules, rituals and rites

about getting married?'' she replied with a sigh. ''I've been getting all kinds of flack for my lack of proper bridelike apparel.''

''Well, honey, you might notice that you're the only female here in boots and jeans and it's your wedding.''

''Exactly. It seems to me that since it's my wedding I should be able to dress as I please.''

He dropped his hands lower on her back, cupping her buttocks and pulling her up tight against him. ''You haven't heard me complaining about those tight jeans, now, have you?''

''Travis!'' She tried to push away from him in the midst of the general laughter, but his hold was too strong.

He nibbled on her ear and whispered, ''Relax and enjoy it, honey. It's all part of the fun.''

When she looked around, she saw the smiles and tender looks between some of the other married couples and realized that he was right. The joking and teasing was just as much a part of all of this as the flowers and the rings.

She relaxed and he immediately let go of her. ''Let's go find some music.'' He took her hand and led her over to the portable tape player.

''I don't know how to dance.''

''Of course you do. You danced with me in Austin.''

''But that was different. They're going to expect something mushy and sentimental for the first one and I can't slow dance.''

''Just follow me, baby. I won't let you down.''

Thanks to Travis, it really was all right. He found a simple melody from a popular country-and-western album and led her to the concrete patio area near the house. After they completed a circuit around the area, the others immediately joined in. By the time the song was finished, the area was filled with dancers.

Another song began and Travis continued to hold her while others began to take part in some line dancing.

"That wasn't so bad, was it?" he asked, his voice pitched below the music.

"No. Thank you for helping me to deal with all of this."

"Hey, the worst is over. We've cut the cake, opened the presents. We can leave anytime now."

"Somebody asked where we were going for our honeymoon. That's the first time I'd even thought about one."

"I told the few who mentioned it to me that we planned to take one later, but that right now there was too much that needed to be done."

Mona walked up to them and said, "Where do you two intend to stay tonight?"

Megan looked at Travis, who seemed to be waiting for her to answer. "I, uh, thought we'd go home—I mean, to the ranch."

"Would you like for me to invite Mollie and Maribeth to stay here? I would imagine you'd like some privacy since—"

"Thanks, Mom, but that won't be necessary," Travis interjected smoothly. "The O'Brien house is plenty big enough for privacy, and we're all going to be living there so we might as well get used to it. However, I do think we're going to slip away from the party now. Megan's tired and I need to take the load of belongings that's piled in the back of my truck over there. Maybe you could have Dad bring the girls home whenever they're ready to leave, if they need a ride.''

''Bobby Metcalf has his dad's truck. He can drop them off on his way home,'' Megan said.

Mona hugged them both and waved them off as they unobtrusively went around the house to where his truck was parked. At least nobody had tried to decorate it for him, which was a blessing.

''I figured you didn't want to hang around for a public send-off, considering everything,'' Travis said, helping her into the truck.

''No, please. I've really had enough of all this.''

''You've been a good sport. But I really think it was necessary for the community to treat this as a normal marriage.''

''Me, too.'' She impulsively leaned over and placed a kiss on his cheek. ''Thanks for being so understanding.''

Megan was pleasantly relaxed, which was surprising, considering that she and Travis were alone once again. She supposed it had to do with his nonchalant attitude, as though getting married and moving in together was just an ordinary occurrence, a logistics problem to be worked out.

They drove to her house once again and stopped near the back door. Travis looked over at her and said, ''I want you to know that what happened here earlier won't happen again. I don't want you worrying about the possibility that I might pounce on you at any moment.''

''I'm not.''

Darned if he didn't look disappointed. She almost smiled at the thought he might be bothered by the idea that she trusted him. The fact was, she trusted him more than she did herself at the moment.

She couldn't forget how his kisses and his touch had triggered all kinds of new and wonderful sensations within her. After all the rites and ceremonies today, she certainly felt married enough to at least consider the idea that there was nothing standing between their sharing the same bed and participating in all the intimacies of marriage.

However, she didn't trust all these new feelings. They certainly weren't reliable, not enough upon which to make such a decision. There was time…a year at least…in which to explore the possibilities of learning more about the pleasures to be enjoyed with her husband.

Megan climbed out of the truck and gathered up some of the bags Travis brought while he removed the boxed cartons and placed them on the porch.

With both of them unloading, it didn't take long to have everything in his room. The bedroom was a corner room and had originally been two rooms. An earlier O'Brien had knocked out the dividing wall and had partitioned part of the larger space to make a walk-in closet and a bathroom.

Megan went to the bathroom door and said, ''You'll find towels and shampoo and soap in here.

Sometimes I use this one when the other one's occupied.''

''Why didn't one of you move in here after your parents died?''

''We talked about it. Several weeks after friends helped us to pack up all our parents' belongings, I considered moving in. The girls were so young at the time, they preferred their own rooms that Mama had decorated for them. The truth is, I felt the same way. Plus, I wanted to be closer to the girls in case they cried out at night. It's very quiet back here. You shouldn't be disturbed.''

The bed was an oversize four-poster. She studiously ignored it. ''There's plenty of drawer space for your things, and as you can see, the closet is huge. Do you want me to help you unpack?''

''Maybe tomorrow. I think we've done enough today.''

''I'll see you in the morning, then.''

''Megan?''

She stopped in the open doorway to the hall. ''Yes?''

''You're still welcome to use this bathroom anytime. I don't mind sharing.''

There was only one lamp on in the room, and his face was in shadows, so she couldn't see his expression. She nodded, not knowing what to say. The casual, friendly atmosphere had disappeared and she could feel the tension mounting between them. With a hasty ''good night,'' Megan retreated to the safety of her own room.

Share the bathroom, share the bed. Share his life.

She couldn't do that. She couldn't allow herself to become vulnerable where Travis Kane was concerned. He had his own life, mostly on the road. She had her responsibilities here. What if she became too attached to him? She couldn't afford to miss him when he was gone, or look forward to his coming home. She certainly couldn't get caught up in worrying about his safety.

She just couldn't.

Early the next morning Megan was hunched over the kitchen table sipping her second cup of coffee when Travis came downstairs. Although it was light outside, the sun had yet to appear. She glanced up at him with a scowl before returning her glare to her coffee.

He grinned at the sight of her sitting there in her sleeveless shirt and coveralls, still barefoot, with her hair uncombed. "You find out all kinds of interesting things about a person you wouldn't have guessed unless you happen to live with them."

Obviously reluctant, she raised her eyes until her gaze met his. "What's that supposed to mean?"

He poured himself a cup of coffee, snagged the leg of his chair with the toe of his boot and turned it to face her before sitting down next to her. "That you get up earlier than I do, and that you're grumpy in the mornings."

She shoved her hand through her hair and reached for her cup. "You're reading a great deal into very little evidence."

He took a sip of the coffee and smiled. She made

a mean cup of coffee. He could forgive a great deal in exchange for that particular talent. "True," he acknowledged. "Where did I go wrong?"

She folded her arms and rested them on the table. "I've been up for a while because I couldn't sleep." She shook her head in disgust. "I heard the girls come home, I heard every rustle in the yard, I heard—" She shrugged. "You get the picture. I've been sitting here trying to decide whether to try to get some work done or to go back to bed and hope to get some sleep."

"Ah. While I, on the other hand, slept very well," he said, stretching the truth more than a little. There was something about sleeping alone on his wedding night that created a certain restlessness, not to mention being aware of his new bride just down the hallway. However, he couldn't resist teasing his grumpy bride this morning. "The bed's quite comfortable, thank you for asking. I came down hoping to find you up and about. I have a suggestion to make. Why don't we spend today outdoors, maybe take the horses and have a picnic?" He took another sip of coffee, hoping to catch her reaction without being obvious.

Megan rubbed her head, wishing her nagging headache would go away. It wasn't fair that he could be so rested and relaxed, that he could sleep like a baby, while she tossed and turned all night.

"It will do you good to get away for a few hours," he coaxed. "Besides, I'm going to have to leave tomorrow. I'd like to spend a little time with you before I go."

She straightened. "You just got here."

"I know. But if I don't stay with my schedule I won't rack up enough points to qualify for world champion, which is what all this traveling is about. I have to enter as many events as I can." He leaned back in his chair. "I had to pass up a couple in order to come home for the weekend."

She gave him a disgruntled look. "I'm sorry if I put you out."

"Are you sure you aren't like this every morning?" he asked with mock suspicion. He had to tease her or he'd grab her and kiss the living daylights out of her. Damn, but she was adorable in this mood. No wonder he'd been unable to resist her when they were kids.

She buried her face in her hands and groaned. She peered at him through her fingers. "Oh, Lord, I don't know. I don't seem to know myself at all, anymore. I lay there last night wondering what I'd done. How could I have thought that marrying you would solve anything?"

Oops. He'd hoped that the ceremony yesterday had effectively moved them past this part of their relationship. "Well," he said, thinking hard, "at least your immediate concerns are taken care of. The mortgage is paid for another year, you've been able to take care of the most pressing repairs, and—" he threw his arms wide "—you got me in the bargain. Doesn't that count for something?"

The look she gave him was quite similar to the ones she used to give him on the school bus all those years ago. "That's what bothers me, if you want to know the truth. Our plans all sounded so cut-and-dried when we first discussed the idea. I mean, let's face it, I know you as well as I know anybody. I trust you. But now that we're actually married, none of it seems real to me.''

He let out a silent breath of relief. If she had to deal with these doubts, he was glad she was looking at them *after* the wedding and not before. At least now he had a better chance of dealing with them.

''Let's not worry about it just yet. I'm no expert by any means but it makes sense to me that marriage takes some getting used to. So why don't we just ease along, continuing with our routines while we spend whatever time we can together, and see what happens? Nothing has to be decided on today, does it?''

She'd been watching him closely during his speech, as though trying to make up her mind about something. He was glad he'd taken the time to shower and shave and put on his best pressed shirt. When she continued to study him in the silence that fell between them he lifted his brows in silent query.

After allowing the silence to stretch, she eventually asked, ''Are you always so bright-eyed at this time of the day?'' as though she really wanted to know.

''Only on alternate weekends,'' he immediately replied. ''The rest of the time I don't hear anybody or anything, much less talk, until the middle of the morning.''

He spotted a tiny grin lurking on her face as she said, ''That's good to know. I'd never realized before that unremitting cheerfulness too early in the day can be quite grating.''

''I'll keep that in mind.'' He got up and refilled

both their cups. "So, how about it, sunshine? You want to run for the hills today? After all, this is officially our honeymoon."

She considered his earlier suggestion, not really finding anything wrong with it. She wouldn't have worked today anyway, which was one of her problems. She didn't know what to do with herself. Her life had changed when she hadn't been paying enough attention. She wasn't sure what to do next. "Do you have a particular place in mind?" she finally asked.

"Yeah, as a matter of fact, I do. I thought we'd take Daisy over to Dad's place by trailer, get my horse and ride back into a part of his property that he doesn't check out much. It would give me a chance to scout around and report to him how it looks, as well as give us a chance to do some exploring in a part of the county you haven't seen."

Megan stood and stretched. Either the coffee or the conversation had helped her mood. "I'd like that," she decided suddenly. She walked over to the refrigerator and opened the door. "The girls brought home enough food from the reception that we won't have to cook for at least a week. I could make up a picnic lunch."

He could feel his relief that she'd agreed to his plan run through his blood like the finest champagne. It was all he could do not to laugh out loud with triumph. Instead he nodded and said, "Great. While you do that, I'll make us some breakfast."

She looked around at him in surprise. "You can cook?"

"Yep."

"Wow. Maybe I got a better deal than I thought. I've often wondered what I'll do once Mollie leaves for college. I really don't function well in a kitchen."

He started gathering ingredients for pancakes. "You've got her convinced to go?"

"Yes. She got accepted at UT in Austin. I'm going to miss her but I'm glad she's going to get away and enjoy people her own age. She's had too much responsibility."

"That sounds funny, coming from you."

"Not really. That's why I understand the importance of a social life, so she won't be like me—awkward and unsure of herself."

He paused in his mixing. "Is that the way you view yourself? I see you as self-assured, filled with self-confidence, knowing what you want and striving to achieve it."

Why did his words remind her of some of the thoughts that had kept her awake most nights these past few weeks—thoughts of when she'd been in high school, wanting to be noticed by this particular man. Her feelings had been buried so deeply back then they were only now beginning to surface, which made her very self-conscious around him.

Megan began to fill a basket with food while Travis put their breakfast on the table. They worked together as though they'd been a team for years.

After they ate and were rinsing their breakfast dishes, Travis said, "Be sure to bring a swimsuit. There's a great place to swim in this particular section. Zack and I used to swim in this stream when we were kids. By the time we get there, we'll probably be glad to rest and cool off some.''

A tingling awareness shot through her once again at the idea that she and Travis were going to spend the day alone together…and that he was leaving again tomorrow.

Hopefully she would get through today and have some time to work through this strange jumble of feelings before Travis came home the next time. She hated the jittery, jumpy feelings that had engulfed her recently. All she wanted was to return to the uneventful life she'd been leading before Travis Kane showed up and turned her life upside down.

Nine

By the time they reached the hidden canyon back in the hills, the sun was high overhead. They'd been riding for most of the morning through rough terrain. The unexpected adventure was just what Megan had needed to get her mind off her strange situation. Horseback riding had always been a way for her to relax and become a part of nature.

Did Travis know her that well to have suggested it, or did he find a similar sense of well-being away from the world? She was too content at the moment to ask him, but filed the thought away for another time.

Megan was surprised to discover that the Kane ranch, although sharing a border with the O'Brien ranch, had a different geological landscape on part of the land. There were more granite outcroppings, the hills were steeper, and she had seen a couple of natural springs that she wished they had on the Circle B.

Cottonwood trees and weeping willows lined both banks of the stream that ran through the canyon, providing shade for the horses and a cool place for a picnic.

The canyon was wide enough to capture the breeze flowing over the land. Since they had been steadily climbing, the air actually felt cooler here, despite the summer sun beating down around them.

"I don't know about you," Travis said, dismounting, "but I think I'm going to swim before we eat. I'd like to cool off some."

"Sounds good to me." She looked around the area and noticed that one of the weeping willows had an abundance of foliage drooping toward the water that could provide a private changing area.

She slid off Daisy and while Travis loosened the cinches on the horses she dug into the bag she'd brought for her swimsuit.

She'd had her suit for more years than she could remember. It was faded and without style, but it had never mattered to her before. Now, she felt a little self-conscious about being seen in it, but there was nothing to be done about it.

By the time she stepped through the leaves once again Megan discovered that Travis had already changed into ragged cutoffs and was already wading into the stream.

"How is it?" she asked, admiring the way his broad shoulders narrowed down into a trim waist. He was already brown from the sun, the muscles in his back gleaming.

He paused and glanced around. "Great, really great. I'm always amazed at how cold the water is, no matter how hot it is. The springs feeding this stream must come from way underground." His gaze took in her skimpy attire.

She self-consciously pulled her suit down over her hips, then hastily readjusted the top. She must have grown some since the purchase of this particular piece of apparel. Since it was all she had to wear, she couldn't be too choosy.

Luckily Travis didn't appear to notice what she was wearing. He had already turned away and dived beneath the water.

She sank into the refreshing depths with a chuckle. This was wonderful! There had been times when she was younger when she'd take the girls swimming in one of the stock tanks but this was so much better— cooler and fresher. She wished the girls were there to share it with her.

That's when she remembered that she and Travis were there together because they were married and people expected them to spend some time alone before he left again.

She was grateful that he'd come up with his plan to remove them from everyone. They hadn't even seen anyone when they'd brought Daisy over earlier in the day. It was almost as though they were the only two people in the world today.

Megan stretched out and floated on her back, closing her eyes. She wasn't prepared for the feel of something brushing her thigh. She let out a squeal as she jerked away and opened her eyes. Travis was standing beside her, grinning.

She'd gone under when she'd started trying to get away from what obviously was Travis touching her, and she came up sputtering. "You scared me to death!" she yelled, taking a swing at him.

He nimbly dodged her and hit the water with the side of his hand, splashing her full in the face.

"Travis!" She hit a spray of water back at him and in moments they were playing and splashing each other as if they were a couple of kids. He dived under the water and grabbed her ankles. She had a chance to grab some air so that as soon as she went under she twisted and hit him hard behind the knees so that he, too, collapsed.

Because of her smaller size, she was much more nimble and was able to give as good as she got. By the time they crawled out of the water they were both weak with a combination of laughter and strenuous exercise.

"I can't remember when I've acted so silly," she said, still giggling, as she grabbed a towel and scrubbed her face and hair. When she uncovered her head she saw that Travis was standing a few feet away, his hands on his hips, watching her with a grin on his face.

"What?" She asked, looking around. "Did you want this towel? What is it?"

He shook his head and without taking his eyes off her reached down and picked up his towel. "I was just enjoying watching you. I can't remember ever having seen you laugh before. I was just thinking about that. As I recall you were generally angry with me about something or the other.''

She leaned over and began to dry her legs. ''That's not surprising, since you always did your very best to make me angry!'' She straightened and saw that he was absently patting his dripping chest, still watching her.

''Did you ever wonder why I pestered you so much?''

''I didn't have to wonder. I knew you hated me. Well, believe me, the feeling was mutual!''

His grin shone white in his darkly tanned face. He shook his head. ''Wrong. Guess again.''

She tied her towel around her waist and began to unload the food she'd stuck in the saddlebags. Travis spread out the blanket he'd tied to the back of his saddle and knelt down beside her, still watching her with amusement.

After setting everything out, she leaned back on her heels and looked at him. ''What do you mean, guess again?''

''I didn't hate you. I've never hated you. So guess again.''

She looked at him, puzzled by his attitude. ''You just like to tease people?''

''Close. I always liked teasing you.''

She snorted and began filling a plate with barbecued chicken, potato salad and spicy baked beans. ''That's for sure,'' she said, taking a bite and giving a sensuous purr of pleasure.

He quickly mimicked her actions, and they spent

the next several minutes indulging their appetites. At one point, Travis got a thermos of lemonade out of his saddlebag and filled the cuplike lid. They companionably shared the icy liquid between them while they ate.

"I'd forgotten how good all of this tastes," she said, licking the barbecue sauce off her fingers. "I guess I was more nervous yesterday than I thought. I didn't eat very much, and what I did eat, I don't remember actually tasting."

He stretched out on the blanket and folded his arms beneath his head. "You didn't act nervous."

She began to gather up their scraps and carefully stored the leftovers. She glanced at him from the corner of her eye. "I thought it was obvious to everybody, especially you."

"Nope. You acted like getting married was something you do all the time." He draped his hat over his nose with one hand while patting the blanket beside him. "Settle down and rest...let some of that food settle. Maybe we'll go swimming again before we leave."

She yawned. "My sleepless night is catching up with me now that I've filled my tummy." After placing the food back in her saddlebag she stretched out on the blanket on the opposite side from him. Within minutes, she was sound asleep.

Travis couldn't get enough of watching her. He could easily spend the coming weeks and months following her around, watching her many moods and listening as she dealt with life on the ranch.

She was so active, so vital, and most of the time

so unselfconscious. He found her fascinating. At the moment she was sprawled bonelessly beside him like a child. Her total innocence and lack of sexual awareness continued to keep him off-balance.

She seemed to take their skimpy attire in stride while he fought to control his response every time he looked at her. That was the biggest reason why he'd chosen to wear the cutoff jeans to swim in. They were more likely to camouflage his unfailing reaction to her whenever he was around her.

Travis had a plan, and he wanted to follow that plan, but he hadn't taken into account just how difficult being with her, living with her, was going to be for him when he couldn't make love to her.

He sighed, and closed his eyes. Even the thought stirred him. He was really in bad shape. It was probably a good thing he was leaving tomorrow.

He must have dozed off. The next thing he heard was a slight murmur from Megan. He glanced over and saw that sometime in the past hour or so, she had turned on her side and was now facing him. The strap to her swimsuit had slipped off her shoulder so that the top drooped across her chest.

Without giving the gesture much thought, Travis sleepily reached over and slipped his fingers beneath the strap to return it to its proper place. Her eyes fluttered open and she smiled at him, still more than half asleep, herself. His hand stilled on her sun-warmed arm. His fingers reflexively moved across the satiny skin.

"Did you sleep?" she asked.

"Some." He continued to stroke her shoulder and

arm. Instead of replacing the strap, his movements slid it even lower, exposing a larger expanse of her breasts.

He kept his eyes on hers as he moved his hand until it slid inside her suit and cupped her. Instead of recoiling from him, she smiled and her eyes drifted closed once again. She arched her back so that her breast pressed deeper into his cupped hand. He bit back a groan.

This was insanity. She was still more than half asleep. He couldn't take advantage of her. And yet... and yet, he wanted—no *needed*—to touch her, needed a tantalizing taste of her sweetness.

Travis slipped the other strap from her shoulder and inched the top down her body until it rested at her waist. She smiled without opening her eyes.

He leaned down, touching the tip of her breast with his tongue, before sliding his lips around her, gently tugging.

She squirmed, her hips lifting slightly as she moved closer toward him.

He knew he didn't dare risk the strides he'd gained by getting her to marry him. However, he also knew he couldn't stop touching her. Not just yet.

He nuzzled her breast, first tugging, then soothing the pebbled tip with quick flicks of his tongue, moving from one to the other, placing soft kisses on the plump underside.

Languidly lifting her hand she touched his head, running her fingers through his hair. Her thumb caressed his ear. She continued moving her legs and hips restlessly.

Unable to resist such a seductive temptation, Travis continued to place tiny kisses in a meandering path across her breasts and down to her waist, eventually pushing her suit down…down…down her body and legs until it was removed.

He continued to caress her with his mouth and tongue, all the while cupping her breast…gently molding and tracing its shape with his hand.

He swirled his tongue in and around her belly button, causing her to moan and spasmodically move once again. When he raised his head to look at her, she was watching him, her eyes glittering.

"You are so beautiful," he whispered, his voice shaking.

"So are you," she replied softly.

He closed his eyes. "I've got to stop this. I can't— I know you—" He opened his eyes again.

"We *are* married," she offered timidly.

"Oh, yes. We're definitely married."

"Well, maybe it would be all right if— I mean…" Her voice trailed off.

He leaned on his elbow and looked at her with a burning intensity. "Will you let me love you?" he asked.

Her eyes seemed to grow larger as she stared back at him. He waited, not wanting to rush her. If she said no, he was determined to leave her alone…but he prayed that she wouldn't say no.

Slowly she nodded her head.

That's when it hit him. This wasn't why he'd brought her out here. He had thought— Dear God, what had he thought he was doing? She watched him, her face flushed, as though wondering what he would do next as she lay there beside him, wearing nothing more than a slightly apprehensive expression.

As though he was waiting for something—or some-one—to stop him, Travis hesitantly placed his hand over her mound of tight curls, slowly slipping his fingers into her honeyed depths.

She was…oh…so warm there…warm…and slick with arousal. With an abrupt movement he reached down and unsnapped his cutoff jeans, then raised his hips enough to shove them down his legs.

Her eyes widened at the sight of his erection. He knelt between her legs, then braced his hands beside her shoulders and began to kiss her—long, possessive kisses…he tried to show her the familiar rhythm with his tongue, hoping she would understand and not be frightened.

When he lowered himself to her she gave a little whimper of impatience, sliding her arms around his waist and holding him tightly.

He rested against her briefly before he entered her, pushing slowly, easing a path. She was so hot and so tight.

She took control by the simple act of raising her hips to meet his careful thrust. Travis could no longer hold back and began to move in an overheated rhythm that quickly set both of them afire.

She clung to him, which further inflamed him, pushing him further and faster until he didn't have the strength to hold back a moment longer.

Megan let out a soft cry and tightened her grip around him and he gratefully recognized the spasmodic contractions that told him she had reached her peak. Her sudden cry had caused him to lose whatever control he'd clung to. His chest heaved in an effort to fill his lungs with much-needed oxygen, and he closed his eyes with a sense of joy and gratitude for what they had just shared.

Megan was his now. At long last and forever, Megan belonged to him. He would never let her leave him, not now. Whatever he had to do to keep her, he would do it.

"Are you okay?" he finally found the air to say.

"Mmm-hmm."

Her face was buried in the curve between his shoulder and neck. "I didn't hurt you, did I?"

"Uh-uh."

He wrapped his arms more snugly around her and rested his chin on the top of her head. "Are you ever going to speak to me again?"

She nodded.

"Then say something. Anything. What is it? What do you want?"

"More?" she asked dreamily, stroking his back from neck to buttocks before leaning back to look at him. Her smile had a definite smirk to it.

The relief he felt was overwhelming. "Oh, baby. You're something else," he whispered. "I was so afraid…"

"Afraid? Of what?"

"That you would hate me. We never really talked about this part of the relationship. I was afraid to bring it up. But when you said you didn't want to share your room, I took that to mean you didn't want to have an intimate relationship with me.''

She sighed and allowed her head to drop back to his shoulder. ''I didn't think I did. I mean—it's all so confusing. The marriage wasn't supposed to be real but somewhere along the way, during all the dress fittings, and plans and all, it began to feel that way to me. I guess I tried so hard to pretend that our marriage was just like everybody else's that I began to believe in it, myself.''

He gave her a leisurely kiss. When he finally pulled a few inches away from her, he said, ''I'm glad, because that's exactly what I wanted all along...a marriage like everybody else's.''

She blinked. ''You did?''

''Oh, yeah.''

''Then why didn't you say something.''

''I did. I asked you to marry me.''

''But not because you loved me,'' she noted.

''Don't ever doubt my feelings for you, Megan O'Brien Kane. I love you, oh, my, yes I do. I have loved you since you wore pigtails down to your waist. Why do you think I gave you such a terrible time? I wanted you to notice me.''

''Oh, I noticed you all right!''

''But you weren't supposed to hate me.''

''Oh, Travis...'' She kissed him. ''This is all so confusing. My feelings are in such a jumble.''

''It's okay, baby. You don't have to explain. If you'll just let me love you, and live with you when I'm home, that's all I ask. I don't intend to change any of the rules on you. Everything is just like it was.''

She rubbed her hand across his chest. ''Not exactly. I've never seen a naked man before. I'm not sure I'll ever forget that sight!''

He grinned. ''Well, maybe being around a naked man on a regular basis will make it less strange for you.'' He sat up, grabbed her around the waist and carried her to the edge of the water. ''Now I'll show you how much fun skinny-dipping can be!''

It was dark when they arrived back at her ranch. He told her to go inside while he put Daisy away. He watched her wander into the house and shook his head.

The older he got the more he realized that he didn't understand women. Not at all. He thought she would be upset with him for pushing the boundaries between them. At the very least, he had expected a stronger reaction when he told her how he felt about her. She'd appeared more bewildered than angry. He had to believe that her willingness to make love with him was a positive sign. She didn't appear to have any problem with consummating their marriage. One hurdle had been overcome.

He wished he hadn't already paid his entrance fees for this week's events. If he could spend more time with her, perhaps he could show her the kind of relationship he wanted them to have.

Then again, maybe they both needed some time apart, just to allow things to cool down. Nothing in their relationship had been normal from the very beginning. Why did he expect something different now?

By the time he walked into the house, Travis wasn't certain what was expected of him next. He felt more confused than ever.

Mollie and Maribeth were sitting in the kitchen.

"Hi, Travis," Maribeth said brightly. "It's weird having a man around the place. But it's kinda nice, too. Are you going to be here long?"

He removed his hat and hung it by the door. "As a matter of fact, I'm leaving in the morning." He forced himself to ask in a casual voice, "Uh, where's Megan?"

Mollie answered. "She's upstairs. She said she thought she rode too long today and she's sore and achy. I think she's taking a bath to ease her muscles."

Travis fought to keep his composure. Hell's bells, what had he done to her? Hadn't she been the one teasing him with—

"Well, uh, guess I'll head upstairs myself. I'll probably see y'all in the morning, then."

"Are you hungry?" Mollie asked behind him.

He paused. "No. We had a lot of food with us today. I'm fine."

"G'night, then."

"Night."

Travis went upstairs and down the hallway to his room. He didn't hear any noise from either the bathroom or Megan's bedroom. He would see her tomorrow, of course, before he left. He'd talk to her then, make sure she knew that he hadn't meant to hurt her or make her feel—however she was feeling at the moment.

He reached the door to his room and opened it. The bedside lamp was on, the covers were turned back and there was the sound of sloshing water in the bathroom. The door to the bathroom was open.

"Is that you, Travis?" Megan asked from inside the bathroom.

"Uh, yeah. I'm sorry. I forgot about your using this bathroom. I'll go back downstairs for a while. Don't rush on my account. I'll just—"

"Don't be silly. This is your room. Come on in."

He tentatively stuck his head around the corner. She had bubbles floating on the water of the old-fashioned tub. She had slid down into the tub so that her chin barely cleared the bubbles.

"There's room enough for you in here if you'd like," she offered.

Travis's heart did a double-time beat at the unexpected invitation. "You don't mind?"

"I wouldn't have invited you if I minded, now, would I?" She gave him a saucy grin. "Are you going to be shy with me?"

"No, of course not. I was just surprised, that's all."

"Well, c'mon in, then." She lifted a soapy arm and gestured to him.

Travis needed no further encouragement. He jerked his boots off, hopping on first one foot, then the other. He got out of his jeans and briefs, and crawled into the tub as he shed his shirt.

Megan was laughing even as the waves he made almost swamped her. She hastily sat up, pulling her knees up to her chest. She watched him settle himself at the other end of the tub, his long legs fitting around her.

"Aaah, this is wonderful," he said, feeling the heat soothe his body. He allowed his eyes to drift shut before he remembered his concerns. He straightened, opening his eyes.

"Are you okay?" he asked.

She smiled. "I'm fine. Why do you ask?"

"Maribeth said you were tired and that you thought you'd overdone the riding today."

Her smile widened to a mischievous grin. "I hardly thought it appropriate to explain to a sixteen-year-old what I'd been doing to create some unaccustomed tender spots on my body."

He leaned forward and slipped his arms around her, pulling her toward him and turning her so that her back rested against his chest. He hugged her to him, loving to feel her pressed so intimately against him. "I didn't mean to hurt you."

"You didn't. Not really. I was just a little uncomfortable for a while, and having to get back on Daisy didn't help matters. I'll be fine. I'll just stay on the ground for the next few days. There's enough work around here to keep me busy without needing transportation."

Their new position gave him access to her and he unashamedly took advantage. He cupped her breasts, leisurely moving his fingers over and around their plump roundness.

Her hands weren't idle, either. She caressed his thighs lazily, from knee to hip, trailing her fingers from side to side, lingering on the sensitive inner thigh area.

"I wish I weren't leaving tomorrow," he finally said wearily. "I never thought that—"

"That I'd fall into your arms quite so easily?"

"No! I didn't intend— Well, of course I'd hoped, but I wasn't going to take advantage—"

"Travis—" She turned her head so that her lips were almost touching his neck. "We haven't done anything wrong, you know. We don't know anything about the future, but for now, we can spend this time together, enjoy each other's company and see what happens."

"If I hadn't already paid my entrance fee, I'd cancel this trip, but this is an important event in the circuit and I—"

She placed her damp fingers across his lips. "I don't want to cause you to have to choose between me and what you do, understand? I wouldn't want to be placed in that position. I'm not going to do it with you."

He wrapped his arms around her waist and squeezed her gently. "We're going to make this work between us. I want our relationship to last."

"I'm glad. I feel like I've been dreaming this weekend. But if I am, I don't want to wake up. I had no idea having a husband could be so great."

He shifted, pulling his legs up and standing, hauling her to her feet at the same time. She turned and looked at him, puzzled.

Travis stepped out of the tub, lifted her out and

briskly toweled her off. After giving his body a few quick swipes he took her hand and led her into the bedroom and over to the bed. He stretched out on the bed and patted the space next to him. She willingly slipped in beside him and he pulled the light covers over them.

Taking her into his arms, he said, "Do you remember my last year in school, when I was playing football?"

"Yes, of course."

"What I've never told you was that I was trying to work up enough nerve to ask you to go to the homecoming dance with me that year."

"Homecoming?"

"Yeah. Then two weeks before the dance..." His voice trailed off.

Her voice sounded strained. "My folks took us to Fort Worth for the weekend. The girls and I had gone to a movie matinee and they were supposed to pick us up after the show...only they never came back."

He held her close to him. "I just wanted you to know that even back then you were very important to me. I just didn't know what to do or say after everything happened. I remember you didn't come back to school for almost a month."

"I know."

"Even when you returned you were so distant. You attended classes, then disappeared back home."

"I was fighting to keep the girls with me. I was determined not to have them placed in foster homes. I was fortunate to be six and eight years older than they were. The added years gave me a bit of an advantage, but even so, it was really tough. I would have quit school if that had helped. Thank God Butch was there to talk to the authorities. He couldn't take legal custody, but he was there and several of Mama's friends insisted they were available to help supervise and offer advice if I needed help.''

"I felt like I let you down during that time.''

"How?''

"Because I wasn't there for you.''

"I wouldn't have accepted your help.''

"I know. I was afraid you wouldn't accept my offer this time, either. I knew you wouldn't believe me if I told you the truth about how I felt.''

"You have to admit that I had good reason. I haven't seen you or talked to you in years.''

"And you made it clear you weren't interested in me.''

She curled up against him and brushed her lips against his. "I thought you hated me, that you lived to torment me. Besides, you always dated the most popular girls in school, the ones who could afford the fanciest clothes.''

"Do you have any idea how sexy you looked— and still look—in your jeans and Western shirts? I got into a fight one time when one of the team members made a suggestive remark about you. After that everyone was very careful about what they said in front of me.''

"I had no idea.''

"Will you forgive me for hiding my feelings from you?''

"That depends on how you want to make it up to

me,'' she said, her fingers wrapping around his rapidly hardening length.

With sudden motion, he rolled until she was beneath him. ''I'll do whatever it takes to convince you that my heart was in the right place. I just wanted to be a part of your life.''

She lifted her arms around his shoulders and pulled him down to her. ''Well, cowboy, you finally got me into your bed. I guess you're going to have to show me some of those skills of yours.''

Ten

A sudden gust of wind rattled the windowpanes and Megan glanced outside. The fierce autumn storm approached the ranch with dark roiling clouds rapidly covering the sky. Mother Nature seemed to be serious about reminding them summer was over.

She had spent the morning with Butch and the other two hands locating some of the stock and bringing them into pastures closer to the ranch building. Other than the wind, there had been no hint of a storm. Thank God they had brought the stock in from the outflung pastures.

Things were definitely looking up for the Circle B. The beef market was marginally better than it had been earlier in the year, and with any luck, the storm coming in would bring some much-needed moisture.

So much had changed in her life since her marriage

with Travis. She wondered what she would have done without him. His generosity in advancing her the necessary money had made all the difference in the world to her. She was now able to meet her obligations, get needed repairs done and had the extra help so that she and Butch didn't have to put in such long, grueling hours.

Everybody had taken a break about one o'clock this afternoon and, since it was Saturday, the three men had gone off for the weekend, although Butch had offered to be home tonight so that she wouldn't be alone.

She insisted he enjoy his time off and spend the weekend relaxing with his friends. He had been working too hard for too long. She was pleased that he could rest more often now. He certainly deserved it.

Mollie was away at school, now. From her letters, she seemed to be settling in a little better now than the first few weeks she'd been gone when she struggled with homesickness.

Maribeth was involved with all the fall festivities in school. She was spending the weekend in town with friends.

The only thing that would have made Megan's day perfect was to have Travis home. She worked to keep those thoughts out of her head. He kept in touch by phone and gave her his itinerary so that she could keep up with his travel plans, but there were times, such as now, when she missed him so much that she ached with it.

Since their wedding, he'd been able to spend several weeks with her, but never more than two or three days in a row.

The last time he'd been home, he'd told her that what he hoped to do was to work with horses once he got too old for the dangerous competitions he presently entered.

He was already designing a new barn where he could board and service horses as well as break and train them.

Megan realized that part of her problem today was that she wasn't used to being alone. She wasn't sure what to do with herself. For years she'd kept a full schedule working on the ranch and looking after the girls. Now, they didn't need her all that much and the ranch was running more smoothly than it had in years.

She supposed it was time for her to discover what she could do if she didn't need to be working all the time. Not that housework or cooking appealed to her, but she might learn to enjoy having some time to read and nap.

She was curled up with a book in the living room sometime toward evening when she thought she heard—between the sudden gusts of wind—the sound of an engine coming down the lane. Maybe one of the neighbors had dropped by for a visit. That was a new event in her life as well, having time to sit and visit.

She hurried through the kitchen and opened the back door. The wind almost grabbed it out of her hand. She let out a whoop at the sight of her visitor, dashed across the porch and made a running leap down the steps.

Travis was home.

He'd backed the truck and horse trailer into the barn and by the time she got inside he had his horse in one of the stalls and was pouring feed into the bin.

"Hi!" she said, pausing in the doorway.

He glanced over his shoulder and grinned. "Howdy, stranger. I was wondering if this place was deserted. Where is everybody?"

He stepped back with the empty bucket, smoothed his hand across the horse's back and joined her in the opening of the stall. She stepped back so that he could latch the door. As soon as it was closed he turned and grabbed her up into his arms, swinging her around. "God, but it's good to be home! I drove most of the night to get here."

She was laughing breathlessly by the time he allowed her feet to touch the ground. "I wasn't expecting you for at least another week. What are you doing here?"

"I couldn't keep my mind on what I was supposed to be doing and I was making dumb mistakes. A guy could get killed not paying attention. So I decided to come on home. I just needed to see you again."

He swooped down and kissed her, a long, possessive kiss that made her blood sing. When he finally raised his head, he asked, "Where is everybody?"

"The men are gone for the weekend. Maribeth is in town."

"So it's just you and me?"

"Mmm-hmm."

With a whoop he grabbed her hand and headed toward the barn door at trot. "That's mighty obliging of everybody to give us some privacy, I must say. I'll have to—'' He came to an abrupt halt and stared out at the ranch yard.

The yard was rapidly filling up with hail that bounced on the ground like thousands of marbles. The wind was so strong the tree limbs were bouncing and swaying. Megan paused just behind him, her head resting on his shoulder as she witnessed the end of the drought.

''Look, Travis,'' she said, pointing at what looked like a wall of water rapidly approaching them. ''The rain is coming.''

The greenish-black clouds continued to roll so low overhead she thought she could reach up and touch them. The wind carried the smell of wetness.

He wrapped his arm around her as they stood there watching. ''We don't dare go out there now,'' he said, his voice barely heard over the howling wind. ''If the hail doesn't get us, the lightning might.''

The hail stopped as quickly as it had started. Within moments the rain hit hard, like a sudden waterfall. Megan took a deep breath, inhaling the scent of moisture that engulfed them.

Without a word Travis turned and, with his arm still around her, went back to the truck. He opened the door to the cab and reached behind the seat, pulling out a blanket. He dropped his arm from around her shoulders and took her hand, leading her to the ladder that gave access to the hayloft.

The expression on his face was all she needed to understand his intent. ''Travis?'' she asked, wondering at his audacity.

"Hey, this rain could set up its pouring for hours. We might as well get comfortable and get good seats to watch."

She started up the ladder and felt his hand brush across her bottom. Grinning, she stepped off the ladder and waded into the loose hay. The window at the end of the loft was open, but facing away from the force of the wind so that little moisture came inside. Sheets of rain swept past the barn.

Travis moved past her and paused a few feet away from the window, spreading the blanket. With his usual grace, he lowered himself to the blanket and lay on his side, holding out his hand to her.

"C'mere, you," he said, his voice sounding husky with need.

Feeling suddenly shy, Megan sat down on the edge of the blanket.

"Is something wrong?" he asked.

She shook her head. "I've missed you."

"Well, honey, I'm here now and you're wasting our precious time. C'mere." He took her hand and playfully tugged her down beside him.

"I forget what it's like being with you," she said, allowing him to unsnap the buttons on her shirt. "After a while, it's like I've dreamed it all...you and me...being married...everything."

"While I spend my nights dreaming of being home curled up in bed with you, holding you, loving you. I've lost my enthusiasm for the road since I married you." He slipped both hands beneath her shirt and slid it off her shoulders. While his hands were on her back, he deftly unfastened her bra and removed both items, leaving her bare from her waist up.

"You are so damn beautiful," he murmured, leaning over and kissing one of her breasts. "I dream of doing this to you." His warm breath gusted over her sensitive skin, creating a stream of chills across her.

Megan felt so strange. She'd been thinking about him, wishing for him, and now that he was here this all seemed too much like her fantasy to actually be happening. With a soft sigh of surrender, she discovered that she didn't care. If she was dreaming, she didn't want to wake up.

She feverishly fumbled to open his shirt and belt. He sat up and jerked off his boots, then reached over and helped her pull hers off as well. Their jeans soon followed.

The cool wind wafted over their nakedness. "What if somebody comes?" she whispered nervously.

"I'm countin' on it," he replied, grinning.

"I mean, company, or somebody?"

"In this weather? Not a chance. Even if they did, who would think to look for us up here?" He drew her back down to him and her thoughts scattered with the distraction of his chest pressed against her bare breasts. "Mmm," he said with obvious satisfaction. He ran his hand down her spine, cupping her buttocks, then pulled her up tight against his heavy arousal.

She shifted so that he was thrust between her thighs. With deep sensuous pleasure she undulated her hips just to feel his slick hardness move enticingly back and forth.

He bit back a groan and flipped her onto her back. Before her head stopped spinning he was inside of her with a hard driving rhythm that almost took her breath away.

She felt as though she was burning up for him, starved for the taste, scent and feel of him. She hung on to him with her arms and legs wrapped convulsively around him, fully expecting to go up into flames at any moment.

The tension climbed...higher...higher...until she cried out just as he threw back his head with a moan, each one triggering the other's release.

She sobbed with the beauty of the moment, wanting to capture and save this particular piece of time when she felt so much a part of him.

He rolled onto the blanket, never letting go of her, still panting for breath. She continued to place tiny kisses wherever her mouth could reach—along his jaw and his neck and his shoulder—even down to his chest where she nuzzled his flat nipple.

He continued to smooth his hands over her back and sides, following the smooth curve of her waist and hips, then lazily sliding to her front where he cupped and squeezed her breasts. Eventually he leaned over and pulled one of the rosy tips into his mouth, tugging lightly, while he caught the other one between his thumb and forefinger, gently massaging her delicate flesh.

She could feel him growing within her once again and she lifted her hips in invitation. A whoosh of breath accompanied his chuckle. ''You're downright insatiable,'' he managed to say between his kisses and caresses.

"Me? What did I do? You're the one who—'' She forgot her line of thought when he tugged on her breast with his mouth once again, then carefully stroked it with his tongue in a soothing movement. "Oh, Travis'' was all she could think of to say.

It seemed to be enough.

The cold, damp air woke Megan and for a moment she was disoriented. Where was she? What time was it? Had she fallen asleep reading on the couch?

As she came more fully awake, Megan realized that Travis was curled around her, spoon fashion, so that only the front half of her body was exposed to the damp wind blowing through the open loft window.

The storm must have blown past them. The rain continued to come down in a steady, earth-quenching drizzle. The yard light that automatically came on at dusk cast its rays into the loft.

"Travis?" she whispered

"Mmm?" he replied without moving. He was still asleep.

"I think we can go inside now.''

He tightened his hold around her waist. In his sleepy voice, he said, "I don't think I want to move.''

"It's too cold to spend the night in the barn.''

"I've got you to keep me warm.''

She smiled into the darkness. "Not for long. I'm going in to take a hot shower.''

"Spoilsport.''

"You could always join me," she offered.

After a moment he stretched and straightened, rolling onto his back with a sigh. "Now there's an invitation and a temptation no man could resist." He began to gather their clothes, tossing hers to her. "C'mon. Nobody's here. Let's make a dash for it."

Giggling like children, they bundled their clothes and boots into their arms and made a mad dash across the soggy ground between the barn and the house wearing little more than when they were born. Once inside, they didn't slow down until they reached the bedroom upstairs.

With the help from the light of the hallway Megan felt her way into the bathroom and turned on the shower, tossing her clothes into the corner. Travis followed her into the small room. She glanced around at him and began to laugh.

"What's so funny?"

"You."

"Me? What did I do?"

"I just wish I had a picture of you standing there buck naked wearing your Stetson."

He grinned and readjusted it on his head. "Well, where else was I going to carry it? I had my hands full."

She walked over to him and with a new sense of assurance placed her hands around him. Her touch made him change rapidly in size. "Now, wait a minute. That isn't some kind of hat rack, woman."

"Of course not," she agreed. Stepping back, she motioned for him to follow her into the shower. He didn't need any more coaxing. He tossed his hat through the door into the bedroom and climbed inside.

The shower stall was roomy enough for two, giving her the space she needed to cover him in foamy soapsuds, from his chin down to his toes. She concentrated on the swirls and designs she could make on his chest, drew diagrams around his belly button and felt a particular sense of satisfaction when she heard him gasp when she meticulously soaped between his legs and around his hardened shaft.

She loved to watch the immediate responses to each of her soft touches. When he finally turned toward the water to rinse off, she wasn't certain which one of them was quivering the most.

''My turn,'' he said with grim determination, taking the soap away from her and making sudsy lather between his hands. Now she understood what he had gone through as she stood there trying to remember to breathe while he covered her breasts with soap bubbles. He lightly pressed...and gently squeezed...and intimately rubbed...until she was gasping.

''Why are you holding your breath?'' he asked in an innocent voice.

She just shook her head because he was already exploring downward. His hands kept rubbing between her thighs, the heel of his hand pressing repeatedly on her mound of tight curls. She gave a quick sigh of relief when he knelt and continued washing and soaping her legs, ankles and arches.

Still kneeling he positioned her under the spray of water until the soap slid away from her body. Only then did he lean over and kiss her at that most intimate spot. She was already so aroused by all that he had done before that she could only moan.

He drew her out of the shower and quickly toweled both of them off, then carried her into the bedroom. Laying her sideways across the bed with her legs dangling, he knelt once again and with slow deliberation kissed and caressed her until she was sobbing with need. She was begging him for relief, for completion, for everything his lovemaking promised them when he finally stood and, wrapping her legs around his hips, joined them with a strong thrust of his body.

With his added freedom of movement he took control, varying his movements and his rhythm until she was once again whimpering. Slowly, stroke by stroke, he moved her into the center of the bed until he was able to stretch his length out on top of her, hastening his rhythm until they both felt the relief grab them, hurling them into completion and utter satiation.

Sometime during the night, Megan was roused by Travis turning them in the bed and tucking the covers around them both. As he hauled her back into the warmth of his body and contentedly curled around her once more, she heard him whisper, "You're going to be the death of me yet." She was much too relaxed to respond.

Eleven

The insistent ringing of the phone eventually drew Megan from a sound sleep. By the time she remembered that Travis wasn't there to answer it she was awake enough to realize it was in the middle of the night.

She fumbled for the phone, which was on his side of the bed. "H'lo?" she muttered, her tongue still asleep.

An agitated feminine voice replied. "May I please speak to Megan Kane?"

Megan blinked her eyes, trying to get them open enough to see the clock. The digital numbers said it was after midnight. "This is Megan. Who's this?"

"You don't know me. My name is Kitty and I'm a friend of Travis's. He's going to kill me for calling you but I thought you'd want to know."

Megan sat up in bed, clutching the phone to her ear. Travis had only been gone a few days. He'd stayed home longer this time than at any time since they had married. He'd been reluctant to leave and she still hadn't gotten used to having him gone again. She leaned over and turned on the bedside lamp. "Know what? What's wrong? Has something happened?"

"Travis is in the hospital here in Pendleton."

"Oregon?"

"Yeah. You knew he was here for the rodeo?"

"Oh God! What happened?"

"He got throwed and gored and stepped on. The doctor has been working on him for several hours. Said he's lucky to be alive. He's got a concussion, some broken bones in his foot, as well as broken ribs and a deep slice along his side. But it's the concussion the doctor's worried about. He hasn't recovered consciousness since he was hurt."

"Oh my God. When did this happen?"

"This afternoon. Maybe nine hours ago. I figured you'd want to know."

"Oh my God," Megan repeated, her thoughts swirling so fast she was dizzy from the sensation.

"If there's anything I can do—"

"What did you say your name is?"

"Kitty Cantrell. I've known Travis since he started on the circuit way back when. He mentioned he got married a while back, so I thought— Well, if it was me sittin' there at home, I'd be wanting to know what had happened to him."

"Oh, yes, Kitty, thank you. You're absolutely right. I'll get there as soon as I can."

"Probably the quickest way would be to fly into Portland and rent a car, unless you want to charter a plane out of Portland to get over here to Pendleton."

"Thanks. I'll see what I can do. Can you give me the name of the hospital? The doctor's name? What room he's in?"

Kitty quickly gave her answers and she scribbled them down on the notepad beside the phone. By the time she hung up the phone, tears blinded her.

"Megan?" Maribeth stood in the doorway. "Who was that? Is something wrong with Mollie?"

Megan threw back the covers. "Not Mollie. Travis."

"Travis! What's wrong? What happened? Is he all right? Where is he?"

"In Oregon. I've got to fly out there. He's in the hospital, unconscious. They don't know for sure— The doctors think he'll be okay but they aren't sure because he hasn't regained consciousness." She rushed over and hugged Maribeth. "I've got to go to him."

"Of course you do."

"But I can't leave you here alone."

"That's not a problem. I'll stay with Kim in town. Her mom won't care. As soon as she hears what happened, she'll insist on it."

Megan tried to remember if she had a suitcase. She never went anywhere, but maybe there were some things in the storage room. She ran down the hall and opened the door to what they had designated the junk room. She found a dilapidated duffel bag in one of the corners and hurried back to her room.

Maribeth was already placing underwear and shirts out on the bed. "Gee, Megan, I hope he's all right. It would be awful if something happened to Travis. Y'all have only been together for such a short time. It doesn't seem fair."

Megan began to dress, not worrying about how she looked. She found jeans and a heavy shirt, then ran a brush through her hair.

"How are you going to get to the airport?"

"I'm going to have Butch drive me."

"Should I go wake him up?"

"Thank you, Maribeth, that would be great. I wasn't thinking that far ahead."

By the time she was dressed and packed, she heard voices in the kitchen and knew that Butch was already up and ready to take her to Austin. Thank God for Butch. He would be at the ranch to keep an eye on things while she was gone.

She hurried into the kitchen and saw him standing there, his hands in his pockets, waiting for her.

"Thank you for this," she said.

"It's the least I could do. You ready?" he asked, taking the bag from her.

"Yeah," she said, knowing that she was lying. How could she ever be ready for something like this? She'd never been out of the state, never flown in an airplane and now she was going to go racing halfway across the country to Travis's side. What had that woman—Kitty—said? That Travis wouldn't like it because Kitty had called her. Why? What didn't she know? Did that mean that Travis had been hurt other times and hadn't bothered to tell her?

She hopped up into the truck beside Butch and leaned back against the headrest as they began the two-hour trip to Austin. She would try to get booked on the first plane to the Pacific northwest. She could only hope that by the time she got there Travis would be awake and yelling at her for dashing up there.

He wasn't.

As soon as she reached the hospital, Megan explained to the nurses at the desk who she was. They told her that he had not regained consciousness, The doctors had done several sets of X rays to determine the extent of his head injury but she would need to discuss the results with them.

"May I see him?"

The nurse nodded. "The doctor will be making his evening rounds later today. He'll be able to discuss your husband's condition with you at that time."

Megan was glad she was alone when she stepped inside Travis's room. Late-afternoon sunlight flooded the room. The other bed in the room was empty. There seemed to be a cluster of machines surrounding Travis, all making their own peculiar sounds.

His skin looked pasty white except where there was massive bruising and for a horrifying moment she thought he was dead. Tears streamed down her cheeks, dripping off her chin despite her attempts to wipe them away. She tiptoed to the bed, uncomfortable with the sound of her boots on the tiled floor.

He had a cast on his foot, which was propped up. Massive bruises covered the side of his swollen face—mottled purple and green and yellow. One eye would probably not open even if he were awake to attempt to see out of it.

She sank onto the chair beside the bed and touched his hand. Megan had had several hours to think about what had happened to Travis during her flight between Texas and Oregon. She'd also had time to look at what had happened to her.

During the five months she'd been married, she'd become used to the idea of being Travis's wife. She'd accepted his long absences, had looked forward to his quick visits home, had reveled in their lovemaking, but until now she hadn't really allowed herself to admit the truth.

She had fallen in love with Travis Kane. It had happened so gradually that she wasn't certain when her attraction to him had become so much more.

Even though he had explained early on that he had loved her for years, she hadn't been comfortable with the idea that he was telling her the truth. She had no way to compare what he'd told her with what other men said when they tried to convince a woman they wanted them.

If they hadn't already been married at the time, she would have thought that Travis said that to every girl he dated, which was why they were so hurt when he walked away.

He hadn't walked away from her. He'd married her. Of course neither of their life-styles had changed much since the marriage. She still ran the ranch, he still traveled. But the routine had worked for them.

She hadn't made any claims on his time, he hadn't tried to push her aside to take charge of the ranch.

Sometime during these past several months, Megan had forgotten the reasons behind their marriage and the fact that she hadn't intended to stay married to him when she originally agreed to the idea.

Now, as she sat beside him, she wondered how she could have been so blind to her own feelings. Was she so single-minded that her concerns were limited only to the ranch and her sisters? How could she have ever seen Travis as a means to an end rather than to love him and appreciate what he had done for her?

Yes, she loved him, but she had never told him. The grim thought that she might not be able to do so shook her tremendously.

Megan continued to sit there with him, willing Travis to open his eyes. She'd come a long way, not only in miles but in emotions, to tell him what was truly in her heart. She prayed that he would wake up soon and be able to hear her.

Hours later Megan stepped out of the room to get some coffee from the vending machine near the waiting room. She had spoken to the doctor who explained the procedures they had taken to check for injuries. He pointed out that the other injuries were healing satisfactorily and that hopefully Travis would regain consciousness soon. Head injuries were always tricky and couldn't be predicted with any degree of accuracy.

Since there was no other patient assigned to the room for the night, the doctor gave Megan permission to stay with Travis. The large overstuffed chair would serve as a place to nap as she waited out the hours for him to regain consciousness.

She stopped at the vending machine and placed the necessary coins into the machine, then punched the button needed for the coffee.

"Excuse me. Are you Megan?"

Megan glanced around and saw a strikingly beautiful woman a few feet away, watching her intently. The woman's hair was so black it glistened. It hung long and straight, cascading across her shoulders and down to her waist. Equally black eyes, delicately tilted at the outer edges, studied her with an expression of curiosity and interest.

She wore a gold satin Western-cut blouse and black jeans that accentuated the long curving line of her legs. Her black boots gleamed.

"Yes, I'm Megan. May I help you?"

The other woman closed the gap between them and said in a low, husky voice, "I'm Kitty. I called you when Travis was hurt."

Megan's heart began to pound in her chest. This woman was Travis's friend? She was drop-dead gorgeous. Struggling to hide her reaction, Megan held out her hand. "I'm pleased to meet you, Kitty. I want to thank you for calling me."

Kitty took her hand. "How is he?"

"The doctor says he's healing nicely."

"Has he regained consciousness?"

"No."

Kitty's expression fell. "Oh. That's too bad."

Megan took her coffee and motioned to the empty
waiting room. "Would you like to sit down?"

"Thanks." Kitty seemed to glide across the room
as she led the way and sank into one of the chairs
with all the poise of royalty. Megan felt awkward and
unpolished, suddenly aware of her casual clothes
she'd thrown on much earlier that day.

And yet—Kitty was also dressed in Western wear.
On her the Western-cut blouse and jeans looked cus-
tom-made to fit her curvaceous body.

Once seated beside her, Megan gripped the paper
cup with both hands. Staring at the black liquid, she
fought to sound casual as she asked, "How long did
you say you've known Travis?"

Kitty's smile flashed brilliantly white in her tanned
face. "Oh, Travis and I go back a long ways."

That's what I was afraid of, Megan thought to herself.

"Are you part of the rodeo?"

"Yeah. I've been riding since I could walk. My
dad was a rodeo bum, trailed around the country for
years. He taught me to ride. I do some of the special
events—trick riding and roping—that kind of thing.
More exhibition than anything. I'm considered part of
the entertainment."

Megan felt so out of place, not only because of the
hospital environment but because she knew so little
about Travis's life. She was certain that this woman
knew her husband much better than she did, and she
recognized that she didn't like the idea at all.

"I'm sure you've heard this a lot," she said, determined to be honest, "but I have to say that you are very beautiful."

Kitty smiled. "Thank you. I didn't have much to do with that. My folks are from Oklahoma—my mom's mostly Cherokee and I look like her, although I got my height from my dad."

"Travis's never mentioned you to me."

Kitty glanced away before answering. "No reason why he should." She shifted her shoulders in a tiny shrug. "I always knew that there was someone waiting for him at home...and that's okay. He's always been there for me, a good friend when I needed one."

Megan swallowed. Hadn't that been what he offered her as well...friendship plus the legal right to sleep together?

She shivered, wondering if she had misunderstood his intentions. Wasn't he the one who had said they didn't have to end the marriage after a year, that he was willing to consider their arrangement a permanent one?

However, now that she was being forced to look at the life he led when he wasn't in Texas, she was beginning to realize that there was a great deal about Travis she didn't know.

She didn't care what Kitty said about her relationship with Travis...the woman was in love with him. It was easy to spot when you suffered from the same ailment.

Kitty spoke. "Where are you staying?"

"Here."

"No. I mean, what motel?"

"I didn't check into one."

Kitty shook her head. "You can't stay here all night. You've got to get some rest, take a shower, that sort of thing." She reached into her handbag. "Here. I checked into the Best Rest Inn down the street once everyone else left to follow the circuit. I usually bunk with one of the gals who has a travel trailer. But I didn't want to leave town until I knew Travis was out of danger. Take my key and go get some sleep. I'll stay here with him until you come back. Okay?"

Once again Megan felt the odd throb in her heart at this further evidence that Kitty was deeply involved with Travis. However, she was exhausted, it was true. Not only the two-hour time difference, but the fact that she hadn't slept since the midnight phone call the night before all added up to a weariness she could no longer ignore.

Megan slowly reached for the key. "This is very kind of you, Kitty. I don't know what to say."

Kitty briefly flashed her beguiling smile once again. "No need to say anything. I don't want Travis to see those dark circles under your eyes when he finally decides to wake up. He'll think you've been in a fight with somebody." She stood and offered her hand to Megan, pulling her to her feet. "G'on, now. I'll stay with him in case he stirs. If he does, I promise to call you immediately."

Megan knew she was right. "Okay." She turned away and took a few steps. "I'll see you early, I promise."

"Don't worry about it. I'll be here whenever you show up. Sleep well."

Unfortunately, once she got to the room and into bed, after she fell asleep her dreams were filled with foreboding images and feelings that haunted her. She kept waking up with a jolt at every unfamiliar sound, and there were many. Even though the motel was set back from the highway, there were still sounds of heavy trucks passing through, as well as local traffic, blasts of car radio music and muffled voices.

She'd spent her life sleeping on a ranch where every sound could be immediately identified. City noises were as foreign to her as a jungle would have been.

Megan forced herself to go back to sleep each time, knowing she had to keep up her strength. Travis would need her and she wanted to be there for him.

When the phone rang she let out a quick shriek before recalling where she was. Light came through the curtained window and she realized that somehow she'd managed to sleep past dawn.

"H'lo?"

"Hi, it's Kitty. He's been stirring some. Hasn't opened his eyes or anything, but the doctor is encouraged to think he's coming out of his deep sleep. I thought you'd want to be here just in case."

Megan was already out of bed, standing by the phone. "Yes. I'll be there right away."

She dashed into the bathroom and turned on the shower. She'd been too tired the night before to do more than fall into bed. Ten minutes later Megan let herself out of the hotel room and hurried up the street to the hospital.

He was going to be all right! He had to be. She

could hardly wait to see him again, to talk to him, to explain how she felt, to let him know how much she loved him.

She slowed her hurried footsteps as she neared his room and quietly pushed the door open. Kitty was standing beside the bed, holding Travis's hand. She glanced around at Megan, her face shining with relief.

Megan immediately looked at Travis and saw that his one good eye was open. He'd been gazing at Kitty, but when Megan stepped into the room, he glanced at the door and saw her.

He shut his eye for a brief moment, then opened it again, frowning. He looked at Kitty, his face registering his shock and disbelief, then back to Megan before saying hoarsely, "Megan? What are you doing here?" There was no sound of welcome.

Megan felt paralyzed as she stood in the doorway, feeling like an intruder. Travis had looked comfortably relaxed with Kitty before he saw her. Her presence certainly changed that. She forced herself to walk toward him. Kitty obligingly stepped back.

"Hello, Travis," she said quietly. "It's good to see you awake. How are you feeling?" She wanted badly to touch him, to reassure herself that he was all right. But the look on his face made her hesitate.

"What are you doing here?" he repeated.

"I was worried about you. I wanted to be certain you were okay."

"How'd you find out I'd been hurt?"

"I told her," Kitty said firmly. "I thought she should know."

Travis muttered something and closed his eyes.

Whatever he'd said beneath his breath Megan knew wasn't particularly complimentary. When he looked at her again, he was still frowning. "I'm sorry Kitty called you. I'm okay. Just banged up a little. You shouldn't be here."

Megan felt as though he had slapped her. "I was worried—" she began but he cut her off.

"I'm fine. Really. This is nothing. You should get back home. If I need anything, Kitty's here."

Megan couldn't look at the other woman standing there so quietly. She kept her eyes wide, determined not to let him see the tears she was fighting.

"If that's what you want," she finally said around the lump in her throat. Afraid that she would betray her feelings at any moment, she spun around and walked out of the room.

After a long silence, Kitty finally said, "You can really be an ass, sometimes, you know that?"

Travis's head was hurting like hell and he didn't need anybody giving him a bad time. He felt as though every muscle in his body was screaming at him. His chest hurt with every breath he took.

"She wasn't supposed to know about any problems I have on the road. I've told you that. She doesn't know anything about the risks. I wanted to keep it that way, damn it!"

"Oh? And if you'd broken your fool neck, I suppose I wasn't supposed to let her know about that, either?"

He tried to shift in the bed and let out a groan before he could control it. "I'm not hurt that bad and you know it."

"No, as a matter of fact, I don't know it. What I know is that you're one stubborn, idiotic cuss of a man who's too afraid of losing his macho image to thank his wife for dropping everything to fly here to see about him."

"I don't want her worrying about me."

"Oh, that's a good one. Of course now she won't be worrying about you at all. She'll be too busy filing divorce papers to give you much of a thought."

He groaned. "You think I was too rough on her?"

"Try cruel. Whether you know it or not, you had all of us, doctors included, worried about you. You've been lying there unconscious for almost thirty-six hours. That's enough to shake anyone. It was stupid of me to think that a blow might have knocked some sense into your head, of course. I've watched you trying to kill yourself for the last several months, pushing all the limits with every event. I should be used to it by now."

"You know why, Kitty. I told you. I need all the prize money I can get. I'm trying to help Megan get her ranch financially back on its feet."

"Does she have any idea the kind of risks you're taking in order to make the money to help her?"

"Of course not. She doesn't need to know. Besides, I'm also saving to buy some horses. Once I've got enough money to invest into some good breeding stock I won't have to stay on the circuit like this."

"Well, if it makes you feel any better, you walked off—or should I say you were carried off—with the prize money here as well. Your scores beat out the other contenders. I picked up the check for you, which is why I've been hanging around, waiting to give it to you."

He touched her hand in a light pat. "You're a good friend, Kitty. You always have been."

She sighed. "Not good enough, it seems. I can't seem to stop you from ruining the relationship you've been talking about wanting so badly for years."

He tried to smile and winced. The entire side of his face was swollen and sore. "Maybe you should go find her for me so I can explain. I guess you're right. I didn't want her insisting on my quitting right now and I knew she would if she knew about some of my injuries."

Without another word Kitty hurried out of the room and down the hallway, looking for Megan. It was too late. Megan was gone.

After carefully checking the hospital corridors and lobby she returned to the room. "You're in worse trouble than we thought, Travis. She took you at your word. She's nowhere to be found."

Travis felt as though a herd of buffalo was trampling his skull. "Damn. I've got to talk to her and explain." He was having trouble concentrating. He closed his eyes, saying, "I'll give her time to cool down, then I'll call her. I've got ten days before the next rodeo. I'd planned to go home but maybe I'll wait until—"

"You're not doing anything with a cast on your foot."

He glanced down at his encased foot. "I've cut those damn things off before. As long as I don't put my full weight on it, I'll do all right."

"You're crazy, Travis. I've always known that. All you rodeo characters are."

"You should know, honey, you're one of us."

She shook her head. "Only because I don't know any other kind of life." She studied him for a long moment. "You want me to stay so I can drive your rig to Wyoming for you when you're ready to leave?"

"Where's your rig?"

"I had one of the guys drive it over to Boise for me. He's got a spread near there. I didn't know how long you'd be laid up, and I didn't want Blaze left unattended. Roy'll look after her until I can get there to pick her up."

"Thanks for the offer. I'll keep it in mind." He closed his eyes once again. "Give me some time to get over this granddaddy of all hangovers. Maybe, then, I'll be able to think better. Megan's going to be furious with me. She's got a temper that won't quit."

"You'll deserve anything she cares to dish out, cowboy. You need your butt kicked."

"Yeah, well, it won't be the first time I've been on her list of undesirables." His grin was halfhearted at best. "At least we're married now. Thank God. I'll make it up to her when I'm feeling better."

Twelve

"What in the hell do you think you're doing?"

Megan recognized the voice coming from below. She hadn't expected him to be home this soon. She wasn't prepared to see him. Not yet. Not now. Refusing to look down from her perch on top of the water tower, Megan concentrated on tightening the fitting of the replacement pipe she'd just installed to stop a leak.

"Megan O'Brien Kane! Get down from there before you break your fool neck."

Once the fitting was tightened enough to suit her, she threw her leg over the side of the supporting structure and began to lower herself down the ladder. She was not coming down because she'd been ordered to do so...she was coming down because she had completed what she'd set out to do.

Megan didn't take orders from anybody, most especially not from Travis Kane.

Travis's hands grabbed her around the waist before her feet reached the ground and he swung her around, causing her to clutch his shoulders for balance.

She hadn't seen him in weeks, not since she'd walked— correction, been *ordered*—out of his hospital room. She hadn't spoken to him since then, either. Not that he hadn't called, but she had always made certain that someone else answered the phone and told him she was unavailable. She'd had nothing to say to him.

She still didn't.

He looked thinner, which wasn't surprising. It was obvious that he hadn't been taking care of himself, which certainly wasn't her problem. He'd made that very clear.

"What are you trying to do, kill yourself?" he demanded.

She lifted her eyebrows as she met his gaze. "And if I am, what business is it of yours?" she asked, stepping back from him and walking over to Daisy.

"Why didn't you have one of the men do that?"

She paused without turning around, gathered the reins into one hand and stepped into the saddle before answering him. "I let them go."

Travis's jaw dropped at her calm announcement. "You did what? What are you talking about?"

She turned Daisy's head. "We can talk about it at the house," she said, leaning forward and signaling Daisy into an easy canter.

Travis lifted his hat and wearily resettled it on his

head. Yep, he had really done it this time. He couldn't believe she'd stayed so angry this long for something he said when he was half out of his mind with pain and a blasted concussion. Hell, he didn't even remember what he'd said to her. The first few days after he'd regained consciousness had been a blur to him. Of course Kitty had been more than willing to repeat everything to him on more than one occasion when he'd been upset because Megan wouldn't take any of his calls.

All right. So he'd messed up. Hell, he was only human. Nobody was perfect, after all. Why couldn't she understand that she was the very last person he had expected to see when he woke up in that blasted hospital? Now she wouldn't give him a chance to explain.

No, wait. Hadn't she said she would discuss it at the house? He'd been so focused on finding her when he first arrived at the ranch that he'd done no more than make sure she wasn't around the house before getting directions from Butch as to possible whereabouts. He'd quickly unloaded his horse and come looking her...for all the good it had done him.

He looked up at the water tower. Damn fool woman had no business clambering around up there. Didn't have a lick of sense. And what had she meant by laying off the help he'd hired? She couldn't take care of things on her own. Hadn't she already learned that?

Travis made no effort to catch up with her. Instead he just followed the trail she'd taken. Man oh man, but he was tired. He'd driven long, lonely hours for several days in order to get back home.

God, he'd missed talking to her, seeing her. This was the longest he'd been gone since they were married. But his injury had set him back and he'd needed to make up for his hospital expenses and his missing some of the other rodeos he'd intended to enter before he'd gotten hurt. His ribs had been slow in knitting, his head had felt as if it was going to topple off his shoulders for weeks afterward and his ankle still bothered him.

Now he was through with the rodeo for the season. He had enough money to start adding to his stock. Who knew? He might decide not to follow the circuit next year. His ankle was still acting up on him. Besides, he was tired of all the traveling.

He missed Megan, he missed waking up with her curled up in his arms every morning, missed falling asleep with her beside him at night.

The problem was he had to get her to understand that he hadn't meant to hurt her feelings when she'd flown to Oregon to check on him. When he'd recovered from his injuries, he'd been touched that she'd cared enough to come…touched and encouraged. He just couldn't get her to take his phone calls so he could tell her so. He needed to explain if she would just get off her high horse and listen.

He rode into the ranch yard and nudged his horse into the barn. Spotting Daisy in her stall, he knew that Megan had already been there and gone on to the house. After unsaddling his mount and making sure he had his feed, Travis headed toward the house.

"Hi, Travis," Maribeth sang out cheerfully as he neared the porch. "How come you're limping?"

"My ankle's still a little sore," he said, negotiating the stairs with care. "Did Megan go inside?"

"Yep," she replied without moving from her position curled up on the porch swing. "She wasn't in the best of moods. Does she know you're home?"

"Uh-huh, which is probably the reason she isn't in the best of moods. I'm not her favorite person at the moment."

Maribeth grinned. "Yep, guess that's true enough. She acts like she never heard of you whenever I mention your name."

He shook his head with disgust and went inside. There was no one in the kitchen. He stuck his head back out the door. "Where's Doris?"

"Oh, Megan let her go. Said we didn't need a housekeeper. She insists she and I can keep up with everything."

"The cooking, too?"

Maribeth laughed. "Yeah. We eat a lot of frozen stuff these days, but I'm getting a little better at cooking. I really miss Mollie, though. She actually liked doing all that stuff. Can you imagine?"

Travis went upstairs to the room he and Megan had shared for the past six months. When he walked inside he immediately noticed that none of her belongings were on the dresser. He opened the closet door and found his things hanging alone. Not a good sign.

He went into the bathroom and stripped out of his clothes. If he was going to see Megan, he wanted to be refreshed as much as possible. He obviously had some serious fence-mending to do where she was concerned. He just wished he wasn't so tired. He felt as though he could sleep for a week.

By the time he returned downstairs, a meal of sorts was waiting on the table. Maribeth was filling the glasses with iced tea. There were two places set.

''Who isn't eating?'' he asked, pulling out one of the chairs.

''Megan told me not to set her a place. She's working in the office this evening and took her dinner in there.''

Travis knew it would be rude of him to join Megan and leave Maribeth to eat in the kitchen alone, particularly when he was fairly certain it was his arrival home that had sent Megan into the other room. He did his best to be polite and visit with Maribeth during the meal. As soon as they were finished, however, he excused himself as politely as possible and went to find Megan. It was time to deal with the situation, make his apologies and put all this behind them.

The office door was closed. Travis tapped lightly and waited.

''Come in.''

He opened the door and spotted Megan working behind the desk. It didn't look as though she'd had more than a couple of bites of her meal.

''Megan, we need to talk,'' he began quietly.

She glanced up briefly, then tore a check out of the register. ''Yes, we do.'' She watched him sit down across from her. ''I managed to sell off most of my beef. Got a fairly decent price, I'm pleased to say.'' She handed him a check. ''Here's the money I borrowed from you. I added the current interest percentage. I think that makes us even now.''

He barely glanced at the check. ''Megan, I owe you an apology and an explanation for the way I behaved in Oregon. I—''

''Not at all,'' she smoothly interposed. ''You were right. I had no business going up there. What you do and who you do it with is none of my concern.''

''Who I do it—? What are you talking about?''

''I've spoken to an attorney, explained our verbal agreement and that we are now ready to dissolve the partnership. He said—''

Travis came out of his chair in a lunge. ''*What?* Now wait a minute! We aren't going to— I mean, you can't just— Megan? What are you doing?''

''Playing by your rules, Travis, just like always. I'm sorry if I misunderstood them for a while. You've been very kind, loaning me the money and all. Now that it's paid back I really think it would be better if you move out as soon as possible. I've already moved my things out of your room. I suppose you have to make some kind of explanation to your folks and will need a place to stay for a few days, but I really think the sooner you move, the more comfortable the situation will be for both of us.''

He stared at her in disbelief. ''Damn it, Megan, will you just listen to me for a minute?''

She folded her hands on the desk in front of her and looked at him. ''All right…I'm listening.''

''I was still groggy when you showed up at the hospital. I had no idea Kitty had called you. It was a shock—''

"Oh, I don't doubt that in the least."

"I realized only minutes after you left that I'd given you the wrong impression. Kitty went after you but she was too late. I didn't mean to sound so—so—"

"It doesn't matter. None of that matters now."

"It sure as hell does to me. You're kicking me out of here just like you got rid of the ranch hands and Doris. Hell, I've never been fired from being a husband before. You're not even giving me a chance to explain."

"Explain what, Travis? That your life is the rodeo? I know that. That Kitty understands your life much better than I ever will? I understand that, too. That on your few visits home you enjoyed playing house with me? Yeah, I finally figured that one out as well. I was very naive to believe that story you told about loving me all those years, but I don't guess I blame you for laying it on a little thick. The thing is, you didn't have to say all of that to me. You never forced me into doing anything I didn't want to do. I just didn't realize that you had someone on the road, that's all. You taught me a lot, Travis, and I—"

"You don't know a damn thing about what you're talking about. I don't have anybody on the road. There's nobody in my life but you!"

"Can you honestly look me in the eye and tell me you aren't involved with Kitty?"

"*Kitty?* Is that what this is all about? You think there's something between us? Well, you're dead wrong! Yeah, we've been friends for years. She's been like a sister to me. I've kept an eye out for her, let guys know that if they tried anything with her, they had to answer to me, but that's it. There's been nothing romantic between us."

"I see."

He eyed her uncertainly. "You believe me?"

She shrugged. "It doesn't really matter. I'm going to be able to make it now, thanks to your loan. I've ordered a herd of angora goats as well as several head of sheep to be delivered next week. I can't afford the extra help your money provided, which is why I let everyone go, but Butch is here. Between the two of us we can—"

"So you want to call the marriage off, is that it?" he asked in a low voice. "Just like that?"

"Yes, I believe that's the only thing to do."

"Why?"

"Because our life-styles just don't mix, Travis. I honestly thought when we talked about this, that you following the rodeo circuit wouldn't bother me, but that's before I saw you lying there unconscious, all battered and bruised, and I understood why you mentioned that others had tried to get you not to do such dangerous work. As long as I closed my mind and imagination to the danger, I was able to handle it, but no longer. It isn't fair to either one of us. You have your life-style and I have mine. They just don't have anything in common."

"What if I told you I was already thinking about quitting the rodeo? I've saved enough to start my horse farm, something I've always wanted. We could—"

"Not *we*, Travis. Not anymore. I think you should

do whatever you want with your life. But don't include me.''

''That's it? You want it over?''

She nodded.

He stared at her for a long time, taking in the shadows beneath her eyes, the tightness around her mouth. ''I really blew it this time,'' he muttered.

''There should be no hurt feelings. That was our agreement, remember?''

''No, as a matter of fact, none of this was a part of our agreement. In the first place, I gave you that money. It wasn't a loan. In the second place, we agreed to stay together for twelve months... *remember?*'' he used her same inflection on the last word. He stared at her but she refused to drop her gaze or respond to him. He spun away from the desk and began to pace, his mind racing furiously for some answers. ''The way I see it,'' he said after a tense silence, ''you still owe me six months as my wife.''

After a long pause, she slowly nodded. ''Technically I suppose you're right. But I thought since I've already paid you that—''

''Well, you're wrong. I don't want the money. I want those six months. I want to prove to you that we can make a go of our marriage, Megan. Will you give me that chance?''

She frowned. ''I don't understand why you should care.''

He gave a frustrated sigh. ''Well, then I'll just have to figure out a way to make you understand during the next six months. I figure you owe this to me, Megan.''

She drummed her fingers on the desk, fiddled with the fountain pen, straightened a stack of papers on her desk and finally sighed. "Do you really think this is necessary?''

"Yes. Yes, I do.'' He watched her intently, praying she wouldn't see his fear. He couldn't lose her. Somehow, he had to fight in every way he could to hold on to what they had.

The silence between them seemed to fill the room with its own tension-filled presence.

Finally she nodded. "All right. But I'm not going to sleep with you, or make love to you. I realize now that I should never have slept with you in the first place.''

He folded his arms and looked at her. "Why not?''

"Because it muddied the water of our agreement. It complicated things. We should have kept it strictly as a business arrangement, without our feelings getting involved.''

"Are you saying your feelings are involved?'' he asked softly.

"Don't worry. I can handle my feelings just fine. It was past time I grew up, anyway. You helped me do that as well. Guess I owe you another thanks for that.'' Her tone didn't sound particularly grateful.

Travis decided he'd gotten as many concessions out of her tonight as he dared push for. He turned toward the door. Just before he opened it, he paused and said, "I'll be home during those months. Since you got rid of the others, plan on using me. Just give me a list of each day's work schedule and I'll do my part.''

She nodded without speaking and Travis walked out of the room.

He was so tired he could hardly walk straight and his damn ankle was throbbing like crazy. But he'd bought himself some time—not a hell of a lot, but it was better than having to move out in the next few days.

Somehow in the next six months he had to figure out a way to convince Megan that they could work all of this out together, if she'd just give them a chance.

He refused to think about the fact that he might lose her from his life. He couldn't lose her now. He just couldn't.

The winter schedule was slow. As more and more moisture fell, in the form of rain, sleet, and occasional snow, Megan found herself with time on her hands.

It certainly didn't help her peace of mind that Travis seemed to be permanently attached to the ranch now. He seldom left the place, giving a list to Butch of anything he needed whenever Butch went into town for supplies.

Maribeth seemed to be almost completely caught up with school activities. She'd gotten the habit of spending a couple of nights in town most every week, which meant that Megan and Travis spent the evenings alone at the house.

At first Megan had been nervous around him, waiting for him to argue with her, expecting him to use his charm to convince her to let him become a bigger part of her life.

He never said anything to her. Of course, there had been one time…

She sighed, thinking about Valentine's Day.

Now there was a day that she'd largely ignored most of her life. When her folks had been alive, her mother used to tease her dad about not being much of a romantic. One year he'd surprised her with a big heart-shaped box of candy. Her mom had been so touched by the gesture that she had saved the box, and used it for years to store special mementos.

In the years since her parents had died, there had never been any reason for Megan to give the day more than a passing thought.

But Travis had remembered.

Travis hadn't given her candy. He hadn't even mentioned the significance of the day to her. But when she went to bed that night she discovered a long-stemmed red rose and a sprig of baby's breath tied with a ribbon lying on her pillow. A square blue velvet box accompanied the rosebud.

She stared at the silent offering with uneasiness. What was he up to? Why was he doing this? Didn't he understand anything?

Reluctantly she approached the bed and picked up the rose, absently bringing it to her nose. Its gentle fragrance made her sigh. She'd never been given flowers before. Wasn't a red rose a symbol of love? Was that what he was saying to her?

Next, she picked up the box and lifted the spring-hinged lid. There, nestled on a bed of white satin was a golden locket on a chain. She stared at it, fighting back the tears that suddenly filled her eyes.

She wasn't a jewelry kind of person. She'd saved her mother's things for the other two girls who dressed up and went out. The only jewelry she owned was her wedding ring.

With trembling fingers Megan picked up the locket, only then noticing a small card that read, ''I love you, Travis.'' She touched a small catch and the locket opened, revealing a carefully inserted snapshot taken on their wedding day. Travis had scooped her up into his arms—she remembered the scene so well—and had twirled her around as though publicly proclaiming her as his prize.

They'd both been laughing when someone—was it Mollie?—snapped the picture.

She'd put the locket and card away, unable to say anything to Travis about them, although she kept the rose until it turned brown.

Meanwhile, he quietly followed the routine she and Butch had, doing the work of both the men he'd hired earlier in the year, and making it look easy.

Being around him was having an alarming effect on her self-righteous anger. She was beginning to look at what happened from his point of view, which made it more difficult to hold him responsible for her hurt feelings.

The fact was that he *had* been concussed when he'd first seen her. He'd admitted to her that it was tough for him to have her see him in such a helpless condition.

What was particularly galling to Megan was her

slow but inevitable realization that it was her jealousy of Kitty Cantrell that had convinced her that Travis couldn't possibly love her, Megan O'Brien, when someone like Kitty was an integral part of his life.

Eventually her sense of fairness made her stop and reconsider. Why didn't she believe that Travis could love her?

Well, of course it was simple. Just look at her.

She stood in front of the oval mirror in her bedroom one night, preparing for bed, and caught a glimpse of herself. She looked more like a twelve-year-old kid than a grown woman. She could still remember Kitty's sultry good looks and voluptuous body. How could any man prefer her to Kitty?

But it was you he married, her mirror image pointed out. *Why do you suppose he did that? If he had wanted to marry Kitty, he's had plenty of opportunities to do so. And what if Kitty is in love with him? Does he have any control over her feelings?*

She was reminded of the girls who'd dated him in the past. It was true they had fallen for him, but he had done nothing to encourage them. Had he?

She shook her head at all the thoughts racing around inside. What was she going to—

"Megan? There aren't any towels in here! Can you bring me one?"

Oh, Lordy, she'd forgotten to replenish the supply of towels in Travis's bathroom. She was always forgetting some household chore or another. At least she'd remembered to gather up all the towels earlier today to wash them.

"Hold on!" she called back, hastily wrapping her

bathrobe around her, "They're still downstairs. I'll bring you some."

She paused long enough to slip on her house shoes, then hurried downstairs and emptied the clothes dryer. Carrying the armful of towels she hurried back upstairs and down the hall to Travis's room.

She tapped on the door.

"C'mon in," he said, his voice muffled.

She fumbled the doorknob, managed to open it and walked into the room, dropping the pile of towels in one of the chairs. The bathroom door was ajar so she picked up one of the towels and stuck it through the door. "Here you go."

Before she could turn away, he opened the door, saying, "Thanks," as he began to dry himself off, seemingly oblivious to the fact that she still stood there.

Megan whirled away and headed for the bedroom door.

"Megan?"

She froze, unable to look around. "Yes?"

After a couple of beats, he said, "Thanks."

She quickly drew in some air. "No problem. Sorry I forgot to bring them upstairs."

He touched her shoulder and she glanced around at him. The towel was now wrapped around his waist and hips. "You don't have to act as though I'm going to attack you," he said quietly.

She turned to face him. "It isn't that, Travis. It's just— It's—" She waved her hand in frustration.

"What?"

She shook her head. "I don't know. This is all so confusing. I don't know what to do. I feel so—"

"So—?"

"Stupid! I mean, I don't know what's expected of me. I don't know anything about being married and in love and I know it's stupid to be jealous but I can't help it because I—"

He caught her by her upper arms and said, "Whoa, wait a minute here. What do you mean you don't know about—what was it you said—being in love? Would you like to help me understand that remark a little better?"

Megan couldn't possibly think with him standing so close to her that way. She was acutely conscious of the heat from his body, the fresh scent of soap he'd just used, and the unsteadiness of his breathing, as though he was just as affected by her. She looked up at his unusual, dark blue eyes and felt a melting sensation sweep over her. "You must know how I feel about you," she said weakly.

He caught his breath. "No. Maybe you'd better tell me."

She swallowed, then, unable to resist, she laid her palm lightly against his chest, feeling his heart race beneath her hand. Concentrating on the strong line of his jaw, she admitted, "I've loved you for a long time, Travis. I just didn't understand what I was feeling. I had a crush on you in high school, just like half the girls around. I tried to convince myself that what I was feeling was hate, but I—"

"Oh, Megan!" he groaned, gathering her up into his arms and holding her tightly against him. His towel immediately slithered to the floor. "Oh, baby, if you only knew how I've prayed that I'd hear you say that to me someday. I was beginning to give up hope."

He began to kiss her—long, drugging kisses that made her go limp. She felt the room tilting before she realized that he had picked her up and carried her to the bed. Her robe had fallen open, revealing that she wore nothing underneath.

Travis lowered her to the bed and quickly followed. He couldn't seem to decide where to touch and caress her next, both his mouth and hands moving restlessly over her.

"Don't you understand?" he whispered brokenly. "I never really saw another woman, not in school, and not on the road. You're the only one I've ever wanted."

"Oh, Travis."

There were no more words between them, not for several, love-filled hours. Sometime in the early morning, predawn, she lay awake, her head resting on his shoulder as he lazily stroked her breast. "Let's don't ever fight again, okay?" he whispered. "Not like that. If you want to yell and scream at me, okay, but don't push me away, babe. Anything but that."

Megan felt completely loved at that moment, as well as cherished and treasured. She smiled in the darkness. "I won't push you away," she admitted. "But I probably will yell and scream. You have a wonderful knack for provoking me to extreme reactions."

"What I can't understand is why you would ever be jealous of someone like Kitty?"

She could hear the sincere puzzlement in his voice.

"She's beautiful, Travis," she said pointedly, feeling much more gracious about the other woman's looks now.

"But she isn't you," he said in such a reasonable tone of voice that she found herself loving him even more than she did before.

"Travis?"

"Mmm?"

"Were you serious about not going out on the circuit this year?"

"Yes, ma'am, I'm definitely serious about that. I was having too much trouble keeping my mind on what I was doing those last few months."

"Can you use the money I gave you to start your horse farm?"

He was quiet for so long that she thought he wasn't going to answer her. She'd almost dozed off before he said, "We can decide that together, baby. From now on, we'll make all our decisions together."

Megan drifted into sleep.

Epilogue

"Uh, Travis, there's something I need to discuss with you," Megan said several weeks later.

It was April once more. The Texas winter had disappeared and the bluebonnets were in full bloom, their color still rivaled by the brightness of her husband's compelling eyes.

Travis was in the barn checking on the new foal. He'd bought the mare knowing she was due in the spring and was quite pleased with the results.

He stepped out of the stall and joined Megan who was leaning against one of the posts, watching him. He leaned down and gave her a quick kiss. "Sure. What's up?"

"It's almost lunchtime. Why don't we go eat now?"

"You're getting more domestic every day," he

teased, dropping his arm around her shoulder and guiding her toward the door. "What are we having?"

She grinned. "Don't laugh at me. At least I'm trying. It's one of Mollie's recipes she left with me during spring break. I'm actually discovering I'm having fun experimenting."

They were halfway through lunch before Travis said, "So, what is it you need to discuss with me? Is it your herd? Do you need more help? What?"

"The herd is fine, the extra hands are a godsend now that Butch is retiring, and yes, I think maybe we are going to need to hire a housekeeper."

"Ah. So you aren't enjoying being domestic as much as I thought."

"Well, it's not that, exactly. You remember when we agreed to discuss everything together before we made any decisions?"

"Uh-huh."

"Well, I'm afraid we're going to both have to accept that we can't always be in that much control."

"What are you talking about?"

"I'm pregnant."

She hadn't meant to blurt it out that way. She'd wanted to break it to him slowly, gently. She'd wanted to be sure that he truly wanted to have a family and that he wanted to start one now. But all of that was a little behind times now.

"Pregnant?" he repeated hoarsely before a smirky grin appeared on his face. "No kidding? I mean, you're sure about that?"

She nodded. "I bought one of those home kits to

make sure, but I already knew. The signs have been too obvious.''

"When? I mean, when is it due?''

"November, I think. I've got to see a doctor to make sure but I think it will be here in November.''

Travis's grin grew wider. He reached for her hand and squeezed it. "Are you okay with the idea? I mean, are you feeling all right? Was this what you wanted?''

"I don't know how I feel. I guess I just never gave it much thought. We certainly never did anything to prevent it!''

His smile was very knowing. "I'm well aware of that.''

"You mean you did it on purpose?''

He shrugged, all innocence. "Who, me? Hey, I'm just a country boy. What do I know about— Ow!'' he said, laughing, as she quickly moved around the table and punched him on the arm.

"You *wanted* me to get pregnant, you sneak!'' she exclaimed, laughing as he pulled her down into his lap.

The kiss he gave her was filled with love and re-assurance and a great deal of longing. When their lips finally parted, both of them were breathing erratically. "Here I've been...wondering how to...break the news, afraid you wouldn't...want a baby this soon,'' she admitted between breaths.

He sobered, his eyes filled with love as he studied her beloved face. "I can't think of anything that would please me more than for us to start our family now. I'll admit that I hoped you'd get pregnant sooner or later, but I figured that the law of nature would catch up with us eventually, so I wasn't giving it much thought.'' He hugged her to him. ''And yes, this means that we are definitely going to get you a housekeeper. You're going to have to cut back on the heavy work, at least.''

She cupped his face in her hands. ''It's so hard for me to believe all of this. A year ago I thought we were going to lose the ranch. I didn't know what to do or where to go or what to plan. And then—'' she kissed him ''—you walked back into my life and nothing's been the same ever since.''

He smoothed his hand across her flat abdomen. ''Hey, babe, I have a hunch you haven't seen nothing yet!'' His hand strayed to her breast and within a few minutes he'd picked her up and started for the stairs, her arms entwined around his neck.

Megan smiled to herself, thinking about the changes. As long as Travis was a part of her life, she knew she'd face all the changes with courage and calm acceptance. His love for her had finally helped her to understand what strength can be gained by accepting love and help from others.

* * * * *

INSTANT MOMMY

Chapter One

"Well, land's sake, if it isn't Mollie O'Brien! My, but it's good to see you again, Mollie. When did you get home from college, my dear?"

At the sound of her name, Mollie paused on the steps of the Agua Verde post office and glanced around. A late spring breeze dancing across the courtyard square caressed her face, providing a touch of relief from the heat of the Texas sun.

"Oh, hi, Mrs. Krueger," she replied, when she saw the woman who had called to her. Lydia Krueger had taught Mollie's eighth-grade Sunday school class. "I came home yesterday for Maribeth's graduation. We have finals next week, then I'll be home for the summer. How are things with you?"

"Can't complain, dear, can't complain. I imagine Megan will be pleased to have you home for the summer. She could probably use some help with that new baby of hers. How old is he now?"

Mollie grinned, always eager to discuss her tiny nephew. "Danny's seven months old and such a cutie. I've really missed not being around him more this past school year. Babies seem to grow up so fast."

"Not only babies," Mrs. Krueger replied with a smile. "Why, it doesn't seem possible that you O'Brien girls have gotten so big. It seems only yesterday that Megan was fighting to keep the three of you together as a family...and you and Maribeth were still in grade school. Now here she is a new mama and both you girls are college age. I swear the time just gets away from me."

"I know what you mean. I'm four years older than Megan was when our parents died, and I'm still not sure I could handle the responsibilities Megan took on back then," Mollie admitted.

"Well, she did a fine job of it, let me tell you. Everybody can see that." Lydia Krueger glanced at her watch and shook her head as though amazed at the time. Starting toward her car, she said, "It was good to see you again, my dear. Be sure to give my regards to the family...and give that baby an extra hug for me."

"I will, Mrs. Krueger." Mollie had already turned away to enter the post office when Mrs. Krueger called to her.

"Oh, Mollie, speaking of babies, wasn't that the saddest thing about Deke Crandall?"

Mollie froze for a moment at the unexpected mention of Deke's name, before she retraced her steps to Lydia's side.

"What happened to Deke?" she managed to ask through lips that suddenly felt numb.

"Didn't Megan tell you?"

Mollie could only shake her head.

"Well, his wife, Patsy, had their baby a few weeks ago," Lydia explained, her voice losing its lilt. She paused for a moment, obviously searching her memory. "Must have been back in April. She had a little girl. I'm not real sure what happened after that. I understand Patsy started running some kind of fever and the doctors couldn't seem to do anything to help." Once again she paused, shaking her head. "I believe the baby was maybe three days old when Patsy died."

"Oh my God!" Mollie whispered, shock racing through her. "How horrible. Deke must be devastated."

Lydia nodded vigorously. "Oh my, yes. It's really just the saddest thing that's happened around here in years. The whole county turned out for the funeral, of course. It was enough to break your heart. Deke just sat staring at her lying there in that coffin. It was like he didn't know anybody else was around. People tried to talk to him, but he didn't seem to hear them. He just sat there…looking at her. He never broke down…leastways, not in front of anybody." She sighed. "I don't know what's going to happen to him and that poor little baby."

"What do you mean?"

"Since the funeral he's locked himself away in his room and won't come out. I know he must be sufferin' and all, but he's got a daughter now that needs to be cared for. We've all been real worried about them.''

''Who's taking care of the baby?''

Lydia paused, blinking the moisture from her eyes. ''You remember the Schultzes live out there near the Crandall place? Well, Cynthia Schultz set up a rotating schedule with her women's group from the church. Each of them takes turns staying a day and a night at a time to care for the baby. They also prepare food for Deke...not that he seems to eat much of anything these days,'' she added with resignation. ''I don't know how long they're going to have to do that. At first, they thought they'd just help for a week or two until Deke got his head back on straight and decided to hire somebody to look after that sweet baby.'' Her eyes filled once again and she resolutely touched a handkerchief to them. ''At this rate, the little darlin' will be walkin' before she even knows who her daddy is.''

Mollie felt stunned. Even when Lydia said no more, Mollie could only stand there in shocked silence, staring at her.

Lydia patted her arm. ''I really do need to go, dear. Time just seems to fritter away on me. It's good to see you back home, Mollie. Once you're settled in, why don't you come over for a visit? I'd love to hear about school and all.''

Mollie glanced at her watch. ''Thank you, Mrs. Krueger. I'd like that. I'll call you one of these days,'' she offered absently before she turned and went into the post office, her mind replaying all that she'd just heard.

Deke Crandall grieving and in pain…Deke's daughter being shuffled between well-meaning but busy women who had their own families to look after.

"Oh, Deke, I'm so sorry," she whispered softly while she gathered the accumulation of ranching magazines, the weekly newspaper and various letters and statements addressed to Travis and Megan that had been her reason for stopping by the post office in the first place.

She continued to the grocery store and mechanically filled the list Megan's housekeeper, Mrs. Hoffmeyer, had given her earlier that morning while she continued to mull over what she had learned.

Once everything was in the car, Mollie drove out of town toward the family ranch, absently following the route she'd learned years ago…while her thoughts replayed the first time she ever saw Deke Crandall.

The day was clearly marked in her mind. She'd been seven years old. It was so memorable because it was one of the few times in her life when she'd spent a whole day alone with her father. Normally he spent his time working on the ranch while her mother looked after the girls. She couldn't remember now where Megan had been, but she did recall that Maribeth had been running a fever and her dad had suggested to her mom that Mollie go with him while he ran a few errands.

Thrilled by the opportunity to spend time alone with her dad, she had accompanied him to town, happily tagging along while he stopped at the hardware store, the bank and stopped to have coffee with some of the ranchers at the little shop on the courthouse square.

Later they'd driven out to the Crandall ranch. As soon as they'd stepped up on the porch, she'd spotted a mama cat and her kittens. Delighted with her discovery she'd gone over to play with them while her dad had gone inside the house.

When the shouting and laughter broke out down by the barn, her natural curiosity had caused her to follow the sound around the side of the house where she had a clear view of the barn and several pens. A group of men were gathered outside one of the pens, hanging on to the railings while they cheered and called out advice to someone she couldn't see.

She'd immediately drawn closer, slipping silently among the roisterous men and peeking between the slats of the railed fence.

A man was riding a horse that was doing everything possible to throw him off. It was just like a rodeo she'd once seen, only now she was much closer to the action. She could almost taste the dust flying in the air.

She studied the man on the bucking horse. He seemed to be enjoying himself immensely, gracefully balanced high on the back of the spinning, gyrating animal. The men watching continued to yell out suggestions, laughingly predicting an unplanned departure from the saddle.

Sunlight glinted off his blond hair. She was mesmerized by the sight.

Eventually the horse slowed, then after a half-hearted stiff-legged jump and a defiant toss of his head, he stopped, his sides heaving. Two of the men vaulted over the fence and ran to the horse, steadying him while the rider climbed off, dusted his pants and walked toward the fence near where she peeked through.

Nobody had paid any attention to her presence. She continued to watch as the man came closer, opening a nearby gate that she hadn't noticed and joining the other men.

Seen up close he was as big as her daddy, his face sun-darkened, his loose-limbed stride like so many men who spent much of their time on horseback.

Then she heard her father calling her name. The blond man looked around in surprise and saw her watching him.

"Well, look here, would you? Where in the world did you come from, honey?" he asked, closing the distance between them.

She dipped her head toward her father's truck.

"What's your name?" he asked

"Mollie."

"Mollie? That's a nice name." Gravely he removed his leather gloves and extended his hand. "Pleased to meet ya, Mollie. I'm Deke."

She had to look a long way up to see his face. He must have realized how intimidating he seemed to someone her size because he immediately knelt, balancing on his heels so that they were eye level. Timidly she touched his hand, feeling the rough calluses on his palm.

"Do you live here?" she found the courage to ask.

"Sure do. At least during the summertime when I'm not in school."

She stared at him in surprise. "You still go to school?"

He threw his head back and laughed, his white teeth flashing in strong contrast to his deeply tanned face. "Yeah, I'm afraid so. I've still got another year to go. Are you in school?"

She nodded.

"How old are you?"

"Seven. How old are you?"

"Almost twenty-two."

She gathered up her courage and said, "You sure do ride a horse good."

"Why, thank you, Mollie. I'm glad you think so."

It was then that her father walked up.

"Mollie, you 'bout scared me half to death, girl. I left you playing on the porch and the next thing I knew you'd disappeared. Your mama would have my hide if I let something happen to you while I'm supposed to be looking after you."

Deke stood and faced her father. "She's okay, Mr. O'Brien. We wouldn't have let anything happen to her."

The two men began to chat and Mollie was able to study Deke to her heart's content. Up close that way she could see that his eyes were a startling green, glittering like jewels. He was as tall as her father, with broad shoulders and lean hips.

He wasn't really handsome or anything, not like men in the movies or on television, but it didn't matter to Mollie. He had spoken to her as if she was his equal. He had shaken hands with her and talked with her. All the other men had gone about their business without paying much notice to her, but he'd taken the time to draw her out.

She had never forgotten that meeting.

Somehow in her child's mind Deke had become more than just another rancher who lived in the county. She had begun to see him as an imaginary part of her life. When she was alone she got into the habit of pretending that he was there, and she would talk to him, tell him about school and about her life.

At the age of seven it was easy to imagine that once she grew up she would be old enough to marry Deke and live happily ever after.

By the age of ten, life's harsher realities intruded into her imaginary, little-girl world. Her parents were killed. Megan fought hard to keep the ranch and the family intact. Mollie, who had always loved helping her mother in the kitchen and with the housework, quickly tried to do her part in the house.

The three girls had clung together in an effort to survive the horrific loss and cherished memories of her childhood hero were put away with other childish dreams.

The final end to any dreams that might include Deke occurred when she was fifteen and heard that Deke had gotten married. It was funny now, looking back to the young girl she'd been just five short years ago, at how hard she'd taken the news after so much time had passed since she'd first seen him riding that bronco.

Oh, she'd seen Deke around town over the years,

but always at a distance. She'd never spoken to him again. She doubted he even remembered meeting her that long-ago day.

But the memory had lingered for Mollie, even after she'd become old enough to know that he'd already been a grown man soon out of college when she'd barely started grade school. Blond hair and green eyes had always held a special kind of fascination for her.

Not that she expected him ever to learn about her early dreams of him, or become aware of the fact that she had been foolish enough to pretend that he would wait for her to grow up before deciding to marry.

She had never known his wife. Patsy wasn't from the area and there'd been no reason for their paths to cross once she and Deke were married.

Driving home, all she could think about was how sad that Deke should lose his wife just as he was becoming a father. Her heart grieved for him. She wished there was something she could do for him, but she couldn't think of anything that others hadn't already done.

She turned into the entrance of the O'Brien spread. There had been lots of changes in the almost three years since Megan had married Travis Kane, but the name of the ranch wasn't one of them. Maybe it was because Travis's parents owned the adjoining ranch and it would be too confusing to use the Kane name on both pieces of property.

Mostly it was known as the O'Brien ranch because it had been in the O'Brien family for over a hundred years. Their ancestor, Paddy O'Brien, had won it in an all-night poker game on one of the paddleboat

steamers that plied the Mississippi back in those days.
According to family legend, he'd been a riverboat
gambler who'd decided to accept the win as a sign
from God that he was to do something different with
his life, so he'd headed west to Texas, eventually married and settled down to become a rancher.

Since there were no more O'Briens to carry on the
family name, only the ranch would be there to remind
people of the O'Brien legacy. Travis had no problem
with the idea. But then, Travis had always had a
healthy sense of his own worth.

As soon as Mollie pulled up near the back door of
the house, Megan stepped out onto the porch from
the kitchen and hurried to help her bring in the sacks
of groceries.

"I still can't get used to finding you in the house,"
Mollie said to her, grinning. "Even Travis couldn't
keep you inside. And yet, all Danny has to do is
whimper and you're right by his side."

Megan had allowed her blond hair to grow long
enough so that she now wore it pulled high in a po-
nytail. She shoved her bangs out of her eyes and took
two of the bags while Mollie brought the last two.
"Just because I was in the habit of working long, hard
days doesn't mean I necessarily prefer them. I'm enjoying my time with Danny," she said, rapidly putting away the groceries. "Of course, I enjoy it a lot
more when he isn't teething, but I guess that's part
of the process."

"Speaking of Danny," Mollie said, "it's awfully
quiet in here. What did you do to him?"

Megan laughed. "I didn't do anything. Mrs. Hoffmeyer used one of her tried-and-true remedies to help babies when they're cutting teeth. Whatever it is, it must have worked. She rubbed it on Danny's little swollen gums and within minutes he'd quietened. He was exhausted, poor baby. Ain't silence grand?'' she teased.

After they'd put away the groceries, Mollie retrieved the ever-present pitcher of iced tea from the refrigerator. Filling two glasses with ice cubes and tea, she handed one to Megan and they both sat down at the large, round kitchen table.

"Speaking of babies, did you hear what happened to the Crandalls?'' Mollie asked.

"You mean Patsy? Wasn't that terrible? How did you hear about it?''

"I ran into Mrs. Krueger at the post office this morning. I'm surprised you didn't tell me.''

Megan shrugged. "Guess it didn't cross my mind to mention it. I mean, it isn't as though we knew them, really, although I think Travis sold Deke a couple of his horses last year. We went to the funeral. It was so sad…Patsy was only thirty-two.''

"Mrs. Krueger said Deke was pretty broken up.''

"Yeah, he was. Travis mentioned that his folks went out to the ranch to check on Deke a few days after the service, but Sally Whitman, who was looking after the baby when they got there, said he wasn't coming out of his room for anything or anybody.''

Mollie was silent for several minutes, wishing there was something she could do to ease Deke's pain. But, as Megan said, he didn't even know them. What could she say or do that could help him deal with such a blow?

"I like the way you are wearing your hair these days," Megan said during their companionable silence. "I've always thought your hair was so gorgeous...that luscious, dark chestnut color. The sun brings the red out in it."

Mollie touched her shoulder-length hair. "It's funny how each of us looks different, yet we're sisters. You have the blond hair and the blue eyes."

"Ugly eyes, you mean. Like a carnival kewpie doll."

"You have beautiful eyes, very expressive."

"What about you? Your eyes are so blue they look artificial. Mama always called them Irish eyes, with the thick dark lashes surrounding them."

"Of course they're nothing like Travis's blue eyes, are they, Megan?" Mollie teased.

Megan smiled. "No. His are almost purple, they're so blue. Yours are more like the sky, or a lake."

"Then there's Maribeth," Mollie said, "with the flaming red hair and flashing golden eyes. We each have our own individual look, and yet, we're alike in other ways."

"Thank goodness we've been able to wear each other's clothes. Remember when I had to borrow a dress from you when Travis first asked me out on a date? I didn't even own one."

Mollie grinned. "I remember. I had to forbid you from wearing your boots with it!"

"Maribeth's almost as bad. She's still running around with the guys like she's forgotten she's a girl…she prefers to wear jeans, and is completely unaware of her striking looks.''

"Is she still dating Bobby Metcalf?"

"Dating? I guess that's what you'd call it. They're always together, but I seldom see just the two of them going anywhere. There's usually a group headed off to the movies or a local rodeo, or some school activity.''

"Does she still talk about marrying him?"

"In some vague future time. Right now they're excited because they both got accepted into A & M for this fall.''

"Mrs. Krueger happened to comment today that the O'Brien girls are all grown up. We made it, thanks to you,'' Mollie said with a smile.

"Nonsense. We wouldn't have survived if you hadn't fed us and looked after us. It was a partnership and we each pulled our load.'' She eyed Mollie for a moment before saying, "Are you still irritated with me for insisting you go off to college?''

"More resigned than irritated. Just because we didn't have the money for you to go to school you seem to feel that Maribeth and I shouldn't be deprived of our education.''

"C'mon and admit it. You've made lots of new friends and you're discovering there's a whole different world outside of Agua Verde County.''

"True, but this is my home and I really miss being here. Let's face it, I'm just a homebody at heart.'' She folded her arms on the table and leaned forward. "To be honest, I'm jealous of Mrs. Hoffmeyer.''

Megan blinked. "You're kidding.''

"Well, maybe I am…a little. You've got to admit that she's got the place running so efficiently there really won't be anything for me to do when I come home for the summer."

"Except relax and enjoy yourself, for a change. That's what summer vacations are for. Maribeth never has trouble finding all kinds of things to do with her time."

"I know, but she's always been sociable, while I'm more content to stay home and putter around the house." She took a sip of her tea. "You know, I've been thinking…"

"About?"

"Deke Crandall."

Megan looked at her in surprise. "Why in the world would you be thinking about Deke Crandall? I mean, I know he's suffered a grievous loss but still…there's nothing anyone can do for him."

"That's just it. Maybe there is," Mollie mused.

"What are you talking about?"

"I've been toying with the idea of asking Deke if I could take care of his baby…I mean, until he could find somebody permanent."

"Do you mean actually live with him?"

"Well, yeah, I'd have to stay there to be able to look after an infant."

"Oh, Mollie, I don't think that's a very good idea."

"Why not?"

"Isn't it obvious? You living there with him, for whatever reason? It just wouldn't look right."

"Megan? When have you ever cared what people think?"

"About me? Never. About my sisters? I guard your reputations with my life."

"Well, maybe it's time to let us do our own guarding. If I don't care what people think, and if I can help Deke out, I'd like to do it."

"I doubt he'll agree to it. From what I hear he's in pretty bad shape."

"Well, then I guess I'll have to beard the lion in his den and discuss it with him."

"You're really serious about this, aren't you?"

"Yeah. I think I am. I couldn't get it out of my mind during the drive from town. Here's this little baby being cared for by strangers, practically orphaned if what I'm hearing is true about Deke's behavior."

"You'll be a stranger to her, too."

"At first, yes, but from what I understand, the women are taking turns keeping her so that the poor little thing isn't getting used to seeing one face she can depend on."

"And what's going to happen when it's time for you to return to school? I'm here to tell you that you can really get attached to them mighty fast."

Mollie shrugged. "That's almost three months away. I may not get the job. Even if I do, Deke may find someone to care for her permanently in a few weeks. I don't see any reason to borrow trouble before it gets here, do you?" She glanced at her watch. "I think I'll go over there and talk to him about it."

"Now?"

"Sure, why not?"

Megan laughed. "You've never been one to sit still since I've known you, but you've got another week of school before you're home for the summer. Why don't you wait and talk to him then?"

"Because I'm afraid I'll lose my courage if I don't do it today." She walked around the table and hugged Megan. "I'm fine, Mama Bear. You can stop worrying about me, okay?" She picked up the car keys and headed toward the door. "Wish me luck. I have a hunch I'm going to need it."

Chapter Two

The sound of women's voices going on and on finally registered on Deke's alcohol-soaked brain.

He groaned.

It must be changing-of-the-guard time again. Each day a new shift arrived, taking over his kitchen, taking over his house, yippin' and yappin' until he wanted to throw something at them.

At least they'd finally learned to leave him alone. He didn't want to see them, he didn't want to talk to them and he sure as hell didn't want to hear any of their well-meaning advice about what he needed to do.

He knew what he had to do. He was just too much of a damn coward to do it quick and clean. Instead he was trying to kill himself with alcohol.

The problem was that he'd never been much of a drinker. His system had slowly been tolerating more during the past few weeks, but he was ashamed to admit that he threw up almost as much as he drank.

Deke sat on the side of the bed and rubbed his face. He couldn't remember the last time he'd shaved…or bathed…or ate. He generally waited until late at night when the house was quiet to leave his bedroom and go to the kitchen. There was all kinds of food in the refrigerator. Everybody and her mother had brought food out here to him.

He didn't have much luck keeping it down, either.

He knew he couldn't keep on this way. He was being a self-absorbed, self-pitying, son of a— But what the hell. It wasn't a crime, was it, to sit down one day and decide that he was tired of fighting it? He'd never had any use for whiners. Now he'd turned into the biggest whiner of them all.

He froze at the sound of a high-pitched wail. He heard the tittering of the women somewhere in the house. They sounded like a gaggle of geese, for God's sake. The baby was suddenly quiet. Of course she'd shut up. With every woman in the county making certain that all her needs were fulfilled before she was even sure what it was she needed, she certainly had nothing to complain about.

Except for the fact that she no longer had a mother and she had a worthless excuse of a man for a father.

He stood, still unsteady from the quantity of bourbon he'd managed to consume the night before, and felt his way into the bathroom. He'd kept the drapes tightly closed over the windows for days. The only light coming in was the thin stripe between the edge of the windows and the drapes. Enough light to see where he was going. Not enough light to have to face his image in the mirror.

He made it to the bathroom without stumbling and reached into the shower to turn on the water. Maybe a shower would help to clear his head.

As soon as the water warmed, he stepped under the cascading spray, feeling it caress his battered body. He stood there for countless minutes, allowing the water to work its magic on bruises that were too deep within him to show.

By the time he turned off the spray, it was running cool, but his body had been scrubbed and his hair was now clean. He toweled off, already feeling exhausted from the unaccustomed exercise.

After draping the towel around his shoulders he returned to the bedroom, seeing the accumulation of bottles, glasses, dirty dishes and disheveled bed-clothes. He was going to have to do something with the place. It was a pigsty. Worse than that. It was a—

A knock on the bedroom door interrupted his search for the proper description of the room he'd turned into his lair.

Who in the hell was stupid enough to knock on his door? Nobody had bothered him in here for weeks now. He thought they understood that—

Another knock sounded. ''Mr. Crandall?''

Who was that? He didn't recognize the voice.

''Go away,'' he growled.

''Mr. Crandall?'' was the immediate reply. ''This is Mollie O'Brien. You probably don't remember who I am but I need to speak to you.''

He glanced down at his bare body and almost

smiled. Whoever the hell Mollie O'Brien was, he'd be willing to bet that he could shock the sweet little dear out of ten years' growth if he invited her in.

"Go away," he repeated doggedly. Deke walked over to the bed and sat down, grateful for the support. Damn, but he was weak! Now his own body was betraying him, which was a hell of a note. Couldn't depend on anything anymore. Absolutely nothing.

"Mr. Crandall. I know you're grieving. I know that this is a very bad ti—"

"You don't know what you're talking about! Now get away from that door and leave me alone."

"I'm not going to do that, Mr. Crandall. I'm going to stand here and pound on this door until you let me talk to you. This is really important or I wouldn't be so insistent."

For one almost uncontrollable moment Deke felt the urge to pick up the empty whiskey bottle beside his bed and throw it against the door. Only some slight sense of sanity reminded him that if he did, he would be subjecting himself to a carpetful of glass slivers.

He closed his eyes for a moment, trying to think around the helacious headache that pounded through his head like a giant kettledrum.

Whoever this Mollie O'Brien was, obviously she was not going to take no for an answer. His only other option was to get rid of her. The sooner the better. Her persistent knocking wasn't even in the same rhythm as the kettledrum in his head.

He stood up and grabbed at a shadowy pile of clothes, knocking them over. He felt around until he recognized the texture of his jeans. The burst of anger that her intrusion had created helped him to shakily step into the jeans and pull them up. He zipped them as he made his way to the door.

"Mr. Crandall?" she was saying just as he opened the door.

She stood there, her fist poised in midair, inches away from his bare chest. He stared at her, frowning. Did he know this woman? He didn't think so. She wasn't the forgettable kind. Eyes the color of a summer sky, surrounded with the longest, thickest lashes he'd ever seen, a complexion that looked like porcelain, and a tumbling mass of reddish-brown hair that framed her heart-shaped face.

She wore a simple, shirtwaist dress the same color as her eyes. *I wonder how long it took her to find a perfect match,* he wondered cynically.

"All right. Here I am. Now what do you want?"

Mollie took a step backward, staring at the large man filling the doorway that had been closed tightly against her an instant before. She hadn't been prepared to confront him in quite this fashion.

He stood there wearing a pair of faded jeans. Period. His blond hair tumbled over his forehead, and he had the beginning of a thick beard covering his cheeks. But it was his bloodshot eyes that silenced her into numb compassion. The man standing before her had seen hell—was, perhaps, still living there.

"Mr. Crandall," she said hesitantly, "I, uh, would like to speak to you, if I may."

"You've made that quite obvious. What I want to hear from you is why. Didn't those women—" he waved his arm toward the front of the house " —tell you I don't want to see anybody, I don't want to talk to anybody, I don't want company, I don't want consoling? What I want is to be left the hell alone!''

"Yes, they told me,'' she said quietly. "However, I still would like to speak to you.''

"You would, would you?''

"Yes.''

With a sigh he turned around and stalked back into the room. "Well, come on in, if you must. And close the door behind you.''

Gingerly she stepped into the darkened room, her eyes working to adjust to the gloom before the closing of the door reduced the visibility even further.

Deke threw himself down on the rumpled bed and lay there, watching her without expression.

Mollie couldn't remember a time in her life when she'd felt so out of her depth. But she refused to turn away now. Not after she'd seen Deke's baby daughter. From the time she'd walked into the house and had seen the tiny infant greedily pulling on her bottle, Mollie knew she was in real danger of losing her heart to another Crandall.

Jolene had her dad's glittery eyes and a shock of almost white hair, which stood up from her tiny little face as though brushed into a spike. Her eyes had locked with Mollie's and she'd watched her every move. How could such a newborn baby be so alert?

Now more than ever, Mollie was determined to accomplish her mission.

Mollie finished closing the door and felt her way to a straight-back chair she'd spotted nearby. She brushed a pile of clothes off it and, once seated, clasped her hands together in her lap, straightening her spine. "I've come to apply for the position of housekeeper and to care for your daughter."

"No," he replied immediately. "Now get out."

"But, Mr. Crandall, you're going to need—"

"It's none of your concern what I'm going to need. I don't want some high school baby-sitter trying to look after—"

"Mr. Crandall, please. If you'll just give me a moment to explain. I'm twenty years old. I've just completed my second year at UT in Austin. My sister Megan had her baby last November and I've had some experience looking after him. I—"

"O'Brien...of course. You're one of the O'Brien girls. I remember now. You were just a kid when your folks were killed."

"Yes. I was ten. I grew up fast. I looked after the household until I left for college. I believe that I could help you until you're ready to begin interviewing for a full-time permanent caretaker."

"What makes you think I need someone? The baby's being cared for."

"Yes, but you can't expect these women to continue interrupting their schedules indefinitely, whereas I have nothing else to do this summer. I can give you three months in which to look for a replacement."

Deke stared at the shadowy figure of the woman seated across the room from him. She certainly hadn't been scared off by his manner and he knew he was being a complete bastard.

He knew. He just didn't care.

But something inside reminded him that a part of him had to care, for the baby's sake. It wasn't her fault that his life had turned to—

Deke sat up and swung his legs to the floor. Facing her now, he asked, "Mollie? Is that your name?"

"Yes."

"I don't guess I understand. Why would you want to tie yourself down with so much responsibility? You aren't that old, after all. Why aren't you making plans to spend the summer socializing with your friends? You're young. You're attractive. Surely you have a busy social life."

"I left my so-called social life in Austin where I'm certain it will be waiting for me when I return in the fall. In the meantime, I'm used to responsibility and there's nothing for me to do at my sister's place. She already has all the help she needs."

Deke pushed himself up and made his way barefoot into the bathroom without saying anything. He ran some water, rinsed out a glass, then filled it. He looked into the medicine cabinet until he found some over-the-counter pain medication. Tipping out three tablets, he swallowed them, then chased them down with the water.

For the first time in days he stared into the mirror in front of him. Light from the frosted glass of the bathroom window illuminated the room.

It was not a pretty picture. Black puffy circles decorated his eyes, making him look like some damn raccoon. He was well on his way to having a full-fledged beard when he'd been clean shaven all his life.

Let's face it, Crandall, he thought to himself. *You're messed up. Really messed up. Here's a chance to get back on track. Are you going to blow this off, too?*

He took his time before returning to the other room. He was giving her a chance to leave. When he walked back into the bedroom he saw that she hadn't moved.

"Do you know how to make coffee?"

"Yes."

"How about putting on a pot of coffee while I shave? After that we'll talk in my office, away from all those women."

At least he was willing to talk to her. Without saying anything more, Mollie left Deke's room, quietly closing the door behind her.

She walked to the kitchen and immediately had everyone's attention.

"We tried to tell you, honey. Don't take anything he said personal. He's just hurtin' and—"

"He asked me to make him some coffee," Mollie said, walking over to the cabinets and searching for the necessary ingredients.

The women exchanged a look. "He did?" one of them asked in surprise.

"Uh-huh." She quickly found what she needed and started the coffeepot.

"Well, I wouldn't have believed it," another one muttered.

"Of course you know, Mollie, that you can't possibly stay out here all by yourself like that. It's real sweet of you to offer to help him and all, but it just wouldn't look right for you to stay out here."

"Why is that, Mrs. Ferguson?" she asked, leaning against the cabinet and facing the three women sitting at the table.

"Well, it's obvious, of course. I mean here you are a good-looking single girl and then there's Deke in there…" She allowed her voice to drift off.

"Who has just lost his wife," Mollie added, "and who is in complete despair. Somehow I don't think he's going to be in the least interested in who's keeping Jolene."

"That's the truth," one of them muttered.

"Anyway, he hasn't said he'd hire me. But I will talk to him about it." She filled a large mug with black coffee and walked into the hallway. She spotted his office off the long living room and went inside.

She wondered if he would really come out of his room or whether he'd just decided to say whatever was necessary to get rid of her. She placed the cup of coffee on the desk and wandered over to the window.

From there she had a panorama of the rolling Texas hills that were part of the Crandall ranch. Closer, she saw the large barn and holding pens surrounding it where she'd seen a much younger, happier Deke for the first time.

He'd changed in many ways. His broad shoulders were heavier, more muscled. Or maybe it was just the fact that she'd now seen him without a shirt for the first time. Seeing him again after all these years had been a real jolt to her system.

She was no longer seven years old, but he still had a strong effect on her.

Maybe everybody—Megan, Mrs. Ferguson, Deke—was right. Maybe she had no business trying to care for Jolene or Deke. She was already too emotionally involved. It didn't matter that he hadn't known who she was. It didn't matter that he had no idea how he had become an imaginary childhood friend to her while she was growing up.

She smiled at the memory of the many nights when she'd lain in bed and talked to him, just as though he were there in the room with her. She would tell him about her day, the good things and the not so good things. He would always listen, applauding her when she had a triumph, consoling her when she'd been hurt in some way.

Now that she'd been confronted with the real man, Mollie had to face how much she'd idealized him over the years. In person, he was much bigger, much more male, and certainly not the image conjured up by an innocent child's need for a companion.

The sound of the door closing behind her caused Mollie to turn around.

He'd shaved and dressed. He walked over to the desk in that long-legged stride of his that she remembered, then sank into the chair behind the desk. He picked up the cup with both hands and brought it to his mouth.

Mollie slowly walked over to the two chairs arranged in front of his desk and sat down in one of them.

He didn't look at her. Instead he concentrated his attention on the contents of the cup. It was only after he'd drained it that he spoke, and that was merely to ask, "Is there any more coffee?"

She gave him a long look before she quietly said, "Of course. There's a whole pot...in the kitchen."

He flinched at her words. She couldn't believe it. This large specimen of manhood actually appeared intimidated by the prospect of going into the other room to get more coffee.

She took pity on him. "Would you like for me to get you some more?"

His bloodshot gaze looked at her as though she had offered him untold riches. "Please," he murmured fervently.

She took his cup and left the room.

Only one of the women remained in the kitchen and she was in the process of changing the baby. "I'm going to put Jolene in her room for a nap," the woman said.

"The others have gone?"

"Oh, yes. They've got to get home to their families."

Mollie poured the coffee, then on impulse picked up the carafe and took it back into the other room with her. When she walked inside, she saw that Deke was resting his head against the back of his leather chair, his eyes closed.

The harsh light coming in from the window was cruel to his features. His eyes were sunken and surrounded with dark circles, while deep lines scored his face on either side of his grim mouth.

She set the cup and carafe on the felt pad in front of him and silently reseated herself.

He opened his eyes and stared blankly at her. Slowly his gaze focused and sharpened. He reached for his cup and took a long swallow. "You make a mean cup of coffee, I'll give you that...but you're too young," he finally said.

"For what?"

Her calm rejoinder seemed to catch him off guard, for his cheeks grew ruddy with color. "To be anybody's nurse or housekeeper," he muttered. "You're too damn young."

"All right," she replied agreeably. "Maybe I am. But you need somebody and I'm the only one volunteering at the moment. You need some help. There's nothing wrong in admitting it. Who's looking after your ranch?"

He glanced over at the window. "I have a foreman."

"When's the last time you spoke with him?"

"What's it to you?"

"Nothing. I'm just wondering how long you're going to keep hiding in that room, pretending that—"

"I'm not pretending anything, damn it! I know what's happened. I know I can't change anything. I know..." His voice drifted into silence.

"You can change a few things, Mr. Crandall. You can change what you're doing today. You can come out of that room and start showing some interest in your daughter and in your ranch. You can—"

"Who the hell do you think you are, that you feel you can sit and preach to me? You don't know anything about what I'm going through...what it's like to—" He suddenly caught himself, realizing what he was saying and who he was saying it to. "Sorry," he mumbled. "I forgot about your folks."

"All I'm saying is that you have a good reason, a very good reason, to keep going. You've got a daughter who needs you. And you need her, even if you don't think so at the moment."

They sat in silence and stared at each other for a long while before Deke gave a deep sigh and finally spoke. "I can't deny what you're saying, but I just can't deal with all of this right now."

He got up and walked out of the room. Mollie continued to sit there as she heard his booted footsteps echo down the hallway. The bedroom door slammed, causing Jolene to give a brief *"wahh"* of surprise from her room. Mollie could hear the woman with her murmur something in a soothing voice. The baby made no more protest and the house was silent.

After several moments, Mollie eventually stood and slowly left the room. She walked through the empty kitchen and let herself out of the house. Once she reached her car, she stood and looked around at the cluster of buildings.

What a shame, she thought. If he could only understand how much he still had to be thankful for. Well, at least she had tried.

Mollie drove away from the Crandall ranch, her heart heavy. Perhaps she could think of something more she might be able to do to help, but at the moment her mind was blank.

Deke was in bad shape. She wished it didn't hurt so much to see him that way. There was no rhyme or reason for her to have such a strong reaction to a man she really didn't know. She had no explanation for it. She just knew that she hurt for him, and she'd had to walk away.

Chapter Three

"I wish he weren't so stubborn," Mollie said that night over dinner.

"The man's got to be hurtin', Mollie," Travis said in his deep voice.

"Of course he is, but that doesn't mean he has to shut himself away and stop living."

"I'm just relieved he turned you down," Megan said. "That's way too much responsibility for a young girl like you to take on."

"I can't believe I'm hearing you say that, Megan," Mollie replied. "You were four years younger than me when you took on the responsibility of this entire ranch and Maribeth and me, besides."

"Which certainly qualifies me to be able to voice an opinion in the matter," Megan immediately retorted. "Don't you see, honey? I don't want you to have to give up so much of your youth when you don't have to. I had to do what I did if I was going to hang on to the ranch for all of us as well as keep the family together. It was worth it to me.''

Mollie looked down at her empty plate. ''Maybe this is worth it to me,'' she said quietly.

After a charged silence, Travis said, ''I'm not certain that I understand why, Mollie. I didn't even know you knew Deke.''

She shrugged. ''I don't. I mean, I knew who he was, but that's all. I just keep thinking about that baby, needing someone in her life.''

''But it isn't your problem, honey, as long as Deke's neighbors are helping out.''

''I suppose,'' she said, knowing her reluctance to the idea of giving up on Deke made no sense, not even to her. She was an adult now, too old to confuse her childhood imaginary friend with the man of the same name.

''Good,'' Megan said, pushing away from the table. ''Who's ready for some pie and coffee?''

Mollie knew that the subject was over.

Three weeks later Mollie was playing with Danny when the phone rang. Since she was the closest, she grabbed it.

''H'lo?''

''Is Mollie there?''

She recognized the gruff voice immediately. Bouncing Danny against her hip to keep him quiet, she replied in as calm a tone as possible, ''This is she.'' She could feel her heart racing.

''Uh—Mollie—uh, this is Deke Crandall.''

''Yes, Mr. Crandall?''

She heard a noise that sounded suspiciously like a groan. "Would you mind calling me Deke? I mean, I know I'm old enough to be your father, but damn, I hate being called mister. I feel like I should be hobbling around."

She grinned. "You would have had to be a terribly precocious fourteen-year-old to have been my father...Deke."

He grunted. "I'd probably been better off than this," he muttered, as though to himself. He cleared his throat. "The thing is, all these women are driving me plumb out of my head with all their cackling and yacking. I was wondering if... Well, if maybe you'd... What I mean is, if you could just come over and help me out for the next few days." He coughed. "I kinda lost it this morning and went stompin' into the kitchen and told 'em all to get out of my house and give me some peace and quiet...so they did...and now I don't know what I'm going to do. So far the baby's still asleep but when she wakes up she's going to expect somebody to feed her and dress her and do all those things..." He waited but Mollie didn't say anything. She heard a heavy sigh. "So what I was wondering was...I mean, if you're still willing to help me out for a few days like you once mentioned... would you consider coming over here, uh, now?"

It would serve him right if she said no. His neighbors had just been trying to help him. However, she had to admit that he'd seemed to be shaken by the presence of the women the last time she'd seen him.

Of course, she really didn't have anything else to

do with her time, which had really been dragging since she'd gotten home.

Besides...she *had* offered her services, hadn't she? Anyway, it would only be for a day or two... probably.

"Uh, hello? Mollie? Are you still there?"

The man sounded desperate. "I'm here. I was just thinking about your offer."

"Look, I'd be willing to pay you whatever you want. I know I wasn't very gracious when you were here before and I'm really sorry."

She didn't want him groveling, for heaven's sake. "I suppose I could come over and help out, if you'd like."

He didn't try to disguise his sigh of relief. "Thank God. Please come right away. I'll be watching for you."

I'll just bet you will, she said, hanging up and going to find Megan to tell her that she was leaving. She already knew her sister would be less than overjoyed with the news of her latest employment opportunity.

Deke stepped out onto the porch as soon as she hopped out of the car. He looked as bad, if not worse, than he had when she'd last seen him. That was probably the last time he'd shaved.

"Is she awake?" she asked, coming up the steps to where he stood.

"No."

She looked at him and shook her head. "When's the last time you ate?"

The glare he gave her was obviously meant to an-

nihilate her. She ignored it and walked past him. "Go
get cleaned up. You look like a grizzly bear. No wonder you ran the women off. They probably didn't realize you were human."

He followed her into the kitchen. "So why aren't
you scared off? I've yelled at you a few times, haven't
I?"

She just shook her head and started opening cabinets and cupboards. "I don't scare easy," she said,
not looking around. "Don't forget to shave."

Mollie began to mix up a batch of biscuit dough,
found some bacon in the deep freeze and rummaged
in the refrigerator for eggs. There were several par-
tially eaten casseroles that she guessed had been
brought over by well-meaning neighbors.

Something had to be done about Deke. Enough was
enough. Somebody had to get through to him and it
looked as if the only person left around him was her.

When she heard him coming down the hallway
some time later she asked, "How do you like your
eggs?"

"Over easy." His voice sounded very muted.

She removed the bacon from the pan. "Sit down.
Your breakfast is almost ready."

"Breakfast? It's almost two o'clock in the afternoon."

"So what?" She placed a heaping platter on the
table, filled with steaming biscuits, hash browns and
bacon. She returned to the stove to prepare his eggs.

Deke sat down and stared at the plate in front of
him, wondering what he was doing sitting there look-

ing at food when all he wanted was another glass of bourbon and permanent oblivion.

Slowly he began to eat. The biscuits were so light they almost floated off his plate. Patsy had never been able to—

No. Thinking that way lay madness. Stick to the moment. That was the only way he was going to be able to survive—moment by moment.

"Thank you," he murmured to his plate.

"For what?"

"For coming over as soon as I called. For continuing to kick my butt when I've been nothing but rude to you and everybody else."

She set a plate of perfectly prepared eggs in front of him, then sat down across the table from him. "I really do understand what you're going through, Deke. But enough's enough. Taking out your hurt and anger on everybody else isn't going to get you anywhere."

He kept returning his gaze to her in silence while he methodically continued to eat, bite by bite, until everything on his plate was gone. "Yeah," he finally said, "I guess you do understand, at that."

Deke noticed with a sense of surprise that he had eaten everything on his plate. His stomach hadn't forgiven him for his latest bout of bourbon, but it was calming. If he remained quiet for a while, perhaps his stomach wouldn't rebel against him this time.

"I didn't take time to pack anything because you sounded rather desperate, but sometime today I'm going to have to—"

"No," he immediately said. When he saw the look

of surprise on her face, he said, "I mean, you can't go and leave the baby. She might wake up before you can get back here."

She smiled. "You don't have to be afraid of her. I can show you how to—"

"No! You stay here. I'll go pick up your things."

She could see that he was very serious. She thought about what he was offering to do. According to what she'd heard about him, he hadn't left the ranch since Patsy's funeral. He'd stayed locked up in his room. She didn't know what had set him off this morning, but she was glad that something had broken through his apathy. Maybe he hadn't really meant to run the women off, but at least he'd taken some action rather than staying sunk in his dispair.

She nodded. "All right. I can call Megan and have her pack a few things for me."

A sound from the other room made both of them turn toward the hallway. When Mollie glanced back at Deke, he looked panicked. "I don't know anything about babies. Nothing. If you'll go check on her I'll be on my way to get your things, okay?" Deke pushed away from the table and stood. He paused for a moment, as though he was still having a little trouble moving too fast. "I'll be back shortly."

Mollie watched him cross the ranch yard to a long low building where she could see a pickup truck. Then Jolene let out a wail, reminding Mollie of why she'd been called to the rescue.

Jolene would be the person who would help ease Deke's pain, if he would let her. Mollie hurried into the other room.

"Hello, there, little one," she said softly as soon as she reached the side of the crib. "It looks like it's just you and me, babe, for the next few days. Shall we get acquainted?"

Mollie had already seen the schedule that the women had posted on the refrigerator and knew that it was time for Jolene's next feeding. She'd already prepared a bottle, so all she needed to do at the moment was to replace the wet diapers and get acquainted with her new charge.

Jolene watched her with a solemn expression, her green gaze appearing more direct and knowing than Mollie would have expected from a tiny baby. Her hair stood in a peak over her brow. Mollie smoothed her hand over the crown of her head, pressing the tuft down, only to see it spring upright as soon as she moved her hand.

"All right, cutie, it looks like your hair is going to do exactly what it wishes. Is that a hint to your personality as well? Something tells me you're going to be as stubborn and strong-willed as your daddy. I'm lucky I won't be taking care of you for more than a few days."

Within a few minutes Jolene was sucking determinedly on a nipple that seemed too big for her rosebud mouth. Her concentration was intense as she kept both her tiny fists and her eyes closed.

Still holding her, Mollie went to the phone and called Megan. As soon as her sister answered, she explained that Deke was on his way over to get her things.

"I doubt I'll be here more than a few days. It looks

like he's ready to start rebuilding his life. I'm sure he'll start interviewing housekeepers soon.''

Megan sighed. ''I wish I felt better about all of this.''

''Why don't you keep your mothering instincts for Danny and let me deal with this, okay?''

Megan chuckled. ''Ah, to be twenty again, that wonderful age when we know everything about everything and life can be controlled and directed to suit our preferences.''

''You don't have to talk as though you're in the twilight of your years, Megan,'' Mollie replied with a hint of irritation. ''You're not even close to thirty yet.''

''Oops, there goes Danny. I'll talk with you later. I may be able to get over to see you tomorrow or the next day, in case you need some help. That is...'' she paused, then said in a wry voice, ''if you don't think I'm trying to mother you too much.''

Mollie grinned to herself. ''No. That would be great. I want you to see Jolene. She's a real cutie and already looks just like Deke. Besides, I'm sure I could use some pointers on how to take care of her.''

''Really? Well, it's good to know I can help you with something!''

''Oh, you! Goodbye, now,'' Mollie said, replacing the phone in its cradle. She gently pulled the bottle away from Jolene and placed her on her shoulder, gently rubbing her tiny back to get rid of any air bubbles she might have swallowed in her vigorous efforts at eating.

Mollie glanced around the kitchen. The women had

done a good job of keeping everything clean and polished. However, she had a hunch that nobody had been in Deke's room since she was here and it had already been a complete mess then. As soon as she finished feeding Jolene, she'd attack his room before he returned with her things.

Once the baby was fed, rediapered, and put down for another snooze, Mollie went down the hallway and opened the door to Deke's bedroom. The drapes were still drawn and the air was stale.

She walked over to the windows, pulled the drapes and opened the windows wide, then turned to survey the room. It looked like the site of a natural disaster. She shook her head and gathered dirty clothes, pulled rumpled sheets from the bed, then carried the bundle she'd gathered to the laundry room.

Another trip had her gathering dirty dishes and empty bottles. She started her actual cleaning in the bathroom, surprised at how modern it looked. Deke must have had it remodeled in the past few years. Mirrors lined the walls, an oversize tub with water jets was below a large frosted glass window. A separate glass shower stall was in another corner.

The white and hunter green tiles matched the green towels and throw rugs.

As soon as she finished the bathroom, she made sure Jolene was all right and then started on the bedroom. By the time she had vacuumed, dusted, put clean sheets on the bed and found a summer bedspread to replace the heavier one that needed to be dry cleaned, the room was filled with light and fresh air.

While cleaning the bedroom she'd found a shattered glass-framed picture of Patsy lying almost under the bed. After making sure she'd gotten all the pieces of glass that had fallen into the rug, Mollie carefully removed the photograph from the frame. It had been sliced by the broken glass but she knew Deke would want the picture when he was over the worst of his grief. She would see about having it mended and reframed and would give it to him later.

She stared down at the laughing woman in the picture, wishing she'd known her better. Of course there was a large gap in their ages—Megan had said Patsy was thirty-two. She looked like she would have been fun. Her brown eyes sparkled and her smile was mischievous, as though she'd been teasing the person who had snapped the photo.

Mollie felt the sadness of what such a loss would mean to Deke and Jolene. Sometimes it was extremely hard to understand why these things had to happen.

She hoped that her presence would help him to continue to deal with his new situation. She wanted to do whatever she could, not only for Deke, but for his baby daughter as well, who was too young to understand what had happened, what it meant not to have a mother.

Mollie knew only too well what that was like.

Deke had no sooner stopped his truck in front of the O'Brien homestead than Travis Kane appeared in the doorway of his horse barn and started toward him in long strides.

Deke hadn't spoken to Travis in months. Even though they lived in the same county and each owned a ranch, their paths seldom crossed. Travis bred and raised quarter horses while Deke ran cattle and sheep on his place. At one time Travis had also built himself a reputation as one hell of a bull rider and calf roper. According to county gossip, though, Travis now devoted himself full time to the ranch. Deke appreciated his eye for good horseflesh after buying two of his horses.

Deke stepped out of the truck and waited for Travis to reach him.

"Deke. It's good to see you out and about," Travis said, holding out his hand to Deke. "We were all saddened by your loss. I want you to know that." When Deke looked away without saying anything, Travis added, "So, how's that baby girl of yours doing?"

"She's okay," Deke finally muttered gruffly. "That's why I'm here. Mollie's agreed to stay over at my place and look after her until I can hire somebody permanently for the job. She was supposed to have called Megan to get her stuff together for me."

Travis pushed his Stetson to the back of his head and scratched his temple, frowning. "Nobody mentioned anything about any of this to me."

"We just decided, kinda suddenlike."

"Who is we?"

"Me...Mollie."

"Have you spoken to Megan?"

Deke stiffened. "Why?" he growled. "Is she her sister's keeper?"

Travis kept his voice quiet. ''You might say that. She was made her legal guardian a few years back.''

Deke leaned against the truck, crossing his arms across his chest. ''The way I understand it, you don't need a legal guardian when you're twenty years old.''

''Are you sure having Mollie over at your place is a good idea, Deke?''

''Hell, no. I'm not sure of anything anymore,'' he said, looking off toward the hills.

Travis studied the older man for a longer moment before he companionably touched his shoulder. ''C'mon into the house. We'll have some coffee and talk to Megan.''

Deke shook his head, wondering how the hell he'd gotten into this situation. He was at least five years older than Travis, more than that older than Megan and yet here he was docilely allowing the younger man to lead him into the house where he was no doubt going to be vigorously interviewed by Megan Kane before he could be considered as a possible temporary employer for Mollie. What's wrong with this picture? he asked himself.

All he wanted to do at the moment was to find himself a full bottle of bourbon and return to his darkened room. He wasn't ready for any of this. He should turn around right now and get the hell out of there.

Instead he followed Travis up the steps, across the wide porch and into the kitchen of his home.

''Hi, Deke,'' Megan said, sitting at the table and spooning food into the mouth of a baby sitting in a high chair. ''Mollie said you were on your way over.

Unfortunately I had to stop and feed Danny-boy here before I had a chance to do much.''

"We came in for some coffee, anyway," Travis said, filling two cups with steaming black liquid. He placed them on the table and motioned for Deke to sit down. Deke chose the chair farthest from the baby, keeping his eyes averted.

As soon as he took a sip, he glanced at Megan and said, "So this is why Mollie makes such good coffee," he said with a solemn nod of approval.

"She taught me, I'm afraid," Megan replied. "Mollie's the domestic one in this family."

Travis dropped an arm around his wife's shoulders and leaned over to give her a brief kiss. "You're doing just fine, honey. Just fine."

Deke watched the interplay between the two and felt his stomach clench. This was the way couples acted when they loved each other. Had he and Patsy ever acted that way? Maybe at first, when he'd been foolish enough to believe that she'd actually loved him, and that she'd married him out of love. But he'd found out quick enough she was real good at lying. Much too good.

Travis sat down beside Megan and smiled at his son. "Looks like you're wearing as much as your eating, boy," he said.

The baby slapped his hand on the high-chair tray and gurgled, showing a flash of white.

"Boy, that tooth is really showing up, isn't it?" Travis muttered, leaning closer.

"Plus two more coming in at the top. He's miserable. Can you blame him?"

Deke closed his eyes, wishing he could close his ears, as well. He didn't want to hear about babies and teething and pain. He didn't want any part of the whole scene.

"Are you okay?" Megan asked, her voice sounding concerned. Deke opened his eyes.

"Yeah. I'm wrestling with the granddaddy of all headaches at the moment, but I'll live through it."

Travis got up and walked over to the cabinet, found some pain medication and set it down in front of Deke along with a glass of water. "That should help."

He shook out a couple of tablets and swallowed them before murmuring his thanks.

"I'm a little concerned about this idea of Mollie's to help you out," Megan said, "but once you get to know Mollie, you'll discover that she has a mind of her own. She's quiet, but as stubborn as a mule."

"I don't really understand why she's offered to help me. Like you say, I don't know Mollie. Not really. I guess I know most of the kids in the county, either them or their folks, but I don't remember much about her."

Megan finished cleaning Danny's hands, hair, neck and face before she gave him a teething ring and returned her attention to Deke, saying, "Now that I've given her idea more thought, I realize that I shouldn't be surprised that she would offer to do something like this. Mollie is a natural-born homemaker. There's nothing she'd rather do than to putter around the kitchen trying new recipes, baking, sewing, that sort of thing...and she's been wonderful with Danny the little she's been home since he was born."

"But she's too young to be living there with me," Deke said pointedly. "It doesn't look right."

"I agree," Travis promptly added.

After another sip of coffee, Deke said, "The thing is, I've put myself into a bind of sorts. Having the neighbor ladies in and out of the house all the time was about driving me crazy. I finally exploded at 'em this morning, told 'em to get out, which of course they did. I'm really ashamed of myself, but you can't believe how peaceful and quiet it is around there now that they're gone. I'm just not used to all the ruckus. But I hadn't hired anybody to look after the baby. It was a dumb thing to do. I'm the first to admit it. That's when I remembered that Mollie came out a while back and offered to help me out. So I decided to take her up on her offer. The truth is, I don't know what I'm going to do without her."

"We could look after Jolene here, if you'd like," Megan said.

"No. Thank you, but she's my responsibility. I can't just farm her out like some unwanted puppy. Besides, you've got your hands full already." He looked over at Travis. "I want you to know that Mollie will be perfectly safe staying with me."

"If I didn't already know that, she wouldn't be over there right now," Megan said quietly. "This has nothing to do with you, personally, Deke, and you know it. But she does have her reputation to consider. She's really unaware of what talk can do, how much it can hurt."

Megan left the table and picked up the coffeepot, refilling their cups. "I'll go finish packing her things.

It won't take much longer. That's another thing about Mollie. She's very organized and neat. You'll find it easy to get used to having her around.''

Once she left the kitchen Deke muttered, ''That's what's worrying me. She's a damn attractive woman. That's the last thing I need in my life at the moment.''

''Thanks for being honest about it,'' Travis said with a half smile.

Deke got up abruptly and turned away. He walked over to the screen door and stared outside. ''I've always lived by a strong code of honor, Travis, no matter what. Mollie will be as safe at my place as she's been here with you and Megan. I wish I could prevent any comments about the situation, but people being who and what they are, I know there's bound to be talk about us staying out at the ranch together. All I can say is, I'll do my best to find someone to come in and take over as soon as I can.''

''If there's anything Megan or I can do for you, let me know,'' Travis said from behind him. ''I'll go see if Megan's finished packing.''

When Deke finally looked around, he was alone in the kitchen, except for the teething infant watching him steadily from across the room. His chest tightened. What was it about babies that got to a person so? Their wide-eyed gazes seemed to look straight through him, seeing the hollowness inside.

He didn't have anything to give. There was nothing left. And yet he was supposed to learn how to care for a child, how to nurture one. He shook his head. He was way over his head.

Patsy had been the one who'd suddenly decided

that she wanted a child. Not him. Never him. He'd been adamant about starting a family. They'd talked about the idea of a family as soon as they'd discussed the possibility of marriage. He'd made his views quite clear. She'd agreed at the time, but later changed her mind without bothering to let him know. She'd been amused at his shock when she'd told him she was pregnant. As though she'd managed to pull off a wonderful practical joke. She'd ignored his anger and blithely made plans for the new arrival, laughing at him when he'd attempted to discuss how betrayed he felt about her decision to get pregnant without telling him of her intentions.

There were times when her laughter still rang in his ears, as though she were still amused at his predicament. He'd continued to drink to drown out the sounds, but nothing had worked.

Hiring Mollie was probably another mistake, but it certainly wouldn't be the first one he'd made. Marrying Patsy had been his biggest one. He'd paid for that one over and over.

From the looks of things, he'd be paying for the rest of his life.

Chapter Four

Mollie heard the truck coming up the lane and was waiting at the end of the walkway when Deke pulled in and parked. He wore mirrored aviator shades that concealed his gaze, but there was no ignoring the grim expression around his mouth and jaw.

Knowing her sister and brother-in-law, she had a hunch she knew why.

She watched him get out of the truck, then reach behind the seat and pull out the suitcase she used for college. Mollie drew in a deep breath and approached him. "Thank you for getting my things for me."

"You aren't going to be here long enough to use that much," he replied, stepping around her and continuing up the path.

"It's the only suitcase I have," she explained, following him into the house. "I doubt Megan packed for more than a few days."

He paused halfway down the hall and pushed open

a door. The room was obviously a guest room that
looked unused. He nodded toward another door. "The
bathroom's through there. It opens into the other bedroom where the baby is. You'll be able to hear her
from in here."

"Thank you."

He glanced around. "No need to thank me. I
haven't done anything." He spun on his heel and disappeared from view but it didn't take long before she
heard from him. "What the he—? What were you
doing in here in my room?" he bellowed.

She followed the sound of his voice and found him
standing in the middle of his now-clean bedroom.
"Earning my living," she replied in a mild tone of
voice.

She could see that he wanted to say more, much
more, but was equally determined not to, for which
she commended his restraint. She'd done nothing
more than she'd said she would do.

"I have a roast in the oven. We'll be eating in
another hour," she announced before turning away
and leaving him standing there.

Deke knew he was in trouble and it didn't have
anything to do with the fact that he now had a clean
room, with fresh sheets on the bed and no doubt
newly washed towels in his bathroom.

He wasn't ready to deal with all these changes. He
couldn't handle it. Unfortunately he was being forced
to.

He spun on his heel and strode down the hallway
and out the door, ignoring the woman who now held
his daughter in her arms. He had to get out of here.

He got back into his truck and took one of the ranch roads up into the hills where he could be guaranteed some solitude. He had to get away. He wasn't certain he could survive the next few weeks, much less the coming months and years.

Deke followed the road, which was little more than a rutted track up into the hills, following along a ledge that gave way to more hills dropping away in the distance.

At the top of one of the ridges he stopped and got out of the truck. He walked over to a large outcropping of stone and sat down. Now that he was here he wondered why he'd spent so much time hidden away in his room. This was where he belonged. Here was a place where he could breathe, where he could see for miles, where he could remember the past without being stifled by the pain.

His grandfather had worked for many long years to put this place together, taking any profits he made and investing in more land. His only son, Deke's father, had never shown an interest in the place. He'd gone into the service and never returned home.

Deke would never forget the first time he saw this land and the man who turned out to be his grandfather. He'd been little more than seven years old when his mother had taken him by bus from Greensboro, Mississippi, to Agua Verde, Texas. They had gotten off the bus in the small town and somehow she'd managed to find somebody to drive them out to the ranch.

The man he was today could better understand what had happened back then, but at the time the little boy had been confused and bewildered. All his mother had told him was that he was going to see his grandfather. Of course he'd been excited at first... eager, even, to meet a new relative. He'd never known his father. He'd only seen some blurry snapshots of him, taken before Deke was born.

He would never forget standing there in the driveway, holding his mother's hand, and watching the lean old man walk slowly toward them.

"Hello," his mother had said. "My name is Lena. You probably never heard of me but I've heard lots about you and this place." She looked around at the cluster of buildings surrounding the ranch yard. She tugged on Deke's hand, pulling him forward. "This is your grandson, Mr. Crandall. I named him Deke. Me and Roy got married just before he shipped out, even though he wasn't any too happy about it, but I wanted my baby to be legal and all and he is. I brought all the papers to show you. The military sent me an allotment for a while, then it stopped. I never heard from Roy again. Have you?"

His grandfather had looked at her for a long time without speaking, then he'd knelt in front of Deke so that they were eye level. He'd held out his hand to him, just as if he was another adult, and had said in a gruff voice, "I'm very pleased to meet you, son. You have no idea how glad. Nobody ever told me about you, I'm sorry to say."

He'd looked up at Deke's mother and said, "Young lady, you're welcome to stay here as long as you want, but if you ever decide to leave, just know that the boy stays here. This place is his heritage."

His mother had started crying then—big, heart-breaking sobs that had confused Deke even more. His grandfather had straightened and she had hugged him for the longest time, tears still pouring down her face.

"What's wrong, Mama? What did he say? Can't we stay, Mama?"

"Of course you can stay, son. Your mama's just tired, I expect. No doubt she's been struggling with a heavy load on her own for quite a spell." His grandfather had nodded toward the house. "Come on in and I'll show you where you'll be staying."

Deke had been preparing to go away to college before his grandfather ever explained to him the reasons behind what he'd witnessed that day. His mother had been told that she had inoperable cancer and she had done the only thing she knew to protect her little boy. Because of Roy's view of the place and his father, she hadn't been certain of her welcome, but she'd come anyway, determined to do whatever she could to provide for him.

All Deke had known growing up was that his mother had never seemed to have much energy and that as time went by she got thinner and thinner. His grandfather had taken her to several doctors but there hadn't been much of anything they could do for her. She'd managed to live until a few days past Deke's eleventh birthday.

He wouldn't have made it without his grandfather. Without his grandfather he wouldn't have this place, either. Deke had been in his senior year at Texas A & M when he got the call that his grandfather's heart had finally worn out. He'd gone to sleep one night and had never awakened.

Deke had graduated from college, getting the degree his grandfather had wanted for him, then he'd returned home to the ranch that was his legacy from the old man. He'd lived there alone in that old house for several years before he had met Patsy. She'd been everything he wasn't—warm and vivacious, filled with life and a love of excitement. Why hadn't it occurred to him at the time that the ranch offered very little in the way of excitement?

They'd been married almost a year before she told him the truth about her past, who she was, why she'd been willing to bury herself on a ranch. By then she'd given up pretending that he'd been anything more than a safe haven to run to. That's when he knew that there was something really wrong with him, something that people couldn't love. Of course his dad hadn't tried, and his mama had died. His granddad had done his best, but Deke knew, he just knew, that there must be something lacking in him that people sensed.

He'd left Patsy alone after that, pretty much. At least she'd finally decided not to lie to him anymore. She'd leave for a few months at a time, then return home, saying she missed him, saying she was ready to settle down for good. After a while she even insisted that she loved him. But he knew better by then.

After she told him she was pregnant, she kept saying that a baby was just what they needed to make their marriage work.

He knew better.

He didn't know anything about being a father. He'd never had one, even though his grandfather had meant everything in the world to him. In the most secret part of his heart, he'd lived with the fear that he was too much like his father. He couldn't handle the thought of bringing a child into the world, of being responsible for another person.

None of that mattered to Patsy, of course. The baby was already on the way.

She'd been so blasted determined to do things her way. As though having a child would make their relationship work better, would keep her from being so lonely away from the city lights and entertainment, would solve all their problems.

And now Patsy was gone. His grief had arisen out of guilt that he hadn't loved her enough, that he hadn't been capable of being the husband she wanted and needed. He'd let her down. He'd let himself down.

Now he was left with a baby girl to raise on his own.

He'd never been so frightened in all his life.

Mollie O'Brien was right, though. He couldn't stay locked away in his room forever. He was too much of a coward to take his life and too afraid to live it. Living it meant making more mistakes, this time with an innocent child who would suffer from his poor judgment.

What was it they said about the sins of the fathers? Well, here was another generation of Crandalls, still suffering the sins of their fathers, and there wasn't a thing he could do about it.

The sun was setting by the time he turned his truck around and headed back to the ranch. Thank God he had a foreman who knew how to take care of the place. Otherwise he'd be in worse shape than he was. His grandfather had been an astute businessman and had made some wise investments over the years. Deke had never had to worry about the ranch paying for itself, even though it did.

Ranching would never make a person rich, but it was in his blood, just as it had been in his grandfather's. His grandfather had done everything he could for Deke. Somehow, Deke would have to do the same for his tiny daughter.

The problem was that at the moment he just didn't have any idea how.

Mollie was in the kitchen baking something when he stepped into the house. She glanced around and smiled at him. "You must be starved. Let me warm up your dinner" was all she said about the fact that he'd disappeared several hours before.

The funny thing was, he was hungry for the first time since he could remember. "I'll go get washed up" was all he replied before going through the doorway into the hall and on to his room.

The room still reflected its newly cleaned image. He had to admit to himself that he kind of liked it now that he was getting used to it. There was an un-opened bottle of bourbon in his office. He might open it later to help him sleep, but in the meantime, he'd clean up a little and try some of Mollie's cooking. If it was as good as her coffee and biscuits, he'd really lucked out. She was going to make some lucky fellow a hell of a wife someday.

Deke couldn't sleep. He'd tossed and turned for hours, fighting the restless dreams that kept sweeping over him. After the last one he threw back the covers with a groan and sat up.

Times like this he wished he'd started smoking, but his grandfather had been so adamant about his not starting the habit that he'd never been tempted before now. He was fairly certain it was too late for him to find any real satisfaction from cigarettes.

Even though his mother's cancer had not been in her lungs, his grandfather had convinced him as a young boy that if cigarettes could cause that kind of suffering as well, he would leave them alone.

He'd started drinking after Patsy died, when he couldn't sleep, thinking it was better than taking prescription drugs, but now he wasn't so sure. He couldn't seem to sleep without it.

Without turning on a light he pulled on his jeans and stepped into the hallway to go to his office. He paused when he saw light coming from the baby's room. Taking a couple of silent steps, he stopped in front of the half-open door and peered inside.

Mollie was lifting the baby from her crib and giving her a bottle. He hadn't heard the baby. He was too far away with the door closed between them, but Mollie had obviously heard her stirring. He watched unseen as the woman he barely knew held his baby in her arms.

Only then did he realize that she wasn't wearing

much of anything. She hadn't bothered to grab a robe. Instead she wore a sheer cotton nightshirt that stopped at midthigh in front and back, but came up higher on either side, barely covering her hips. It was sleeveless with a scooped neck. Her breasts were youthful—firm and full, their darker tips apparent through the thin material.

She sat down in the rocker, her movement calling his attention to her long, shapely legs. Only then did he realize that he was standing there like some sleazy voyeur ogling the woman he'd hired to take care of his infant daughter.

Taking care that she didn't see or hear him, he retreated to his room, thankful he was barefoot. Once closed, he leaned against the door. Damn. His heart was racing as though he'd been in a footrace, and he was more than a little aroused.

What in hell was he thinking of, standing there spying on her that way? Didn't he have an ounce of decency left in his body? Hadn't he just reassured her relatives that she was perfectly safe staying there with him?

Well, now he knew better. So he'd just have to do something about the situation immediately. Tomorrow he'd place an ad in all the newspapers within a hundred miles. He had to get permanent help as soon as possible.

Forgetting his original destination, Deke threw himself back on the bed and burrowed his head into the pillow. It was unfortunate that his dreams for the rest of the night gave him glimpses of long legs, full breasts and the shining sparks of red in a mass of tumbling dark hair.

Despite having to get up with the baby during the night, Mollie felt wonderfully rested when she awoke. Granted, it was the sounds of the baby that had pulled her out of a dreamless sleep, but she willingly went into the adjoining room and took care of her new charge.

Once again Jolene was wide-eyed and watching her every move.

"I'll never admit it to Megan, sugar," she said in a cooing voice, "but you are just about the prettiest baby I've ever seen, bar none. Of course, Danny doesn't need to be pretty 'cause he's a boy, but just to be on the safe side, let's keep my secret between the two of us, okay?"

Jolene waved one of her arms and gave an energetic double kick with her feet.

"Oh, aren't you smart! Just look at you go. I can't get over how alert you are and how wise you look, just like you're understanding every word I'm saying."

Jolene made a little squeak and after much effort, a tiny coo.

"I was right. You're having a little trouble letting me know, but you understand everything, don't you?"

As soon as she fed the baby, Mollie took her into the kitchen and placed her in the bassinet out of the traffic area in the room. She put on coffee and began to make biscuits as well as fry up several strips of bacon. She would wait until Deke came into the kitchen before she prepared his eggs.

Mollie had no reason to suppose he'd come in, for that matter. Just because he'd stayed out of his room once he returned with her things the day before didn't mean that he didn't intend to continue to hibernate in there now that she was there to care for Jolene.

Everybody had their own way of dealing with pain. It didn't just go away because a person wished it to do so. She certainly wasn't going to judge the method he used, even though his bourbon consumption, if the empty bottles were any indication, concerned her. She'd heard about people trying to drown their sorrows but this was the first time she'd ever witnessed it.

Oh, well. That wasn't part of her concern. After dinner last night they had sat down and discussed her salary as well as her duties. Deke had been polite but distant.

Not that she blamed him. After all, he didn't know her. He'd probably be shocked if he ever learned that she used to have a tremendous crush on him. She'd be mortified if he or anyone else should ever find out, but there was little chance of that. She'd never shared that particular secret with anyone, not even her sisters.

Who would have believed back then that one day she would actually be living in the same house with him, taking care of his beautiful and bright daughter? It was strange the way things worked out sometimes.

She was taking the biscuits out of the oven when she heard a sound behind her. Since the baby was in the other direction, she knew it wasn't Jolene. Mollie straightened and looked around. Deke stood at the counter pouring himself some coffee.

He looked fresh from the shower, his hair still damp, newly shaved, wearing clean jeans, a chambray shirt and well-worn boots.

"Good morning," she said to his back. "You're about the quietest person I've ever been around. I never heard you come in." She removed the biscuits from the oven and placed them on top of the stove. "How would you like your eggs this morning?"

He gave her a brief glance then looked away. His gaze also avoided the area where Jolene lay sleeping. He sat down at the table and took a careful sip before replying, "Same as yesterday, I guess."

So he wasn't much of a morning person. Lots of people weren't. She felt blessed that she could hop out of bed and within minutes be wide-awake and ready to face her day. She remembered how Megan used to grumble at her cheerfulness. Oh, Megan was always up early, she had to be to take care of the chores, but she was a bear until she'd had at least two cups of coffee.

So Mollie, based on past experience, wisely chose not to make conversation with her new employer. Instead she carefully broke three eggs into the skillet and finished preparing his breakfast.

Once she'd set his plate in front of him, she made another one for herself. Then she sat down across from him and diligently ate, unobtrusively checking on the baby from time to time.

When he finished, Deke picked up his plate and took it to the sink where he rinsed it and placed it in the dishwasher. He refilled his cup and sat down again before he spoke.

"Mollie?"

She'd gotten so used to the silence that her heart leaped in surprise. "Yes?" she asked, taking a quick sip of coffee to wash down the bite of toast she'd almost swallowed wrong.

"I want you to know that I appreciate your immediate response to my call yesterday," he began in his soft-spoken drawl. "The thing is, I've had some time to think about it. I guess I really blew it yesterday with those ladies and I want you to know that I'm grateful that you came to my rescue." He paused and sipped his coffee while she warily watched him. "But after sleeping on it, I realize that Megan and Travis are right. This isn't going to work, you being here with me like this."

She waited and when he didn't say anything more, she said, "I don't understand. I thought we discussed this last night and you were agreeable to my staying until you could find somebody permanent. What did I do? If I've offended you in some way, just tell me. I can follow any routine you prefer. I can stay out of your way, I can—"

"No, it's not any of that." Mollie wasn't sure that she wasn't imagining it, but she could almost believe that Deke was blushing. She stayed silent and he began to haltingly say, "You and I know that you're much too young for me, but the fact remains that you're a very attractive woman and I— Well, I just can't—" He shook his head. This time there was no doubt that his cheeks were ruddier and that he was very uncomfortable.

What was he saying here? That he found her attractive? Mollie fought not to give away her reaction to his words.

"Anyway," he went on after clearing his throat, "I realized last night that I've put us both in a rather uncomfortable situation. I'm really sorry about that." Once again he cleared his throat. "Until I can find someone to stay permanently, I'm going to be spending my nights out in the cabin with the single men." She could see that it was an effort for him to meet her gaze. "I'm really sorry for getting you involved in all this."

Her gaze remained steady. "I'm not. I'm happy that I can help. I'm just sorry you're uncomfortable about my being here."

"It's nothing you've done, Mollie, believe me."

"It's okay. I understand." She got up from the table and began to gather the dishes. "I hope you find somebody that will be good to Jolene."

He nodded abruptly. "So do I." He pushed away from the table, grabbed his hat and headed toward the door. "Thanks for understanding," he said before almost racing to his truck.

Molly watched him, shaking her head. Men were really funny creatures. Yesterday he was begging her to come help. Today he could hardly wait to get rid of her.

Guess she'd never understand them.

Chapter Five

A week before Christmas vacation was due to begin, Mollie pushed open the door to her dorm room and dispiritedly crossed to her desk, tossing her books on the paper-covered surface. With a sigh she slumped down onto the side of the bed and stared at the papers scattered across the desk's surface.

"I hate this," she muttered to herself. "I really hate it."

Her fall class schedule included several business classes—statistics, finance, economics—all of which she was failing or near failing. Why? Because she had little or no interest in business.

So why was she taking the courses?

That was the question of the century. Why had she allowed Megan to talk her into majoring in a subject for which she had no aptitude nor interest?

Partly it was because Megan had always taken the lead in their relationship. The six-year edge made an enormous difference while they were growing up, not to the mention the fact that it had been Megan's strong determination to fight for the family unit that had kept them together.

So she had felt that she owed Megan something... that she owed it to Megan to go on to college, since Megan hadn't gone. Now that Megan and Travis could afford to pay for college, neither one of them had asked Mollie if she wanted to go, or what subjects she might want to take. Instead it was a foregone conclusion that Mollie and Maribeth would have the opportunity that Megan never had.

So here she was, Mollie thought with disgust, in her third year of school, hating every minute of it. The next biggest question was, what did she intend to do about it? There were options, of course. She could change her major, or she could drop out of school entirely. Since Megan wouldn't be any too happy with that particular choice, Mollie knew she would have to come up with something else she could do with herself, instead.

An image immediately formed in her head of those few short weeks last summer when she'd taken care of Jolene and attempted to provide Deke a place where he could begin the healing process.

She leaned back on her pillow, remembering those days with a smile. Despite all his intentions, Deke had discovered that it wasn't all that easy to find a permanent replacement for Mollie, which gave her the opportunity to truly fall in love with Jolene as well as her daddy.

Jolene was so easy to love. Her father much less

so. Jolene was a happy baby most of the time. She just wanted her needs met immediately, that was all. In exchange, Jolene did whatever she could to entertain Mollie—cooing, grabbing on to her hair or nose, chuckling every time Mollie tickled her tummy.

Jolene would be so different now—almost nine months old. Danny had been walking by that age. She wondered if Jolene had decided to explore her world so quickly?

Mollie also wondered about Deke. Had he changed his attitude toward Jolene, shown any more interest in her? She hoped so. While Mollie had been there on the ranch, Deke had ignored them both. Once he'd left the sanctuary of his room, he'd spent all of his waking hours working with his men on the ranch or buried behind his accounts in his office.

His nights were always spent across the ranch yard in the bunkhouse.

He did little more than nod at Mollie whenever he was brought face-to-face with her, and it was obvious that he would have avoided those encounters if possible.

Whenever she tried to talk to him about Jolene he would leave the room. He never looked at his daughter or asked about her.

So how could she possibly love a man like that? she wondered. But she knew. Oh, yes, she understood why…because she saw his pain, no matter how much he tried to hide it. She saw the agony that he was going through every time Jolene wailed, or squealed, or blew bubbles. Jolene represented a loss he couldn't come to terms with, and he couldn't bear to be reminded.

Eventually he'd found a woman from Austin who agreed to move to Agua Verde—a Mrs. Franzke. She was a very pleasant woman and Mollie knew that Jolene no doubt had adapted quickly to yet another face in her life, but it had taken Mollie most of the summer to adjust to not seeing Deke and Jolene on a daily basis. Thank God Danny had been there for her. She'd spent the remainder of the summer helping Megan with Danny in an attempt to get on with her life.

She envied Megan, having a husband and son, being where she wanted to be, doing what she wanted to do. If Mollie had her choice...but exactly what would she choose? At the moment all she could do was to study harder in order not to flunk out of school. Perhaps after the Christmas break she would look into switching majors.

Instead of doing the assignments she'd been given earlier, she curled into her pillow and dozed off, awakening only when someone tapped on her door.

"Mollie?" It was Sharon from across the hall. "You in there?"

Mollie sat up. "Come on in, Sharon. I must have fallen asleep."

Sharon peeked around the door, grinning. "You've got a caller downstairs."

Mollie was puzzled by Sharon's tone of voice and her expression. "Who?"

"I didn't ask. But whoever he is, I've gotta tell you, he's got every gal in the place finding some reason to wander through the reception area. Talk about a hunk.''

Mollie grabbed her hairbrush. ''Does he have a woman with him? Maybe it's Megan and Travis.''

''Uh-uh. All alone, looking a little harried with all the attention he's getting. He's rolled and unrolled the brim on his Stetson so many times, it'll never be the same.''

Mollie froze, her eyes widening. ''Deke? Could it possibly be—?''

''Only one way to find out, gal. Go check him out.''

It couldn't be Deke. Why would he be here? She hadn't heard anything from him since she'd left the ranch at the end of June. But who else could it be? She wasn't dating anyone these days.

When she walked into the reception area she saw him with his back to the room, staring out the window. There was no mistaking those broad shoulders or the lean, muscled back and buttocks. Her heart was working overtime in an effort to get blood to her head. Even so, she felt light-headed at the sight of him.

''Deke?''

He spun around at the sound of her voice. He hadn't removed his sheepskin-lined denim jacket, although it hung open, revealing the plaid flannel shirt beneath. He clutched his hat in one hand while his other hand was fisted. He jammed it into his coat pocket as he strode toward her.

''Is there somewhere private where we could talk?'' he asked, without bothering with a polite greeting. Yep, it was Deke, all right. He looked around the busy area with an expression bordering on desperation, reminding Mollie of his behavior last summer around the group of women who had taken care of Jolene. "If you have time," he added as an obvious afterthought to the social niceties of polite behavior.

Mollie carefully hid the smile that was hovering around her mouth. "I've got time," she replied, astounded at how thrilled she was to see him again. Here she had thought she'd managed to get over her feelings for the man, darn it. Now all she could do was try not to embarrass herself with her eagerness. "Why don't we go for coffee? There's a place not too far from here where we won't be disturbed."

"You'll need your coat" was all he said. Definitely a man of few words, but she managed to detect a slight relaxation in the taut lines around his mouth.

She nodded. "I'll be right back." She waited until she was out of his line of sight before racing to the stairs, taking them two at a time, and running down the hallway to her room. She wasn't in the least surprised to see Sharon stick her head out of her room.

"Well?"

"He's a friend from home." She tossed out the answer as she grabbed her jacket.

"Yummy. Wish I had friends like that. Are you going to introduce him around?"

"He's shy."

Sharon laughed knowingly. "Oh, I'll just bet he is!" Her last words followed Mollie as she dashed back to the stairs.

Mollie had given the first excuse she could think of, but as she returned to Deke she realized that it was the truth, at least where women were concerned. Why else would he have felt so ill at ease with the women who'd come to tend to Jolene? If she hadn't been so persistent the day she'd gone out to see him, he would have avoided her, as well. In the end, she had been the means to save him from the other women.

As she approached him for the second time today, she realized that once again her presence would rescue him from another gathering of interested females, several of whom were attempting to draw him out in conversation. They were having little success, however, and Mollie knew it was time for her to get him out of there.

She moved to his side and looped her arm through his. "Ready?" she asked brightly, just as though she was used to taking such liberties with him, when the truth was she had never been this close to him before.

He glanced down at her, his expression a mixture of relief and surprise, no doubt startled by her unaccustomed familiarity with him. With a curt nod, he jammed his poor hat back on his head and headed toward the door in his long-legged stride. Once there, he shoved the door open and waited for her to walk through. Mollie slipped her hands into the pockets of her coat before she was tempted to touch him again.

He looked so good to her after all this time. He had regained some of his weight, so that he didn't look quite so gaunt, although there were new lines on his face. His hair was still overlong, as though he couldn't be bothered to have it trimmed.

Mollie led the way to the student hangout off campus waiting for him to speak. After a prolonged silence she mentally shrugged and asked, "How's Jolene?"

"She's okay," he replied gruffly. "Not sick or anything."

"I bet she's really grown. I've thought about her over the months, wondering what she looks like now."

Once again she waited, but he showed no signs of grabbing his wallet and revealing an abundance of baby pictures for her to admire.

She gave a tiny shrug of acceptance, then asked, "And Mrs. Franzke?"

He let out a deep sigh of frustration. "Oh, *she's* all right. It's just…" He seemed to run out of words and breath at the same time. He adjusted his hat, pulling the brim down even lower over his eyes. Uh, oh. Something was definitely wrong, but then she'd known that. Why else would he have turned up here on the UT campus looking for her?

"What is it, Deke? Why are you here? What's wrong?"

He just shook his head, more in weariness than in denial and said nothing more until they reached the café. The place was cavernous, but there weren't many people inside at the moment. After all, it was Friday afternoon, with only a few days before the Christmas holidays and most people were either studying, shopping, or getting ready for a date. Since

Molly had already made all her gifts and had only one more test before school was out, she had not lied when she told Deke she had time for him.

They found a booth in the back and waited for their coffee to be delivered without speaking. Mollie knew that Deke would answer her questions, but in his own time. There was no pushing the man, that much she'd learned.

So she waited.

"Mrs. Franzke's sister had a stroke a few days ago," he finally said, not looking at her. "She's doing better, but once she's released from the hospital she's not going to be able to look after herself any longer. Mrs. Franzke feels that she has no choice but to move in and help."

"Ah," Mollie said, immediately understanding why Deke had shown up on her doorstep. At the least the guy was predictable! "So you need me to take care of Jolene until you can find someone else," she concluded for him. "Well, that shouldn't be a problem. I'll be coming home next Wednesday for a couple of weeks, which should give you time to—"

"Mollie, I need your help." His voice sounded desperate and strangled, as though he was trying to remember lines he'd been rehearsing but hated having to give.

Hadn't he just heard what she'd said? Without conscious thought, she reached across the scarred table and touched the back of his hand with her fingertips. "It's okay, Deke," she said in a soothing voice. "I can help you out. It won't be a problem for me."

He studied her hand as though he'd never seen one

before and she glanced down, seeing how her neatly shaped nails and pale skin contrasted with his scarred knuckles and callused fingers. He slipped his hand from beneath hers as though he'd been made uncomfortable by her touch.

After gripping his hands in a tight clasp in front of him, Deke shifted on the bench seat of the booth and met her inquiring gaze with narrowed eyes. "Before you so freely volunteer, maybe you should hear what I'm going to ask of you."

Mollie folded her hands in her lap. She'd been trying to ease his tension, but it hadn't worked. So she smiled at him when she would have preferred to kick him in the shins. Why did he have to make the most simple conversation such a strain?

He looked away from her, then reached for his coffee. After taking a gulp of the hot liquid he said, "Ever since we got the call about Mrs. Franzke's sister, I've known that I was going to have to do something about my situation. I was damn lucky to be able to find someone like Mrs. Franzke and I know it. Nobody's interested in living out so far in the boonies these days. Not people qualified to care for children, anyway. There are too many jobs in cities where they can enjoy their time off doing stuff besides staring out at the rolling hills and listening to the howls of coyotes."

Mollie grinned. She couldn't help it. He sounded so disgusted. "I never minded," she stated softly.

His gaze met hers for a moment, then danced away. "Yeah, I know. I guess that's because you were raised on a ranch, grew up in that kind of place, know what to expect.''

''There's another reason, Deke, besides my background. I happen to love your little daughter. She's easy to love, you know.''

A muscle flexed in his jaw but he didn't say anything. Instead he straightened in the booth, pressing his shoulders against the back. After a weighty silence, Deke rubbed his forehead as though he might be dealing with a headache. She could tell this interview, if she could call it that, was tough for him, but she didn't know what she could say or do to make it any easier.

His voice was gruff when he spoke again. ''I can't have a young woman like you working for me. We've already covered that territory last summer.''

Now she really was confused. If he wasn't here to offer her a job, even on a temporary basis, then what did he want? Mollie felt unnerved without understanding why. What could Deke want from her?

''I want to make you an offer, Mollie,'' he said through his clenched jaw. ''I've been thinking about this for a while. You'll probably think I'm crazy, and maybe I am. I don't know much about anything anymore. Nothing in my life has gone as I thought it would, so now I'm grasping at straws. Don't think I don't know that.''

She was even more unnerved by his grim expression. ''All right,'' she managed to say.

''I'm asking you to marry me, Mollie,'' he began and continued to speak in that deep voice of his, but Mollie heard no more after those first few words.

Deke was asking her to marry him? Deke? Asking her? For a moment she was convinced the room had started to sway before she realized that his words had put her into shock. She stared at him, only then realizing that he was still talking and she hadn't heard another thing he'd said.

"I'm sorry," she managed to blurt out. "I'm sorry, but I wasn't keeping up with what you were saying. Did I hear you correctly? Did you just ask me to marry you?"

Now it was Deke's turn to look taken aback. He frowned, as though his carefully rehearsed words had suddenly deserted him.

"Yeah," he drawled, grabbing his cup and draining it before adding, "that's what I'm trying to say here."

"I don't understand," she finally mumbled. "I mean, we really don't know each other very well. You've never given me any reason to think that you—" She swallowed, unable to find the words to describe the usual sentiments that went along with a marriage proposal.

"I know I'm doing this all wrong, but I've never proposed to anybody before, besides the fact that this isn't really a—"

"What do you mean, you've never proposed before? You were married to—"

"Yeah, I know. But I wasn't the one who suggested getting married. She did. She convinced me that nothing would make her happier, so I kinda went along with it."

He was definitely blushing, which eased her discomfort a little.

"Is this your way of protecting my reputation so I can take care of Jolene?"

"So what if it is? People get married for all kinds of reasons, not just because they think they're in love with each other." He shoved his hand through his hair. "You don't need to tell me how unfair I'm being to you. You're too young for me. I know that. You've got your whole life ahead of you. You're a beautiful woman, intelligent— It was a stupid idea, I see that now." He looked around as though wanting to leave. "Why don't we just forget all about it, forget I said anything. Put it down to not enough sleep and working too hard." He looked back at her. "You ready to go? I need to head back to the ranch. There's no reason for me to—"

"Deke?"

He eyed her warily. "Yeah?"

"Can we talk about this offer of yours for a minute or two before you withdraw it, please?"

"What do you mean, withdraw it?"

"Well, you haven't given me a chance to even think about it before you've decided it's a bad idea."

"I shouldn't have said anything."

"I'm glad you did, Deke," she said, deliberately reaching out and taking his hand, clasping it firmly in hers. "I'm glad you trust me enough, have faith in my abilities enough to want me to be a full-time mother to Jolene."

She could feel the tension in his hand but refused to let go. She needed to touch him. Needed to feel his warmth, to know that whether or not he loved her, or wanted her in the way a man wants a woman, that Deke Crandall needed her in his life.

"It wouldn't be like a real marriage or anything," he blurted out, his eyes looking everywhere but at her. He cleared his throat. "What I mean is, if you're seriously considering my offer I want you to know that I don't expect you to pretend to love me or anything like that."

"I see," she said, watching him closely.

"You'd still have your own room, if you wanted it. I…uh…know that sounds like a strange way to go into a marriage, but sometimes maybe it's better to be straight with each other up-front…and not pretend feelings we don't have."

"A marriage of honesty, is that it?"

"Well, yeah, at least we don't have to pretend with each other." He studied her for several moments in silence before adding, "I'm way too old for you, honey, don't think I don't know that. And what I'm suggesting is almost criminal, because I'm stealing your youth."

She smiled. "That's a little dramatic, don't you think? You aren't stealing anything. Whatever I decide, it will be my choice." She released his hand and leaned back in her seat. "I want to be as honest as I can with you, Deke. I can't imagine anything I would rather do than to live at your ranch with you and care for Jolene." She gave a little chuckle. "I'm really not into all this higher learning, I don't mind admitting to you. It's just that I never thought you'd insist that we be married in order for me to live there.''

The waitress came by and refilled their cups. Deke cupped his hands around the hot mug and studied the steaming liquid, allowing the silence to draw out between them once more.

When he looked up at her, his eyes seemed to shoot off sparks of green fire. ''I'm not going to lie to you and tell you that I'm making this offer just because of Jolene, because I'm not. But she is a large part of why I decided to marry again. I'd also planned to wait a while, at least until next summer, before mentioning it to you. This thing with Mrs. Franzke has thrown everything into turmoil.''

Mollie couldn't believe what she was hearing.

''Then why did you decide on me?''

He rubbed his nose, then scratched his jaw. ''I—uh—can't seem to get you out of my mind. I'm not going to pretend that I'm not attracted to you… because I am. For the past six months I've been telling myself that it was just what I was going through last spring that made you seem to be the only bright spot in my life. But it's more than that, Mollie. Even though you were only at the ranch for a few weeks, you left your touch there. Everywhere I look around the place, I see something that reminds me of you, and the time you were living there.''

Mollie couldn't believe her ears. Was it possible that Deke was as attracted to her as she was to him?

When she didn't comment, he went on in a low voice. ''I've been trying to convince myself all this time that you're what Jolene needs.'' He cleared his throat. "But being around you reminds me of some of my needs, as well." In a rush of words, he explained, "That was the trouble I was having last summer. I didn't want to take advantage of the situation, or make you feel that I'd gotten you out there under false pretenses, but I discovered quick enough that you have a very strong effect on me." His gaze flickered back to meet hers. "I want you to know that I would never force myself on you or anything like that." The tips of his ears glowed red. "It would be your choice if, at a later date, you maybe wanted to have a real marriage with me. I promise you right now that I would never mistreat you in any way. I would always show you respect as my wife and the mother of my child regardless of what happens or doesn't happen between us."

A lump formed in her throat, she was so touched by his words. Here was this man, so big and tough, trying to reassure her. She had known that there were depths to the man not easily seen. Otherwise, he would not have been in so much pain.

She didn't want to make too much over the fact that he had decided to ask her of all the women he knew to marry him. From his point of view, it was a sensible choice, since he'd already seen her in his home and caring for his child.

What gave her hope was his telling her that he was attracted to her, despite himself. Hearing him speak of his needs made her tingle. He was determined to be honest about his feelings. She wondered how he would feel if he knew that she was already halfway in love with him? If he knew that, would he be so eager to have her as his wife?

What he was suggesting was more than she ever expected him to offer, but was less than what she wanted from him. Could she make do with what he proposed?

She gazed across the table at him and smiled. Deke Crandall had talked more to her today than during all the time they'd spent together last summer. Now he sat there watching her in silence, as though he had run out of words.

"Deke," she began, feeling her way. "This is much too important a decision for me to make without giving it some thought."

"I know. Talking about it makes it seem really farfetched."

"No," she replied firmly. "It sounds very sensible and practical. I understand your reasons and I appreciate your being candid with me." She folded her arms and leaned on the table. "I know you said that you needed to get back, but I was wondering if you'd let me sleep on your suggestion overnight? If you would stay in town tonight, maybe we could meet for breakfast in the morning."

"You mean you're seriously considering my offer?"

His obvious surprise made her grin. All right, so it wasn't the most romantic proposal she'd ever heard about, but she was far from saying no to the possibility.

Mollie wasn't going to pretend that she wasn't intrigued by his offer. All right. More than intrigued.

Nothing like this had ever happened to her before. It was as if someone had listened to her childhood prayers and dreams and was now offering them back to her.

The problem was, she was no longer a child. Any decision she made would have a profound effect on each of them as well as on Jolene. She had to think all of this through very carefully...unemotionally...rationally, and not be influenced by the look in his eyes or her regrettably strong reaction to him.

"I'm not sure I'll have an answer by tomorrow, but I promise to give the idea considerable thought." She glanced around. "In the meantime, are you interested in ordering something to eat? They make the best hamburgers and fries here you've ever eaten...just dripping with all kinds of fat and cholesterol."

He lifted one of his eyebrows. "Is that supposed to be a recommendation?"

She grinned. "They're the most delicious thing you've ever tasted, I'll guarantee you that much."

He looked around and saw that while they'd been talking the room had gradually filled up. "Now that I think about it, I haven't had anything since breakfast. Sure. Let's go ahead and order."

Mollie hoped that she had convinced him that an unexpected marriage proposal was a common day occurrence to her, one that she could blithely file away to consider at a later date.

At least he was considerably more relaxed now than when she'd first seen him. Why, he'd almost smiled at her enthusiasm for her menu choice. *That's it*, she reminded herself. *Keep it light. At the very least, he's offering you the possibility of a friendship with him. He admires you. He's also attracted to you. There were worse things than that on which to base marriage.*

Don't think about it now. You've bought yourself some time. She forced herself to smile at him while he gave their order to the admiring waitress. If Deke intended to marry in order to provide Jolene with a stable home life, and if she decided not to marry him, Mollie had a hunch there would be plenty of women who would jump at the chance.

Would she—at some later date—be able to live with the knowledge of all she'd given up when it was too late to change her mind?

Did she have the courage to accept what he offered in the hope that someday it would grow into something more?

Chapter Six

Mollie opened her sleep-starved eyes and foggily focused on the digital clock beside her bed. It was just past three o'clock in the morning.

She groaned.

This had to be the longest night she'd ever spent. She kept dozing off and waking up, tossing and turning in an effort to get comfortable. It was useless for her to try to rest. Every time she fell asleep she dreamed the craziest dreams. She wasn't certain if she even wanted to go back to sleep.

By the time she'd left Deke at the front door to her dorm, she'd known how foolish it would be for her to enter into a loveless marriage, regardless of the mitigating circumstances. She wanted a marriage like Megan's. Travis obviously worshiped his wife. Mollie had hoped to be able to have the same kind of marriage someday.

However, Deke was offering her something considerably less.

Would being married to her childhood romantic ideal be enough for her? What if she discovered too late that it wasn't?

After weighing all the reasons, pro and con, her logical, orderly mind told her to forget about his proposal. It would never work and she could quite possibly end up being very unhappy.

So. There it was. She'd made her decision.

Hadn't she?

If so, then why didn't she feel better?

Because every time she closed her eyes she could see Deke's seductive eyes staring at her with reproach…or she would hear a baby crying on and on… and no one was responding.

She punched her pillow. It wasn't her problem. Just because she'd had a crush on the guy most of her life didn't have anything to do with reality. The reality was that he could very easily break her heart if she attempted to get closer to him than the boundaries he'd set between them.

So…now that she'd wisely dealt with the issue, she could go back to sleep.

Sure. Just like that, she could forget that Deke Crandall needed her, that he was giving her a chance to live with him, to get to know him better, to help him learn how to live again, how to love again…if she had the courage to try.

She pulled the pillow over her head and held it against her ears. What a ridiculous idea. How could she teach him anything? What did she know?

She knew how to love. She'd been given years of instruction by example...from her parents and from her sisters. Maybe Deke hadn't had the benefit of similar teachings. What, after all, did she really know about him?

Besides, he'd obviously been deeply in love with his wife, hadn't he? That had to count for something.

Slowly she withdrew her head and sat up on the side of the bed. This was getting her nowhere. Why was she having such an argument with herself? What was this all about? Why couldn't she make up her mind?

It was then she understood what was happening. Her head was arguing with her heart and neither one was willing to back down. She could list all the logical, rational reasons against accepting Deke's offer...or she could admit, at least to herself, that there was nothing in the whole wide world she wanted more than to marry Deke, to be his wife in every way, and to be a part of Jolene's life.

As long as she was being so blasted honest with herself, she also wanted to give him more children. She shivered, thinking about the possibility of sharing his bed, of making love to him.

Once again Mollie stretched out on her bed, pulling the covers up to her chin, and stared at the ceiling. She'd never thought of herself as anything but practical, down-to-earth and rational. This time, none of that was enough. This time, she had to believe in something that wasn't tangible, but was real, nevertheless.

Despite all the evidence pointing to the contrary,

Mollie knew that she would never know any peace unless she found the courage to go with her heart.

Mollie was watching for Deke the next morning from the reception area window. She stepped outside just as he approached the door.

A blustery norther had blown in earlier that morning. She pulled up the hood of her jacket and noted that he'd turned his collar up and his hat brim down.

He looked surprised to see her waiting. "Were you watching for me?" he asked warily. "Or hoping to sneak away before I showed up?" She could see a glint of amusement in his eyes.

"I thought I would save you the trial of being the object of everyone's interest inside." She stuck her hands into her coat jacket.

He slipped his arm through hers. "I didn't know I was that easy to read."

She grinned. "I remembered how you reacted to the women at your house last summer."

He rolled his eyes. "Please don't remind me. I'm only now getting some of them to speak to me again. I was way out of line and had to do some mighty tough apologizing."

"Good for you. A little humility is good for the soul. Builds character."

He nodded toward his truck. "I thought we might take the truck, if that's okay with you."

"Anything to get out of this wind." She walked arm and arm with him to where he'd left the truck and got inside. It was still toasty warm, and as soon as he started the engine, the heater kicked out a gust of hot air across her feet and ankles.

"We may get some snow before the day's out," he said, backing out of the parking space.

"I guess you're eager to get home, aren't you?"

"Yeah. I never like being away for long. Guess I'm a homebody."

"That's something we have in common," she stated quietly. "It was very tough for me to adjust to being here at school."

He was quiet for several blocks before he said, "How much longer do you have to go before you graduate?"

"If I pass all my subjects this semester, another year and a half."

"It makes sense you'd want to see it through," he offered. She could only nod.

Neither one said anything else until after they reached the famous A-shaped building that was known for serving breakfasts around the clock. They gave their orders to the waitress and Mollie immediately sipped her coffee without looking at Deke again. She didn't have to, since her first glance at him this morning seemed to have noted the changes in him from the evening before.

He looked more rested, as though the hardest part for him had been finding a way to put his offer into words. The lines around his mouth weren't as severe, and he'd mentioned that he was hungry.

"You look a little tired this morning," he finally said. "Were you studying late last night?"

She made a face. A gentleman wouldn't have been

so quick to point out her pale face and the circles beneath her eyes. Ah well, so much for looking for a gentleman.

"I've got one more final before the holidays," she replied truthfully enough, even though it had nothing to do with her looking as though she'd stayed awake all night.

"Mmm" was all he said before finishing his first cup of coffee and pouring another one from the carafe left by the waitress. He'd practically inhaled the first cup.

Deke leaned back in his chair and studied her, as though he were meeting her for the first time. Self-conscious, she pushed a lock of hair behind her ear. When she forced herself to meet his gaze, he gave her a lopsided smile.

"You don't have to say anything, you know," he said softly. "I never should have made such a crazy suggestion yesterday. Put it down to worry, overwork, not enough sleep and skipping too many meals."

What relief, was Mollie's first thought. *I don't have to say anything. He understands. Thank God. I don't have to explain or—* "So you're withdrawing your offer," she blurted out, sounding irritated. What in the world was the matter with her?

It didn't help that his smile moved into a slow, definitely sexy, grin. "If I didn't know better, I'd swear you were disappointed," he teased.

"Of course not! It's just that—" She glanced at him, then away. "I just worry about Jolene, that's all."

His smile disappeared. "So do I."

"So you're going to probably look around until you find a woman you really want to marry, right? Not somebody like me who you still see as some kind of schoolgirl who doesn't know her own mind or—"

"Whoa! Whoa! Wait a minute. What's going on here? I was just trying to help us over an awkward moment or two, that's all."

"Oh." She studied her hands, realigned her coffee mug on its paper doily before casually saying, "But you don't really want a wife. You're wanting to provide a stable home for Jolene."

"True enough. It does seem odd, now that we're talking about it, that I'd even consider getting married again. You'd think I would learn, huh? One disaster was enough."

"Disaster?"

He sighed and shook his head. "Patsy never thought I was much of a husband. I guess she was right. I didn't know the first thing about making a woman happy. Still don't. All I know is ranching. Arranging a marriage between us was strictly for your protection. Very selfishly, I wanted you to be willing to stay with Jolene, that's all." He looked away, no longer meeting her gaze. "I apologize for coming up with such a harebrained idea."

"What if I agreed to it?" she asked slowly. "What then?"

He had his coffee cup halfway to his mouth when she spoke and he froze, looking as though he'd been caught in suspended animation. Slowly he moved his gaze from his cup until he was staring at her for a long, silent moment.

Deke very carefully set the cup back on the table. "Are you kidding me?" His voice sounded gruff and strained.

"I'm willing to marry you, Deke, for however long you want it to last, for whatever reason you want to put on it...to look after Jolene...to protect my reputation...whatever."

There was no sign of the relaxed and smiling man now. "But why, Mollie? I should have been taken out and shot for coming up with the idea in the first place."

Mollie got a reprieve from having to come up with an immediate answer by the arrival of their breakfasts. She'd already forgotten what she'd ordered and stared at her plate as though she recognized nothing there.

She ignored his question while she carefully cut up her ham, seasoned her eggs and sipped her orange juice. When she glanced over at him he was already eating, so obviously this conversation hadn't disturbed his appetite any.

In fact, Deke waited until the waitress cleared their plates before he refilled their cups and faced her once again.

"Why would you be willing to leave school now and marry me?"

She lifted her chin slightly. "Maybe I've always wanted to get married and yours was the first offer."

He chuckled and shook his head. "Somehow I doubt that."

"Or maybe I've just been waiting all these years for you to notice that I've grown up," she said more slowly.

He raised an eyebrow at that one. "What do you mean? I didn't even know you before last summer, and you looked grown up enough to me then."

"Not really. You thought I was a high school student." When he didn't comment, she said, "Actually, we met many years ago when I was just a kid. You were breaking a horse one day when my dad and I came out to your ranch. It was when your grandfather was still alive."

His brows drew together slightly, as though he was searching his memory. Finally he shook his head. "I'm sorry. I don't remember."

"No reason for you to. But I feel like I've known you all my life."

"That isn't a very good reason to decide to marry me."

"Like you said," she stated in a casual tone, "it isn't like it's a real marriage offer, with love on either side. I'd be there to look after Jolene."

He stared at her quizzically. "Surely you want more than that out of a relationship."

She folded her hands and forced herself to meet his intent gaze. "Well, if it would make you feel any better, we could always have an understanding that when I meet someone I would like to have a real marriage with, I could tell you. Would that work?" She fought to keep her face composed as she waited for his reaction.

She was pleased by his frown. He didn't like that idea very much, which she considered to be a good sign.

"I guess that would work," he said after a long silence.

"So when do you want to do this?"

His brows went up. "You sound like you're in a hurry."

"Not me. You're the one who has to replace Mrs. Franzke. I don't see any reason to come back to school after the holidays, so I think we should plan a small wedding between Christmas and New Year's."

"Well, uh, I'd been thinking that— Well, if we did actually decide to get married…that we could do what Patsy and I did and just go to the courthouse to get married."

She was already shaking her head. "No. I want my family to be there. And I want to wear the gown that Megan was married in. It's a family tradition for us girls."

"What do you think your family's going to say about us suddenly deciding to get married? They're pretty protective of you."

"They just want me to be happy."

Silence stretched between them. "So do I, Mollie. I don't want to take advantage of you in any way."

She smiled. "Don't worry about it. I won't let you."

"Mary Katherine O'Brien! Have you completely lost your cotton-pickin' mind? Where is your head these days? I thought you'd gone bonkers last summer and that was for a summer baby-sitting job. But this! What could you be thinking of!"

Mollie, Megan and Maribeth were wrapping

Christmas packages in the living room while Danny played in his toy-filled playpen. He threw one of his stuffed animals down and pulled himself up, peering over the side to see what had his mama so riled.

"I don't remember your asking me or Maribeth whether or not you should marry Travis, and you managed to pull that one off in a hurry."

"Not in less than two weeks! And besides, Travis and I— Well, we—"

"You always professed to hate Travis with a great deal of vehemence Megan, me-girl."

"Exactly! And I clearly recall how upset you were when you found out I'd agreed to marry him!"

"I see. So this is payback time, is it?"

"Of course not!"

"Then why are you so upset?"

"Because you don't know Deke Crandall, that's why! At least I grew up with Travis. Except for those few weeks you spent caring for Jolene last summer, you've never been around him."

"True."

"Well, then," she said in her most reasonable tone of voice. "Don't you want to get to know him better?"

Mollie gave her sister a very wicked grin. "Don't worry. I fully intend to…after we're married."

"You know perfectly well that's not what I'm talking about!" She glanced at Maribeth who was grinning. "And you could be helping me out here, you know."

Maribeth shrugged. "It's none of my business."

Mollie leaned over and hugged her younger sister.

"Thank you, thank you, thank you. Now all we have to do is convince big sister that she doesn't have to concern herself, as well."

Megan wadded up a piece of wrapping paper and threw it at her. "All right. So I'm a busybody. So sue me."

"I just want you to quit worrying about me, okay? Please? If I'm making a mistake, it will be my mistake and I'll live with it."

"But he's too old for you!"

"Who says? I think he's the perfect age for me...and the perfect height for me...and the perfect—"

"Ah, love," Maribeth sighed theatrically, clutching her chest and falling back in her chair in a mock swoon. "Ain't it grand!"

Megan threw her hands in the air. "Oh, I give up."

Mollie and Maribeth immediately began clapping and cheering until all three burst into hearty laughter.

"Sounds like you're having a party in here and forgot to invite me," Travis said from the doorway. All three looked around. Danny saw his daddy and immediately started squealing and trying to crawl out of the playpen. Travis reached over and hauled the tot into his arms and began to nuzzle his neck, much to Danny's delight.

Megan scrambled to her feet. "You aren't supposed to be in here! There are things you aren't supposed to see until Christmas."

Mollie had already wrapped most of the gifts Megan had bought for him, but she carefully covered what was still unwrapped that she and Maribeth had found, a routine they'd fallen into years ago since Megan had no patience for making fancy bows and neatly folded corners. She'd only been there today to give them moral support.

Megan slipped her arms beneath Travis's heavy coat and hugged him despite the fact he had his arms full. The gesture was so familiar the sisters thought nothing of it. Travis stepped back long enough to put Danny into his enclosure, then wrapped his arms around her, resting his chin on her head, and looking like a very contented man.

Mollie had a sudden pang of envy at the closeness they shared. Would she ever be able to share a moment like that with Deke? Would she ever dare be so familiar with him?

"So, what was going on in here a while ago?" he repeated, smoothing his hands along Megan's spine. "I heard your voices clear outside."

Maribeth laughed and nodded her head toward the other two women. "That was just Megan shouting at Mollie again."

"My mild-mannered wife raise her soft voice to yell at someone? Why...*ouch*...that doesn't sound like...*ouch*...my sweet— Ow! Stop pinching me!— wife."

"Then stop making fun of me," she replied in her sweetest tone.

"Hey, that's my most favorite thing to do in all the world, woman! Always has been, always will be. Now, stop changing the subject. What's got you gals going in here?"

Megan sighed and reluctantly stepped back from

her husband. "Mollie has just announced that she intends to marry Deke Crandall right after Christmas."

"What?" Travis bellowed. The three sisters immediately began laughing all over again. "You can't be serious! Why, you can't possibly— You don't even know— Mollie, that's the most—" He looked at the three of them for a moment, then grinned sheepishly. "That's why you were yelling, right?"

Megan nodded her head, still laughing at his predictable reaction.

"Well, hell. I don't blame you." He strode over to where Mollie was sitting. "How long has this been going on? Have you been seeing him since last summer?" Then, as though suddenly struck by a thought, his face darkened. "Mollie," he began in a menacing voice, "you aren't—"

"Don't even say it, Travis." Mollie interrupted, hastily coming to her feet. "There's no reason to play the outraged father here. Deke has always been a perfect gentleman with me."

"Speaking of fathers, he's old enough to be—"

"Watch it, Travis! I'm warning you. I don't want to hear any cracks about Deke's age, do you hear me?"

"All I'm saying is—"

"I don't want you saying anything...except whether or not you'd be willing to give me away."

That stopped him cold. He stood there looking at her, blinking in surprise. Then he swallowed. Hard. "You're really serious about this, aren't you?"

She looked him in the eye. "Yes. I really am."

He staggered back and fell on the couch, groaning.

"Megan, our chick is trying to fly from the nest. What are we going to do?"

"Honey, I'm afraid she's already flown. She doesn't intend to go back to school. She's going to become a wife and mother in a matter of days."

Travis's head jerked up for a moment, then remembered. "Oh, yeah, that's right." He straightened. "Is it because of the baby, Mollie? I know you got real attached to her last summer, but—"

She held up her hand. "Travis. I will tell you just as I told Megan. I am doing what I want to do and no one is going to stop me. I am twenty years old. I don't need anybody's permission to get married. This is what I want. Just be happy for me, okay?"

Shaking his head, he gave a weary and very disgusted sigh. "Stubbornness seems to run in the O'Brien family," he offered to the room at large, then ducked as three women launched themselves at him in full attack.

Chapter Seven

Today was her wedding day. Mollie was having more than a little trouble accepting the fact that the day had arrived so quickly.

Where had all the time gone? There was so much she'd intended to do, so many things she'd wanted to say—to her family, to Deke. Why, she hadn't even seen Jolene. How was it possible that she was only a few minutes away from repeating vows to a man she hadn't seen since their breakfast together in Austin almost two weeks ago?

At least she had these few minutes alone. Megan had darted out of the small room at the church where Mollie had changed into her wedding gown, looking for Travis. She also wanted to make sure that Deke had actually arrived.

Mollie knew that Megan was hoping he'd had a change of heart. Mollie knew better. She'd spoken to Deke last night. He'd called to see how she was doing, and if she'd gotten all of her packing done and to let her know how much he appreciated what she was doing for him.

She'd been touched by his concern. He'd called her each day since she'd been home. Once he'd suggested that he come over, but she had hastily explained that she was too busy, what with making slight alterations to the wedding gown, which she didn't want him to see, and going through a lifetime accumulation of belongings, wondering what to pitch and what to keep.

What had been more important to her, though, was that she kept Deke and her family as far apart as possible before the ceremony. There was no reason to let Megan and Travis offer their opinions to Deke about the marriage. Of course he'd asked her, but she'd laughingly pointed out how no family is ready to let go of younger siblings. No doubt he knew they weren't pleased and why, but he'd accepted her explanation without comment.

And now, here she stood before the mirror staring at the image of a calm-faced bride, surprised that her nervousness didn't show.

Having the wedding so quickly had had the effect of keeping everyone too busy to try to change her mind.

Mollie had discovered that the only time between Christmas and New Year's the church chapel would be available was Wednesday morning at ten o'clock. The wedding was small, only their closest friends were told about it, and no reception was planned. Megan had taken care of the arrangements at the church, Maribeth and her friends had prepared flowers and candles to be used as decorations, while Mollie sorted through her belongings, getting ready to move away from the O'Brien ranch.

Megan had never had to do that. She still lived in the same house where she'd been born. It was tougher than Mollie had thought it would be...to know that she would be leaving the ranch for good, instead of for just another school term.

Mollie heard a soft tap at the door and Maribeth's voice, saying, "Mollie, it's me."

"Come in," Mollie replied, carefully adjusting a fold in her skirt.

Maribeth slipped in and closed the door. "Oh, Mollie, you look absolutely beautiful."

Mollie grinned. "All brides are beautiful, didn't you know that?"

Maribeth sank into one of the chairs. "I suppose," she said wistfully. Folding her arms, she added, "I don't care what Megan says, I think this is so romantic."

Mollie glanced into the mirror and looked at her sister. Although there was only two years' difference in their ages, Mollie felt years older than Maribeth. It really wasn't Maribeth's fault that both Mollie and Megan had worked hard to protect her from the harsher realities of their orphaned lives. She'd been the baby, only eight when they'd lost their parents. It wasn't that she was spoiled. Maribeth wasn't the type of person who asked for much out of life. She enjoyed her friends, was involved in school activities and was totally oblivious to her startling good looks and her effect on the entire male population. She'd been a tomboy all her life. There was nothing she'd rather do than to hang around with the 4-H group or practice roping and riding with the boys.

Megan had bought Maribeth a dress the soft color of her golden eyes to wear to the wedding. Mollie had gathered her flaming red hair into a cascade of curls at the crown of her head. Maribeth had no idea how stunning she looked, nor did she care.

Mollie smiled at the expression on Maribeth's face. "Are you looking forward to the day you wear this dress?" she asked, more than a little curious about her sister's dreams and fantasies.

"Sure. I mean—" Maribeth shrugged slightly. "I guess I am…when the time comes. Bobby and I want to finish college first, but after that, I guess it will be fun to get all dressed up and have a big reception and all the things that go with it. Aren't you a little sad not to have waited to have a big wedding?"

"Not at all. I've never wanted anything like that." She eyed her sister thoughtfully for a moment, then turned away from the mirror. She walked over to where Maribeth sat. "Have you ever had any doubt about wanting to marry Bobby?"

Maribeth laughed. "Of course not. I've always known that someday we'd get married, from as far back as I can remember."

"You've never been interested in any other male at all?"

"Are you kidding? Most guys act so dopey… stuttering and stammering and saying crazy things— like comparing the color of my hair to the sunset, really stupid things like that, or wondering if I wear contacts to make my eyes sparkle. I can't believe they can act so dumb.''

"Does Bobby ever pay you compliments?"

Maribeth looked up at her in surprise. "Well, yeah, of course he does. He always brags about me when I do a good job riding or roping. Don't you remember how excited he was for me when I won the barrel race at the county fair rodeo? He's real proud of me.''

Mollie grinned and gave her head a tiny shake. "Sounds like true love, all right.''

"Why do you ask? Doesn't Deke pay you lots of compliments?''

Mollie was determined not to chuckle at the idea of Deke saying anything more personal to her than complimenting her coffee and biscuits. "Oh, he has his moments,'' she replied lightly.

"You know, Mollie, Megan's still upset that you wouldn't at least wait until summer to get married. I mean, if he loves you enough, he'd wait for you to at least finish another year of school. I can't believe you wouldn't want to get your degree, though. But then you'd have to wait almost two years, I guess.''

Mollie looked into Maribeth's concerned eyes. "I know, but it can't be helped.''

"Your getting married now or her being upset?''

"Both,'' Mollie admitted with a sigh.

There was another tap on the door.

"Come in, Megan,'' Mollie said, facing the door.

Megan stepped inside, holding Danny in her arms. "Deke's here. He and the pastor are waiting in the chapel, so I guess it's okay for you to come out now.''

"Is Mrs. Hobson here to play the organ?''

"I think she's in the church office."

"Okay. As soon as she's ready, have her start playing the prelude we picked and I'll come out. Is Travis handy?"

"He's waiting at the door to the chapel."

Mollie took a deep breath, then smiled at both her sisters. "Okay, here we go. Wish me luck."

Megan slipped her free arm around Mollie and hugged her. "You look just beautiful. I wish you would have let us have the photographer come take pictures."

"I don't think Deke would have been comfortable making a big deal over this."

"Well, that's just too bad. Just because Deke's already gone through all this once doesn't mean—"

"I didn't mean that. And he didn't go through anything like this before. They were married at the courthouse."

"Oh."

"I just know that he's not all that comfortable about having the church wedding and knowing you guys are disturbed about the suddenness of our plans. I didn't see any reason to make things any more tense than they already are."

"Well, I brought my camera. Would you mind if I take some pictures after the ceremony?" Megan asked.

"I'd love to have them," Mollie admitted.

Maribeth stood and came over to them. "Go find Mrs. Hobson so we can get this show on the road, okay?" she said to Megan. Glancing down at her dress, she added, "I can hardly wait to change back into my jeans. I feel half naked in this thing."

"You've got beautiful legs, Maribeth. You should enjoy showing them off," Mollie said.

Maribeth glanced down in surprise. "I do?"

"Yes, you do," Megan replied. "They're very shapely."

She frowned. "So? Legs are legs, aren't they?"

Mollie and Megan shared a glance and a smile. "I'll see you in a few minutes," Megan said, giving a quick squeeze to Mollie's hand and slipping out the door.

Maribeth adjusted the short veil around Mollie's face. "You look so calm."

"I'm glad. I don't want Deke to think I have any concerns about marrying him." And of course she didn't. Not really. But her whole life was going to change as soon as she stepped out of this room. It would never be the same again.

Deke couldn't believe that he was standing there in front of these people wearing a formal suit and tie. He never wore ties. But this was what Mollie had wanted and he couldn't say no.

He stood next to the pastor, a man he'd known for years, and watched the doorway for Mollie and Travis to appear.

He'd felt a definite frost in the air from the family when he'd showed up this morning. They'd probably been hoping he'd changed his mind. Mollie had already told him about their reaction and he couldn't blame them.

He saw a shadowy movement at the back of the chapel and the organist immediately changed the quiet background music to the familiar strains of the wedding march.

His heart felt as though it was in his throat. He tugged at the collar of his shirt and tried to swallow. There she was, dressed in a long gown that revealed her small waist and curving breasts and hips. A short veil hid her expression from him. He fought not to show how uncomfortable he was in this setting. Thank God there were only a few people there to watch them.

Then she was standing beside him and he looked at the pastor for direction.

Soon the words of the traditional ceremony flowed over him—soothing, compassionate, a blessing for the future, much more loving than the terse words once said to him at the courthouse.

He learned that Mollie's real name was Mary Katherine, while she and everybody there learned that his real name was Dewayne Kenneth, an embarrassment for him his entire life.

Travis spoke up in his firm voice to give her away and diplomatically remained silent when the question was asked if anyone objected. Before Deke knew it, he was putting a ring on Mollie's finger, a gold band that he had purchased in Austin the day she'd agreed to marry him.

It was time for him to kiss the bride. How strange to realize only in that moment that he had never kissed her, but then, there had been good reason for not doing so. It would have been out of place and unconscionable to have shown a personal interest in her last summer, and their visits together in Austin had been more like a business deal than a romantic date.

Regardless of how it had been arranged, the fact was that Mollie O'Brien Crandall was now his lawfully wedded wife.

He could feel his blood racing. He reached over to lift her veil and noted that his fingers trembled slightly. When he folded the netting back over her head, he met her gaze and his heart thundered in his chest. She looked up at him with eyes filled with so much trust. Never had she looked at him with that kind of warmth and—could it possibly be?—affection.

Carefully he brushed his lips against hers, feeling them quiver. For a brief time he allowed his mouth to linger on hers, reassured by the contact and the slight return of pressure. At least she hadn't flinched or drawn away from him.

Slowly he straightened, still holding her hands clasped in his. Only then did the organ burst forth with a fanfare of chords. The people attending the service all stood when the pastor turned the couple to the gathering and introduced them for the first time as Mr. and Mrs. Crandall.

A flash suddenly went off nearby and he glanced at the front row where Megan stood, snapping pictures. Maribeth held Danny while Travis and several friends came toward them, laughing and wishing them well.

Thank God it was over! was all he could think as

the visitors shook his hand and kissed Mollie on the cheek. It was the most natural thing in the world for him to slip his arm around her waist, cupping his hand over her hip.

Was it his imagination or did she lean slightly into him? He glanced down at her but she was listening to one of the women who had taken care of Jolene last summer.

Thankfully people had other places to go and things to do, and Deke heard himself talking about getting everyone together for a party at the ranch once the weather warmed up. He'd never done anything like that before, but the more he thought about, the better he liked the idea.

After everyone but the family had gone, Travis drew Deke aside.

"I wanted to do something for the two of you to help get this marriage off in a traditional way," Travis said to him in a low voice, "so I've made reservations for you and Mollie to stay at one of those fancy hotels along the river in San Antonio for the next two nights, all expenses paid. I figured y'all could use some time together away from the ranch and the baby."

Deke was dumbfounded. He couldn't think of anything to say. How could he explain that he and Mollie wouldn't be sharing a room in the foreseeable future? Mollie turned toward them and Deke realized that she had heard Travis. Her face was rosy.

"Oh, Travis, you didn't have to do that!" she said, and Deke wanted to add his agreement but couldn't seem to find the right words.

Travis shrugged. "It's my wedding present to y'all. You didn't give us much of a chance to do anything more."

Mollie looked at Deke, obviously waiting for him to deal with this latest situation. What could he say, after all?

"That's mighty nice of you, Travis," he murmured, shaking hands with his new brother-in-law. "I really appreciate the gesture." Once again he dropped his arm casually around Mollie's waist and gave her a gentle squeeze. "Sounds kinda fun, doesn't it, honey?" he asked, causing her to blink at him in surprise.

Her bright color and stammering response could be taken for a new bride's shyness.

Travis smiled at Mollie and winked at Deke. "Looks like you have a blushing bride, all right. Guess it's part of the tradition, after all. I just wanted to say that while you're gone, I'll see that all of Mollie's things get out to your place. Megan and I will make sure Mrs. Franzke doesn't need anything. If she does, she can always give us a call."

Deke glanced down at Mollie and wasn't surprised to discover that she wouldn't meet his gaze. "I don't know about you, honey," he drawled, "but I'd be much more comfortable if I could change into something else before we head down to San Antonio. How about you?"

"Oh! Yes, of course. I wouldn't want to wear this. I'm afraid it's a little too conspicuous." She motioned toward the back of the church. "I brought something to change into. Did you?"

"Guess I wasn't that prepared. But once you've changed, we can run out to the ranch, tell Mrs. Franzke our plans and let you see Jolene while I change clothes. That sound all right with you?"

She nodded, then turned away. For a moment he wanted to follow her, to ask her what she wanted to do, but this wasn't the time, so he watched as she retreated up the aisle, her sisters following her. Travis now held Danny who was showing signs of restlessness.

"They sure grow up quick, don't they?" Travis said, finally allowing the toddler down and firmly holding his tiny hand. "He's gotten to be quite a handful since he's been walking. We have to watch him every second."

Deke looked at the baby. He was a sturdy little boy, nothing babyish about him, with his dad's dark good looks. Deke swallowed and looked away.

"Is Jolene walking?"

"Uh, yeah, she's beginning to."

"We'll have to let them play together once they're a little older. Megan and I want a large family. We're already talking about our next one," he said with a grin.

Deke wanted no part of this conversation. "I'll go check on Mollie to see if she's changed," he managed to say. "Thanks again for the trip. I hadn't given much thought to what we'd do after the ceremony. I guess I just assumed—" He stopped, not wanting to get into that particular subject, either. He shrugged and headed toward the back of the chapel.

* * *

He was standing in the church foyer when he caught movement out of the corner of his eye. He turned and saw Mollie coming toward him. She wore a blue, heavy knit sweater and a matching blue plaid woolen skirt and blue high heels. She looked stunning. Blue was definitely her color. He'd never noticed her legs before, and fought to control the impact she'd made on him. "I'm ready whenever you are," she said, not quite meeting his eyes.

"Then let's get out of here," he growled, grabbing her hand. He heard Travis chuckle behind him. Megan and Maribeth had followed her from the dressing room, carrying her wedding gown and veil.

"Give us a call when you get back," Megan said, her voice wobbling.

Maribeth grinned. "They aren't flying around the world, you know."

Mollie laughed and turned back to give each of them a quick hug. "Thank you for everything. I couldn't have put this together without you. I love you so much."

"Now don't start that," Megan said. "I was determined not to cry, darn it!" She grabbed her purse and started searching for a handkerchief.

Deke added his thanks to everyone, then took Mollie's hand and led her outside to his truck. "Hope you don't mind me rushing you, but I've got to get out of these clothes," he said, pulling off his tie. "I can't understand why anybody would want to wear them."

"It's okay. I'll see them again in a few days. Wasn't it sweet of Travis to offer to get my things over to your place for me?"

"I don't know that I'd call it sweet, exactly, but it was a thoughtful gesture. I should have thought of that. Guess I haven't been thinking too clearly this week. I never gave a thought to our going off anywhere. I guess I was planning to bring you home and put you to work immediately," he said in disgust.

"Don't feel bad...that's what I thought was going to happen, too. When is Mrs. Franzke leaving?"

"Oh, she said she could stay a couple more weeks if I needed her, so there isn't a problem with that." He glanced at Mollie out of the corner of his eye. "I just wasn't thinking about a honeymoon, that's all."

Mollie folded her hands in her lap and looked straight ahead. "Honeymoons are part of the tradition."

"Well, sure, if it's a real wedding and all."

Next she trained her gaze on her clasped hands. "Ours was a real wedding, Deke."

"You know what I mean."

Mollie didn't say anything more and darn if he could think of anything to break the silence. Why was it that he felt he had done or said something wrong? Didn't they have an understanding, after all? They were married, but not really. She would be staying in her room and he would be staying in—

Damn. He'd forgotten. She wouldn't have a room as long as Mrs. Franzke was there. He turned off the highway onto the ranch road, already feeling the beginnings of a headache. There were several things he hadn't thought through, obviously. Somehow, they'd get through these next few weeks. It was just that, at the moment, he wasn't certain how.

* * *

Mrs. Franzke greeted them as soon as they walked through the door. ''Oh, there you are! I tried to keep Jolene awake but she was so fussy I finally fed her and put her down for her nap.'' She smiled at Mollie. ''You must be eager to see her again.''

''Oh, I am! I'll just peek in on her,'' she said, heading down the hallway.

Deke pulled off his suit coat and started down the hall, then paused and turned to Mrs. Franzke. ''Mollie's brother-in-law has arranged for us to spend the next couple of nights in San Antonio. He said they would be available if there's an emergency of any kind.''

Mrs. Franzke smiled. ''What a lovely thing for him to do. You and Mollie will enjoy some time alone, I'm sure.''

He wanted to argue that point, but knew better. ''Yeah, right. I, uh, thought I'd change clothes and, uh, pack a few things to take with me.''

''You're a very lucky man, Deke, to get such a loving woman as Mollie. She's going to make a wonderful mother for little Jolene.''

His guilt gnawed at him. ''I know,'' he muttered and escaped down the hallway. He paused at the door to Jolene's room and watched Mollie as she carefully rearranged the covers over the baby. Her tender smile caused a lump in his throat. He moved away, thoughtfully going into his room to get ready for his wedding trip.

He knew he was way over his head on this one, but there wasn't a thing he could think of to do about it at this point. Somehow, he had to believe that everything would work out all right for the three of them.

However, it was definitely a long shot in his book.

Chapter Eight

The winter sun had already disappeared by the time they reached San Antonio that evening. Mollie could feel the beginnings of a headache coming on, no doubt due to the strain of the past two hours—the length of the drive from Agua Verde to San Antonio.

She'd tried to make conversation but Deke was obviously distracted. He showed no interest in any of her casual comments so that eventually she gave up trying to get him to talk. With a hint of desperation, she turned on the radio, wondering if he was upset because Travis had arranged this trip.

She was glad they had come. After all, this was her wedding, the only one she would ever have, no matter what she had teased Deke with when they'd first discussed the possibility. For some reason she had thought that Deke would be more relaxed after the ceremony was behind them. Wasn't this what he'd wanted? It wasn't as though she'd come up with the idea and forced it on him.

Perhaps he was being reminded of his first marriage, comparing the two, and finding Mollie considerably less appealing than he'd first thought.

Well, if that was the case, then she would have to show him that he hadn't made a mistake in choosing to marry Mollie O'Brien. She was determined to make him a good wife and Jolene a loving mother.

They found the hotel with no trouble. It towered above the surrounding buildings. Mollie couldn't help but be impressed. She'd never stayed in a hotel before, of any kind. She was pleased that her first experience would be in luxurious surroundings.

Deke found a parking space and pulled in. He turned off the engine and lights, then turned to face her. "Mollie—" he began, then stopped.

"Yes?"

"Maybe this wasn't such a good idea, after all."

She waited for him to continue. When he didn't, she probed with a question. "Are you talking about our marriage or coming to San Antonio?"

Her question seemed to disconcert him and he gave her a lopsided grin as he reached for her hand. Folding it into his much larger one, he said, "Both, probably, but I was talking about staying here." He nodded his head toward the entrance to the hotel.

She glanced in the same direction. "Why? It looks quite nice."

He leaned his shoulder against the door of the truck, then carefully laced his fingers between hers. She found the handclasp surprisingly intimate. The warmth of his fingers surrounded hers, and the palm of his callused hand caused hers to tingle.

"When I was considering all the reasons for getting married and how we might make it work, I kept seeing us at the ranch, much as we were last summer—you looking after Jolene and me working outside. I figured that I could stay at the house this time, since there was no need to worry about your reputation, but the thing is, I never gave a thought to the possibility of us sharing a room."

"Oh."

"Yeah. Oh. It hit me this afternoon that until Mrs. Franzke leaves, your room won't be available. Now, here we are ready to check into the hotel as Mr. and Mrs. and we'll be expected to share a room."

Somehow his voice seemed to have dropped a couple of notches during his explanation. The tingling that had begun in her palm was now running up her arm until she felt it all through her body. She shifted slightly, her knee coming to rest against his thigh.

"Well," she finally said, feeling a bit breathless, "I guess that's fairly normal for married people, isn't it?"

"Sure, if this was a normal marriage."

"But you don't want a real marriage."

He muttered something under his breath, then raised their clasped hands and brushed his mouth against her knuckles. "I never said that."

Her body seemed to be vibrating to some silent tune playing around them. "Uh, does that mean that you *do* want us to have a—uh—" She couldn't quite find the words to use and stumbled to a halt.

Deke nibbled on her knuckles, then gently soothed them with his tongue. "It doesn't matter what I want," he said. "You're the one calling the shots here."

She straightened in surprise. "I am?"

His chuckle sounded a little pained. "Oh, yes. There's no doubt about that. From planning the wedding to when and where it would take place, to—"

"But I only wanted—"

"I know," he said soothingly, "I wanted you to be happy with the arrangements. I still do. So I'm willing to play this out any way you want."

A bubble of excitement seemed to grow in her chest. Deke was offering her choices. He was willing to accept whatever she decided. So now all she had to figure out was what she wanted.

That didn't take much thought.

"Then could we get something to eat?" she asked. "I'm starving."

He stared at her in disbelief. "You're hungry?" he drawled, as though never having heard of the condition.

"Aren't you? We skipped lunch, you know. I thought about saying something once we got on the road, but then I thought... Well, you seemed so quiet and I didn't want to—"

Deke began to laugh, a hearty sound she had not heard from him since the day she first saw him many years ago. She couldn't believe the change it made in him. He looked years younger, and actually happy. She soon joined him.

"I guess I'm not being very romantic, am I?" she finally asked.

"But oh, so very practical." He pulled her into his arms and gave her a hug. "God, I'm lucky you came into my life. I can't believe how lucky."

She tucked her face into his shoulder for a moment, loving the feel of his arms around her, before she leaned back so that she could once again see his face. His eyes were dancing and his smile flashed bright in the darkened cab of the truck. "You didn't seem all that thrilled when you finally came to the door," she reminded him.

"True. I should have known then that you're used to getting your own way."

Before she could do more than sputter, Deke opened the door and stepped out of the truck. "C'mon, woman, let's go find you some food before you start looking for something else to sink your teeth into."

His grin and the heat in his eyes made her blush, even if she wasn't certain exactly why he looked so amused.

Deke found their reservations waiting at the desk. He also inquired about the restaurant that they could see through wide doors off the lobby and was told they could go eat while their luggage was sent up to their room.

Deke took her hand and escorted her into the dimly lit restaurant. There was a small musical combo playing and a few people were dancing. He glanced down at her.

"Do you like to dance?"

"Yes, but I've never danced anywhere but at school functions."

"Let's get you fed, then maybe we can do a couple of turns around the floor. What do you say?"

She knew her heart must be in her eyes when she replied, "I'd like that...very much." All at once all the dreams and fantasies of her childhood had leaped into being, but this was even better than a child's wild imaginings. This was real. She was here with Deke Crandall and she was his wife. A dream come true.

Deke had definitely gone through an abrupt mood change since they'd left Agua Verde. After communicating in monosyllables during the drive down, he was now keeping the conversation going by asking her all kinds of questions. Unfortunately they were about her, a subject that couldn't be more boring.

"You actually took over the cooking when you were ten?" he was saying, his voice echoing his amazement, his eyes as he watched her still warm and glowing.

"They certainly weren't gourmet meals, if that's what you're thinking. You have to remember that I was always fascinated watching my mother in the kitchen, until she finally put me to work. She showed me how to measure, how to follow simple recipes. I found it all great fun. Lots of little girls play at cooking. I was lucky enough that my mother was willing to let me use real ingredients."

"Was Megan interested in all of that?"

Mollie chuckled. "Hardly. No, Megan has always been the one who followed Dad everywhere. She was probably riding a horse by the time she could walk.

Remember she was a few years older than me, so we didn't have much in common.''

"But you got along?"

"Sure. Probably because we were so different. I admired her skills that were honed working the ranch, knowing I could never do any of it. She seemed to admire what I did around the house, even though she claimed not to have any patience for it.'' Mollie grinned. "Of course, now that Danny's here, her domestic side is certainly showing up. She dotes on him.''

"Travis mentioned that they're already talking about having more.''

"Now that's news! She hasn't mentioned it to me. How did he happen to say something to you?''

Deke shifted uncomfortably in his chair. "Ah—well, I'm not really sure, now that you mention it. I think he said something about how fast babies grow up.''

"Oh, yes, that's true. I should be getting used to it after seeing how much Danny changed while I was away from home, but when I saw Jolene I was still amazed at how much she's changed.'' She glanced around the softly lit room. "I'm not sorry to get to see and experience all of this, but I can't wait to get back to see Jolene, to get her used to having me around, you know what I mean?''

Deke's smile faded. "Yes.''

"Deke?''

"Yes?''

"Why don't you show more interest in Jolene? I

know it was really hard on you at first, and you probably blamed—''

''Look, Mollie, I don't want to talk about Jolene,
okay? I think it's great that you love her and were
willing to commit to marrying me in order to care for
her. But I don't want to discuss her with you.''

The formidable expression had reappeared and
Mollie felt totally lost. What had happened? They had
been having a lighthearted conversation just minutes
ago, and then— Ah. The conversation had been about
her and her family. He could handle that. But any
reminders of his life, which would include Jolene,
was obviously off limits.

Mollie fought to hide her disappointment at his
rapid mood change. The fast rhythm of the band came
to an end and they immediately shifted into another
song, this time a slow blues number.

On impulse, Mollie asked, ''Are you ready to
dance with me?''

Deke glanced at the dance floor where several couples were circling, then back to her. ''Sure. Why
not?'' He rose and pulled her chair out for her, then
guided her to the dance floor. Once there, Mollie
turned and waited for him to take her into his arms.

She certainly wasn't disappointed now. With prac-
ticed skill Deke slipped his arm around her waist and
snuggled her to his body. He took her hand and
clasped it against his shoulder, then looked at her with
an unreadable expression. ''This may not have been
such a good idea, after all,'' he murmured.

Mollie had never been so close to anyone before.
She tentatively placed her other hand on his shoulder,

glad that she was wearing high heels. His lips rested against her forehead and she could feel his warm breath, not to mention the hard, muscled length of his body.

"What's wrong?" she managed to whisper, suddenly feeling very unlike herself. Her breasts were pressed against his chest and they had become unbearably sensitive to every subtle shift of his body.

The movement of his thighs guided hers in the agonizingly slow pace of the song being played.

"Let's just say that I'm glad it's fairly dark in here, otherwise we might both be embarrassed."

Only then did Mollie realize what he must be referring to, and she could feel her face burning. It wasn't as if she didn't know and understand all about human anatomy and the difference between the genders. It was just that this was the first time she'd had a physical demonstration of the phenomenon. Despite her embarrassment, Mollie felt a surge of excitement. Holding her this close, Deke couldn't hide his response to her. He wanted her, at least on the most basic level, but it was enough at the moment to make her feel ready to take the next step.

Deke wasn't ready to share his life and his heart with her. She could only hope that once he accepted their new relationship that he would someday open up to her.

In the meantime, she was going to do whatever she could to show him that she loved him unconditionally.

Deke edged away from her in a turn and she unobtrusively stepped closer.

"Mollie—" His voice held a definite warning.

"Mmm?" She'd closed her eyes to better savor the sensation of being so close to him.

"The trouble with playing with fire, honey, is that sometimes you can get burned."

She went up on tiptoes and kissed his ear. "Really? But sometimes the beauty of the flames is worth it, don't you think?"

Before he could reply, the song ended to a polite patter of applause. "C'mon," he said gruffly, "let's get out of here."

Since he was leading her off the dance floor toward their table, he didn't see her delighted grin. Pausing only long enough to sign their dinner tab, he led her to the bank of elevators without looking at her.

The elevator was crowded and he placed her directly in front of him. She deliberately leaned back against him, shifting her weight so that her bottom rubbed enticingly across him. She heard a hiss of air being drawn between clenched teeth and smiled to herself.

Once they reached their floor, Deke wasted no time striding down the hallway until he located their room. He opened the door and motioned for her to enter. He wouldn't meet her eyes.

A lamp glowed across the room by the sliding doors that led out onto a balcony. The drapes were open and drew Mollie's attention to the view. Deke disappeared into the bathroom, firmly closing the door behind him and leaving her alone.

The room was large, which was a good thing, since the mammoth bed took up so much space. There was also a love seat and a round table with two comfortable-looking chairs.

Mollie opened the sliding glass door and stepped out onto the balcony. The city lights twinkled back at her. Down below the winding river made its picturesque way through the heart of the city.

She heard the bathroom door open and without looking around she said, ''Oh, Deke, come look at the view. I can't believe it's so beautiful.''

She could feel his presence even though he didn't say anything when he first stepped outside. They stood in silence for several minutes before he spoke. ''Yes,'' he said in a low voice. ''Very beautiful.''

When she glanced around she saw that he wasn't looking at the view. His gaze was fixed on her. She straightened from where she'd been leaning on the railing and slowly turned to face him.

''Deke?'' she whispered.

He edged her back until she was pressed against the smooth siding of the building, then placed his forearms on either side of her head. ''You're driving me crazy. You know that, don't you?'' he replied, but didn't give her time to respond before he captured her mouth in an explosive, mind-numbing kiss.

He allowed his long length to rest against her, not hard enough to be heavy, but to make her fully aware of him and his present condition. Then he deliberately shifted so that he rubbed against her.

The effect on her was electrifying. A bolt of excitement shot through her, making her groan with pleasure, and she wrapped her arms tightly around his neck.

He leisurely explored the shape of her mouth with his tongue, stroking lightly, then nipping at her bottom lip. When she couldn't hold back a slight gasp, he took advantage of her parted lips and took his exploration deeper.

Mollie's knees refused to bear her weight and she sagged against him. Without releasing her mouth, he swept her up into his arms and carried her back into the bedroom.

He finally lifted his head and stared down at her, breathing hard. "I hope...you haven't just been...teasing me...to see if...you could get a...reaction," he said. "'Cause you may get more than you...bargained for." He leaned his knee on the bed and lowered her to its surface, following her down and leaning over her, his breath still coming unevenly.

Mollie felt as if she was floating. She'd never experienced anything resembling what he was making her feel now. And she wanted more. So much more, even if she didn't know what it was that she wanted. Mostly she didn't want him to stop...for any reason.

With her eyes still closed, Mollie urged his mouth back down to meet hers. She felt—more than heard—a brief chuckle as, once again, he allowed her to have her way.

She tugged at the buttons of his Western shirt, glad that they snapped and so quickly responded to her efforts. With fevered longing she touched his bare chest, her fingertips sensitized to the feel of soft hair snugly curling around them.

Deke kept his weight off her by leaning on his

forearms, which pressed their lower bodies together more tightly. She shifted, moving her legs so that one of his knees slipped between hers. He groaned when she clamped her legs around him.

Mollie had no idea what she was doing and she didn't care. Nothing she and Deke could do together could be wrong. She loved him. Of course she did, or she would never have married him. Someday maybe she'd be able to tell him that. Until then, she would show him how she felt.

Deke sat up, leaning on his haunches. "You've got entirely too many clothes on," he said, his eyes heated pools of emotion. He reached for her sweater and she obligingly lifted until he could tug it over her head. Tossing the garment aside, he reached behind her and unsnapped her bra. Drawing it slowly away from her, he stared down at her breasts with unfeigned pleasure.

"Oh, Mollie, you are even more beautiful than I could possibly have imagined."

Mollie was surprised to discover the pleasure his words gave her. Even more surprised was she to realize she wasn't embarrassed at having him look at her. She was shyly pleased that he found her attractive, grateful to know that perhaps she could give him pleasure, too.

He unfastened her skirt and slid it, together with her slip and panty hose, down her legs, removing her shoes and tossing the bundle to join her sweater. Only her scrap of lace panties remained.

"How about you? Aren't you going to—" She motioned, calling his attention to the fact that he still wore his boots and jeans, his shirt hanging on his shoulders.

He shook his head as he rolled over and tugged on his boots. "You make me crazy. I can't even think," he muttered as though to himself.

Within moments he'd stripped to his briefs, then he paused to pull the covers back. Scooping her into his arms he held her close to his chest for a long moment, looking down at her in wonderment.

"Do you have any idea how beautiful you are?"

"I'm glad you think so."

"But you don't agree."

"I'm average looking, I guess."

He just shook his head and lowered them both to the smooth expanse of sheets. "I'm not sure what it's gonna take to convince you, but I'm sure gonna try."

He touched her as though she were a priceless, fragile piece of artwork to be gently stroked and fondled, but never handled roughly.

Everywhere his fingers trailed, her skin tingled and leaped into a new awareness. She'd had no idea her body had so many sensitive spots. With his tongue he stroked the hollow at the base of her throat, causing her to shiver. He ran his fingertips in a circle around her breasts, moving them in an ever smaller circle until they paused on the quivering tips, hardened with arousal.

He followed the contour of her ribs down to her waist, then leaned over and kissed her belly button, tracing it with his tongue. By the time his fingers slipped beneath the lacy edge of her panties, Mollie felt like a trembling mass of nerve ends, all screaming for a release she knew nothing about.

He took her hand and gently guided her to touch him. Her eyes widened—as she tentatively followed the hardened length—to feel him quiver.

"I don't want this to hurt you," he said, beads of moisture across his brow. "I've never— It's been so— Oh, honey. I want this to be good for you." His fingers continued to explore beneath the only piece of clothing she still wore.

Only then did she discover that she was moist and so hot there. His fingers felt wonderful to her, as though he knew what she needed, what she had to have. Reflexively she lifted her hips to him, encouraging him in the only way she knew, not to stop.

The lamp created an aureole of golden light around him, touching his blond hair, burnishing his deep tan, and she could only marvel at his masculine beauty. Only as an adult could she fully appreciate all this man was. The reality of the man far surpassed any childhood memories that might have lingered.

Deke slipped off the remaining barriers between them and knelt over her, still loving her with his hands and mouth. Too impatient to wait for him, she wrapped her arms and legs around him and clung to him, making him laugh aloud at her eagerness.

Glorious moments later she was rewarded as he slowly and carefully took possession of her. She was so aroused that she scarcely noticed the momentary barrier and could only sigh when he was fully seated deep within her.

"Oh, Mollie, honey, you feel so good. Oh baby, I

can't believe how good you feel to me.'' He held her as tightly as she was holding him while he continued to place hot kisses along her brow, nose, cheek, jaw and finally settled on her mouth with passionate intent.

Mollie felt surrounded by his loving presence. When he began to move slowly in an achingly provocative movement she met him with an equally arousing lift and thrust, matching him, encouraging him until she lost all sense of place…and time…and began to experience the most astounding physical responses.

She clung to him, panting for air all the while she clutched him closer and closer until everything seemed to explode around her, inside and out, her body pulsating and throbbing in a rhythm that was new and yet as old as time.

Deke groaned as he made one final lunge before collapsing over her, his hair damp with perspiration, falling across her cheek as he buried his face in her neck.

They lay that way for uncounted minutes before Deke finally shifted slightly. ''I'm too heavy,'' he managed to say.

''Oh, no,'' she said, unable to contain her emotions so that they overflowed into tears of love and joy. ''You're just right. Please don't move.''

He shifted a little more, so that most of his weight was on his hip as he slid to one side of her. ''I'm not going far, believe me.''

She could feel his heart still racing in his chest.

She placed her palm over it, loving the strong, solid rhythm of it.

She must have dozed because she awoke sometime later when Deke pulled the covers around them. He must have also turned off the light, since the room was now in darkness. Before she could get her brain working again, he gathered her into his arms and she drifted off once again into a deep, dreamless sleep.

Chapter Nine

Bright sunlight shining in her face woke Mollie the next morning. Since the sun didn't come into her bedroom window either at school or at home, she was disoriented. Where in the world was she?

Then the radiating heat along her back and cupped behind her knees reminded her of not only where she was but with whom.

She couldn't suppress the smile that hovered around her mouth.

They'd gone to bed rather suddenly last night, as she recalled with secret relish, without closing the drapes. She glanced at the clock, amazed to see it was after nine o'clock. She was usually awake hours before this. But if you couldn't sleep in on the morning after you'd gotten married, she reminded herself, then there was nothing fair about this world.

She edged away from Deke and carefully slipped out of bed. He never stirred. She turned back to study him for these few private moments. Thick lashes shadowed his cheeks, which were already showing signs of a needed shave. His tanned shoulders made a strong contrast against the whiteness of the sheets.

Wearing a smile of pure pleasure she reluctantly turned away and headed to the bathroom. Once she was moving she discovered a few little aches that were new to her experiences. So what? She didn't mind when so many other sensations had been so extraordinary.

Mollie let the hot water soothe her body for several minutes before she soaped herself, rinsed, then crawled out of the shower. There were matching robes hanging on the door with the hotel's logo on the pockets. As soon as she'd dried off, she slipped into one of them and reentered the bedroom.

Deke hadn't moved.

Mollie stepped out onto the balcony, enjoying the feel of the warm sunshine after the past several days of cold, blustery winter. She turned her face up to the sun and closed her eyes, luxuriating in the simple, sensual pleasure.

A pair of arms suddenly snaked around her waist and she let out a little squeak. "Deke! You scared me."

He nibbled on her ear. "Really? Who did you think it was?"

"I thought you were asleep."

"I was. Then I woke up. You looked too delicious standing out here to be ignored."

Only then did she realize that he was standing out

on the balcony without a stitch of clothing. "Deke! What if somebody sees you like that!"

"Like what?" he asked, all innocence. "You're standing in front of me."

She looked wildly around before relaxing slightly. People from below wouldn't be able to see him, and anyone looking from the buildings across the river would only see his bare shoulders.

She turned in his arms, inadvertently untying the sash of her robe, so that it immediately fell open, leaving her bare skin pressing against his.

"Ah, I must admit that this is even better," he said, his mouth seeking hers while his hands decided to explore.

Her newly tutored body immediately responded with enthusiasm and before long Deke was backing toward the bed while she eagerly followed. The bed caught him behind the knees and he toppled backward, laughing as Mollie tumbled down on top of him.

He wasted no time showing her how much pleasure she could experience while she was in that position.

When she next looked at the clock, it was noon, and they were still in bed.

"Aren't you hungry?" she asked. "We've missed breakfast and it's already time for lunch."

"What can I do about it? I'm being held captive by a love-hungry woman who won't let me out of bed," he drawled. He might have been more convincing if he didn't look so smug.

"Maybe we could order from room service. I noticed there's a full selection. That would be really different, to have someone waiting on us for a change.''

He opened one eye. ''I think I'd be safer if we got dressed and stayed away from any beds for the next few hours.''

''Oh, you,'' she said, poking him in the ribs and grinning.

''Why don't you take a shower with me?''

She gave him a haughty stare. ''Do you dare trust me not to attack you while you're helpless?''

He rolled over and dragged her off the bed with him. ''I'm never helpless, woman. Drained and weak, maybe, but—'' He began to laugh at her expression. ''I can't believe how much fun you are to tease. I may have found a whole new hobby.'' He led her into the bathroom and turned on the shower. ''Maybe tonight we'll try out the tub. Look. It's got air jets, room for two. We could probably spend hours in here.''

''True, but you'd have to take your clothes off for that, as well, leaving you vulnerable.''

''That works both ways, honey. And I intend to enjoy every minute of our time together...starting now.'' He stepped into the shower, helping her to join him, then lovingly soaped every inch of her body before magnanimously offering her the soap to do the same thing to him.

They never did manage to leave the room that day and were thankful for room service. Otherwise, they might have starved.

By the time they returned to the ranch, Mollie felt confident that she and Deke had made great strides in their relationship. She couldn't believe how different he'd been with her once he discovered her eagerness to explore and experience the physical side of their union. He'd become a teasing, delightful lover, considerate of her every need.

When they pulled up in front of the ranch house, she felt certain that the awkwardness of their first few hours of marriage was gone for good.

Mrs. Franzke met them at the door. "I don't need to ask how you enjoyed your stay in San Antonio," she offered, beaming. "You both are positively glowing."

"Glowing?" Deke repeated, arching a brow.

Mrs. Franzke laughed. "Close enough." She turned away to pour them some coffee. "Travis brought Mollie's things. I hope you don't mind that I went ahead and put them in your room," she said, looking at Deke. "I had to make room in your closet for a few things, and I used the chest of drawers that was empty."

Mollie responded. "That was kind of you, but I could have unpacked once I got back."

"I know, but I figured you might have your hands full with Jolene. She seems to have picked up a little cold, probably due to the changeable weather. Sometimes it's difficult to know how to dress a little one. I don't think it's anything to be concerned about, but she's been really fussy. I figured until you settled into a routine, you'd probably want to spend most of your time with her, so I put things away whenever I had a spare moment.''

"Where is she?" Mollie asked. "Is she asleep? Maybe I could go check on her."

"She's in bed, and since I haven't heard anything out of her for the past few minutes, I guess she's still asleep. She'll certainly let you know fast enough when she's awake."

Mollie hurried into the hallway and down to Jolene's room. The baby was sitting up in bed, rubbing her eyes.

"Well, hello, darlin'. Did you have a nice nap?"

Jolene blinked at her solemnly.

"Do you remember me? Oh, I hope so. You and I used to have so much fun together. Remember that?" She reached for Jolene, smoothing her hand across her forehead. "Do you have a fever, sugar?" she wondered, and was relieved to feel the normal warmth radiating from her.

Jolene held up her hands and gave an impatient grunt and bounce.

"Oh, yes, ma'am. You're going to be friendly with anybody who'll pick you up, aren't you? Come on. Let's get you into some dry diapers, then we'll go see your daddy. How's that?"

Jolene stared at her for a moment before she began to babble some kind of language that caused Mollie to laugh. After she'd changed her new little daughter, Mollie gathered her up and took her back to the kitchen.

"Would you look at— Deke?"

Mrs. Franzke was alone in the kitchen.

"Where's Deke?"

"Said he needed to check with the foreman about

what's been going on since he was gone.'' She smiled at Jolene. ''So you remembered Mollie, did you?''

''Either that, or she's willing to make friends quickly. She's really a chunk now, isn't she? How much does she weigh?''

Mrs. Franzke gave her the pertinent statistics and the two of them spent the rest of the day visiting with each other, going over Jolene's routine and helping to get Mollie settled into her new home.

''If you wouldn't be upset,'' Mrs. Franzke said later that day, ''I've been thinking about leaving earlier than I first mentioned to Deke. Of course I'd stay if I thought you really needed me, but it looks like you're already comfortable with the baby and I would like to get over to my sister's in time to help bring her home from the hospital. The doctor is talking about letting her come home in a few days.''

''That's fine with me, Mrs. Franzke. I'm sure Deke would understand.''

''Well, I'll check with him this evening. I guess I'd better get a meal put together.''

''Why don't you sit back and relax now that we're back home? I'd enjoy doing some cooking after all those months at school.''

''Aren't you going to miss going to college, my dear?''

Mollie laughed. ''Not at all. I couldn't be happier doing what I'm doing right now,'' she said as she placed Jolene in her high chair.

Her words echoed in her head as she looked through the freezer and pantry to decide what to make for Deke's dinner. She wondered if he understood

how important it was for her to see him enjoy her
meals, or how good it had made her feel when he
commented on the little touches she'd added to his
home.

He'd left little doubt in her mind during the past
couple of days that he enjoyed her in other ways. In
fact, after being in his constant presence for that
length of time, she'd found herself missing him as the
afternoon wore on.

She knew the ranch was important to him, of
course. He hadn't even waited to see Jolene before
going out there. But then, he expected her to look
after the baby.

Mollie just wished he spent more time with his tiny
daughter. She wasn't certain how, but she knew she
was going to do everything she could to help him
come closer to Jolene.

During the next few weeks, Mollie found herself
making the same resolve on more than one occasion
and feeling frustrated when Deke reverted to the
schedule he'd kept last summer…with one notable
exception. He spent each night with her, not out in
the bunkhouse.

She couldn't have asked for a more loving, giving
husband. He'd willingly driven Mrs. Franzke back to
Austin to be with her sister, he'd spent his evenings
and nights showing Mollie how much he needed and
wanted her, but whenever Jolene was in the room, he
found reasons to be somewhere else.

She wasn't imagining it, that was certain. Whenever she attempted to talk to him about the baby, he'd

change the subject. Mollie couldn't understand how he could ignore such an adorable, happy child.

One evening while Mollie was trying to get everything on the table, Deke wandered into the kitchen after his shower just as Jolene let out a loud wail from her room, long after she was supposed to be down for the night. Glancing over at the timer, Mollie rushed to the oven, saying, "Would you check on Jolene for me, please? I've got to get this roast out of the oven before it dries out."

"I'll get the roast," he immediately replied. "You can see why she's crying."

Mollie had already opened the oven door by the time he spoke. She straightened and looked at him. "I really do believe your daughter is more important than the roast."

"I agree. So it makes sense that you should be the one to check on her and see why she's upset. She's usually out for the count by this time in the evening."

There was nothing actually wrong with what he was saying, but once again Mollie was left with an increasing sense of unease that none of her plans to get him to spend more time with Jolene were working.

Later that night he was propped up in bed waiting for her when she came out of the bathroom. "I was about ready to come in there after you. What happened? Did you fall asleep while you were soaking in the tub?" He pushed the covers back on her side for her to crawl under them.

Absently she did so, saying, "I was thinking."

"About?"

"You."

"Boring subject."

"And why you refuse to have anything to do with Jolene."

He reached over and turned off the light. "I don't refuse. I just don't know anything about babies, that's all."

"And you haven't tried to learn."

Silence greeted her remark.

She checked to make sure the baby monitor was on. It was one of the first things she'd had installed after they were married, explaining to Deke that she wanted to be sure she could hear Jolene from this bedroom.

"Will you tell me why?" she finally asked.

After another weighty silence, he said in a very quiet voice, "How I choose to behave around my child seems to me to be my business. How much time I choose to spend with her is also my business. Just because I married you does not give you any right to concern yourself in my business."

Mollie couldn't have been more shocked than if he'd slapped her. The phrase *"just because I married you"* seemed to echo in her ears.

Just because...the phrase seemed to grow louder and louder with each repetition. He'd made his reason for marrying her quite clear. It was very simple. He'd wanted someone to look after Jolene. That was it. There was no more to be said.

She was the one who had tried to make something more out of the arrangement. She'd wanted them to become a family,...like Travis, Megan and Danny.

She'd wanted—so much, so very much—and as the child she'd once been, she'd spun fantasies and dreams around the fact that she and Deke were now married and they were supposed to be living out their happily ever after.

She lay rigid on her side of the bed, hurting, but determined not to let on to Deke how much. Everything had worked out quite well for him, actually. Not only did he have a built-in baby-sitter, but he also had a cuddly playmate to keep him company in bed each night.

Mollie shot out of bed like a cannonball.

"Mollie? Where're you going?" he asked, reaching for the light. By the time he'd turned it on, she was already opening the door to the hallway. "What's wrong?"

She looked around at him. She felt as if something squeezed her heart, seeing him lying there, looking at her with a quizzical expression.

Of course he was confused. Hadn't she fallen into his arms like a ripe peach the first chance she got? He certainly didn't have to work at seducing her. She'd come to his bed more than ready, actually eager to experience all that they could share.

And they had shared so much. Even now, finally recognizing the futility of all her daydreams, she couldn't forget all that he had taught her, about herself and her own sexuality, as well as how to please him.

He sat up and swung his legs over the side of the bed. That's when she realized he was nude. He'd been waiting for her, as he so often did, to come to their bed to make love. Her throat tightened. *I will not cry,* she sternly reminded herself. Lamplight was very flattering to Deke Crandall, burnishing his bronzed and muscular good looks, highlighting his blond hair.

And she was a fool. An absolute fool.

"I, uh, I'm a little worried about Jolene," she stammered out. "I think I'll sleep closer to her tonight, in case she needs me."

His eyes narrowed. "But you can hear her on the monitor if she stirs at all. Wasn't that the whole point of having it installed?"

"I don't want to take the chance." She looked away, not wanting to see the look in his eyes. "It's much easier to be right next door to her. I'll see you in the morning. Good night." She was already closing the door when the sound of his voice stopped her.

"Mollie?"

"Yes?"

"Is this some kind of punishment because I won't talk to you about every blessed thing you want to know about me?"

"Punishment?"

He ran his hand through his hair and gave a disgusted sigh. "Withholding her favors was one of Patsy's favorite pastimes. Somehow I didn't figure you the type to play those kinds of games."

Mollie wrapped her arms around her waist, glad to be wearing her flannel nightgown that covered her from chin to toes. She forced herself to take a long, hard look at Deke. "You're absolutely right," she finally said. "I don't play games. Good night, Deke," she said, stepping into the hallway and closing the door behind her.

She was shaking so hard her teeth were chattering but somehow she managed to convince herself she'd gotten chilled from standing there in the cool hallway for so long after her hot bath.

It was true that she was concerned about Jolene. She was running a slight fever. The doctor said it wasn't all that unusual, but if it persisted to bring her in and he'd make sure she wasn't harboring an infection.

Concentrate on Jolene, she reminded herself, tiptoeing into the baby's room. Mollie knew that she was no match for Deke. He had years of experience on her that she would probably never have, regardless of the difference in their ages. Besides, he knew how to have a relationship. She, on the other hand, had never been involved with another man and had nothing to compare.

She was only now beginning to understand just how unhappy his marriage with Patsy had been. Some of his remarks sounded so cynical to her. And yet, he'd been so upset when Patsy had died that Mollie had assumed he was overcome with grief because his heart was broken. Even if that hadn't been the case...even if they hadn't been getting along, it made sense that he hadn't wanted her to die.

Mollie leaned over the railing of the crib and carefully smoothed Jolene's hair back from her cheek. She seemed to be resting well enough, thank God. It was amazing how the older Jolene became, the more she looked like Deke. They had the same hairline and the same eye color and shape.

Jolene also had a tiny dimple that flashed in her cheek when she smiled. Mollie had noticed it for the first time just last week. Deke had one, too, which only showed up when he grinned a certain, mischievous way.

After making sure that all the doors between their two rooms were open, Mollie crawled between the cold sheets of the spare bedroom.

Brrrr.

She'd forgotten after only a few weeks what it was like to sleep alone. How could she have so quickly succumbed to living and sleeping with Deke? She was such a fool, living in her own little world, believing that everything would turn out all right because that's the way she had everything planned.

Mollie forced herself to go to sleep, knowing that she had to make some changes in her life, starting tomorrow.

Remember, Jolene is the important one here. At least you can take care of yourself, she grimly pointed out to herself. At the moment, however, she wasn't feeling much more capable than Jolene. There was a deep, aching hole in her chest that she wasn't certain could ever be mended, but she had to try.

At least she'd had experience dealing with the grief of a lost loved one. The experience didn't make it any easier to face; it just assured her that she could get through this loss, too.

"Say, boss, I noticed one of the fence lines is down over in the back section," Deke's foreman mentioned the next morning. "You want me to send someone out there to restring it?"

"Let me go take a look. We may have to replace all the fences in that section. Good thing you noticed it. It will be easier to repair if we catch it before it gets any worse."

The back section was the toughest one to reach on the ranch since there was no road back in there. Deke saddled up one of his horses and rode out that way, knowing he would be gone for several hours. It was just as well. He had several things to think over. A day alone helped him do that.

Mollie was at the top of his list.

Damn, but she was stubborn. He'd learned that about her first off, of course, and had never been given a reason to change his mind about her since.

Take this morning, as an example. By the time he woke up, he could already smell the savory scent of bacon frying and the mouth-watering aroma of coffee brewing.

He'd slept like hell, twisting and turning, reaching out to the empty space beside him all night. What the devil had been wrong with her, that she'd suddenly got some burr under her saddle about sleeping in the other room?

Okay, he obviously must have made her mad last night. Well, that was too damn bad. Why did she keep poking and prying into things that were none of her damn business, anyway?

He was taking care of Jolene, wasn't he? He made

sure there were qualified people to look after her. She certainly didn't need him following her around.

He guessed he would just let Mollie stew over whatever it was that had her marching out of his bedroom. If she didn't want to sleep with him, that was fine and dandy with him. He'd spent most of his life sleeping alone, for that matter. Hell's fire, he'd done a lot of that while he was married to Patsy. Women! Who needed 'em?

His thoughts were a variation on that theme for the rest of the day.

Deke didn't bother to ride back to the house at lunchtime. Instead he spent the day reattaching the wire he'd found lying on the ground as a makeshift barrier until they could order some new supplies to bring out to this area. There were several rotted posts that also needed replacing.

After mending that part of the fence, he spent the rest of the day riding along the boundaries of the entire section, making note of the number of new posts they would need as well as the number of feet of wire required.

It was almost dark when Deke finally returned to the house, cold and hungry. He walked into the kitchen and was greeted by savory scents that made his mouth water.

Mollie glanced up from stirring something on the stove and gave him a cheerful smile as soon as he walked inside. "Hi. Your foreman told me where you were. You should have said something to me before you left. I could have packed a lunch for you."

He shrugged out of his coat. "No problem. I made

it okay, but I sure am hungry now,'' he admitted, inhaling deeply. His stomach growled to punctuate his statement.

''Dinner's ready now if you're ready to eat.''

He glanced down at his filthy clothes and made a face. ''Let me get cleaned up a little, first. I'm too dirty to sit down at the table at the moment.''

Deke made a beeline for his bathroom, peeling off his clothes and relaxing beneath the soothing spray. He wasted no time scrubbing and rinsing himself off, then hurriedly drying himself off.

He returned to the bedroom for clean clothes and was pulling on a pair of jeans when it occurred to him that something was different about the bedroom. He reached for one of his flannel shirts and thoughtfully fastened the buttons down his chest while he looked around the room, puzzled.

And then it hit him. He looked back into the closet and started cursing. He walked over to the chest and started pulling out drawers. Empty. Every one of them.

He sat down on the edge of the bed and jerked on his socks, then strode back into the kitchen without bothering with his boots or slippers.

''Did you lose something?'' she asked when he walked in. ''I heard you slamming drawers and doors in there.''

He leaned his shoulder against the doorjamb and folded his arms across his chest. ''What could I have possibly lost?'' he asked. ''Everything is always put away in exactly the same place.''

She put the last serving bowl on the table before

turning to look at him. "Do you have a problem with that? I thought that was part of my job, making certain you had clean clothes when you needed them."

"Your job?" he repeated slowly, his eyes narrowing.

"Well, whatever you want to call it."

"What I call it is…you are my wife, not an employee."

She turned away and started cleaning off the countertops. "Well, yes, that's true, technically speaking."

He dropped his arms and straightened. "Maybe you'd better explain 'technically' to me. I'm just a country boy, remember."

She spun around and glared at him. "Don't you dare patronize me, Deke Crandall. Don't you dare! I am keeping your home, I am providing you with meals and I am caring for your daughter. That's what you wanted and that is exactly what you are getting."

"And no more?" he added softly. "Is that what you're saying? Is that why you moved out of our bedroom?"

"Not *our* bedroom. *Your* bedroom. I have my own, thank you." She went over to the table and sat down. "Your dinner's getting cold."

"And we can't have that, can we? I might dock your pay, or even worse, fire you. Is that what you think?" He strode over to the table, jerked out his chair and sat down, glaring at her.

She held her napkin in a stranglehold in her lap for several long minutes before she quietly said, "I'll tell you what I think, Deke. I think I totally misjudged you. And the funny part is that I have no one but myself to blame.

"You see, when I was a little girl I idolized you. You were the hero of every story I ever read or movie I ever saw. You were the central figure of every childhood fantasy I made up. Why, I thought my heart had been broken forever when I heard that you had gotten married, because in that hidden place in my heart where I stored my most secret dreams and desires, I had hoped that someday, if I did everything right in my life, I would grow up to marry my prince. Only the prince didn't wait for me to grow up."

She stood and placed her napkin beside her plate. "Too bad that after all these years I was given my chance after all, only to find out the prince had never been a prince in the first place. He was actually a frog."

Mollie walked out of the room, leaving Deke sitting alone at the table, stunned.

Chapter Ten

Deke wiped the back of his gloved hand across his sweaty brow, then paused to look at his watch. He and his men had been working since early morning on one of the most hated jobs on any spread—digging postholes and stringing new wire. It was now almost two o'clock. They'd been working steadily except for a short break to eat whatever they'd brought with them for lunch.

In fact, they'd been working on this project off and on for several weeks, soon after Mollie had moved out of his bed and pointed out his failings as Prince Charming.

That had been in January. Now it was mid-March. Spring was already showing up in patches of protected hillsides in the form of fresh green grass and colorful spring wildflowers.

Of course they might get some more cold weather before winter gave up for the year, but there were more warm days than cold. The worst of winter was over.

Not that he missed it. He still got plenty of frost whenever he walked into his house. Mollie was frigidly polite to him. She was careful to respond to anything he said to her, but she kept her distance and made sure that she and Jolene were around him as little as possible.

He'd thought at first that he would wait a few days for her to cool off before attempting to make amends. Not that he was exactly sure what he'd done wrong, but hell, he was willing to listen to a list of his shortcomings if she'd take the time to point them out. But she never gave him a chance to say anything about anything.

Whew! but that woman had a temper.

He grinned to himself, just thinking about her. As far as that went, he spent most of his time thinking about her.

He missed her. He missed the way she used to be with him. He missed looking into those beautiful eyes of hers, seeing the—all right, he'd admit it—the adoring expression in them. So what was wrong with enjoying having someone adore you? he'd like to know. The irony hadn't escaped him. He'd lived with Patsy for almost a year before he discovered that she had never loved him. He'd lived with Mollie only a few short weeks before he discovered that she'd been in love with him for years.

Too bad he'd only found out when she'd discovered he wasn't worth loving. He could have told her that years ago and saved her the trouble.

He'd managed to figure out on his own that it probably had been her love for him that had caused her to come pounding on his door, offering to help him out. But that wasn't all he'd worked out in his head these past several weeks. He understood her a lot better now that he'd had time to look at their relationship.

It had been her love for him that had caused her to decide to marry him.

It had been her love for him that had caused her to make love with him...beautiful, life-affirming love-making that still caused him to dream the most erotic dreams of his life and wake up trembling and sweating and hurting with need.

He wouldn't go so far as to call himself a frog, exactly, but he was definitely a fool. He had managed to tick her off royally and he didn't have a hope in hell of convincing her to give him another chance.

Once a fool, always a fool, he guessed.

"Hey, boss, can we call it a day? We've set the last of the posts in this section. We can string wire tomorrow, can't we?"

Deke nodded. "Yeah, good idea. Let's call it a day."

The men cheered and immediately gathered their tools together before returning to their horses. By the time they reached the ranch yard everyone was already looking forward to taking a half day off and enjoying their first cold beer.

Deke went into the house, expecting to find Mollie there as usual and was surprised to find the house empty. He looked around. There was no note on the table, but then, she wouldn't have expected him back this early, either. Maybe she'd gone over to see Megan. On a hunch, he picked up the wall phone in the kitchen and called the O'Brien ranch. After several rings, Megan answered.

"Hi, Megan, is Mollie over there?"

"Oh, hi, Deke. She and Jolene were here this morning, but she had to leave for her doctor's appointment about one o'clock. She should be home shortly."

"Oh," he said blankly. "Yeah...guess I forgot."

Megan laughed. "Mollie said it was just a formality, seeing the doctor and all. You guys have known for weeks about the baby. Guess you're excited, huh?"

Deke's knees gave way and he sank to the floor. "Uh, yeah, that's about right," he managed to say. "I'll talk to you later, Megan...thanks," he offered as an afterthought before he hung up.

He pushed himself up off the floor and walked across to the refrigerator on wobbly legs. He found a bottle of beer and made his careful way over to the table to sit down.

Mollie was pregnant? And she'd known for weeks? She'd told Megan...and who else? Everyone but him? Mollie was going to have his baby?

Oh dear God...no.

Deke was still sitting at the table some time later when Mollie walked in with Jolene riding on her hip. "Oh, hi. You're home early. Did you get your ref-encing done?"

"Nope. Just decided to quit early." He waited but

she didn't say anything more. Instead she began to talk in some indecipherable language to Jolene, removing her hat and coat and placing her in her high chair. Jolene babbled back, chuckling and banging on the tray in front of her to punctuate her remarks.

"So—" he finally said when she continued to bustle around the kitchen opening cabinets, going to the pantry, the refrigerator, the freezer "—where've you been?"

"Over at Megan's," she said without pausing or looking around at him. "Jolene and Danny are learning to play together really well. I think it's good for both of them to be around children near their own age."

"You were there all day?"

She paused in the act of pulling a mixing bowl out of the cabinet. "Most of it, yeah. I had a few errands to run."

He continued to sit there and watch her as she rapidly pulled a meal together. Finally she glanced around. "Aren't you going to shower before dinner?"

He looked down at his dirty clothes, only now aware that he had been sitting there for hours without a thought other than Megan's news. He pulled himself out of the chair. "Guess so."

"Deke?"

He paused in the doorway and looked around at her. "Yeah?"

"Is there something wrong? Did you get hurt today?"

He studied her for a long moment before he said,

"Yeah, in a manner of speaking, but I'll probably recover."

"Do you need any help with bandages?"

He just shook his head and walked away.

Deke stood under the hottest water he could stand, trying to come to terms with what he'd learned. He'd never been so frightened in all his life when he'd heard that Mollie was pregnant.

Dear God, not Mollie, too! I can't lose Mollie. Even if she hates me, even if she'll never let me near her again, I can't lose her, too. Don't you understand? I love her! Maybe it was me that didn't understand, because what she makes me feel is so different from anything I've ever felt before. I know the doctor said that what happened to Patsy was a freakish thing, but that doesn't mean it couldn't happen to Mollie, too. I felt so bad losing Patsy because of the guilt for not loving her. Please don't take Mollie away from me as punishment. I'll do whatever I can. Will you please help me, God?

Mollie was feeding Jolene when he returned to the kitchen. She glanced up, looking a little harassed. "I'm sorry. I try to have her fed and in bed before you get home, but I guess the time slipped away from me today and then you came home early and—"

"It doesn't matter. I'm not that hungry, anyway."

He sat back down and watched Mollie feeding Jolene. The baby was almost a year old now. She was beginning to look like a person to him now, not a faceless little blob of humanity.

Jolene giggled, flashing two teeth in her bottom

jaw, as well as a dimple in her cheek. Deke froze, suddenly intent on the baby's face. He studied her hair, her eyes, the shape of her brow, and watched for that betraying dimple. There! He saw it again.

Jolene didn't look anything like Patsy, he realized. Instead she was beginning to look more and more like…his mother. Her hair had grown quite a bit in the past few months, but it was still as light as it had been when she was born.

His mother had been a natural blonde, as well.

Deke felt as though he'd gotten a one-two punch to the gut today. He was still reeling.

"Upsy daisy, sweetie," Mollie said to Jolene. "Let's get you cleaned up and ready for bed…yes, I know you're tired. You've been such a good girl today. Let's get you a bath and then it's beddy-bye time." She lifted Jolene to her hip. "Dinner's almost ready, Deke. Why don't you go ahead and dish up something?"

"That's okay. I can wait for you."

"I'm going to be a while. She enjoys her bath and I usually let her play for a while."

"It's okay."

She shrugged. "Well, if you get tired of waiting, it's all there on the stove."

What had he done to himself with his stiff-necked pride? He'd deliberately denied himself the first year of his daughter's life. He'd made no effort to get to know her or to let her get to know him. Who had he thought he was punishing? Patsy? Himself?

When he heard the sound of laughter and water splashing down the hall Deke followed the sounds and ended up in the doorway of the bathroom watching his daughter destroy the entire area with unabashed glee.

After a particularly big splash she glanced up at him and broke into a toothy grin. "Dada! Dada-dada-dada." She bounced and splashed both hands into the water.

Mollie glanced around in surprise, then smiled at Jolene. "Yes, honey, that's your daddy, come to see what a big mess you can make," she said casually. "Now, then, don't you think it's time you get out? I'll let you play an extra long time tomorrow, but I think that's enough for today. You've worn me out and I—"

"Why don't you let me take over?" he blurted out, surprising himself and Mollie. "I mean, at least let me dry her. Do you have her nightclothes laid out?"

"Uh, yes. They're lying on the dressing table." She lifted the dripping little girl out of the tub and wrapped her in a towel. "Are you sure you want to do this?"

"Oh, yeah. I'll probably make a mess of it, but I definitely want to try."

She sighed. "Thanks. I think I tried to cram too much into my day today. I'm beat." She handed him the squirming baby, saying, "Go to your daddy, honey."

Just like that he had his daughter in his arms for the first time.

She was a solid little bundle, and Deke could understand why Mollie could be exhausted from hauling her around. Was it good for her in her condition? Oh

God. He didn't know. He didn't know and what if it wasn't? What could he do to help?

Jolene quickly demanded his entire attention as he attempted to dry her, powder her and place a diaper on her. The baby was in constant motion. She never once paused. The diaper was hanging around one leg when Mollie walked in. ''Well, at least the bathroom's cleaned up a little. Here, let me help.'' She quickly flipped the baby back down and anchored both sides of the diaper, before sitting her up once more and dropping her nightgown over her head.

Deke was amazed at Mollie's dexterity. She was a natural at dealing with a perpetual-motion machine that pretended to be a baby. She lay her down into the crib and patted her back until Jolene's eyelids fluttered closed for the last time.

Deke took Mollie's hand and led her back into the kitchen. ''Why don't you sit down and I'll fix both our plates. No reason to put everything out on the table tonight.''

He knew it was a measure of how she must be feeling that she didn't argue with him. Instead she sank into her chair with a sigh. ''Everything's probably cold by now.''

''No. It's just fine. You really amaze me, the way you can put together a delicious meal in such a short time. That's a real talent you have.''

She yawned. ''Not really. It's just something I've done all my life. It comes second nature to me.''

He waited until they finished eating, then suggested she get ready for bed while he cleaned up the kitchen. Once again she docilely followed his suggestion. This was not the Mollie he knew, fierce and independent, and he was becoming more and more concerned.

After everything was in its place in the kitchen, Deke went looking for Mollie and discovered her in bed fast asleep. She looked pale to him, and there were dark shadows beneath her eyes. God, he was such a jerk. She'd been pushing herself for weeks. He remembered Patsy's first few weeks. She'd been so sick. How had Mollie kept her condition from him? Things were beginning to make a little more sense to him now. That was why she spent so little time around him.

She was always up before he was, and then he was gone all day. He seldom came in for lunch. Perhaps she'd been able to nap when Jolene was down. He hoped so.

Thank God she'd decided to go to a doctor. He'd probably put her on the necessary vitamins and minerals.

Deke lost track of time as he stood there watching her sleeping. Then he made his decision.

Taking care not to awaken her, he scooped Mollie up into his arms and carried her down the hallway to his bedroom. He flipped the covers back with one hand before he gently lowered her to the bed, then stripped out of his clothes and crawled in beside her.

She didn't stir. He reached over and turned out the lamp, then gathered her into his arms. He had so much he needed to say to her. And he didn't want her out of his arms until he could tell her what was in his heart.

* * *

Mollie was having the most wonderful dream. She and Deke were somewhere; she wasn't sure where they were. There was a white sandy beach, a deeply blue lagoon, palm trees, tantalizing music…and Deke was holding her in his arms.

She ran her hand down his chest, feeling the muscles ripple and move beneath her fingers. Her hand continued to drift downward until she discovered his wonderfully aroused condition.

She moaned—or was it he who moaned?—as her fingers brushed across him, outlining and caressing him.

Then he was kissing her—hot, passionate kisses that made her shiver with need. He was touching her, finding her warm and ready and—

Mollie's eyes flew open. This was no dream! Deke was in bed with her and he was… Oh, my, yes, he certainly was…she clutched him to her, holding him tightly as he carefully moved over her, joining them once again.

Oh, yes, this was what she had been missing for so long. She'd spent so many sleepless nights thinking about holding him and loving him and now…and now…it was real.

She was quickly propelled into a fierce release, sobbing into his shoulder as he followed her lead. He rolled, still holding her tightly against him, until she was lying on top of him, draped across his relaxed body. Only then did Mollie realize they were in his bed.

"How did I get in here?" she asked sometime later when she could gather enough energy to inquire.

"I kidnapped you, I'm afraid. You're probably never going to believe that I didn't intend for us to make love when I brought you in here. That wasn't the plan I had in mind, anyway. But when I woke up and found your hand wrapped around me like that, I'm afraid I lost whatever control I thought I had."

She smiled, her head resting on his shoulder. "I thought I was dreaming."

"I *knew* I was."

They broke into soft, shared laughter before they settled into a companionable silence once again.

"Mollie, there's something I need to tell you."

"Now?" she drowsily protested.

"Not necessarily now, but that was my reason for bringing you in here. I don't want you out of my sight until we've had a chance to talk, okay?"

"I'm not going anywhere," she murmured before she gave a little wriggle and settled herself more comfortably on top of him. He smiled with relief and a heart full of love, wrapped his arms around her and fell back asleep.

Everything else could wait, as long as Mollie was in his arms where she belonged.

"You thought what?"

Mollie was sitting in the middle of his bed, hugging a pillow to her middle and staring at him in disbelief.

Although it was morning, neither one of them had given a thought to getting out of bed. Thankfully Jolene had taken her early-morning bottle and gone back to sleep.

Deke had been trying his best to explain, but he

was obviously not doing a very good job. "I know. I know it sounds like I'm making all of this up, but you need to understand about Patsy and me."

"Yes. I guess I do."

"After the first year of our marriage, she admitted to me that she'd married me on the rebound. That she was really in love with somebody else. A guy who had dumped her. He'd never been the most stable character and she was tired of trusting the wrong kinds of guys. She figured I was different. I owned this property. I was alone and lonely. She convinced both of us that she was madly in love with me. So we got married. I think she really did try, but she was bored here.

"After telling me the truth she left and was gone for several weeks. Then she came back and said she wanted to make our marriage work. That's the way our relationship was for years. The last time, she'd been gone for six months before she came back and I thought she was gone for good. In a way, I was glad. I was tired of the emotional turmoil, tired of trying to be what she wanted when even she wasn't sure what it was she wanted.

"Then she suddenly showed up one day, saying she'd finally gotten all of that out of her system. She said she wanted to settle down and raise a family. I told her I didn't want a family. That things were too rocky between us and that I wasn't sure I wanted to even make the effort anymore. I wouldn't even touch her again until she convinced me she was on the pill. Even then, I did my best to ignore her."

He sighed, scratching his jaw. "Then one night she

caught me in a weak moment and seduced me. I know that sounds like a dumb way to put it—''

''Not really. I find you very seducible, myself. I can understand her reasoning perfectly well.''

''Well, anyway, soon after that, almost too soon I always thought, she admitted to me that she had lied about being on the pill because she'd wanted to get pregnant. And she was. So what was I supposed to think?''

''That she was pregnant, perhaps?'' she teased.

''Well, yes, I believed that part of it, all right, but I also believed that the only reason she'd bothered to come back to me was because she'd gotten herself pregnant and needed to make me think it was mine.''

''So you're sitting there—lying there—actually telling me that all this time you've never believed that Jolene was yours? Deke Crandall, that has absolutely got to be the dumbest thing I've ever heard. All you have to do is look at Jolene to see that she looks just like you!''

''Like my mother.'' He gently corrected her. ''Yeah, I know that now. But the thing is, I had never really looked at her before. To see her, I mean. Until yesterday. I was watching you feed her and noticing how much she's changing. And that's when I saw— That's when I realized that— Aw, hell. What can I say? I've been a complete idiot.''

''Well, I guess that explains why you haven't had anything to do with her all this time. You've been thinking that you were raising Patsy's child by some unknown guy. I guess that would be a little hard for any man to take.''

"No. It was stupid. Jolene was an innocent baby who had lost her mother and needed at least one parent. I was too stiff-necked to see that before yesterday. But don't worry, I've paid for my attitude. I've missed out on all these months, almost a year, of her life. What I needed a long time ago was a good, swift kick in the rear."

"That thought had occurred to me on more than one occasion, I must admit."

He grabbed her pillow away from her and pulled her back down to him. "C'mere, you. I don't like having you so far away."

She allowed him access to her body but her mind was still racing with his confession. "So. Even though you didn't think Jolene was your daughter, you weren't going to tell anybody. You were just going to raise her like she was yours."

"Well, of course. What else could I do?"

She grinned. "Knowing you, probably nothing."

He eyed her uncertainly. "So. What do you think? Am I still a frog?"

"*We-ellll,* maybe not."

"Could I work on becoming a prince-in-training?"

"If I hadn't been so mad, I would have never told you about all that. I am so embarrassed. The idea of telling you of all people!"

"I'm glad you did. I just wish I'd known you back then when you were growing up, your eyes filled with starry visions and dreams. If only I'd been aware of you, I know I would have waited for you to grow up."

"But then you wouldn't have had Jolene."

When he didn't say anything, she said, "I know she's going to be a touchy subject for you."

"It's not that. I was thinking about how angry I was with Patsy during her pregnancy, then how guilty I was when she died. I kept thinking that maybe it was my fault. If I hadn't been so cold and distant with her maybe she would have lived... If I'd done something different, she would have been different."

"Well, I have to say that you have cold and distant down to an exact science."

"You're not exactly a heat wave, yourself, you know. Has anybody ever discussed your temper with you?"

"Me? Temper? I don't have a temper."

"I stand corrected." He eyed her for a long moment. "What do I have to do or say to get you to move back into my bed permanently?"

"What would you like to do or say?"

"Well, I'd like to tell you how much I love you, and how much I've missed having you in my bed, and how touched I am by your devotion to my daughter, and how I've been waiting ever so patiently for you to break the news to me that you're having my baby, and how—"

"What? What did you say?" She slid off him and started hitting him with a pillow. "How did you know? How could you possibly have figured out that I—"

"Megan told me."

She stared at him in horror. "Megan told you! When?"

"Yesterday when I called to see if you might be

over there. She spoke as though I already knew and I didn't want to make her feel like she'd said something she shouldn't have. So when did you intend to tell me?''

"Oh, Deke," she whispered. "I didn't mean for you to find out that way. I'm so sorry."

He stared into her eyes for a long time before he replied. ''Yeah. Me, too."

"I wanted to move back in here the very first night but I was hurting so badly, and I needed some space. Then after I realized that I might be pregnant, I didn't want to move in just because I was going to have your baby. You probably don't believe me, but I had intended to tell you just as soon as the doctor confirmed it. I knew that we were going to have to talk about what was going on with us, and I was scared. We'd never discussed having a family of our own. I was afraid you were going to be so angry and yet, I certainly had some help in getting into this interesting position." She paused, watching him closely. "Did you really mean it?''

"Mean what? That I want you to move back in here? You're damn right, I mean it."

"No. Did you really mean it when you said you love me? You don't have to pretend, you know, just because of the baby. It's okay with me if you just like me at first. I can handle that until we've had more time together, and learned to get along better."

"Come here, you," he said, pulling her back into his arms. "It's okay if I like you?" he repeated in a falsetto. "How kind, how noble you are, Mrs. Crandall. A regular saint, I must say. Well, I'm telling you right here and now that I want a lot more than that from you, don't kid yourself. And I intend to spend each and every day of the rest of my life showing you exactly how much I love you.''

She sighed with unfeigned pleasure, allowing him to cuddle her against him. ''I'm finding it all a little hard to believe. I guess I was hoping that eventually you'd want to make love to me again, but other than that—''

''Eventually? I've wanted you every single night since you moved into the other room, but I wasn't going to beg. If you didn't want to sleep with me, I was trying my best to behave like a gentleman and accept your decision.''

''Could it be possible that we both have rather strong tempers?''

''And that we are both rather stubborn?''

She laughed. ''Oh, our poor baby. He'll be quite a handful.''

''He?''

''Well, that's what I'm hoping for, anyway. Don't you think Jolene needs a little brother?''

''I think Jolene is luckier than she'll ever know. Thank God Mollie O'Brien came marching into our lives, a crusading spirit determined to teach us both more about love, loving and being loved.''

''And have I?''

''Oh, yes, ma'am. More than I can ever show you. But that doesn't mean I'm not going to keep trying,'' he replied, his hands roaming over her body and causing her to quiver.

She kissed him while she did some exploring of

her own. When she finally pulled away to catch her breath, she gave him a beatific smile. ''Then I guess I've accomplished my mission, after all.''

Epilogue

"Mollie? Are you in here? I can't find you for all these flower arrangements!"

Megan came bouncing into the hospital room, grinning from ear to ear. "What did Deke do? Buy out the entire supply at the florists?"

"Of course not. These are from friends, members of the church and that one over there has your and Travis's names on it." She grinned. "You see? Chad and I are very popular these days."

"I don't know how to break the news to you, honey, but you're playing a poor second these days. Deke's been pointing out Chad to everybody who passes by the nursery window, handing out cigars, looking like he personally delivered him."

"Oh, Megan, you should have seen him at the delivery. He was so sweet, trying to hide how uptight he was. You know how worried he's been ever since he found out I was pregnant. He tried hard to hide it, but it was always there. And yet he insisted on being with me through all the stages, including delivery. The doctor had to take him aside and convince him that I was doing fine, the baby was doing fine and that there hadn't been any complications.''

''I know. He's been talking to Travis about his feelings these past few months. I think it's been good for both of them. They've grown quite close to each other.'' She patted her protruding tummy. ''I just hope they haven't decided to go into some kind of competition here. I swear, ever since Chad was born Travis is acting like he thinks we're behind in this baby business, with you already having two.''

''Speaking of babies, who's watching Danny and Jolene?''

''Maribeth. She said she'd come up tonight and see you. Another week and she would have been back at College Station.''

''She seems to be enjoying college.''

''Yes, thank God. She's really eager to finish up so she can get her degree.''

''I can always go back and get mine if I want to. Deke has already mentioned it more than once.''

''But you hated college, didn't you?''

''Yeah, to be honest with you, I really did.''

''I'm sorry I kept pushing you into doing something you didn't want to do. I hope I don't make the same mistake with Maribeth.''

''She'll stand up to you.''

''Just like you did.''

''Yeah.''

They smiled at each other in complete understanding and harmony.

Once again the door to Mollie's hospital room opened. This time, Travis walked in, holding a cigar. "I swear, woman, that kid of yours got here more than half growed. He's huge. Figure he'll be walking out of here on his own steam?"

"I wouldn't put it past him. He's already letting everybody around the place know whenever he's hungry. I've been used to a dainty little girl. Chad's going to whip us all into shape."

While they were chatting, Megan had been wandering around the room, reading the cards on all the flower arrangements. She paused in front of a planter in the shape of a frog with a large knapsack on his back. He sat with long, bony legs dangling over the side, crossed at the ankles. He wore a golden crown cocked over one eye, while the other eye was closed in a wink. He wore a very smug-looking smile on his face.

"This one doesn't have a card," she said pointedly.

Mollie grinned. "It didn't need one."

"Who's it from?"

"Deke. It's kind of a private joke between us."

"Ah. As in kiss the toad and he becomes a prince?"

Mollie laughed. "Close enough."

"Well. I'm glad that Deke has turned out to be such a wonderful husband for you. He looks years younger than he did last winter. You must be good for him."

"He's been good for me, too."

"And he's so good with Jolene. I offered to keep her at our place while you were here, but he said he didn't mind looking after her. He wasn't going to get anything done around the ranch until he had you back home, anyway."

"Well, at least I had enough warning to get her over to you before I had to come to the hospital. I don't think he could have been at both places at once."

"Knowing Deke, he'd try. I wonder if he'll ignore Chad his first year like he did Jolene? You know, some men are really uncomfortable around babies. Maybe Deke's one of them."

"Somehow I doubt it. He just had some healing to do, first. I get the feeling he's looking forward to learning how to care for a newborn."

Deke peeked around the door. "Hi. Thought I'd let you know I'm leaving. I need to pick up Jolene and give Maribeth a rest."

Travis took Megan by the arm. "Hey, we'll get on out of here and give you a minute alone with your wife." He rubbed his hand across Megan's stomach. "If this keeps up, the family's going to have to add a larger maternity wing to the hospital."

Deke walked over and leaned over the bed, kissing Mollie. "I don't think we need any more, do you, honey?" He smiled at the other couple. "I'm too old for all this. I think I'll leave the bigger families to you young people," he said, causing them all to burst into laughter. He looked at the others. "What? What was so funny about that?"

Travis thumped him on the shoulder. "The idea

that you're too old for anything…right, Mollie?'' he asked, disappearing through the door with Megan before Mollie could think of a reply.

''What was that all about, anyway?'' Deke asked his smiling wife.

''Just my crazy family. You should be used to them by now.''

''I'm getting better, I think. I never had much of a family before. Being around the O'Brien clan has been a whole new experience for me.''

''Do you mind becoming an honorary member of the clan?''

He leaned over once again and kissed her, slowly, with a great deal of feeling. ''I wouldn't have missed it for the world.''

* * * * *

THE GROOM, I PRESUME?

One

Chris Cochran slowed his late-model sports car and turned into the lane leading to the O'Brien ranch. He hadn't visited the ranch since he and Maribeth O'Brien had graduated from Texas A & M College. That had been four years ago.

Four years could be a long time in a person's life.

Seeing the ranch triggered all kinds of memories for him. In many ways, he was revisiting his childhood…the happiest times of his childhood.

Four years. He wondered what kind of changes had taken place in Maribeth's life in that time.

The ranch certainly looked prosperous these days. He wasn't surprised. Travis Kane, married to Maribeth's oldest sister, Megan, had built a fine reputation as a horse breeder and trainer since retiring from following the rodeo circuit.

As Chris followed the lane to the ranch headquarters located on a rise of one of the hills, he noted several new outbuildings had been erected on the place. In addition, there were new pastures fenced and neatly whitewashed. The lane, previously graveled, was now blacktopped.

The place looked good. Chris was pleased to know that the O'Brien family was doing all right.

Actually, Maribeth was the last member of the family still using the O'Brien name. When Megan had married Travis, there had been some talk around the county that the family might change the name of the ranch. That kind of talk was quickly stopped when the O'Brien sisters had reminded their friends and neighbors that the property had been known by that name for more than a hundred years. As long as any member of the original family continued to live there, the place would be known as the O'Brien ranch.

Chris pulled up and parked in front of the fence that separated the sprawling, native-stone-covered house from the rest of the buildings. He unfolded his long, rangy body and stretched. He'd left Dallas about five hours ago. Not too bad a driving time between the city and the hill country of central Texas.

"Well, look who's here!"

Chris smiled at the woman loping across the shaded lawn of the backyard toward him. "Chris Cochran, I almost didn't recognize you, it's been so long since you showed your face around here!" She opened the gate and waved him through. "City life must agree with you, cowboy. You're looking real good these days."

"It's good to see you, Megan," he said, giving her a quick hug. If she thought he was looking good, he could say the same about her with complete honesty. Married life definitely agreed with her.

He'd always liked Maribeth's sisters. They were loving, unpretentious people who made him feel accepted for himself. In the circles he now inhabited, he was cynically aware that the type of gushing attention he generally received was because he was Kenneth Cochran's sole heir.

"You remember Mollie, don't you?" Megan asked, motioning toward the other woman who now approached them. "We've been enjoying all this nice sunshine—after all those storms we've been having lately—by sitting outside and letting the kids play together. With the size of our families, we could start our own day-care center with no problem at all."

Chris nodded to the other sister and adjusted his Stetson, pulling it low on his forehead so that it rested just above his sunshades. "H'lo, Mollie."

"I take it you came down a few days early to visit with your mom and grandparents before the wedding, huh?" Megan asked, grinning. "You ready to get all duded up for everybody to stare at?"

"I imagine I'll be able to muddle through all right," he drawled. "Speaking of the wedding, is Maribeth around?" He glanced around the area, not seeing her with the children who were still playing well together, despite their mothers' momentary lack of attention.

"Of course she is," Megan replied. "Since we finished the new barn for the horses, she practically sleeps out there, looking after the new arrivals. Maybe you'll have better luck getting her out of there than we have. You can tell her we've got fresh lemonade up here for both of you."

Chris looked back at the newest and largest building on the property, before returning his gaze to Megan. "I'll see what I can do, but I'm not promising anything. Maribeth is a law unto herself."

"Don't I know it," Megan agreed.

She *should* know, Chris thought as he crossed the ranch yard to the building that sprawled across the way. Megan had been both mother and father to Maribeth since their parents had been killed. Megan had been barely sixteen at the time, while Mollie had been ten years old and Maribeth eight.

He felt nothing but admiration for that kind of family love and loyalty, neither of which had been part of his childhood. Perhaps that was why he'd sometimes envied Maribeth when they'd been children together.

She took for granted all the love and mutual respect that surrounded the three sisters and their families. He, on the other hand, considered the many warm relationships something of a miracle. He could only witness their interactions with a certain amount of awe.

Chris studied the horse barn as he approached it, amazed at how well the structure had been designed. Stalls ran the length of the barn on either side of a wide walkway. Each stall had two doorways—one that opened out into an enclosed pasture, while the other gave access from inside.

He heard Maribeth before he saw her. She was softly crooning, no doubt getting one of the newborns used to the touch and presence of a human being.

Chris's pulse automatically picked up in anticipation, even before she came into view. He was amused by his reaction, but not surprised by it. He'd had the same reaction around her ever since they were kids. Some things just never changed.

He paused at the gate to the stall where she was grooming a colt, her voice a steady stream of honeyed endearments while she gently stroked the animal with both hands, only one of which held a currycomb. Since she was unaware of his presence, Chris took the rare moment to study the woman he'd been in love with since he'd first seen her when they were in the third grade.

She'd always reminded him of a shooting star—a blazing flash of light across a darkened sky—once seen, never forgotten. As a child, she'd been filled with vitality and exuberance, eager to embrace the world. The years had subdued very little of that spark, thank God.

The bright red hair of early childhood had darkened gradually over the years, but it maintained its vibrant shade, no doubt still causing heads to turn for a second glance.

Not that Maribeth ever noticed.

One of her most endearing qualities was her blindness to her own beauty. She was totally unconscious of the fact that her tall slender figure, her fair, creamy skin and her wide-set golden eyes could have easily graced the covers of innumerable magazines around the world.

She'd always been oblivious to her looks. Instead she'd grown up wearing boots and jeans, a typical tomboy who enjoyed ranching life and gave very little thought to the world outside of Agua Verde.

Maribeth had been aware of only one male since Chris had known her—Bobby Metcalf. She'd always been Bobby's shadow, while growing up. And Bobby Metcalf had been Chris's closest friend from grade school through college.

So Chris had contented himself with being a part of a small group of friends who spent their time together, never letting on to anyone how he truly felt about Maribeth.

He'd just been grateful for both of their friendships. Without them, his childhood would have been very lonely.

Bobby had given Maribeth an engagement ring for Christmas their senior year in college. Not that anyone who knew them had been surprised. They'd been talking about getting married someday as far back as high school, but for some reason, the ring made everything more real to Chris, symbolizing all that he would never be able to share with her.

Once the three of them had graduated from college, Chris had deliberately stayed away from Agua Verde. He'd recognized that the time had come for him to make a clean break and to get on with his life.

No doubt Maribeth had made the right choice for her. He couldn't really say that his heart had been broken. How could it be? They had never been more than friends. She'd never given him any reason to suggest that she saw him as anyone other than Bobby's best friend.

No. His heart wasn't broken. Maybe dented a little, but there had never been any doubt in his mind that he would recover.

Bobby should be here now, not me, Chris thought with more than a little frustration. He'd lost track of the many times in their lives when he'd wanted to wring Bobby's neck, but never had he felt the urge more strongly than today.

"Hello, Maribeth," he finally said to the woman he'd come to see. He kept his voice low in order not to startle either the woman or the colt.

At the sound of the familiar deep voice Maribeth froze. She hadn't heard it in years, but once heard, Chris Cochran's voice could never be forgotten.

She spun around and saw him standing in the shadows of the barn. For a moment she forgot to breathe. What in the world was the matter with her? This was Bobby's friend, Chris.

He looked different, somehow, standing there watching her impassively. His youthful good looks had matured into a formidably handsome, mysterious man. She recalled that nobody had been able to figure out what Chris was thinking. He made a great poker player for that reason.

A tiny shiver danced along her spine. He'd always affected her that way. She wasn't certain why. There was just an air about him, an aloofness that had always made her feel the slightest twinge of nervousness whenever he was around. And yet...there was no one in her life whom she trusted more.

"Chris," she whispered, almost to herself, while she slipped through the gate to where he stood. She paused, gripping the currycomb tighter. "You're early!" Then she felt really stupid to have blurted out such a statement. "I mean, you must be here to visit your mother and grandparents. It's good to see you."

His dark eyes always seemed to look deep into her soul. She felt as though any secrets she might have would be easy for him to read.

"Looks like life's been treating you fair enough," he said, deliberately covering his intense reaction to her. "You look as frisky as one of those fillies out there." He motioned to one of the enclosed pastures with a nod of his head.

She chuckled nervously, and used the back of her wrist to shove wisps of curls off her forehead. "I look like a saddle tramp, and I know it. As you can see, I wasn't expecting company." She looked around as though unsure of what to do next. "I, uh, didn't expect to see you for another couple of days. I suppose Bobby told you the wedding rehearsal and dinner are scheduled for Friday." She turned away and began to straighten various items hanging on the side of the stall.

"Yeah, he told me." He glanced around the barn. "Looks like you've got enough to keep you busy these days."

She picked up a saddle blanket and motioned him to follow her back to the tack room. "Well, I needed to do something. Once Bobby decided to follow in

Travis's footsteps and take up the rodeo circuit, Travis offered to give me a job as one of the trainers."

"He's doing well, isn't he?"

"Travis? You bet. Things couldn't be better."

"I was thinking about Bobby."

She continued to be too busy to look at him. "Yes. He's making a real name for himself."

Maribeth put the currycomb and saddle blanket away before leading the way to the entrance of the barn. Pausing in the wide doorway, she looked out at the view.

"You know, Chris, sometimes it's hard for me to realize that the three of us are twenty-six years old. You and Bobby left and started working on your careers, while I seem to have gotten caught up in some kind of time warp." She turned and faced him, wrapping her arms around her waist. "All I've done is stay here on the ranch. I've spent most of my life here." She gave her head a tiny shake. "Not that I'm complaining. Bobby and I always planned to live on his family's place after we got married. It's the only life I know, after all. It just seems a little strange to realize that four years have gone by and I've done nothing more with my life."

"When was the last time you talked to Bobby?"

She tilted her head back and closed her eyes. "Let me think. He called last week. He was in Nashville at the time. He'd done well and was high on his success. However, he made a cross-his-heart-and-hope-to-die promise that he would be here no later than noon on Friday.'' She looked at him as though daring him to doubt Bobby's word.

Chris nodded, unwilling to comment on that particular subject at the moment. "He's still winning a goodly share of the bull-riding events, I suppose."

"Yep, trying his best to win world champion. You know that's been his dream for years." She grinned at Chris. "I doubt that he'll ever beat Travis's record, but he sure wants to try. He deserves that chance."

Chris had his own opinion of what Bobby deserved, but once again, he refrained from sharing it with her. Instead he motioned to the new pastures and their occupants with a sweeping arm gesture. "Speaking of Travis, this is quite an operation he's got going here. I'm impressed."

"Isn't it amazing? He's really done well. Of course he'd built a name for himself in the business while he was following the circuit, which didn't hurt when he decided to stay home. Every time I ask Bobby when he's going to head back home, he reminds me of the legend of Travis Kane and how much effort he needs to work in order to make as big a splash."

"I guess I've lost touch with what's been happening in Agua Verde county these past few years. I thought Bobby was already working with his dad until he called to ask me to be his best man at the wedding. I guess I'd sort of figured you'd gone ahead and gotten married without inviting me."

"You should know better than that, Chris. Bobby would never get married without you by his side. Y'all used to talk about that. You'd each be there for the other."

"I remember. I'll admit I was surprised to find out he'd been traveling for most of these years. It must have been hard on you."

Maribeth heard the sympathy in his voice. Darn it. Seeing Chris again so unexpectedly was bringing up all kinds of emotions that she wasn't ready to deal with. But wasn't that normal for a bride-to-be? She wasn't having any doubts. Of course not. Why, she'd loved Bobby forever and then some. In three days she would be married, after years of making plans.

"I'll admit that I've missed him during some of his longer road trips. At first, he'd come home every week or two. Then later, it was mostly a month at a time before he'd make it home." She could no longer hold Chris's steady gaze and looked away. "It will be different once we're married."

"Will it?"

She glanced back at him. "Well, of course it will. We'll be living together, then. He'll be home more."

"Has he told you that? Or is that what you're hoping?"

"Well, if he's still traveling, then I'll go with him." She tilted her chin slightly. "There won't be anything wrong with his wife traveling with him. He just needs a little time to settle down, that's all. He's still young."

Chris raised one of his eyebrows quizzically. "We're all the same age, remember?"

Maribeth smiled. "Maybe so, but you were born old, Chris. I swear. When I look back at some of the things the three of us did together when we were kids, I figure the only way we managed to scrape by as well as we did was because you always saved our butts.''

''Well, you have to admit that you and Bobby are a bit impulsive.''

She shook her head emphatically. ''Not me. Not anymore. I'm grown up now.'' She waved to the row of stalls behind them. ''I'm steadily employed, thanks to Travis. I have a fulfilling job, a great family and a whole passel of nieces and nephews. Why, my life couldn't be better!''

What could he possibly say to that? He let the silence that fell between them speak for itself. When it stretched into an uncomfortable length, Chris reached over and gently tugged on the thick plait of hair draped over her shoulder. ''How about taking a ride with me?'' he asked. ''I'll show off my newest toy.''

He could almost see the tension leaving her body. She pushed the wisps of hair off her forehead with a gesture that made him ache with a sense of tenderness.

''Sounds great,'' she said. ''Let's go.''

''You won't get in trouble for sneaking away from work, will you?'' His tone was teasing and she responded with a lighthearted chuckle.

''Are you kidding? Travis is always complaining that I spend too many hours out here, and that by comparison I make him look like a lazy bum.''

They strolled toward his car. ''I'm amazed at the number of changes that have been made to this place since I was last here.''

She gave his arm a gentle tap with her fist. ''All that shows is that you haven't been visiting often enough. I figured that once you'd moved to Big D, you didn't have time for us country yokels.''

"That's not true. I've just been really busy.''

"Doing what? You used to talk about working for your father after graduation. Is that what you're doing?''

"In a sense. I pilot one of the company planes whenever they're shorthanded. I guess you would call me a troubleshooter. I fill in wherever I'm needed.''

Maribeth stopped in her tracks. "You're a pilot? I never knew that!''

"Yeah. I started taking lessons as a teenager while I spent my summers in Dallas with my dad.''

"You never said a word about it.''

"It wasn't something to be tossed into a conversation.''

"But it was something you were interested in, something obviously important to you. I remember you would listen to me when I was going on about all my pet projects whenever we got back together after summer vacations. But you never said a word.''

"It was no big deal, Maribeth. Really.''

She just shook her head. "Sometimes I think you work at being a mystery man.''

"What are you talking about?''

"You know. I remember in school how all the girls acted around you. You'd come back each year with this big-city polish, rarely talking to anyone, and never about yourself. It used to drive us crazy.''

He laughed. "Well. Now you know one of my deep, dark secrets. I was spending summer vacations playing up in the clouds. Feel better now?''

They had paused by his tomato red sports car. He leaned past her and opened the passenger door. She got a whiff of after-shave that brought back even stronger memories of the young man she used to know. She'd always liked that particular scent. When she'd asked him about it once, he said it was a gift from his father one year and he'd used it ever since. It smelled expensive, woodsy, and infinitely male.

She searched frantically for something casual to say. "I'm a little surprised that you're content to stay in a large city after spending so many years living here on a ranch."

"That was more my mother's choice. She never liked living in the city."

She tapped his large, silver belt buckle. "You still dress like a country boy, what with that hat, fancy buckle and boots. What is it they say? 'You can take the boy out of the country, but…'"

"I suppose I'll always be a country boy at heart, but I don't think I could ever make ranching my life. I need a challenge that I can come to grips with…not worrying over the price of beef and the uncertainties of the weather." He motioned for her to get into the car.

She paused, and waved to the two women who were watching them from comfortably reclined lawn chairs.

"Megan, if Travis comes looking for me, tell him I'll be back in a little while." With a wink toward him, she added, "Chris is going to take me for a ride in his fancy little car."

"Are you going to take that from her?" Megan

asked without moving. "She doesn't deserve such courtesy if she's going to make fun of your trusty steed."

Chris walked around the car, saying, "The woman has no taste. We all know that, now, don't we?"

They pulled away amid the laughter of the three women. Ever curious, Maribeth scrutinized the dash, peeked behind the seats at the area that was little more than a shelf, then settled back into the luxurious leather seats with a sigh.

"I should have been watching you closer. How in the world did you manage to get into this thing? With a shoehorn?"

"It's not so bad once you get used to it." He pointed to the floor. "At least there's plenty of leg-room once you're inside."

She just shook her head. "It'll never take the place of a full-size pickup truck." She glanced around her once again. "Why, you could barely haul anything in this dinky li'l ol' thing."

Chris tried to stifle his laugh, then gave up, allowing the laughter to ease the tension he was feeling. "Maribeth, you are definitely one of a kind."

She looked at him in surprise. "What's that supposed to mean?"

"Just that. You're definitely unique."

"Is there anything wrong with that?"

"Not at all. There are times when I find myself envying your attitude toward life. You're content with what you have. I've never known you to yearn for something someone else has."

She grinned. "That's because I already have everything I want."

After a pause, he said in a more sober voice. "Everything?"

She glanced at him in surprise. "What more could I possibly want? I have my family, and in three days I'm marrying the man I've loved most of my life. As the old saying goes—'who could ask for anything more?'"

"I know you must have had a tough adjustment, coming back to Agua Verde while Bobby took off to follow his dream. That took a lot of courage for you, not objecting to his plans when you expected to get married as soon as we graduated."

"I was really naive back then, wasn't I? Just because I was ready to get married didn't mean that Bobby felt the same way. I guess that's the biggest difference between men and women. Men want to take longer to find themselves or whatever." She looked out the window, then back at Chris. "I probably wouldn't admit this to another soul, but when Bobby first left, I thought I would die from missing him, missing all the fun times the three of us used to have together."

"I know what you mean. It felt really strange to live in Dallas year-round."

She looked at him, surprised. "You missed us? I find that hard to imagine. You always seemed to be content with your own company...sort of a loner, you know?"

"Yeah. I know."

They rode along in silence for a while before Maribeth began to speak, her voice very soft. "For those first few months after he left, I would lie in bed at night, thinking about him being so far away. Wondering if he missed me as much as I missed him. Then I thought about how it would have been if we had gotten married, and he'd gone on the road afterward. Finally I consoled myself with the fact that at least we'd never been—" She paused and cleared her throat. "Uh, we'd never had—been intimate." Talking faster, she said, "I think that would have made it so much worse, knowing what I was missing while he was away. It was bad enough just imagining what it might have been like to…" After a longer pause, she muttered, "Oh, you know what I'm trying to say."

Chris turned off the highway they'd been on and followed a little-used road until it ended at the top of bluffs overlooking one of the rivers in the county.

"Why don't we get out here and enjoy the view while we talk, okay?" He reached behind his seat and grabbed a blanket.

"Sure. Why not?" Maribeth hopped out of the car and looked around. "I haven't been here in years. We used to come here when we were kids, remember?"

"Oh, yes. I remember everything we ever did together."

He spread the blanket on the ground and they sat side by side, looking across the Texas hills to the horizon.

Chris waited to see if Maribeth was going to say anything more. When she didn't, he cleared his throat, then gruffly said, "I know it's none of my business, but I'd just assumed that you and Bobby had already been intimate. I mean, neither one of you has ever dated anyone else, through high school or college. I just figured that kind of commitment was because— Well, you know what I'm saying. I guess that's why I've been so surprised that he could stay on the road for so long, all the time knowing that you were here, waiting for him.''

He gave her a quick, sideways glance in time to see her face turn as rosy as her hair.

''Um, well, I guess lots of people have assumed that.'' She turned so that she was facing him. ''I'm not sure that anybody else but you could possibly understand this, Chris—'' she began, then stopped.

Chris swallowed. Well, hell. He'd brought up the subject, hadn't he? And it looked as though she was going to unburden herself. He just wasn't certain he was ready to hear all that she was going to say.

He was still reeling from the sudden knowledge that she had never made love to his childhood buddy. That news went a long way toward helping him forgive Bobby for his thoughtless behavior.

She leaned back on her elbows, still looking off into the distance. ''You remember how it was when we were growing up. Bobby and I never really paired off. We were always with the group, or at least with you.''

Chris thought about that before drawling, ''You never seemed to mind.''

Her eyes quickly met his and she shifted, as though slightly restless. ''Oh, I wasn't trying to imply that you were in the way. It was just the way things were for us. You remember.''

He nodded, allowing himself to relax a little.

''It seems strange talking to anyone about it. I mean, really, there's nobody that I could have talked to about it, even back then. Maybe there was something a little weird about us. I know of other couples in high school who were quite open about their relationships, and there were several. But Bobby and me—I don't know. We just didn't fool around. Of course we did our share of parking and necking, but for me at least, I was a little afraid of the whole idea of it. I mean, who could I talk to about it, anyway? Can you imagine what Megan would have said or done if I'd asked her any questions about it? Besides, Travis and Deke would have used Bobby for coyote bait if they'd thought he was fooling around with me when we were in school! Just the thought of accidentally getting pregnant would freeze my blood. There was no way I could have faced Megan with that kind of news.''

She gave him a quick glance from beneath her lashes and chuckled. ''I guess I was lucky that Bobby never really pushed the limits I set. I'm not sure why, exactly. We never really talked about it.'' She sat cross-legged, her elbows resting on her knees.

''Looking back to that time, what I remember was how much fun we had together, the whole group of us. Remember how it was? We were always going places, doing things, having fun with the gang.'' She seemed to be thinking out loud, as she said, ''Growing up the way we did on a ranch, it wasn't as if we didn't know what's supposed to happen and all, but still— Knowing about it isn't the same as actually doing it, is it?''

Her face glowed with embarrassment but she kept her gaze steady as she faced him.

''I think you were very wise, myself,'' he said with a great deal of sincerity.

Maribeth felt a wave of an unidentified emotion sweep over her at his words, as though she'd been seeking his approval, which was ridiculous. What was the matter with her today, anyway? Although Chris had been a part of her life for years, she'd never been so open with him before. Hoping to turn the tables, she suddenly demanded, ''What about you?''

''Me!'' He almost strangled spitting the word out. ''What about me?''

Good. She'd managed to get past his guard that time. ''You know exactly what I'm talking about. If I'm going to be confessing all about my nonexistent sex life on the eve of my wedding, I figure you owe me a tale or two in return, just so I won't feel alone.''

He eyed her warily. ''Such as?''

''Such as filling me in on some of your activities while we were at A & M. I remember you dated several classmates during that time.''

He cleared his throat and then smiled. It was the sexiest, most seductive smile Maribeth had ever witnessed. Her heart began to pound in her chest. Darn, but this man had a lethal charm that she was much too inexperienced to know how to handle. ''My mama always told me that a gentleman keeps his mouth shut,'' he finally drawled.

She fought to control her responses. Working to sound as unaffected as she knew how, Maribeth murmured, ''Mmm-hmm. And you're always a gentleman, right?''

''I try my damnedest, ma'am. I most sincerely do.''

They laughed together, effectively breaking the tension that had suddenly sprung up between them.

Maribeth impulsively reached over and touched his hand, then jerked back as though she'd accidentally touched a hot coal. ''I'm glad you came to see me today. I've missed having you as part of my life.''

He deliberately took her hand and held it firmly in his. ''I've missed you, too.''

The tension immediately surrounded them once again.

Maribeth nervously began to talk. ''You know, being the youngest sister hasn't always been the easiest thing for me, especially as I've gotten older. Do you realize that both Megan and Mollie were married and had children by the time they reached my age?''

Her palm was tingling where it was pressed against his. She looked down at his darkly tanned hand. It was strong, engulfing hers. She forced herself to look into his dark eyes. There was a warmth there that made her feel accepted.

Impulsively she asked, ''Have you ever wanted a brother or sister in your life, Chris?''

She could almost see his withdrawal although his body hadn't moved in the slightest. ''Not really. Being an only child was complicated enough, given my family history. Although, looking back, it might have been nice to have someone else there.''

"As much as I fuss about Megan always playing mother-hen with me, I'm really grateful to have her in my life. Mollie, too. It's strange to think about it. Mollie's only two years older than me, and she's already been married eight years and has three children. Wow. It's hard to realize time has gone by so quickly."

"She seems happy enough."

"Oh, yeah. Deke's obviously crazy about her and it's easy to see how she feels about him." For a moment she was caught up in her memories. "I wouldn't have dreamed when I watched them get married that I would still be single so many years later."

Chris watched her through his lashes. Damn, but it was good to see her, to be with her again! He'd pushed his feelings for her away for so long that he'd almost convinced himself that they were no longer there…or real. This time with her had quickly disabused him of that notion.

They'd been out there on the bluffs for almost an hour and he still hadn't told her what he needed to tell her. Dear God, but he hated this.

She was staring out over the river to the surrounding hills, looking relaxed enough. He still held her hand in his. She might look relaxed, but there was a slight tremor in her fingers.

"Maribeth?"

She slowly turned her head toward him. "Hmm?"

"Bobby called me last night." His voice sounded harsh to his ears.

He felt her hand stiffen in his. She tugged, silently requesting release, which he reluctantly gave her.

She watched him warily, and he knew that on some level she had been expecting something like this. Regardless, it didn't make his job any easier.

"He was in Las Vegas."

She had been bracing herself for something, even though she wasn't certain what it was. All kinds of thoughts had dashed around in her head. He was hurt. He was going to postpone the wedding, he was—What? Why would he have called Chris and not her? Why—?

"Las Vegas? What in the world is he doing there? He said he'd be in Oklahoma this week and would be through there by tomorrow."

"He asked me to come down here to see you."

She fought to hang on to her composure. "Why? What is it, Chris? Just tell me."

He reached for her hands, already feeling the coldness that had washed through her. "He wanted me here because he didn't want you to be alone when you heard his news."

"What?" she whispered.

"Bobby got married last night."

Two

She stared at him blankly for a long moment without blinking. When the silence seemed as if it would stretch into infinity she silently mouthed the word "married?" as though it was a foreign word she'd never heard.

Chris waited, knowing there was nothing else he could say. There was no way to make this easy for her. He could almost see the pain as it seemed to inch its way into her consciousness.

As though finally remembering to breathe, she took a quick breath, then released it. Another moment passed, another gasp of air followed, as though she had to remind herself of her lungs' continual need for life-sustaining oxygen.

"I don't understand," she finally said. Her mouth quivered, then was still. As though searching for words that might make some sense to her, she asked, "Why would Bobby call you and say such a thing? Bobby would never..."

What little breath she had, suddenly deserted her. She paused, her hand pressed against her throat, her eyes mutely pleading for him to tell her that this was all a joke.

Chris could feel her pain just as surely as if it was his. In many ways, it was. He would have done anything in his power not to hurt this woman.

"Chris, surely he was teasing. Surely he didn't really mean that he—" Her breath was coming in short pants, as though she'd been running hard.

"He said that a bunch of the group had been out celebrating, partying. He admitted that he didn't remember too much about the night. Vegas was mentioned, it was like a joke or something. He couldn't fill in details and I didn't ask for any. When he woke up the next day he realized what he had done. He knew he had to let you know. He found that he couldn't call you and just tell you like that. So he called me, instead."

She looked at Chris with dawning awareness. "All this time you've been here...we've been talking about the past, and the wedding..." Her voice trailed off. She spoke as if to herself. "I was even discussing my sex life with you, for Pete's sake." Her eyes suddenly filled with tears and Chris felt as though he'd been punched in the gut. "All this time you knew that Bobby had— That Bobby—"

Suddenly she jerked away from him, jumping to her feet. "I don't believe you," she said in a hoarse voice, her back to him. "Why, the whole idea is absurd. The invitations have all gone out, everything's been planned for months...for years! Bobby wouldn't suddenly do something so—" Her voice broke. Without looking at him, she walked back to the car. In a low voice, she said, "I'd like to go home now."

Chris reluctantly followed her. "I don't think that's a good idea right at the moment, do you?" he asked reasonably. "That's why I brought you out here. So you could have some time alone, to get used to the idea."

The look she gave him was chilling. "Get *used* to the idea? How, exactly, do you propose I do that? Am I supposed to calmly dismiss and forget the past fifteen years of my life?"

"No. Of course not. Damn it, Maribeth. I know I didn't do this right, but how the hell do you tell a person something like this? You had to know. He sure as hell left it a little late to pull a stunt like this, then leave it for me to tell you. I came as soon as I could."

"Fine." Once again she turned away, this time opening the door to the car and getting inside. "You've told me. Thank you very much. Now I'd like to go home."

She'd left the door open. Chris took advantage of that by hunkering down beside her. Taking her hand, he said, "Don't shut me out, honey, okay? I know you're hurt by this. But I'm here for you. You've got me. Does that help?"

Gentleness from this particular man was more than she could handle. The tears she'd desperately been fighting to contain finally spilled over and rolled down her cheeks. She could do nothing to stop them.

Awkwardly he pulled her into his arms. The sudden reminder of his after-shave teased her senses, whisking her away to a younger, more innocent time.

"I don't want to cry," she said fiercely into his shoulder, ineffectually wiping her eyes.

"You're entitled," he murmured. He fumbled in his back pocket and brought out a crisp, neatly folded handkerchief, silently offering it to her.

She straightened, taking the handkerchief and energetically wiping her eyes and cheeks. "How could he do something like this?" Her voice broke and she jammed her fist against her mouth to muffle a sob. She waited until she could gain some control before saying, "It's like a nightmare, a scary dream brought on by prewedding jitters. It's like some kind of a test. What would you do if you planned a wedding and your fiancé didn't show up? It's a giant, cosmic joke. Isn't the bride being left at the altar a cliché?"

"Look, why don't we go back over there and sit for a while? I know I'd be more comfortable," he added lightly, glancing down at his awkward position beside the small car. "Maybe we can work out some kind of plan."

Maribeth glanced at Chris and tried to smile. She wasn't certain how successful her attempt was, but she reminded herself that she had to stop thinking of herself for a moment. Bobby had put both her and Chris into a horrible situation here. Why should she take her feelings out on Chris? He was only trying to help.

With a nod, she moved her legs to get out of the car. Chris immediately stood and offered her his hand. When she was standing beside him, he put his arms around her.

"I know you're hurt, but you and I both know that Bobby has never been a role model for responsibility. In a way, this is very typical of the kid I used to know. I had just assumed he'd grown up some…until that phone call last night."

Maribeth was furious that she couldn't stop crying. The tears slid down her cheeks quicker than she could wipe them away. This was so stupid, getting upset this way. It certainly didn't solve anything.

She leaned against Chris, grateful for his warmth and for his understanding.

He turned and with one arm still around her shoulders, guided her back to the blanket. He helped her to sit, then lowered himself beside her.

They sat there in silence. Maribeth lost track of the time. So many thoughts raced through her mind, none of them making much sense. Chris was no longer touching her, but she knew he was there.

Eventually she asked, "Did he say who it was?"

For a moment, she thought he wasn't going to answer. When he did, his voice was low. "No. I didn't ask. That wasn't the purpose of his call."

"I suppose." After another lengthy pause, she said, "It's probably somebody who follows the circuit. She's probably been there for him whenever he needed consoling or cheering. She's probably—"

"Don't, honey. Don't start to imagine stuff that you have no way of knowing if it's true or not. Trying to second-guess the situation doesn't do any good. It will only make you feel worse.''

Her attempt at a laugh was a dismal failure. ''Feel worse? Surely you're kidding.''

Silence fell between them once more.

Eventually Chris said, ''I know you don't believe this right at the moment, but I know that things are going to be okay for you eventually. It isn't the end of the world, even though it may feel like it. Someday, you'll be able to look back at all of this and see how God's plans for us aren't necessarily what we had in mind at the time. Maybe He has other plans we aren't aware of at the moment. Just give yourself some time to deal with what's happened, and I think you'll do fine.''

There was nothing more he could think of to say. So he sat there beside her, staring out over the hills, and waited for her to deal with the news in her own way. He knew she was crying, but she never made a sound, other than her uneven breathing and an occasional sniff. She was handling it as well as anyone could. He'd never been more proud of her.

And now she's free, a small voice in his head reminded him.

So what?

So now's your chance.

Oh, sure.

Think about it. Maybe something can be salvaged from this mess Bobby has created. Just think about it.

The sun sank lower in the west, tinting the sky with wisps of pastel colors. He'd forgotten how beautiful the Texas hill country was. The gentle breeze cooled them, wafting the scent of cedar across the hills.

He had no idea how long they had been sitting in silence when she finally spoke once again.

"He was right."

"About what?"

"Not telling me over the phone."

"Yes. At least he did something right."

She sighed, her breath still catching. "I'm glad you were here, Chris." She gave him a quick glance before looking away. "It would have been even tougher if I'd been at home, with the family, trying to explain." She sighed. "I just feel overwhelmed at the moment. I don't know where to start."

Her voice sounded stronger. She was more in control of her emotions. He took the chance of resting his hand on her back. When she leaned into him slightly, he began to massage the area between her shoulder blades.

"Start what?"

"Telling everybody the wedding is canceled." The tears that had dried up earlier suddenly reappeared. She impatiently wiped them away, then blew her nose on the handkerchief. "I feel like such a dope, patiently waiting for years for him to return home to marry me when all this time he— He's been—"

There was no reason for her to finish that particular line of thought.

"You know what?" he said, making the effort to sound brisk and matter-of-fact. "What you really need to do is to get away from here for a while. Why don't you come back to Dallas with me? I've got a big place with plenty of room. It would give you a chance to distance yourself from the situation until you can come to terms with what's happened.''

His suggestion brought a quiver to her lips, as though she was attempting to smile. "You've got to be kidding, Chris." Yes. Definitely a watery smile. "I'd never hear the end of it from my family if I went off somewhere with you."

"We could get around that."

Her expression when she cut her eyes around to look at him clearly showed her doubt.

"I have a suggestion that might solve some of this for you."

"What? Put a notice in the paper? I already thought of that, but it's too late. The weekly paper will be out in the morning."

"No. I'm suggesting that you go ahead with the wedding."

"What in the world are you talking about? I can't have a wedding without a groom."

"I know. So I'm volunteering."

She straightened away from him, pushing herself up until she was standing, looking down at him. With a disbelieving shake to her head, she said, "You can't be serious!"

Chris took his time getting up. When they were facing each other once again, he met her bewildered gaze with a level one of his own. He let her see what was in his eyes, what he was feeling, before he replied, "I'm very serious, Maribeth."

If she lived to be a hundred, Maribeth knew that she would never experience a day like this one.

"Why?" Blurted out that way, her response had sounded almost insulting.

"I have many reasons, none of which matter in the least if you find the idea repulsive."

Marriage to Chris Cochran repulsive? Many feelings came to mind, but repulsion wasn't one of them. For a day filled with shocking disclosures, this one was as great as any she'd heard so far.

Marriage with Chris? Why, she'd never thought of him in that way. At least...not exactly. Even though she had teased him earlier today about the women in his life, he'd always seemed too much of a loner for her to ever imagine him married to anyone.

He made her nervous in a way she couldn't quite describe. What would it be like to be married to him? To live with him? To sleep with him? To make love—

Well! He'd certainly taken her mind off the news he'd brought. She'd gotten so caught up in his proposal—and that was exactly what it was, she realized with a dazed fascination—that she had momentarily forgotten that the entire county was going to turn out for her wedding in three days, unless she got busy and explained to everyone what had happened.

Chris wished he knew what she was thinking. Her expressive face revealed a bewildering series of thoughts and feelings, none of which he'd been able to decipher.

"This doesn't sound at all like you, Chris," she finally said. "You're not the impulsive type. So why would you suggest something so unusual?"

He took her hand, placed it on his palm and traced

the length of her fingers with his other hand. "What's so unusual about it? Think about it for a moment. You've been planning to get married for sometime now. You can still get married. You've known me for almost as long as you've known Bobby, so it's not as if we're strangers. You pointed out earlier that you had spent most of your life on the ranch. Well, now you can come with me and see something more of the world."

"I can't take advantage of you," she said slowly, her gaze fixed on their linked hands.

Chris couldn't help but be amused. She sounded so earnest. And so scared. "Sure you can. You have my permission to take advantage of me at anytime, starting right now." He released her hands and tipped her chin up so that she could see his face. He'd never been more sincere in his life when he said, "I can't think of anything that would give me more pleasure than to marry you, Maribeth."

Her expression was difficult to make out. It was only then that he realized the light was fading rapidly from the sky.

"Oh, Chris," she said in the gathering darkness. He could hear the tears in her voice. She wiped her hand impatiently across her eyes once again. "I don't know what to say."

A surge of exultation shot through him. She hadn't turned him down cold. Was it fair to take advantage of her while she was so vulnerable?

Something needed to be done. And done quickly.

Giving in to temptation, Chris slid his arm around her waist and with his other hand, tilted her chin up—

ward. Moving slowly in order to give her time to stop him if she wished, he leaned closer until his lips brushed hers.

She didn't flinch and she didn't pull away. That was enough encouragement for him to put all the yearning he felt into the kiss that he'd fantasized giving her for more years than he could remember.

Her lips were even softer than he had imagined. She tasted of tears and temptation. He took his time molding his mouth to fit hers, easing his way as her innocence imprinted itself on him.

He pressed her against him, his hands exploring her back from her nape to the base of her spine while he nudged her lips apart and dipped into the sweetness of her mouth.

By the time Maribeth understood that Chris intended to kiss her, he was already doing it. The first touch of his mouth froze her into immobility. This was Chris Cochran kissing her! She would have known it was him even if she'd been wearing a blindfold because of the tingling sensation she'd experienced as soon as he touched her. Her body must be some kind of tuning fork where he was concerned!

That was her last coherent thought. Maribeth had thought that she was experienced in the art of kissing at least, but she'd never experienced anything like this before. All she could do was wrap her arms around his waist and hold on.

By the time he drew away from her with obvious reluctance some untold time later, she was having trouble getting her breath. He seemed to be having a similar problem. He leaned his forehead against hers.

"So what do you say?" he whispered. "Shall we shock everybody and do it?"

She was already in shock, and all she'd done was kiss Chris Cochran. Perhaps it would be better to say that Chris had kissed her.

Her head was still swimming.

In a few short hours everything she thought she knew and understood about herself and her life had been turned upside down. She'd been grieving over Bobby one minute and wholeheartedly participating in a kiss with Chris the next.

Had the whole world gone mad, or was it just her?

"Oh, Chris. I can't make a decision like that right now. I can't even *think* right now."

He couldn't see her face, but he could hear the pain and confusion in her voice. He wasn't certain what to say. He knew better than to kiss her again. That way led to madness if he couldn't place her on the blanket nearby and make passionate love to her.

"I need to get back home," she said, only now stepping away from him. "Everybody will be wondering why I've been gone so long."

"You're twenty-six years old, Maribeth, not sixteen. Believe it or not, you don't have to account for every moment of your life anymore."

"You're right, of course. I guess it's a habit."

"I sometimes wonder if you don't feel as though you're in some kind of suspended time frame, like Sleeping Beauty, waiting for your prince to come claim you. You've been content to stay here with your family working on the ranch while you waited for Bobby to return home."

"Perhaps. I don't know. I've stayed here because this has been my life. I never envisioned another kind. There was no reason to, until now. I never would have guessed that Bobby would do something like this. I knew he wasn't in any hurry to come home, which is why I didn't push him to set a date for the wedding. After four years on the road, I thought he was getting ready to settle down. How could I have known...?" Her voice trailed off, leaving her feeling so empty. The life she thought she'd had was no longer there. What could she do to create an alternate future? The thought was scary, no matter what she chose.

"Come with me, Maribeth. Give me the opportunity to show you what's out there on the horizon. Will you do that for me...and for yourself?"

"I don't know, Chris. Everything is happening at once. This must be how a person would feel when they're enjoying the scenic countryside and then suddenly step on a land mine. My world's just exploded into little pieces."

He kissed her again, a gentle, soothing touch that still set all her senses on red alert.

"Give me the chance to help put your life back together, will you?" he murmured. "I don't want to leave here with you feeling so shattered."

"And how do I explain the switch to people?"

"It's too late to say much, isn't it? If you agree to marry me, you don't really need to make any explanations. Everyone will come to see you get married as planned. You'll still be getting married. Only the groom will be different."

"You don't think they'll notice?" she asked, almost laughing at the idea. ''Chris, this isn't some kind of play where suddenly the understudy has to fill in.''

''Maybe not, but it would certainly give the people in the county something to talk about for years to come.''

''Oh, Chris, how could I have forgotten your crazy sense of humor?''

''If you'll marry me, you'll be able to stay in closer touch to be reminded.''

''I must be out of my mind. I'm actually considering the idea.''

That was as much as he could hope for. He didn't want to push his luck. ''Why don't I take you home? You're exhausted and still in shock. I'll spend the night at my family's place and we'll talk tomorrow. See how you feel about things then. A good night's sleep will do wonders for you.''

''I'm not sure I could sleep. I don't know how I could get my mind to slow down. It seems to be running off in all directions.''

He gathered up the blanket and led her back to the car. Once inside, he took her hand. ''I just want you to remember that you don't have to deal with this on your own. I'm here for you. I want to help. You know that I'll accept whatever you decide, but I want you to consider my offer. Will you do that for me?''

Her face was a pale blur in the dark. He couldn't read her expression. ''I can't believe you'd be willing to make such a sacrifice.''

''Sacrifice?''

''Marrying me.''

His laugh was self-mocking even though she

wasn't aware of it. "Someday I hope to convince you that marrying you is definitely not my idea of a sacrifice."

He started the car and backed around, taking the road back to the highway. He was encouraged by the fact that she had left her hand in his. It remained there all the way back to the ranch.

"Well, there you are," Megan said when Maribeth walked into the house. "I was wondering if we needed to send out a search party for you."

Maribeth kept her head down, hoping Megan wouldn't notice her face. She still clutched Chris's handkerchief in her hand.

"We just got to talking," she replied, her voice sounding hoarse in her ears, "and didn't notice the time."

They were in the kitchen and Maribeth opened the refrigerator as though looking for something to eat.

"Well, it's a good thing Bobby's not the jealous type. Otherwise he might have something to say about his fiancée disappearing for hours with his best friend." When Maribeth continued to stare sightlessly into the refrigerator, Megan added, "I saved you a plate. It's on the bottom shelf."

"Thanks." Maribeth's reply was muffled.

"Are you getting a cold? You sound funny." Megan took the plate out of Maribeth's hands and looked at her. "And your face is all blotchy. Have you been crying?"

"For Pete's sake, Megan. I'm twenty-six years old.

I don't need you mothering me any longer. Would you give it a rest?''

Megan blinked in surprise. Maribeth knew she was acting out of character, but she wasn't ready to discuss the news she'd received with anyone at the moment. For that matter, she couldn't imagine a time when she'd be ready to tell the family that Bobby Metcalf had cared so little for her that he had blithely run off and married somebody else days before their wedding.

She watched Megan put the plate of food in the microwave and set the timer. The silence in the kitchen became oppressive to her.

''I'm sorry I snapped at you,'' Maribeth finally said, sitting down at the table and gently rubbing her swollen eyelids. ''My eyes have been watering. I guess I could be getting a cold.''

Megan poured a glass of iced tea and set it down in front of her. ''At the risk of sounding too motherly once again, I'd suggest that you take a hot bath after dinner and get to bed early. You certainly don't want to be coughing and sneezing on Saturday.''

The microwave pinged and Maribeth jumped up to get there first. ''Good idea. I think I'll do that,'' she muttered, carrying her plate and silverware to the table.

''Do you want me to stay with you while you eat?''

Maribeth knew that her sister was just trying to be polite. Normally Maribeth would have enjoyed her company. But not now. Now, all she wanted was to be left alone.

''That's okay, sis. But thanks for the offer.'' She kept her eyes on her food.

Once Megan left the kitchen Maribeth tried her best to eat. She knew she couldn't choke down much of it, but Megan's attitude was just a small sample of what she could expect, magnified a few dozen times, if she told her family what had happened. She could almost visualize what would happen. Megan would immediately get on the phone to Mollie. Then her sisters would tell their husbands. She wouldn't put it past Travis and Deke to round up a posse of angry friends and neighbors and go after Bobby with the intention of lynching him.

Even the children would get into the act in their own way—trying to comfort her with pats and special little gifts.

How could she possibly deal with all of that? Chris was right. She needed to get away from here. Maybe she *would* leave for a while. She could go anywhere. She'd been faithfully saving the money Travis paid her, knowing she'd need money once she and Bobby were married. She could take the money and go to Houston, or maybe San Antonio...or Dallas.

Of course, she could go to Dallas without actually living with Chris. At least he would be there close by. She could find an apartment, maybe find a job somewhere. She could—

Just who was she fooling? She'd never been on her own in her life! She'd always had friends and family around her, looking after her, caring for her, babying her.

The truth was that she'd been spoiled by everyone.

She barely remembered her parents. What stood out in her memory from that awful time was how upset Megan and Mollie had been. It was only later that she understood that the three of them could have been split up and put into foster homes.

None of those memories seemed real to her now. She'd grown up with Mollie taking care of the house and meals and Megan working the ranch.

What, exactly, had she contributed to the group?

A big fat zero.

She'd blithely played with her friends, tagged along behind Bobby and Chris, worked with her 4-H projects and planned her future around Bobby Metcalf.

It was almost as if Bobby's actions had forced her to stop and take a cold, hard look at herself.

She didn't like what she saw.

By the time Megan and Mollie had reached her age, they were wives and mothers, running households, being responsible.

She was still playing with her animals and getting paid for it.

Maribeth looked down at her plate and realized that she'd eaten every bite of food on it. So much for all the agonized suffering she was doing. It certainly hadn't affected her appetite.

What she was doing was sitting there feeling sorry for herself, feeling picked on because she had a sister who was concerned about her, knowing how the family would rally around her if she told them the truth.

What she needed to do was to grow up...and Chris had offered her a way to do that. She could marry him, even though her family would never understand it, and she could set out to prove to herself and everyone else that she was an adult.

The fact was she *was* a coward. She didn't want anyone in Agua Verde to know what Bobby had done, especially while she lived there. She didn't think she could face any of them knowing how easily she'd been duped.

There was no way she could make a decision tonight. Tonight she would take Megan's advice. This was her reality, whether she liked it or not. Maribeth O'Brien was not going to marry Bobby Metcalf, despite all her hopes, her plans, her dreams. It was not going to happen.

Now she had to decide what she intended to do with the rest of her life.

A sudden memory of Chris's kiss flashed into her mind and she shivered. What she had felt stunned her. She had kissed Bobby many times and had enjoyed it, but his kisses had never affected her the way the one Chris had given her.

Just thinking about it made her body react in a new, unexpected way.

She was shaken by the realization that she wanted it to happen again.

Three

"I don't see how you can stand there looking so calm," Megan said to Maribeth with mounting exasperation three days later. "Haven't you heard a thing Mollie's been saying to you?"

Maribeth studied her pale reflection in the full-length mirror, deliberately concentrating on her image in an effort to remain as calm as Megan thought she was. She was too pale. Weren't brides supposed to be glowing or something? Her hair was the only thing about her giving off any color. Her eyes, wider than normal, stared back at her.

Who was this woman? She didn't recognize her at all. She fingered the veil. From this distance it looked like a cloud hovering around her head.

An appropriate piece of symbolism.

Obviously she'd had her head in a cloud for years,

ignoring what had been happening between her and Bobby, refusing to deal with the reality of her life.

She was tired of passively waiting for her life to begin. She was ready to plan an entirely new one, away from Agua Verde and everything that was familiar to her.

Her decisions had brought her to this place at this time. The three sisters now waited in a small room off the foyer of the church they had attended all their lives. Her wedding was set to begin in another few minutes. A wedding without the designated bridegroom.

"I heard her," she finally replied, her eyes still focused on the image in the mirror while her thoughts were elsewhere.

"Don't you understand what this means?" Megan asked, her voice wobbling just a little. "Nobody, and I mean absolutely no one in this town, has seen Bobby Metcalf this morning. Having Chris fill in for him at the rehearsal last night is one thing, but if he doesn't appear in the next few minutes, you're going to look foolish walking down that aisle and not having a groom waiting. Time is running out. What are you going to do, Mary Elizabeth? Now's the time to call off the ceremony, before you actually walk down that aisle." Megan was actually wringing her hands.

Of course Megan was right. She could still call off the ceremony right now if she wanted. No one was forcing her to marry Chris, even though they had gotten their marriage license the day after he arrived, swearing the clerk to strict secrecy until after the ceremony. Not wanting to test the restraint of the small town's gossip mill any further, Chris had driven to Fredericksburg to get her a wedding band yesterday.

Was she out of her mind? Had the shock been too much for her? Or was Chris's offer too tempting to resist? At the moment, she didn't have a clue.

"Oh, leave her alone, Megan," Mollie said. "If the bride isn't concerned, why should you be?"

Maribeth almost laughed at the absurdity of the situation. Concerned? She was terrified! Of her own choices, her judgment or lack thereof, of the future, of breaking down in front of all of these people and admitting that she was a complete fraud—that Bobby Metcalf thought so little of her that he hadn't bothered to get in touch with her directly after marrying someone else.

She wasn't sure she could have gotten through the past three days without Chris. He'd been very matter-of-fact when she told him she would marry him, making arrangements for the license and ring. He'd even laughed when she told him she hadn't told anyone that Bobby wasn't going to be there.

He'd carried off his role of substitute groom at the rehearsal with a casual acceptance of the situation, so that everyone else in the wedding party had accepted Bobby's absence with little more than raised brows and questioning looks at one another.

Megan went over to one of the folding chairs lined up along the wall and threw herself into the chair. "I swear, I'm going to have gray hair before this day is over."

"Megan! You're going to crush your dress," Mollie said, shaking her head in exasperation. "Do you realize that you're acting more like a nervous bride than Maribeth is? You didn't act this hyper when you and Travis got married!"

Megan ran her hand nervously over her dress. "Well, at least Travis was at the church when it was time to get married! Do *you* realize that the chapel is crammed full of people, waiting for us to start this thing? And does your sister care? Oh, no. She's just been humming to herself all morning, as though she didn't have a care in the world."

Maribeth turned away from the mirror and looked over at her oldest sister. "Everything's going to turn out all right," she said, "Please don't be upset, Megan."

Mollie leaned over and straightened the train on Maribeth's gown. "Well, if no one else is going to comment, I guess it's up to me. I think you make a beautiful bride, Maribeth," Mollie said.

"Thanks to you," she replied, hugging Mollie. "At least I didn't have to worry about finding a wedding dress." She glanced back into the mirror. "I'm glad that each of us wore the same dress. I remember watching you make it, Mollie, when Megan got married. I was so excited, thinking about the day that I would be wearing it, too."

Maribeth forced herself to keep playing the role of the ecstatic bride for just a few more hours. She'd discovered a hitherto unknown talent for acting in the past three days.

"I think it's time to—" she began just as someone tapped on the door.

"Maybe Bobby's arrived," Mollie said, hurrying to the door.

As soon as she opened it, Travis peeked inside, saying, "I just got the signal. We're ready to begin. You ladies better get out here, so I can escort the bride down the aisle."

Megan jumped up at the sound of her husband's voice. "Oh, good. Bobby's here, then," she said, joining Mollie at the door.

"All I know is that Chris and the pastor signaled that it was time to start," Travis replied.

Mollie picked up the bridal bouquet and handed it to Maribeth, then kissed her on the cheek. "Here we go, sweetie. I'm getting Megan out of here before she has a heart attack."

Travis must have heard her, because he was chuckling when Maribeth joined him at the door. They could hear the organ pause, then begin the music that was the signal for her sisters to start down the aisle. Only then did Travis look at her and say, "Exactly what are you up to, baby sister?"

She tried to meet his steady gaze, but couldn't hold it. "I don't know what you mean."

"I mean that Bobby is not here and you're not at all surprised. It's my guess that you would be shocked if he were to suddenly show up."

"Fat chance," she muttered under her breath.

"So what's this all about?"

She glanced around the foyer. There was no one there. Everyone was inside waiting for her entrance. Oh, what the heck. It was too late to back out now. She could tell him something of the truth.

"I've decided to take charge of my life."

That certainly got his attention. He stared at her in bewilderment. "What are you talking about?"

She sighed, trying to find the words that would make some sense to him. "I'm leaving home, Travis. It's past time, don't you think? You created a job for me so I wouldn't feel quite so useless around the ranch, but the truth is you don't need me there."

"Has all this wedding hoopla been too much for you, honey? I swear you're not making a lick o' sense. What does your working for me—and you do a damn fine job, I might add—have to do with your bridegroom not showing up?"

"There's our cue. It's time to go," she hurriedly whispered.

She adjusted the veil so that it was over her eyes. She had no trouble seeing, and the netting made a great camouflage for her expression.

The chapel was small. As soon as she stepped into the doorway she saw Chris in a tuxedo standing beside the pastor, both of them watching for her entrance. In that moment, Maribeth felt she was seeing Chris Cochran, the man, for the first time.

He was taller than the pastor by almost a head, probably around six feet tall, with broad shoulders tapering to a slim waist and narrow hips, his long, muscular legs slightly apart and braced.

She'd always taken his dark good looks for granted. Until now. His black-eyed gaze met and held hers. The light from the frosted windows above him emphasized his dark hair, high cheekbones and strong jawline. He was a stranger to her. There was so much she didn't know about him.

How could she possibly be considering marriage to him?

At that moment she saw a tiny muscle in his jaw jump, and she realized that he was as nervous as she was. That made her feel a little better.

They both might be out of their minds for jumping into this, but they were in it together. She made a silent vow to do everything in her power to make their relationship work, starting now. No matter what he said, Chris was giving up a great deal to help her through a bad time in her life. She didn't ever want him to regret his out-of-character impulsiveness.

Maribeth kept her eyes on Chris, although she could feel the gaze of everyone upon her. No doubt they were wondering if she was too nearsighted to notice that the prospective groom was conspicuous by his absence at the front of the church.

She waited until she and Travis had almost reached the altar before whispering, "Would you fill in as Chris's best man?"

Travis glanced down at her in surprise, then looked at Chris who was watching them with narrowed eyes. As usual, Travis was quick to grasp a situation. With a slight squeeze of her hand and a brief nod he escorted her to where the pastor and Chris stood, then stepped back.

There wasn't a sound in the chapel. As far as she could tell, everyone there was holding his and her collective breath, no doubt waiting for her to become hysterical at the sudden realization that Bobby Metcalf had failed to materialize.

Chris stepped forward and firmly took her hand in his.

Maribeth heard several gasps from behind her. Good. They were bound to need air by this time.

"Dearly beloved," the pastor intoned, and began the service as though nothing at all was out of the ordinary. But then he'd been informed of the change as soon as Chris arrived at the church that morning.

When the pastor asked who offered the bride, Travis quietly replied, "Her sisters and me," with such sincerity and love that Maribeth suddenly had a lump in her throat.

Then, as though it had all been rehearsed, Travis stepped over and stood beside Chris instead of returning to the seat reserved for him. She saw Chris slip something into Travis's hand...no doubt her wedding band.

So far, so good.

Maribeth found herself holding her breath when the pastor asked if there was anyone present who could give good cause why the two of them should not wed, and if so, to speak now. From the corner of her eye, she glanced at Megan who stood beside her. She wouldn't put it past her sister to interrupt the ceremony right then and there to demand an explanation. Instead Megan stood staring at the pastor as though watching a white rabbit perform tricks. She obviously didn't know what to expect next.

Only silence greeted the ritualistic question and Maribeth was able to breathe once again.

At the appropriate time Travis calmly offered Chris the ring to slip on her finger. She hadn't seen it until now. It was beautiful—a broad band of intricately carved gold that glowed with a burnished gleam in the suffused light.

She smiled at him when he slipped it onto her finger.

After Chris repeated his vows, the pastor requested the ring she was to put on Chris's finger be presented. But she hadn't bought him a ring! They hadn't discussed it.

Before she could think of what to do, Chris unobtrusively slipped a ring into the palm of her hand, a matching one to the one she now wore.

Startled, she looked at him. His dark eyes held hers with a steady gaze as he held out his hand to her. With trembling fingers she carefully eased the ring over his knuckles while repeating the vows.

Maribeth had never been so aware of another human being in her life as she was of Chris at that moment. She felt as though more than hands had been linked, more than words had been spoken. Something had passed between them, a sense of unity that no mere ceremony could have caused.

"I now pronounce you husband and wife," the pastor said, smiling. To Chris he said, "You may kiss the bride."

She turned to Chris. This part hadn't been rehearsed the night before. This time everything was for real. Even the kiss.

Chris took his time carefully folding the veil back from her face. With a gentleness that continued to startle her, a gentleness she would never have expected from this man, he slipped his arm around her waist and tilted her chin slightly upward with his other hand.

"Hello, Mrs. Cochran," he whispered. "Welcome to my world."

His lips felt warm and even softer than she remembered as he brushed them, oh, so lightly, across hers.

She couldn't seem to control the trembling that suddenly overtook her. She felt flushed and fought the inexplicable urge to cry. When he released her, he took her hand, holding it firmly in his.

When the pastor turned them and introduced Mr. and Mrs. Christopher Cochran to the congregation, she saw that she wasn't the only one experiencing an acute sense of shock and bewilderment.

The triumphant recessional music began and Chris took her arm. By the time they reached the church foyer Maribeth felt surrounded by a sea of people. She leaned against Chris, who immediately wrapped both arms around her, holding her closely against his chest.

She felt light-headed and very strange. She'd never compared the two men before, but now she realized how physically different Bobby and Chris were. Bobby was shorter and more compact, only a few inches taller than she. Standing this close to Chris, Maribeth noticed that the top of her head barely cleared his chin. He was a much larger man than Bobby, his shoulders wider.

She allowed her head to rest against his chest, feeling a sense of protection that was new to her. Through the expensive material of his suit she could feel the rapid beat of his heart. Once again, his outward calm was deceptive. She'd never known anyone so good at hiding what he was feeling.

She wished she knew how he did it. "I'm not at all certain I'm going to be able to carry this off much longer," she murmured beneath the sounds around them. "My knees are shaking so hard I can scarcely stand."

Chris brushed his lips against her neck in a very loverlike expression of affection. "Would you like for me to carry you across the street to the reception? I think my back's up to the job." She could hear the amusement in his voice, even though his expression remained suitably solemn.

That was all either of them had time to say before the crowd began to press in around them, seemingly all talking at once.

Maribeth was glad that the O'Brien sisters had decided to hold the reception at the community center, which was directly across the street from the church. She was in the midst of trying to explain to Chris that she was fairly certain she could walk that far when he suddenly swooped her up into his arms, causing another ripple of reaction in those around them.

Glancing at the gathering crowd he said, "Shall we adjourn this meeting across the street?" Without waiting for a response, he left the church with Maribeth in his arms. She clung to him, almost grateful for his decisive action. For this moment, at least, nothing more was expected of her than to hang on to him.

"The sooner we cut the cake," he murmured into

her ear, "the sooner we can get out of here. I don't know about you, but I'm more than ready to blow this pop stand." The smile he gave her was an intimate one, as though he had already determined what he would prefer to be doing at the moment.

She could feel her face heating up. What in the world was wrong with her, anyway? This was someone she'd known for years. Why was she having such a strong, physical reaction to him when she'd never felt that way toward anyone before?

She laughed a little shakily. "I can't believe we actually went through with it," she replied, looking back over his shoulder at the people continuing to stream out of the church and follow them. "Have you ever seen so many expressions of shock on people's faces? It's quite possible Megan may never forgive me for this."

"Sure she will. It's your life, after all. Besides, everybody needs a little shake up every once in a while. Keeps a person out of a rut."

"Well, I think I've been tossed out of my rut quite adequately this week, thank you very much. I'm really not the adventurous type, you know."

Chris chuckled, allowing her feet to touch the ground once again. "Stick with me, kid, and you'll find it gets easier as you go along." They walked into the decorated community center, which was rapidly filling with family and guests. A small combo was playing in one corner. The music was soft and unobtrusive.

"The place looks great. Did you help with the decorations?" Chris asked.

"I think half the women in town were here, volunteering their services. One of Mollie's friends made the bridal cake, someone else brought the punch."

"Well, I guess it's time for us to face everyone. Are you up for the receiving line?"

"Let's hope. I'll just be glad when today is over and done with."

"Hey, don't wish away your wedding day, Mrs. Cochran. It's supposed to be a happy occasion." He placed a tiny kiss on her temple. "I want you to be happy, Maribeth."

She closed her eyes, inhaling his distinctive aftershave. She went up on tiptoes and kissed his jaw. "Thank you, Chris. For everything you've done for me."

His eyes seemed to be filled with mysterious glints when he smiled at her. "Believe me. The pleasure has been all mine."

Megan rushed up to them. "C'mon, y'all, you've got to get into the receiving line. This whole affair has been crazy enough without forgetting to greet people coming in." She moved off, muttering something about darned kids. For some reason Maribeth didn't think she was referring to her own offspring.

Maribeth exchanged a glance with Chris who grinned back at her. He was right. This *was* her wedding day. It wasn't the one she'd expected to have, and Chris certainly wasn't the man she'd thought would be standing by her side. Nevertheless, the deed was now done. It was too late for regrets or second thoughts. It was time to celebrate the union.

Maribeth tucked her arm through his and said,

"We might as well go face all the curious stares. I wonder if anyone is brave enough to demand explanations?"

"There's only one way to find out. Shall we go?"

She and Chris received many blessings and well-wishes from friends in the next hour. No one was impolite enough to actually ask what happened to Bobby Metcalf, whose name had been on the wedding invitations, but several admitted to being surprised at the way things had turned out.

However, it was Travis who summed up everyone's attitude when he paused long enough in the line to give Maribeth an exuberant kiss before shaking Chris's hand and solemnly asking, "The groom, I presume?" which caused a great deal of nervous laughter.

Chris thanked him for filling in as best man, but Travis waved his thanks away. "Hey, I was glad to be of some help. Maribeth has continued to be a source of surprise to this entire family on more than one occasion. I don't know why we should be surprised that she'd pull off something like this."

Maribeth began to relax after that, believing the worst was behind them. She saw Chris's mother and grandparents come in after the receiving line had disbanded. She took Chris's hand and led him over to greet them.

"I'm so glad you came to the wedding today, Mrs. Cochran, Mr. and Mrs. Lambert. I suppose Chris told you about our plans before you came."

His grandmother was the first to speak. "At first I didn't really believe he was serious, Maribeth. I suppose that's one reason I had to come today. Not that I wouldn't have wanted to see you get married and all, but I haven't been getting out much lately."

Maribeth could see how frail the older woman had become since she'd seen her last. She carefully hugged her. "I'm so glad you managed to be here."

His grandfather didn't say much. He just awkwardly patted her hand, shook Chris's hand, then helped his wife to one of the chairs arranged nearby.

Maribeth turned to say something to Chris's mother, but found her already in conversation with him. "I don't know why I should have been surprised by your actions," she was saying in a low, caustic voice. "You are your father's son, after all. It must be gratifying to grab the prettiest girl in the county away from your best friend. I tried my best to raise you with some kind of morals and a sense of ethics, but I can't fight genetics."

Maribeth glanced at Chris, surprised at the venom in the woman's voice. This was her only child she was talking to, after all. His face registered no response to her words. He looked at her as politely, as impassively, as he'd greeted everyone there.

Maribeth couldn't just stand by and let his mother think so wrongly about Chris. He'd done nothing wrong. His actions had been highly honorable. "Mrs. Cochran, you don't understand. Chris was—"

"Don't explain," he said, firmly cutting off her words. "It doesn't matter." To his mother, he said, "Thank you for coming despite your feelings."

"I wouldn't have come if I'd thought there was a

chance your father might be here. You assured me he wouldn't be.''

"That's right. He doesn't know about the sudden switch in my plans. When I left Dallas on Wednesday, I was coming down to be Bobby's best man. I haven't spoken to him since then.''

She looked amused. "It was smart of you to marry her before your dad gets a glimpse of her. Otherwise, he might have tried to snap her up himself.'' As though feeling the need to explain her remark to Maribeth, she smiled brilliantly at her and said, "You see, Chris's father trades in wives like most men trade in their cars—always for a newer, flashier model. So far, Chris seems to be determined to be just like his father with his fancy cars and his fancy women.''

Maribeth almost choked in surprise. "Are you talking about me?'' she asked. "I'm the last person to be considered fancy.''

"You can't help being what you are, Maribeth. You've always been beautiful. You can't be anything else. I'm sure Chris is going to enjoy showing you off to all his rich, snobbish friends...until he gets bored. Being his father's son, that won't take long.''

"Let it go, Mother, okay? I've been married a little more than an hour. Try not to make too many predictions about the future of my marriage at this stage. Who knows? Maybe I'll surprise you.'' He glanced around. "The photographer is waiting for us to cut the cake so he can finish getting pictures. Would you like to join us at the head table?''

"No. I'll sit with the folks. They aren't going to want to stay long.''

Chris hugged his mother. "I'll be in touch." He took Maribeth's hand and led her to the head table.

She looked over her shoulder at his mother. "Chris, don't you think we should—"

"There's nothing we can do, Maribeth. I know her attitude must seem strange to you, being raised in the kind of family you have. I'll explain later."

There was no more time for talk. Once again, they were caught up in the traditional routines of a wedding celebration.

The photographer took pictures as they cut the cake and fed each other a bite. Then Mollie took over and helped them pass out pieces of the tasty confection to each guest.

Toasts were made and the traditional first dance was performed, Maribeth nervously following Chris's lead. "I don't know how to dance," she murmured when he took her out on the dance floor with everyone watching.

"Something else I can teach you how to do," he replied with a wicked glint in his eye. He wrapped his arm firmly around her waist and guided her through the simple steps that kept time to the music.

His words successfully distracted her from her self-consciousness. "Something else?"

"Mmm-hmm."

"What else do you intend to teach me?"

He grinned. "Oh, I don't know. I'll try to think of something."

"Are you trying to say that you have more experience than I have?"

"In some things. Perhaps."

"Perhaps! Are we talking about what your mama warned you no gentleman talks about?"

He began to laugh. "Ah, Maribeth. What a delight you are. You have made me a very happy man."

"I have?"

"Oh, yes. I will be forever grateful to Bobby Metcalf for stepping aside and leaving the field open for me."

"Grateful! How could you possibly feel that Bobby's behavior could be—"

"We'll talk about it later…say, on the ride to San Antonio."

"San Antonio? I thought we were going to Dallas?"

"I'm a little embarrassed to have to admit that as soon as we're through here, I have to get back to work. I forgot about that when we were talking earlier this week. Not that my working would have stopped me from marrying you. It's just that you're going to get an immediate taste of what my life is like."

She could hear a rueful acceptance in his voice that she'd not heard before.

"I don't understand."

"Another thing to discuss on our way. At least our life together won't be boring, right?"

Then it was time for more photographs. This time the groom was to remove the bride's garter and toss it to the male guests.

He took his own sweet time about removing it from her thigh. "Chris!" she hissed. "For Pete's sake, hurry up." Her words created a great deal of laughter and ribald remarks about her impatience. From the look in his eyes as he grinned at her while kneeling in front of her, he knew exactly why she was bothered.

Maribeth lived in jeans. She wasn't used to wearing dresses, or hose, or garters. And she certainly wasn't used to having a man slide his fingers along her calf, her knee and her inner thigh. His touch was causing strange sensations all over her body. Her breasts were tingling and butterflies had lodged in her stomach.

She was relieved when he finally retrieved the garter and blithely tossed it over his shoulder. He stood, grabbed her in his arms and gave her a robust kiss, much to the delight and applause of those watching.

"Throw the bouquet!" was the next directive.

In moments the single women were gathered in front of her. She tossed it high in the air, but didn't see who caught it because Chris whisked her back onto the dance floor. "They're playing our song," he explained, gathering her into his arms.

"We don't have a song, you idiot!" she managed to gasp when she'd caught her breath.

He sighed in contentment after aligning her body to his. "We do now." Both of his arms were wrapped around her waist, so that she had no choice but to rest her hands on his chest.

"How much champagne have you had today?" she asked suspiciously.

"None. I never drink when I know I'm going to be flying."

"Is that what you meant about going to work?"

"Mmm. One of the company planes is in San Antonio. I'm flying it back to Dallas tonight, so that it will be ready to leave tomorrow."

"You're leaving tomorrow?"

"Unless I can get another pilot to take it. We rotate, and it's my turn."

"Where will you be going?"

"Atlanta...then Miami. My dad does considerable business in that area."

"Oh."

"I figure either place is as good a spot for a honeymoon as anywhere else."

"Then you can take me with you?"

"That's right. Or I'm not going."

"But what about your car?"

"One of the mechanics will get it back to Dallas for me. Believe me, they won't find it a hardship."

"Oh."

She'd wanted a different life, hadn't she? Well, that was what she was getting. Whenever she'd considered her postmarriage plans she'd seen herself in Dallas, finding a job, brushing up on her cooking skills, waiting for Chris to come home. It only now occurred to her that he might not have a nine-to-five occupation.

He glanced around at all the other couples now taking the floor. "Do you think we can sneak away for you to change out of that dress? I think you'll be more comfortable in something a little less formal for the flight back."

She, too, glanced around. "I don't think anyone is going to miss us." They took their time leaving the dance floor, stopping to speak to several couples, but eventually they were able to slip out a side door.

''Where are your clothes?'' Chris asked, standing on the curb. It was almost dark and the streetlights offered circles of light along the street.

''At the church. I'll go over and change. I won't be long.''

''Do you need some help?''

Before she could answer both Megan and Mollie joined them. ''We thought you might need help changing out of that dress,'' Mollie said, smiling.

''Yeah, I distinctly remember it took two people to get out of it,'' Megan said, obviously amused about something.

Maribeth and Chris exchanged glances and she shrugged. ''Thanks. It would probably save time.'' She didn't see why Megan found that remark funny, but Megan laughed and agreed with her.

''Deke hid your car at our place,'' Mollie said. ''He should be back with it any minute.'' She eyed her new brother-in-law ruefully. ''Here we thought you were being so generous, loaning your car to Bobby and Maribeth. Little did we know.''

Chris didn't bat an eye at her teasing admonishment. ''I appreciate y'all taking care of it for me.''

They heard the sound of a high-powered engine coming slowly toward them. Deke drove up in Chris's car and paused by the group standing by the side of the street. He double-parked and got out of the car. ''What's the matter? Am I late?''

''Not at all,'' Chris assured him. ''Maribeth needs to change before we can take off. Your timing couldn't be better.''

''That is one sweet baby to drive,'' Deke admitted,

giving him the keys. "Thanks for letting me have the opportunity to drive it."

The three women left the men talking cars and engine performance and hurried into the church, where Maribeth had stored the summer dress she'd intended to wear once the ceremony was over. She wished now that she'd opted for her jeans. She needed something that was familiar to her.

She also knew that she wasn't going to escape the questions and comments any longer, now that her sisters had gotten her alone.

They didn't disappoint her.

"I just hope you know what you're doing," Mollie began the subject while she quickly unbuttoned the back of the gown.

"Me, too," Maribeth replied with devout sincerity.

After a lengthy silence that led her to believe they weren't going to make any other comments, Megan suddenly spoke up.

"What did you do with Bobby, anyway?" Her tone couldn't have sounded more casual.

Maribeth could feel her cheeks going red. "I didn't do anything with him, for Pete's sake! What in the world do you think I would have done with him?"

Mollie helped her to step out of her gown while Megan handed Maribeth her dress, then helped her slide her arms through the sleeves before answering.

"You can't really blame me for wondering, can you? After all, you've talked about marrying Bobby Metcalf for years. And yet I just watched you marry Chris Cochran despite all your plans. Pardon me for being confused about what's going on."

All right. So she owed them an explanation. What did it matter, anyway? The deed was done. Nobody was going to talk her out of her decision now. Was that what she had been afraid of? How strange.

Maribeth found her other shoes and put them on, then began to pull the pins out of her hair. Megan and Mollie watched her in silence.

"Do you remember when Chris stopped by the ranch on Wednesday?" she finally asked, brushing her hair out, then absently braiding it into her usual thick plait.

Megan was the first to answer. "You mean when you stayed out with him until all hours? Of course I remember. I should have known something was up then, shouldn't I?"

Maribeth turned away from the mirror and sat down in one of the chairs. She motioned for her sisters to join her. "Chris came down from Dallas to tell me that Bobby had called him the night before from Las Vegas. It seems that Bobby suddenly got the urge to elope. So he did. I never found out who the bride turned out to be. I just know it wasn't me."

Her sisters stared at her as though they'd been caught in suspended animation. She looked at each of them before glancing down at her fingers, which were nervously toying with her belt. "Chris offered to step in and become the groom. After thinking it over, I took him up on his offer."

Mollie was the first one to find her voice. "But, Maribeth! Why didn't you tell us? Why would you decide to jump into a new relationship rather than face what had happened between you and Bobby? It certainly wasn't your fault that Bobby did something so crazy. It seems to me that you've just compounded the problem, impulsively jumping into marriage with somebody you don't know.''

"I know Chris," Maribeth immediately replied, knowing she sounded defensive, but not being able to help it. "I know him as well as I know Bobby."

"I guess that isn't saying all that much, now, is it?" Megan drawled. "I thought you were happy living with us. I had no idea you were so desperate to leave home that you'd go to such lengths to get away."

Maribeth jumped up from her chair and knelt beside Megan. She couldn't stop the tears that suddenly filled her eyes when she hugged Megan.

"Please don't take what I've done personally, Megan. Please. You know I love you and Travis and the kids. It's just that it's past time for me to be out on my own. I—''

"Out on your own!" Megan repeated incredulously. "Is that what you think you've done? Honey, I don't know quite how to break the news to you, but you'd better think again. You are Christopher Cochran's wife. You are not out on your own."

"I know. It's just that—''

"Don't you have any idea who his family is?"

"Well, his mother—''

"No. I don't mean his mother. I'm talking about Kenneth Cochran." Megan shook her head. "I don't think you have a clue what you're going to find as the daughter-in-law of Kenneth Cochran. That man moves in some pretty high-and-mighty circles. And you've never even met him, have you?''

''No, but what difference does that make?''

Mollie patted her hand, then pulled her to her feet. ''Hopefully everything is going to work out just fine for you, Maribeth. All we want for you is your happiness. You know that, don't you?''

Once again Maribeth's eyes filled with tears as she and Mollie hugged.

They pulled away at the sound of a knock on the door. It was Chris. ''Maribeth? Are you about ready to go?''

She looked at her sisters, then at the door. The time had come for her to take her first step away from her family and toward her future. She wasn't ready. Suddenly she knew that.

All Maribeth wanted to do at the moment was to be twelve years old again, feeling safe and secure with her sisters.

She swallowed. ''Sorry to keep you waiting, Chris,'' she said, opening the door. Her voice sounded a little ragged, but she couldn't help it. She turned to Megan and Mollie. ''I've gotta go.'' She hugged each of them one more time. ''I'll give you a call soon. I promise. Things are going to work all right. I know they will.''

She turned back to Chris, who stood in the doorway watching her with a sympathetic smile on his face, just as though he knew how difficult this moment was for her. However, his voice sounded light when he asked, ''Ready?''

She nodded, suddenly unable to make a sound.

"Good. I moved the car around to the back, but we're pushing our luck the longer we stay. I have horrible visions of my car covered with streamers and the windows soaped with messages."

She turned back to her sisters. "Thanks for everything. You've been wonderful. I'm going to miss you."

Megan shooed them out the door. "I know, I know, for all of two minutes. Call us and tell us where you'll be, give us a phone number or an address so we won't feel that you've dropped off the face of the earth."

"I will." She turned to Chris who took her hand and led her down the hallway to one of the doors that led to the back parking lot.

"You okay?" he asked softly.

Thank God it was too dark for him to see her face. "Of course."

"I know it's tough, leaving home for the final time, even when it's the natural cycle of events."

She was glad he understood. But then Chris seemed to understand her very well.

When they pulled out onto the street they found a small group, mostly family, standing on the curb waving. Maribeth waved back until they were out of sight, then slowly turned around in her seat and faced the road.

"I left my packed bags at the ranch. There really isn't much there. I was appalled to discover that everything I own could be packed into two suitcases."

"Don't worry about it. We'll go shopping once we get home."

They reached the ranch and picked up the suitcases

that she'd left just inside the kitchen door. Within minutes they were back on the road.

Chris's casual comment kept echoing in her head. *When we get home*... Home. At the moment Maribeth knew that she no longer had a home. Oh, she was sure that eventually she would be able to call Chris's place home. Someday. In the meantime, she had left the O'Brien ranch—the only home she'd ever known—for good.

She looked at Chris, seeing his profile as he watched for the highway that would take them to San Antonio. He was a good man. She knew Megan and Mollie couldn't understand how she could have been so impulsive. After all, both of them had married men they loved and who loved them. She was glad they hadn't questioned her about her feelings for Chris because the truth was, she wasn't at all certain of them.

Today had been filled with all kinds of revelations. Nobody, not even Bobby, had affected her in quite the way Chris did when he gave her a certain look, a look she'd seen more than once today...as though she was a very tempting banquet and he was a starving man.

The look unnerved her and yet... It called to her to find out more. What, exactly, would it be like to be able to satisfy a man's appetite? To fulfill all his intimate longings? The realization that she wanted to find out truly unnerved her. She was tired of wondering about that part of life. She wanted to learn everything that Chris was willing to teach her.

She shivered.

"Are you cold?" he immediately asked, verifying—if she'd had any need—that he was acutely aware of her.

"Oh, no. I'm fine."

"I can turn down the air-conditioning if you'd like."

"No, really. It's quite comfortable."

"If you're sleepy, try to get some rest. We'll be in San Antonio in a couple of hours."

She closed her eyes. Not because she was sleepy, but because she was stunned by her feelings. She was just as aware of Chris as he was of her. Bobby's betrayal had freed her in some very basic way that she wasn't able to understand. He'd hurt her badly. But by his actions Chris had made her feel that Bobby's desertion wasn't the end of the world after all.

Perhaps if she'd had more time, she wouldn't have gone through with this marriage, but at this moment she could not make herself regret it.

Four

Chris interrupted her musing when he reached over and turned on the radio. "I suppose I might as well start confessing now," he said. "You'll find out soon enough."

She glanced at him warily, a little unnerved by his seriousness. "All right," she responded, mentally bracing herself for she knew not what.

"Despite the fact that I was raised deep in the heart of Texas, my musical preference is jazz. Is that going to upset you?"

She rested her head in her palm and groaned. "I thought you were going to tell me something awful!"

"Well, ma'am, confessing that I'm not a fan of country-and-western music is enough to get me run out of the state and my birth certificate revoked. If

I'd told you any sooner, you might never have married me.''

She shook her head. ''I can see that I'm going to have to get used to your weird sense of humor.''

''Among other things,'' he drawled.

''Maybe you'd better tell me about some of those others things so I won't have any more rude surprises.''

''Oh, nothing earthshaking. Just your usual, run-of-the-mill habits that people who live together have to get used to in another person. You have to remember that you don't know if I'm messy or neat, whether I'm a morning person or a night person, if I snore, what my favorite meal is, my—''

''All right,'' she replied, amused by his attitude. ''Are you messy or neat? Do you snore? What is your favorite meal?''

He chuckled a little. ''Actually I'm fairly neat, but not obsessively so. I'm definitely a morning person, but since I don't need much sleep, I'm fairly late in going to bed. As far as snoring, I really couldn't answer that one.''

''What about your favorite meal?''

''A big ol' thick T-bone steak, with lots of French fries and mushrooms.''

''That sounds Texan enough for you to be allowed to live here. It also sounds fairly simple. As long as we're confessing our deepest secrets, I guess I never mentioned that I'm not much in the kitchen.''

His grin flashed white in the shadows of the car. ''Nope. You never did.''

''That's because I never had to be. Mollie's the

homemaker in the family. I manage to get by.'' She thought about some of the other things he mentioned. ''I'm used to getting up early, but I have to admit that I end up doing things out of habit and not because I'm awake. I don't know about the snoring part.''

''Do you have a favorite meal?''

''Not really. I'm willing to eat whatever's there.''

They lapsed into silence after that but it was more companionable, somehow. Maribeth felt herself relaxing, the soft music a soothing background to her drifting thoughts. She didn't realize she'd fallen asleep until she opened her eyes when the car slowed down. They were pulling into the gate of an airfield. She straightened and looked around in surprise.

''I must have been more tired than I thought,'' she said, feeling more than a little self-conscious. ''I didn't expect to fall asleep.''

''You needed it, I'm sure. You've been under quite a strain these past few days.'' Although he was obviously speaking to her, Chris's attention was on the airfield. He was looking around the area, his gaze not missing much.

''It hasn't been a picnic for you, either,'' she murmured. If he heard her, he chose not to comment.

They pulled into a small parking area beside one of the hangars. ''It looks like everything's ready for us,'' he commented. He reached into the back of the car and retrieved his coat jacket and tie. Once out of the car, he tossed the jacket over his shoulder and came around the other side. The lights from the open hangar cast long shadows across him. He leaned over and opened her door.

"I'll get our bags out of the trunk," he said, once she was standing beside him.

"I can help."

Without saying anything more, he opened the trunk and handed her the smallest one, which happened to be his. Then he led the way across the tarmac to the hangar. She had to hurry to keep up with his long-legged stride. "None of these people expect you to have someone with you, do they?"

"It doesn't matter. They work for the company and do what they're told."

Was it her imagination or was there a trace of bitterness in his voice?

"What about your father? Does he care when you take people with you on these trips?"

"You're the first, so it's never come up."

She liked the sound of that and smiled to herself.

When she got a glimpse of the plane Maribeth blinked in surprise. She hadn't been around planes before; in fact, she'd never flown in her life. But the thought didn't frighten her. Instead she was excited to be here.

It was her wedding night, and anything was possible.

Chris placed the luggage inside the plane, a jet that was smaller than the commercial ones she'd seen, but considerably larger than a private plane. He took her hand and led her inside an office where he spoke with two of the men there.

After handing his car keys to one of them, he picked up some papers and they entered the hangar once again.

The plane was now sitting out front. Chris helped her on board. The interior looked like a luxurious lounge. She'd never seen anything like it outside of movies and television. Was this what Megan had meant? Chris seemed to be at home with all of this.

"You can sit wherever you like. It's a short flight. We should be on the ground and on our way to my place within the hour."

She could see that his mind was already on the trip ahead. "I'll be fine. Thanks."

He moved toward the front of the plane, then hesitated. He spun around and in a few quick strides returned to where she had sat down. He leaned over and cupped her face in his hands. "I'd let you up front with me except you're entirely too distracting." He gave her a hard, possessive kiss, then quickly retraced his steps, closing the door to the cockpit behind him.

She stared at the closed door, dazed by his sudden, unpredictable behavior. She was quickly learning that there was nothing she knew about Chris that could help her in this situation. There was no trace of the boy she'd once known.

Like it or not, she was married to a stranger. Mysterious, attractive and sexy. *Her husband*.

The flight to Dallas fascinated her. She'd been too enthralled in all the sensations of a first-time flight to be frightened.

Knowing that Chris was at the controls gave an added sense of adventure. She spent the time looking out the porthole window at the lights below, amazed at the number of cities scattered across the landscape.

By the time they landed she was filled with all kinds of questions for Chris. The whole experience had been fun. Who would have believed that she would be flying for the very first time on her wedding day...? Or night, as it was by now. Chris had teased her about teaching her new things, hadn't he?

She felt a little inadequate, actually. There was so much she didn't know. In a way she was glad she'd already confessed her lack of sexual knowledge to Chris. She was so glad that she and Bobby had never been intimate. She didn't think it would have made any difference to Bobby's choices and ultimate behavior, but it would have made his betrayal so much harder for her to bear.

She peered out the window at this larger airfield. When the door from the cockpit opened she was still safely buckled into her seat.

Chris walked over to her. "Well? How was it? Do you think you're going to enjoy flying?" He flipped open her seat belt and helped her to her feet.

"Oh, Chris, it was wonderful! I had no idea that—"

The sound of the outside door opening stopped her. They both glanced around in time to see three men step through the opening.

"Well, son, looks like you made it back from San Antonio just fine," the man in the lead said to Chris.

This must be Kenneth Cochran. He made a very imposing figure. Maribeth could see the family resemblance between the two men—both were tall with dark hair and eyes. There were flashes of gray in the older man's hair. He had a piercing gaze, sizing up the situation and prepared to deal with whatever was going on. He looked like a man who was used to being in control. There was an aura of power about him, enhanced by the expensive suit that must have been tailored for him.

The other two men with him were equally well dressed, no doubt successful businessmen. Each of them carried briefcases as though the bags were extensions of themselves. They probably were.

Chris kept his arm around Maribeth's waist. "I didn't expect you to meet the plane." She'd never heard him sound so cool. "Is this a welcoming committee?" he asked dryly.

The older man showed no reaction to his son's less-than-friendly greeting. "Not at all. Just a slight adjustment in plans. We decided not to wait until morning to go to Atlanta. I've already had them file your flight plan leaving as soon as you're ready to go." Two men dressed in khaki coveralls appeared in the doorway carrying luggage.

Chris glanced at Maribeth before he spoke. "In that case, would it be possible to get someone else to take the flight? I'd made plans on being home tonight."

The smile Kenneth Cochran gave his son wasn't a friendly one. His dark gaze flicked to Maribeth before returning to Chris, his eyes revealing nothing of his thoughts. In a light tone, he said, "Ah, you brought company along, did you? Importing them these days." He stepped closer to them, not missing much about either one of them.

Maribeth had never felt more rustic or uncomfortable in her life. She had a sudden vision of what this sophisticated man must see. She wasn't used to wearing dresses, but Mollie had insisted she start off for her honeymoon wearing one. Instead of leaving her hair in the elaborate arrangement Mollie had worked on so diligently, she'd absently rebraided it in its usual style. Suddenly she felt embarrassed and out of place in these luxurious surroundings.

That laser gaze paused in its inspection of what he must consider her many shortcomings. She felt as though he was peering deep into her soul. "My son seems to have lost whatever manners he ever had," he said, his tone tinged with irony. He held out his hand. "As you've guessed, I'm his father. And you are—?"

Out of habit she used the name she'd had until a few hours ago. "Maribeth O'Brien…"

"Cochran," Chris smoothly added when she paused. "Maribeth and I were married earlier today."

Whatever his father's reaction to this news, Kenneth hid it well. His gaze veered to Chris. His voice, which he used with the skill of a musician playing an instrument, now carried a hint of amusement. "Really? I could have sworn you said you were attending a school chum's wedding. What happened? Did the bug suddenly bite you, as well?"

Maribeth couldn't believe this conversation. It was totally bizarre. It was as if the father was baiting his son about something as important as his marriage. She glanced at Chris to see his reaction, but like his father, Chris gave nothing of his thoughts away.

"Something like that" was all he said. "I'd like to take a few days off, if it's all right with you. Maybe Sam would be able to fill in for me on this trip, considering the circumstances."

Kenneth continued to ignore Chris's request. "Rather sudden, wasn't it?" This time his intent gaze on her was deliberately provocative. She felt as though he was assessing everything about her, from the color and texture of her hair and the way she was dressed to the sandals on her feet. "You two known each other long?"

Maribeth wasn't sure who he was talking to, but it didn't matter because Chris immediately answered, "Long enough." His voice gave nothing of his thoughts or feelings away.

Kenneth laughed shortly and turned to the two men with him. "I swear, the kid's becoming more like me every day."

Maribeth almost shuddered. She couldn't think of anything worse. She was beginning to better understand his mother's comments. Kenneth Cochran was one of the most intimidating men she'd ever met. What must it have been like being married to him?

Kenneth turned back to them. "Hell, Chris, you can honeymoon as well in Atlanta as you can in Dallas. Better, even. I'll put you up in the fanciest suite they've got there. Once we land, you won't need to do anything for me until we fly to Miami later in the week. What could be better?"

Maribeth could feel the tension emanating from Chris and wondered about it. She wasn't certain if he was angry or whether he didn't like having to be in a position to ask anything of his father.

She didn't want to cause trouble between the two men. "We could do that, couldn't we, Chris?" She smiled at Kenneth. "I've never been to Atlanta."

Once again Kenneth laughed. "Why doesn't that surprise me? From the looks of you, honey, I'd say you were freshly hatched." He winked at Chris. "You've got the right idea, son. Get 'em young and teach 'em yourself, right?"

A ripple moved through Chris and for a moment Maribeth was afraid he might lunge at the other man. He didn't. Instead he waited a moment before glancing at Maribeth. He smiled, but his eyes glittered with anger.

"In that case," Chris said, as though his father hadn't spoken, "We'll go to Atlanta tonight if you think you'd like that." He glanced around at the other men before his gaze rested on his father. "I'll need to get some clean clothes. I only took a few things with me when I packed earlier this week. I was counting on being able to repack before we left in the morning."

Kenneth reached into his inside breast pocket and pulled out a wallet. "No time for that. Here. You and your little missy can go shopping once we get to Atlanta." He handed what looked to be several hundred dollar bills to Chris. When he didn't reach out to take them, Kenneth calmly folded them and stuck them into Chris's shirt pocket. "Consider it the first of my wedding presents to you. I'm proud of you, son. You finally took a piece of my advice, may wonders never cease. I have to admit that you've surprised me. You've never shown much interest in being a dutiful son before.'' He glanced at Maribeth and winked. ''I'm pleased you at least listened to me on this one. You've got a fine eye for quality, boy, I'll certainly give you that.''

Kenneth turned to the other men. ''Well, gentlemen. Find a place to get comfortable. You're in safe hands with Chris here flying us. He's the best there is, I've made damn sure of that!''

Chris took her hand. ''C'mon. I'll show you around while I make sure everything's ready for this leg of the trip.''

She was glad he didn't leave her in the plane with his father and friends. Things were happening faster than she could quite handle at the moment.

Maribeth slept most of the flight to Atlanta. Once she awakened, she kept her eyes closed rather than having to make conversation with Kenneth Cochran. Not that he paid her much attention once they were on their way. She dozed off with the sound of his voice filling the area around her. She couldn't make out much of the conversation, but it sounded as though he was persuading them to either invest with his company or to buy products he sold. He was quite a salesman, she would give him that. He wore his confidence and self-assurance as if it were a royal robe.

So this was Chris's father.

She'd learned more about Chris and his family today than in all the years they'd been friends. Thinking back, she realized that when they were children, she, Bobby and Chris rarely talked about their home life. She'd known that Chris lived with his mother during the school year and spent his summers in Dallas with his father.

Once he returned at the beginning of the new school year, the three of them took up where they'd left off when school was dismissed for the summer. Now that she thought about it, Chris had never talked about what it was like to live in Dallas, or what he did during those summers he was away. He just seemed eager to join in the group activities once he returned to Agua Verde.

Was that why he'd seemed such a loner? Had he made friends in Dallas? Had it been difficult to be pulled between the two parents? She didn't know because he never talked about himself.

He'd been a good student, much better than she was…or Bobby. Chris seemed to thrive on challenges back then.

Well, he'd certainly picked a new challenge to face now. Although she'd been planning for her marriage for most of her life, it now seemed Chris had never given it much thought.

Friendship was one thing. Marriage was a very different matter. She still didn't understand why he'd been willing to help her save face.

If she'd had more time to think it through, she wondered if she would have married him? At the time he'd offered her a short-range solution.

Only time would tell if a marriage between them would create more problems than it had solved.

* * *

Chris slipped the card into the slot of the hotel suite and opened the door, then turned and lifted her into his arms. "This wasn't exactly how I'd planned this, but I'm determined to carry you over the threshold," he said, his eyes smiling into hers.

"The bellhop's going to know we just got married," she whispered as she heard the elevator *ping* announcing that someone was getting off on this floor. At this late hour, it was a good guess that it was their luggage being delivered.

He stepped inside. "Who cares?" He spun her in a circle before allowing her to stand once more. "So, Mrs. Cochran. What do you think?"

She was still trying to take it all in when the bellhop brought in their luggage. He opened another set of double doors into a large bedroom area. She watched as he walked over and flipped on a light, then closed the draperies across the wide glass doors that went out onto a balcony.

"Does your father treat all his pilots this well?"

He laughed. "Hardly. He was showing off tonight. It doesn't matter who the audience is, he's immediately 'on.'"

"Does it bother you?" she asked, then waited while he tipped the bellhop and closed the door behind him.

"Does my father bother me? Sometimes. You'd think by now that I'd be used to him."

"How long have you worked for him?"

"About eight months."

"Oh! I thought— I just assumed that you went to work for him once we graduated."

"No. I never intended to work for him. It's ironic how things happen sometimes." He slowly paced back to where she stood in front of the bedroom doorway. "Are you hovering here in the doorway for a specific reason?"

"Uh, no, not really." She looked around uncertainly. "I'm not sure what to do next, that's all."

"Well, since it's after two o'clock local time, I don't think we'd be out of line to consider going to bed. What do you think?"

Although his tone was gentle, he made no effort to hide his amusement. She knew her face must be flaming but she refused to look away from him. "All right," she managed to say.

"Which suitcase do you want?"

"The smaller one."

He placed it on the rack. "There you are. I'll be a gentleman and let you have first use of the bathroom."

This was getting worse and worse. She felt so awkward. Was it like this for everyone? She wasn't used to sharing a room. She hadn't had to share a bathroom since Mollie got married. Why couldn't she feel more casual about all of this? After all, she was married. This was all perfectly normal. Or at least it would be once she got used to it.

She gathered up her gown and toiletry bag and hurried to the bathroom, closing the door behind her. Her image stared back in the mirror. Maribeth had never seen herself look so flustered and uncertain. She couldn't believe that she was acting so silly.

By the time she came out, she had changed into

the white, tiny-pleated, full-length satin-and-lace nightgown Mollie had given her together with a matching robe. She concentrated on trying to feel relaxed and at ease with the situation. She was almost able to pull it off until she saw Chris.

He'd taken off his shirt, socks and shoes and was stretched out on the turned-back bed, his arms behind his head, watching her.

Maribeth felt as though she'd just received a body blow. Feeling winded, she could only stare at the wide expanse of muscled chest. He swung up and off the bed and when she would have stepped aside he stopped her with a touch. Leaning to kiss her, he said, "I'll be right back. Don't fall asleep on me."

She was still standing there when the bathroom door closed behind him. *Fat chance of that,* was all she could think of in response to his comment.

Hastily discarding her robe, she slid beneath the covers and fought the urge to drag them to her neck. Her gown adequately covered her. There was no reason to be embarrassed, she kept reminding herself.

The sound of the bathroom door opening made her jump before she could restrain herself. She glanced around and saw that Chris had removed his trousers. He was now wearing a pair of black briefs that clung to him as if they were a second skin.

She hastily averted her eyes, but couldn't seem to control the urge to glance back at him. He was gorgeous! Trim and lean and muscled, in obvious good physical condition.

As soon as he got into bed, she reached for the light the bellhop had turned on earlier.

"Would you mind if we leave the light on?" he asked.

"Uh, no. I, uh, just assumed that—"

He laughed. "Oh, I don't need a night-light, if that's what you're thinking. I'm just not quite ready to go to sleep. I want to see you...if that's all right with you."

She almost strangled herself trying to swallow. "Mmm," was the best she could manage as an answer.

"The bed's quite comfortable, don't you think?" he asked, smiling.

She nodded vigorously and made another strangled sound.

"Is the temperature all right for you? Would you rather have it warmer...or cooler?"

This time she vigorously shook her head. "It's fine," she said, sounding a little hoarse.

"Maribeth?" His voice was very soft.

"What?"

"You don't have to be afraid of me, you know. I'm not going to pounce on you."

"I realize that," she admitted. "I just don't know what to do."

"If you'd rather go on to sleep tonight, we can. I don't want you to feel pushed into anything—"

"Sleep! How can I possibly sleep? I've never slept with anybody in my whole life!"

He grinned. "Well, neither have I. It will be a new experience for both of us."

She stared at him with patent disbelief. "But you

told me that— Well, I know you've had more experience than I have.''

''Maybe,'' he conceded. ''But probably not as much as you're imagining. And I've never actually slept with anyone. I've been looking forward to doing that with you, actually. Just the idea of sleeping with my arms around you is a fantasy I never thought to experience.''

She relaxed a little, and slid back down beneath the covers. ''You've fantasized about me?''

''Oh, yes. Many times…all kinds.''

''Will you tell me about some of them?''

''I'd much rather show you,'' he said, and moved closer until he was lying close enough to touch her.

Five

She could feel the heat of his body radiating down her entire length and he hadn't as yet touched her. This man was potent stuff. She couldn't remember a time when she so desperately wanted to be relaxed and at ease. Instead she was so rattled, she couldn't think of anything to say or do in this situation.

Why hadn't she asked Megan or Mollie about what to expect? The truth was, none of them had ever discussed this aspect of marriage.

He placed his hand lightly on her stomach and she almost shot out of bed. "Try to relax," he murmured. "There's no rush, you know. I want you to feel comfortable."

She was feeling several different things at the moment, none of which came remotely close to comfortable. She took a deep breath and exhaled, a time-honored remedy to bring on a sense of relaxation.

Nope. It didn't work.

She was too aware of his hand. His thumb rested just beneath her breasts, while his fingers lay along the bottom of her rib cage. The silk covering her had never seemed so thin. She could almost feel the material heating. It would be a wonder if there weren't scorch marks soon.

She swallowed, hard.

''What would you like to do?'' he asked.

''Do?'' she croaked.

''Have you any fantasies you'd like to check out?''

Despite what she'd expected, she was beginning to adjust to his warm hand resting against her. He was propped up on his other elbow, his expression very tender.

Hesitantly she touched the curls on his chest with her fingers. He made a soft noise that sounded suspiciously like a purr.

''You like that?''

''Yes, ma'am, I certainly do. You have my permission to touch me as much as you'd like.''

Maribeth was pleased with the idea of being the one touching, of being in control. She shifted so that she could face him. His hand quite naturally continued to move around her waist and rested lightly on her hip. He allowed his fingers to drift lazily back and forth, sliding the silken material over her skin. She liked the feel of that as well.

She brushed her fingers across his chest, feeling the smooth surface covering the muscled expanse. When she touched his nipples hidden in the mat of curls, he took a quick breath. She could feel his heartbeat increase.

A sense of power swept over her, one she'd never felt before. She forgot to feel nervous in pursuit of this new pleasure she'd discovered.

He sighed and relaxed back against the pillow. She traced the shape of his brows and nose, his cheek and jaw, and the sensuous curve of his upper lip. He made that purring sound again.

Acting on impulse she placed her lips over his. They were as warm as she remembered and quickly responded to the light pressure. He wrapped his arms around her and took over the kiss.

By the time he pulled away slightly, they were both breathless. In addition, Maribeth knew exactly how she affected him. He was holding her pressed tightly against him so that there was no doubt.

He slipped one of the straps off her shoulder and lingeringly stroked a line from her ear down to the top of her breast. Her nipple hardened in response. As though to appease it, he rubbed his thumb across the pebbled nub in a soothing gesture that didn't do a thing to soothe her.

She shifted restlessly, feeling warm and wanting. What, she wasn't sure, but she knew that he was stirring something inside her.

He kissed her again, this time leaning over her, his chest rubbing against her sensitive breasts. As though her hands understood what she wanted better than she did at the moment, they stroked his back from shoulders to buttocks. His briefs now seemed to be an unnecessary barrier. She slipped her hands under the thin cotton material and squeezed the taut muscles beneath.

"Do you want them off?" he whispered, suddenly breaking the kiss.

"Mmm-hmm."

"Then take them off."

She immediately responded to his suggestion by sliding his briefs down as far as she could reach. He lifted and she reached around to pull the front down and found a whole new world to explore.

Chris helped her by shoving the offending garment down his legs and off his feet. Maribeth was already otherwise occupied exploring what she had found. She forgot her shyness in discovering how each touch affected him so strongly.

She'd had no idea that a man's body could feel this way. She'd never seen a man nude, but wasn't ignorant of the male shape and form. However, a tactile exploration revealed additional information—the smoothness, the sensitivity, and the involuntary movement of his hips as he surged into her hands when she lightly moved her fingertips from base to tip.

She gazed into his eyes, caught up in a delicious sense of awe. "I had no idea," she whispered.

"What?"

"I don't know, exactly. How wonderful it feels just to touch you, to hold you, to have you trust me, to experience your response. All of it. I had no idea that lovemaking could feel this good."

Her candid explanation must have pleased him be-

cause he kissed her again. This time his tongue kept
the same pace as his hips as he moved against her.
When he slipped the other strap off her shoulder she
felt his bare skin brush against her newly uncovered
breasts.

He raised his head and she was startled to see the
look on his face. There was nothing impassive about
him now. His eyes glittered and his face was flushed.
She felt a surge of pleasure sweep over her at the
sight. He was no longer the aloof loner he appeared
to be with others. At least not here. Not now.

He lowered his head once again, his lips encircling
the tip of her breast. When he gently tugged, ever-
new sensations swept over her and she almost cried
out with the feeling. She ran her hands through his
thick hair, holding him to her, silently encouraging
him.

He moved to her other breast, alternating his movements of slightly tugging, then soothing them with his
tongue. Maribeth surprised herself with her own reaction. She lifted her hips slightly, her excitement ac-
celerating when Chris met her movements with ones
of his own. The feel of him pressed so wonderfully
close to her filled her with such an intensity of emotion that she wasn't sure she could handle it.

"Oh, Chris," she whispered, her breathing broken.
"Oh, Chris" was all she could think of to say.

When he slipped his hand beneath her gown and
trailed it lingeringly up to the top of her thighs, she
shivered and almost cried out. She didn't know her
own body anymore while he seemed to know exactly

what to do to elicit an ever-stronger response from deep within her.

He touched her where no one had ever touched her before. Instead of feeling embarrassed or shy, she welcomed him, lifting to the palm of his hand, where it massaged across her tight curls in a circular motion.

When his fingers explored further, she opened to him, breathlessly begging him to help her deal with what was happening to her. She felt as though she were being wound tighter and tighter inside.

"It's okay, honey. You're doing fine...oh, so fine," he whispered, his breathing not much better than hers.

He lifted the gown so that he could rest his lower body between her thighs. Oh, yes. That was what she'd wanted. She reached for him and he immediately took her hand and held it beside her head.

"Not now, honey, or it'll be all over." There was a rueful chuckle in his words.

He felt even bigger than she'd expected, but she didn't care. She wanted him closer. She wanted him inside her. With frustration fanned by untutored desire, she raised her hips, forcing him closer. Her move, together with his own, more careful motion thrust him into her.

She felt the discomfort but didn't care. Instead she wrapped her arms and legs around him, silently pleading for she knew not what.

He knew what she wanted. Even so, he held himself motionless, gazing down at her with a mixture of amazement and need. She was so beautiful, and he'd wanted her for so long. Now that she was actually his, he wanted her to share what he was feeling, now that he was finally with her.

He concentrated on pacing himself, while he continued to stimulate her. She came apart in his arms, her soft cry triggering his own release. All he could do was hold on.

The next thing he was aware of were the muscles quivering in his arms and legs due to the effort of keeping his full weight off her. Sighing, he lowered himself to the bed, holding her tightly against him.

Only then did it occur to him that he'd never bothered to completely remove her gown. It was bunched around her waist. When he could find enough air to speak, he said, "Your beautiful gown may never be the same."

She still held on to him, her face buried against his neck. She muttered something.

"What?"

She raised her head, her eyes shining. "It was worth it."

Damn! But she was beautiful. Her fiery curls trailed across her shoulders and over her breast. He ran his fingers through the silken mass, finding that even that took almost more energy than he had at the moment.

"That was more than I could have possibly fantasized," she admitted after a long silence. "I feel so strange, as though I've turned into somebody else."

He continued to play with her hair. "There was nothing wrong with the other one."

"I didn't know my body could feel so—I don't know—tingly and achy. It was like you started building some kind of fire deep inside of me that took over.''

''I didn't want to scare you by moving too fast.'' He closed his eyes. ''I was worried that I would disappoint you.''

She shook her head. ''Never.''

After another few minutes he was able to get out of bed. He went into the bathroom and after a moment returned with a warm, damp washcloth. Slipping into bed once again he slowly and carefully touched her. This time she was very aware of what he was doing and her cheeks glowed.

''Thank you,'' she whispered.

''It's my pleasure.'' His gaze caught hers and they laughed together, their voices soft and intimate. After returning the cloth to the bathroom, he helped her with her gown. ''Off or on.''

''Would it be brazen to admit I'd like to sleep all night with our skin touching?''

''Not brazen at all. However, I have to tell you that we may be able to fall asleep that way, but I can bet you any amount of money I'll be aware of you all night.''

''Oh, well, if it bothers you—''

''Oh, it will. I'm looking forward to it.'' He pulled her into the curl of his body, her back against his chest. ''How's that?''

''Wonderful,'' she said, sounding sleepy.

He smiled to himself and closed his eyes. That was as good a word as any to describe it.

Maribeth lay there, listening to Chris's breathing even out into deep sleep. She wished she could do the same. Everything was too different for her to relax.

Her mind was filled with racing thoughts, none of which she seemed able to control.

This was her wedding night. She'd just spent an incredible time with Chris. Now she lay next to him, his arm across her waist, in a totally new environment to what she was used to.

She'd wanted to leave home and grow up. Meeting Kenneth Cochran had been one of many shocks she'd received today.

Why hadn't she realized that Chris came from a wealthy background? Was it because they each had been raised on a ranch, not known as a get-rich occupation? She couldn't recall that he had dressed differently from other schoolmates. There had been no indication to give her a clue.

So she looked as though she'd just hatched, did she? She didn't care what Kenneth Cochran thought about her, but she didn't like the idea that he was using her to put Chris in an indefensible place.

She'd never bothered with fashion or the latest styles. But she could. She was intelligent, educated and knew she could hold her own with anyone.

Chris shifted slightly, momentarily tightening his hold around her. Even asleep, he made certain she was there beside him.

It was also time for her to take a good, hard look at what she had done—and what she had admitted—by marrying Chris.

Bobby's actions had been inexcusable and she had

been justifiably hurt. However, if she had been truly heartbroken, she could not have married Chris. She wasn't going to kid herself about that.

She had never felt toward Bobby what Chris had caused her to feel tonight. She'd never been tempted to explore this side of her nature before. And yet she had wanted Chris to make love to her. She'd wanted to know what it was all about.

What was it about Chris that made him so different from everyone else she'd known?

She wasn't certain she knew what it was, but it called to her in ways she didn't understand.

She yawned, enjoying the warmth of his chest and legs behind her. Her last waking thought was wondering if Bobby had discovered all these new feelings with someone else. If so, she could better understand his behavior.

A sliver of light across her eyelids woke her several hours later. Maribeth forced her eyes open and stared at the closed draperies that didn't quite meet in the middle. She was too comfortable to get out of bed and adjust them, so she turned away, burrowing her head into the pillow.

Except this particular pillow was a great deal more firm and was breathing. That was enough to bring her fully awake.

Chris lay asleep beside her. The light didn't touch him. She propped herself up on her elbows and stared at him, enjoying looking at this man she'd married.

He had impossibly long, thick lashes. His skin was tanned, as though he spent time working out in the sun. His thick, black hair tumbled over his forehead, looking boyish.

Chris never looked boyish, even when he'd been one. He'd always acted so much older than the rest of them. Perhaps it had been his expression more than anything.

The sudden ringing of the phone made her leap. Even more surprising was Chris's immediate reaction. He was reaching for the phone on his side of the bed before it finished the first ring, his eyes already open. He'd gone from sound sleep to awake in a heartbeat.

"Cochran," he muttered into the phone.

That was all he said for the longest time. He'd rolled away from her so she was watching his back and saw the muscles tense as he continued to listen.

"Is there a possibility he could be mistaken?"

Once again there was a long silence while he listened.

"I understand" was his final comment before hanging up the phone. With his back still to her, Chris sat up on the side of the bed and propped his elbows on his thighs. He dropped his head into his hands.

"Bad news?"

Slowly he straightened and looked around at her. His dark eyes looked bleak. "I'm sorry. Did the phone wake you?"

His voice sounded flat. Maribeth was suddenly aware of her lack of clothing. She tugged the sheet a little higher on her chest. "No. I was watching you sleep."

That elicited a half smile from him. "That sounds boring. You should have awakened me." He stretched out beside her once again, the sheet haphazardly drawn across his loins. "Good morning, Mrs. Cochran," he murmured, kissing her lightly. "Did you sleep well?"

He was saying all the right things, but there was something wrong. It showed in his eyes. "Fine."

"Do you think you can get used to sharing a bed with me?"

There. She could see more life, more heat in his gaze now. "I think so," she replied absently. "Is something wrong?"

His eyes narrowed. "What do you mean?"

"The phone call."

"Oh. Work related."

"I thought your father wasn't going to need you for the next few days."

There was a long pause, as though he was searching for a reply. When it came, it didn't seem to have anything to do with their conversation. "I wasn't thinking very clearly this past week or I would have realized that this wasn't an ideal time to get married."

She froze. "I see."

"It has nothing to do with you. It's just that—" He paused, obviously searching for words. "My life's a little complicated at the moment."

"You forgot it was complicated?" she carefully repeated.

"I tend to forget a lot of things when I'm around you," he admitted, sliding his hand along her arm to her shoulder, then allowing it to slip down to her breast. His breathing changed, and his expression was suddenly filled with longing.

"Chris? What is it?"

He turned to her fully, his thigh finding the space between her legs and claiming it. "Honey, I would tell you about it if I could. But I can't. Not now, at any rate. There was nothing unusual planned for this trip. I saw no reason not to bring you along. And now—" He sighed. "It looks like I may be busier than I thought."

She almost laughed with the relief she felt. "Is that all? Oh, Chris, I don't mind. If you need to go somewhere, don't worry about me. I can entertain myself. I'm not helpless, you know."

He nibbled on her earlobe, causing shivers to run up and down her body. "I don't want to leave you for a minute. I finally have you exactly where I want you...in my bed."

"You're going to find me in your bed. Never fear."

Then there were no other words. Chris made love to her almost desperately, holding her, whispering hot words of passion, making her quiver with her own need. The gentle lover of the night before was gone. In his place was an erotic, passionate man who sent her spinning into orbit.

She clung to him, too overwhelmed with feeling to do more than hang on while he guided them both into ever-expanding sensuous pleasure.

When he collapsed on the bed beside her, she was too limp to do more than slide her fingers across his moist chest.

They lay there together, the only sound in the room their harsh breathing. When he could find his breath, he said, "I'm sorry. I didn't mean to hurt you."

"You didn't."

He rolled out of the bed and strode to the bathroom, pausing at the door. "I'm going to have to go out for a while. I'll leave you some money. Maybe you'd like to look around, see a movie or something."

"Okay."

"I'm sorry. It's a hell of a thing to do to you the first day of our honeymoon."

She was having a little trouble concentrating on his words while he stood there so unconcernedly naked. Her gaze kept darting over his long, lean frame, pausing to admire the way he was put together. "I'll be all right. Really."

In a few quick strides he returned to the bed and scooped her up. "Let's shower together. That should save some time."

Unfortunately for whoever might be waiting on Chris, a shared shower did nothing to shorten his leaving the suite.

Six

Maribeth was fascinated by the types of stores in the mall not far from their hotel. She'd eaten a salad in the hotel coffee shop before venturing out.

When she got a glimpse of herself in one of the shop windows, she couldn't believe there were no outward changes to reflect how differently she felt inside.

Chris had made her feel like the most beautiful woman in the world. And the sexiest. However, the plait and simple dress she wore still spoke of the country. She wanted to change that. She wanted to look her very best when Chris returned to the hotel.

She spotted a store that had several attractive outfits in the window. Once inside, a salesperson appeared, offering assistance. Maribeth candidly explained what she was hoping to do and the woman agreed to help her.

Two hours later she walked out with several bags and the telephone number of a salon that offered, in addition to hairstyles and makeovers, such things as manicures and massages.

She returned to the hotel and put all her purchases away, then called and made an appointment at the salon.

Instead of attending a movie, she spent several hours having her hair shaped, shortened and layered, having a full body massage, a pedicure and manicure.

After that, she shopped for shoes.

By the time she reached the hotel, she'd learned things about herself that she'd never known before.

The woman who'd helped her select clothes complimented her model-slender shape. The man at the salon rhapsodized over the color and texture of her hair. The woman who gave her tips on makeup couldn't say enough about the unusual color and shape of her eyes, her sparkling smile, her flawless complexion.

None of those things made any difference to her, but Maribeth was pleased that she wouldn't be an embarrassment to Chris. By the time she slipped into one of the dressier outfits she'd bought, there was no sign in the mirror of the country girl Chris had married.

She postponed eating dinner, choosing to wait in the comfortable suite until Chris returned.

Chris glanced at his watch once he stepped into the elevator and frowned. He'd been gone much longer than he'd wanted to be or intended to be. The series of meetings he'd attended hadn't put him in the best of moods. It didn't help any that those attending the meeting had already heard of his sudden and unexpected marriage. He'd had to listen to a bunch of sophomoric comments from several of them, and a chastisement from his supervisor about the poor timing.

Well, how was he to know that all hell was going to break loose during his honeymoon, for God's sake? He'd been a part of this operation for two years. He'd managed to wring a very grudging permission from his supervisor that afternoon to share some of what he was doing with Maribeth. Not much, but enough so that she would understand his periodic disappearances.

He opened the door to their suite and saw Maribeth sitting on the sofa reading. His breath caught in his throat. What had she done to herself?

She glanced up at the sound of the door opening. By the time he'd shut the door, she'd tossed her book aside and stood.

"Hi. I hope you haven't eaten. I waited for you."

"I haven't eaten...what have you done? Where did you find that dress? Your hair...you've cut your hair." He couldn't seem to take in the transformation from the young woman he'd left this morning to the sophisticate standing before him.

She chuckled and turned in a circle. "What do you think? Do you like it?"

Her hair now fell in waves around her face and

shoulders. The dress she wore clung to her figure, the color bringing out the golden topaz hue of her eyes.

He had trouble concentrating on her eyes.

The dress emphasized her full breasts, slender waist and curving hips. It also showed off a considerable length of her legs.

"Like it?" He cleared his throat. "You look, uh, different. That is, very glamorous. You—"

"You don't like it, do you?" she asked, coming closer. "I'll admit it takes some getting used to."

Her eyes looked larger. They sparkled with a mysterious glow. He touched her hair. It still felt silky and so soft. Standing this close to her was having a predictable effect on him.

"They really didn't cut all that much off of it, except around my face."

"You look stunning, Maribeth. I'm not sure how I'm going to handle the reaction you're going to cause when we go downstairs."

"I don't understand. Who's downstairs?"

He grinned. "The entire male population. You're going to start a stampede…at the very least have them drooling."

She kissed him. "I thought you were being serious."

"I am very serious." He slid his hands over her hips and rested them in the small of her back. "Are you wearing any underwear?"

"Of course." She moved as though she intended to show him. He stopped her hand.

"If you intend to have dinner anytime soon, you'll

get out of arm's reach of me and give me a chance to change clothes.''

She obediently—much to his disappointment—stepped back and waved to the bedroom. "I'll wait here.''

"Good idea," he growled, striding into the other room. His reaction to her had caught him off guard. It wasn't as if he hadn't made love to her several times in the past twenty-four hours. He certainly wasn't love-starved, but he was acting like it. If he didn't watch it, he'd be howling at the moon any moment now.

By the time he changed into one of his suits, he was in better shape to be seen in public. The hotel had a very nice restaurant on the top floor. He called to reserve a table, then returned to the other room. "Ready?''

"Oh, my. You look sensational.''

"You're just not used to seeing me in a suit.''

"That's true." He opened the door for her and she stepped out into the hallway. "I thought you looked smashing in the tux, but this isn't bad. Not bad at all.''

He took her hand on the way to the elevator. "Don't say I didn't warn you," he said, pushing the Up button.

"About what?''

"That dress.''

"Is it that conspicuous?''

"No. It's what you look like in it.''

The elevator let them off in the foyer of the restaurant. Chris gave the maître d' his name, and they were immediately led to a table for two by one of the large windows looking out over Atlanta. The city sparkled with lights.

"This is wonderful, Chris."

The table had a single rosebud in a vase as well as a candle glowing. Maribeth was having trouble taking it all in. "Have you been here before?" she asked.

"Yes. My father prefers staying here when he's in town."

"Speaking of your father, did you remind him that he promised not to disturb us until it's time to fly to Miami?"

So. There it was. The opening he needed to tell her.

Just then the waiter arrived with the menus. "Are you hungry for anything in particular?" Chris asked.

"Anything's fine."

"Would you like me to order for you?"

"Please."

It was strange, the things he knew about her. He remembered her favorite foods, as well as those things she didn't like, so that it was easy enough to glance through the menu and choose their meals.

Once alone, he said, "There's something I need to tell you."

"It sounds serious."

"It's about today. My business had nothing to do with my father."

"I'm afraid I don't understand."

"Remember I told you I never intended to work for my father?"

"Yes."

"For the past three and a half years I've been working for an agency of the government that's working to prevent drug trafficking across our borders. My pilot license has come in handy on numerous occasions, but it also created the situation I'm in now."

She was looking at him as though she'd never seen him before. "You're a government agent?"

"Yeah."

"Like a spy?"

He shrugged. "Sometimes. It depends on the operation."

"Then your father—"

"That's what I need to tell you. My father knows nothing about my government work. When my supervisor found out that my father wanted me to work for him, in any capacity, I was assigned the job."

"Meaning you weren't given a choice."

"That's right. My supervisor felt it as too good a cover for me to pass up." The waiter appeared with their wine. After signaling that it was acceptable, Chris waited until they each had a glass. He touched his glass to hers. "To us."

She took a sip, her mind obviously on their previous conversation. "Why couldn't you tell your father about your other job?"

"Because he might not have taken me on, otherwise. My supervisor didn't want to take a chance on blowing the cover."

"You mean he's never known what you did for a living?"

"No. I have as little to do with my father and his

life-style as possible, even though he still insists that he intends to turn his empire over to me someday.''

She stared at him in disbelief. ''You mean you don't want it?''

''Not if it means working for him on a permanent basis. The less I have to do with him, the better I like it.''

''Is he a part of the investigation you're presently working on?''

Silence stretched between them. He reached for his wineglass and took a sip before he spoke again. ''What makes you ask that?''

Now she felt uncomfortable. Was she treading into areas that were none of her business? Surely Chris would say something to that effect. Deciding to take his question at face value she said, ''I'm not sure, actually. Just little things. Mostly the way you are around your father. You don't act as though you like him very much. That attitude may go back to something that happened in your childhood, but somehow, I feel it's more than that. I get the feeling that you don't like him very much as a man, not just as a father.''

He looked at her for a long time before saying, ''You're very astute.''

''And you haven't answered my question.''

He leaned back in his chair and casually glanced around the restaurant. ''I really can't discuss any more of this. I'm sorry. The reason I'm telling you anything at all is because some things are suddenly heating up in this particular operation and, like it or not, I'll be spending most of this week in meetings.

For the record, I don't like it and I've lodged my complaint with the powers that be, for all the good it does me. They seem to find it amusing that I'm not going to be able to spend much time with my bride on our honeymoon. As far as my father is concerned, though, that's exactly what I'll be doing…lazing around."

"Is that what he thought you were doing before you went to work for him, lazing around?"

His smile was brief but amused. "Something like that, yeah."

"I get the impression you enjoy doing things that your father disapproves of."

"I don't care what his opinion of me is."

The waiter arrived with their salads. They began to eat in silence. When Chris appeared to have dropped their conversation Maribeth finally asked, "Could you actually use evidence you uncover while you're working for him to build a case against your father?"

"Maribeth. I told you, I can't discuss that aspect of the investigation…not with you or anyone else. I'm just doing my job, doing what I'm told to do. Whatever happens, happens."

She touched his hand lying on the table. "Oh, Chris. You can't make me believe that you don't care what happens to him. He's your father, no matter what ill will is between you. Whether you'll admit it or not, this must be terribly painful for you."

He looked down at her hand, then turned his over so that he could hold hers. "I can deal with it, Maribeth. I've been dealing with it for several months, now. It's just that, now that we're married, you need to know the truth about what I do.''

"This is what you meant this morning, wasn't it, about the timing of our marriage?''

"Yeah. It would have been much wiser for me to have postponed getting married until all of this was tied up. To be honest, from the time Bobby called me, I never gave my job a thought. All I was thinking about was what you were going through.''

"I'm sorry. If I'd known, I probably—''

"I'm not sorry in the least and I'm glad you made the decision you did. We'll get through this. It won't be much longer from the looks of things.''

Their dinners arrived. This time neither one of them went back to the conversation, although Maribeth could think of little else.

She felt as though she'd stepped into another dimension. Chris a government agent? That was the last thing she'd been expecting to hear from him.

Her new husband was definitely full of surprises.

Kenneth Cochran was alone when they met him at the plane on Thursday.

"My God!'' he said, taking off his sunglasses to look at Maribeth. "You look stunning, woman. Marriage obviously agrees with you.''

"Thank you,'' she said, secretly pleased that she'd been able to make such an impression on him. She was finding that she rather enjoyed creating a stir, such as the one in the lobby when they'd checked out this morning. Chris had been amused that she'd been caught off guard by the looks she'd gotten.

"I warned you, didn't I?" he'd teased, helping her into the cab later.

That teasing man was nowhere in sight at the moment. She noted that the two men didn't bother to exchange greetings when they met.

"I guess I don't have to ask if you enjoyed your stay in Atlanta," Kenneth said. "You're positively glowing."

She glanced at Chris from the corner of her eye. "I enjoyed it very much."

Once on board, Kenneth waved to the seat where she'd sat before, then took the one beside her when Chris went to the cockpit. Kenneth reached for her hand. "I'm glad to hear you enjoyed Atlanta," he said, giving her hand a squeeze. "I want the two of you to be happy. The room was all right?"

"The suite was extraordinary. Thank you for your generous gift."

He patted her hand, then let go of it. "That's just the beginning, my dear. You'd be a very easy lady to spoil, I must say. I never thought I'd ever find myself envying my son, but I'm coming very close to it."

His tone was teasing and she tried to take his comments that way. However, she used the need to fasten her seat belt to ease away from him.

"Have you ever been to Miami before?"

"No. As you pointed out when we met, I'm really just a country girl."

"Now, I didn't mean anything by that. I was just teasing Chris a little. He's always so blasted secretive about his personal life. Why, Bambi and I have the hardest time getting him to come over to the house to visit. I practically have to commandeer him to attend out parties. The rest of the time we never hear from him.''

''Bambi?''

His smile was dazzling. ''My wife. Now there is one luscious lady. You're going to enjoy getting to know her, I'm sure. She's a character. Great sense of humor, loves to have fun. Now that you're part of the family maybe Chris will be a little more sociable.''

Maribeth was thankful the flight was no longer than it was. Once they leveled off, she excused herself to use the bathroom, then deliberately lingered in there. When she came out, Kenneth had moved to a table where he'd spread papers to work on, explaining that he'd be able to chat with her once he checked on a few things. However, they were already approaching Miami before he finished.

She was so relieved to see Chris when he finally stepped out of the cockpit that she wanted to throw her arms around his neck.

''When do you want to return to Dallas?'' he asked Kenneth once they were through at the hangar where they'd left the plane.

''I should be through by noon on Saturday. I'd stay over the weekend except Bambi has this big party planned for that night, which the two of you are expected to attend, by the way. Bambi can hardly wait to meet Maribeth.''

Chris ignored the mention of a party. ''We'll meet you here at one o'clock on Saturday, all right?'' Chris took Maribeth's hand and led her from the hangar, leaving Kenneth standing there. ''We'll get a cab to the hotel,'' he told her, ''and get checked in, then we can spend some time on the beach.''

She clung to him, glad to be with him again. She didn't know how to hide her nervousness around his father, even though he'd never been less than charming to her. Now she could relax, knowing she would have Chris to herself for a few days.

She'd seen very little of him during the days they'd been in Atlanta, but their nights had more than made up for any feelings of neglect she might have harbored.

And now…here they were in Miami. He promised her that morning not to leave her side for the next forty-eight hours. She was already planning on new ways to keep him entertained. She wasn't looking forward to their return to Dallas. Dallas would force her to face the reality of their lives. She would see his home—the place where they would be living. She might also discover that she was hopeless as the proper mate for Chris.

But for now, she refused to look ahead. This was her honeymoon and she intended to create all kinds of memories to look back upon.

''Where will your dad be staying?'' she asked when Chris gave the taxi driver the name of the hotel he wanted.

''He has a condo down here.''

''Have you ever stayed there?''

''A few times, but I prefer to have my own place.''

She leaned back in the seat, looking out the window. ''You know, Chris, I can't help feeling sad that you and your father don't get along better.''

He sighed, causing her to look around at him. She'd never seen his expression quite so pensive. "I learned at an early age that my parents saw me as an object to fight over, a way to hurt each other in their power struggle. My father was determined to punish my mother. He never forgave her for walking out on him."

"She seems to be holding a great deal of resentment against him, even now, if her attitude at the wedding was any indication."

"I know, but there's nothing I can do about it. There's nothing sadder than people who refuse to let go of the past. They miss so much in life that's happening at the moment." He glanced over at her and grinned. "Take right now, as an example. Here we are talking about things that have already happened, over which we have absolutely no control, instead of discussing how we intend to spend the day. Any ideas about what you'd like to see while you're here?"

"Not really. I assumed you had something in mind."

He gave her a lingering kiss. When he eased away from her she was trembling. He had a way of reducing her bones to molten lava. "What I have in mind won't do much for you in the way of sight-seeing," he whispered, nuzzling her ear.

"Well, we can, uh, check into the hotel, maybe get something to eat, then wait until it's a little cooler to walk on the beach. How does that sound?"

"Fine with me. However, that leaves us with several hours unaccounted for."

She glanced at the back of the driver's head before

glancing back at Chris with a grin. "I suppose we can always improvise."

Chris laughed, kissing her again. "An excellent idea."

And an excellent time they had, too!

When they arrived in Dallas the following Saturday the first thing Maribeth saw when she stepped off the plane was Chris's red car parked by the hangar. It was the most familiar thing she knew in the week since she married him.

They were finally home and ready to begin their life together.

His father stopped them on their way to the car. "Don't forget tonight, Chris. I want to introduce Maribeth to all my friends and associates. You don't have to stay long, of course. After all, you're newlyweds, but I expect you to put in an appearance."

Chris glanced at Maribeth before saying, "I'll let you know."

"That's not good enough. I want your word that you'll be there."

Maribeth could see that Chris was uncomfortable. She squeezed his hand. "I'm sure we can drop by for a while."

Without looking at her, Chris said to his father, "All right."

Kenneth slapped him on the shoulder. "You might surprise yourself and find that you actually enjoy it. I know Bambi will be thrilled to see you. I talked to her last night. She can hardly wait to meet Maribeth."

Chris said nothing more when they got into the car.

Maribeth could feel her excitement mount now that they were actually driving toward her new home.

"Tell me about your house," she said. "You mentioned that you bought one. Isn't that a little unusual, being single?"

"I suppose, but I was never one who enjoyed apartment or condominium living. I lived on the ranch too long to feel comfortable close to other people. I happened to hear about this place through a mutual friend. The couple who owned it were divorcing and wanted a quick sale. I offered them what they wanted without having to go through a Realtor so it worked out well for all of us."

"How large is it?"

"The house is comfortable, about three thousand square feet. Plus, there's a little acreage that went with it, which is nice. I have room for a couple of horses and don't have to deal with close neighbors."

"It sounds wonderful. I wasn't certain what to expect."

They headed north from the Addison airport and were soon into rolling hills with fewer signs of the city. Chris drove with smooth efficiency, following the winding road and making the necessary turns. When he finally slowed, she saw a stone pillar with a mailbox and the name Cochran.

They had arrived. She couldn't control the excitement that seemed to grow within her.

He turned into the driveway and followed the lane up to the house and around it to a three-car garage in back. Hitting the remote, he waited for the door to open, then pulled the car inside.

Turning off the key, Chris turned to her and said, "Welcome to your new home, Mrs. Cochran." He got out of the car and walked around to the other side, opening her door. She took his proffered hand and got out.

He smoothed his hands over her arms, then turned away to unload her bags from the trunk. "C'mon. Let me show you the place," he said, gathering their luggage. He opened the connecting door between the garage and the house and motioned for her to enter first.

Chris led her from the back of the house to a curving staircase in the front foyer. Her eyes grew larger with every step.

By the time they walked the length of the upstairs hallway she knew that once again she'd underestimated the life she had chosen.

He set the bags in the middle of a large bedroom. "This will be our room." He nodded toward one wall. "I thought the stone fireplace a nice touch for the bedroom and the view is great from here."

Maribeth paused in the middle of the room, trying to take it all in.

"Come look at the bathroom. They overdid it a little, but I have to admit it's great to crawl into the spa tub and let those water jets wash the aches away."

She walked across the bedroom and peeked inside the doorway to the smaller room. The large Jacuzzi tub could easily hold three people and the freestanding glass shower an equal number. Two walls were mirrored from floor to ceiling and the floor was covered with the same plush carpeting that covered the entire upstairs.

"I didn't realize—" she mumbled, then stopped. She turned away and began to study the bedroom.

"You didn't realize what?"

"When you described the house, I guess I pictured something like the ranch house that had been around for generations. But this...this is so much newer and obviously more expensive."

He stayed where he was in the doorway of the bathroom and watched as she trailed her fingers over several pieces of furniture, pausing to look with concentrated interest at the pictures hanging on the walls.

Sometimes she was so easy to read. He wasn't sure how to handle this. Didn't she understand that it was her lack of interest in the amount of money he might have that had always endeared her to him?

"Does it bother you?" he finally asked when it became obvious that she wasn't going to say anything more.

She didn't answer right away. Finally she turned and faced him, the width of the room between them. "A little, I guess. I feel stupid not to have known. I should have understood, I mean—" she shrugged "—that car you drive is probably terribly expensive. At least I've never seen one like it before. Now I understand why Deke was going on about it. You must have found if funny that I was comparing it to a pickup truck."

"Not funny in the way you mean. I wasn't laughing at you, or making fun of you because you didn't know. You gave me your candid response to it. That's one of the reasons I appreciate you. You say exactly what you think and feel. There's no pretense about you at all. I like that.''

''I don't really fit with a place like this. I'd be scared to drive your car. And as far as this house…'' She shook her head, unable to find the words to describe what she was feeling.

Chris walked over and took both of her hands. ''I don't want you to ever feel that you don't fit into my life. We go back a long way together. I'm still the same guy. Nothing's really changed.''

He put his arms around her. ''I was able to buy this house because of some money my dad's parents left me, that's all. I decided that investing it in real estate was as good as having it drawing interest somewhere.''

She rested her head on his shoulder. Maribeth wasn't sure how long they stood there before she noticed the light on his answering machine was blinking. She reluctantly pulled away from him. ''It looks like you have some messages waiting for you.''

He glanced over at them. ''Nothing urgent, I'm sure.''

''If you'd like to check them, go ahead. I think I'm going to take a shower.'' She forced herself to smile. ''I hope I don't get lost in there.''

She was already in the bathroom with the door closed when she heard him play his machine messages back. Three were men discussing upcoming meetings. One was a female with a very sultry voice. ''I wish you'd return my calls, Chris, honey. This is the third message I've left. You can't have been out of town all the time. It's really important that I speak to you no later than Saturday, the tenth. Please call me.''

The heat in the voice was enough to curl her hair. Today was the tenth. She wondered how long the message had been on there. Maybe it had been waiting for him to return from Agua Verde.

Maribeth quickly turned on the shower, to drown out anything more. She didn't want to know if Chris returned the call or what he said. After all, he'd had a life that didn't include her prior to ten days ago. She had no reason to think that there was anyone in his life to whom he owed any explanations regarding their sudden marriage.

If there was, she didn't want to hear his explanations.

When she came out of the bathroom, Chris was stretched out on the bed with his eyes closed. Since everything she owned was still packed, she had draped herself with a towel. The temptation to stretch out beside him was too much to resist, so Maribeth quietly lay down beside him.

It did feel good to rest. She would just take a few minutes to…her mind shut off and she was asleep.

Chris woke her sometime later. Freshly shaved and just out of the shower, he lay beside her, smoothing his hand over her body. She was already flushed and trembling, wanting him.

''I enjoyed waking up to find you in my bed. At first I thought for a while there I was dreaming. Then I remembered.'' He trailed kisses down the side of her neck until his mouth covered the tip of her breast.

In the week they'd been together, he'd discovered

many ways to please her. Now he put that knowledge to work. She could no more resist him than a flower could resist opening to the sun.

She had learned a few things, as well. By the time he moved over her, they were both trembling with need. He teased her, lowering himself slightly, then pulling away. She clasped him to her, forcing his weight down until he was inside her.

Blindly she sought his mouth, wanting to absorb him through her very pores. Her eagerness inflamed him and he took her hard and fast, racing them to their climax and toppling them into an aftermath of breathless bliss.

When he was able to speak, Chris looked at her and grinned. "So much for showering early to save time."

"We can always shower together now."

"To save time?"

She gave him an exaggerated, innocent stare. "Does it matter?"

In answer, he picked her up and carried her into the bathroom.

Seven

They were late arriving at Kenneth Cochran's palatial home, but there was still a stream of cars pulling onto the grounds when they turned onto the quiet, tree-lined street. Valet parking waited at the top of the driveway. When it was their turn, Chris helped her out of the car and handed his keys to one of the valets.

"Wow," she said under her breath, looking around at the house and extensive lawns. "How long has he lived here?"

Chris shrugged. "As far back as I can remember."

Now that was unexpected news. "You mean you were raised here?"

"Yeah."

"And your mother lived here?"

"Yes."

His replies were becoming more and more clipped. Maribeth was having trouble adjusting her views of the people involved with what she was seeing. "You're saying that your mother left this to live in Agua Verde?"

"She didn't care for the life-style."

"I get a sense that you don't, either."

"That's right. Ready to go in?"

She glanced down at the black dress she wore, which had seemed perfectly adequate when she bought it, but now she wasn't so sure. "Are you sure I look all right?"

"Maribeth, neither of us has anything to prove to these people. As a matter of fact, that provocative dress may draw more interest than you had in mind when you bought it."

"I just didn't want you to be ashamed of me."

"That could never happen. Come on."

Kenneth Cochran stood just inside the open door greeting his guests. A blond woman, who could have easily made a living as a Las Vegas show girl, stood beside him wearing a flaming red see-through dress that showcased a spectacular figure.

Kenneth spoke as soon as he spotted them. "Well, there you are. I was expecting you to be here before the others so that Maribeth and Bambi could get acquainted."

"We were unavoidably delayed," Chris stated calmly. Memories of what had delayed them caused Maribeth to blush. Bambi looked amused by her reaction. Seen up close, Bambi was stunning. She had dark blue eyes and a friendly smile.

"This is Maribeth, Bambi. I know you two are going to be good friends," Kenneth said.

Bambi held out her hand. "I can't tell you how eager I've been to meet you, Maribeth. I've been in a state of shock since Ken called me with your news. Chris had us all convinced that he never intended to marry."

Maribeth reluctantly accepted the perfectly manicured hand, immediately recognizing the sultry voice that had been on Chris's answering machine. Bambi looked at Chris. "Do I get to hug the groom?" she asked, implying a great deal more than what she said.

Chris just looked at her. She tapped him on the chest with her fist. "You never return my calls, you stinker. It's terribly rude of you."

"Blame it on my upbringing," Chris replied with a shrug.

"I'm just glad Ken was able to tell you about tonight's party. I would have hated for you to miss it." She smiled at Maribeth. "This will be a perfect occasion to announce the marriage to all our friends."

Kenneth took Chris and Maribeth by the hand, autocratically abandoning his welcoming position at the door. "Come on. There's several people I want you to meet."

In the press of people and introductions, Maribeth got separated from Chris. Eventually she wandered over to the buffet tables. She couldn't remember the last time she'd eaten. She was filling a plate with delicious-looking tidbits when Bambi appeared by her side.

"I wasn't joking earlier, you know. You have no idea what a shock it was for me when Kenneth told me that Chris had gotten married right out of the blue like that."

"We surprised a lot of people," Maribeth answered, focusing her attention on the items displayed on the table. She hadn't eaten since a very early breakfast and now she was starved.

After a long pause, Bambi asked, "Has Chris ever spoken to you about me?"

Maribeth glanced around at her and smiled. "No."

"Oh."

Maribeth picked up her glass of wine and turned, still holding her plate. "You have a lovely place here."

"Yes," Bambi agreed absently, "it *is* nice. Is that you natural hair color?"

Maribeth hoped she hid the fact that the candid question startled her. "'Fraid so."

"It's an unusual shade."

What could she say to that?

When Maribeth made no response, Bambi asked, "How long have you known Chris?"

"Since he moved to Agua Verde when we were kids."

"Oh! That's right, he did go to school down there. He told me that once, but I'd forgotten."

"If you'll excuse me, I'm going to go find a table

so I can eat.'' She held up the plate and glass to explain her lack of an extra hand.

Bambi followed her outside to one of the tables grouped around the Olympic-size pool. They sat down. Maribeth immediately began to eat. After a moment, Bambi said, ''Chris and I used to date.''

''Did you?''

''Mmm-hmm. He's terrific in bed, don't you think?''

Maribeth almost spilled her wine from the tulip-shaped glass, but managed to rescue it by clutching the stem. She could only stare at the other woman in wonder at her choice of subjects.

Obviously Maribeth's lack of conversation was not going to deter Bambi from a heart-to-heart talk about the man they had in common. ''I couldn't help falling head over heels in love with him. I mean, what woman can resist him, after all? There's just something about those tall, dark, mysterious types that gets to you. I'm sure I don't have to tell you, do I? So how long were you and Chris engaged?''

''Not long.''

''I just wondered, since he and I were pretty involved once upon a time. And then I met Kenneth.''

''He swept you off you feet?'' Maribeth offered.

''In a manner of speaking. He asked me to marry him, which was more than Chris ever did.''

Maribeth was determined not the smile at the disgruntled tone.

Bambi tossed her head. ''I warned Chris that I'd do it if he refused to marry me.''

''Oh?''

"That was when he told me he never intended to marry."

"Ah."

"Now he shows up with you."

"Mmm."

"So you can naturally understand my surprise."

"Naturally."

"Are you pregnant?"

Maribeth was thankful she had left her wineglass alone after the first surprise. She would have spilled it for sure with that one. "We've only been married a week," she murmured.

"Don't be naive, honey. You know what I mean."

"I'm not pregnant."

Bambi nodded thoughtfully. "I thought about it, thinking that my having his baby might change his mind, but knowing Chris, he probably wouldn't have married me, anyway. Besides, he always made sure there was never a possibility of that."

A male voice immediately behind Maribeth said, "Well, I'm glad to see the two of you hitting it off so well." Kenneth Cochran pulled out one of the chairs and joined them. "I just knew you two would find you had a lot in common."

More than I could have possibly guessed, Maribeth thought to herself. She contented herself to replying to Kenneth's remark with a smile.

"Where's Chris?" Bambi asked, looking around.

"How would I know?" Kenneth answered. "I gave up trying to keep an eye on him years ago."

"I think I'll go find him," she said, jumping up from the table and dashing off.

Maribeth finished off the last stuffed mushroom on her plate and took another sip of wine.

"Have I told you that you're the most beautiful woman here tonight?" Kenneth asked.

The Cochrans were going to be the death of her yet. She almost swallowed wrong on that one. "No, sir, you haven't. I appreciate the compliment."

"Not a compliment. Just a fact. I doubt that Chris is old enough, or wise enough, to appreciate what he has in you."

"I feel very fortunate to be married to Chris."

"But he's hard to get to know. There's no denying that. That mother of his did her best to ruin him. No matter what I did, I never could get close to the kid when he was growing up." Maribeth suddenly saw the bleakness in the man's eyes and realized that much of his brusque behavior around Chris was based on pain.

"I'm surprised you never had more children," she said after a moment.

"Are you kidding? And let them be held for ransom when the marriage ended?"

"Is that what happened with Chris?"

"Actually, no. His mother wanted no part of me or my money. She didn't want Chris anywhere around me, either, but I wouldn't let her get away with that. I fought her for custody, and lost, but at least I got him for the summers. Not that having him here did much good. He spent his time counting the days until he could return home to his friends."

"Did he ever talk to you about his life in Agua Verde?"

"Only if I cross-examined him. And then, he gave the barest details. He refused to make friends up here. He's just like his mother. There was absolutely nothing he wanted from me. As you can see, none of that has changed. Chris has never seemed close to anybody. That's why his getting married was such a shock."

Obviously there was a lot of that going around. "You didn't appear shocked. Just amused."

"Good. I would never want him to know how easily he can hurt me. Nobody wants to be thought vulnerable where another person is concerned."

"The two of you are alike in many ways."

"Don't ever let him hear you say that. He'd consider an opinion like that grounds for divorce."

"Is that what you think? That we'll end up divorced?"

"Well, I haven't set him a very good example, I'm afraid. You'd better hope he doesn't take after me in that respect."

"I would never try to hang on to him if he didn't want to be with me, Mr. Cochran."

"Mr. Cochran? If you can't call me Dad, at least use my first name."

"What does Chris call you?"

"He makes certain he never has to address me. I can't remember that last time he called me Dad."

"I find that really sad. I lost both my parents when I was eight years old. There's nothing I can do about that. So I don't understand family who don't attempt to get along, don't try to work out their differences.

I think that family is the most precious gift we can have.''

"Chris is much luckier than he knows, to have a wife who feels that way. Hopefully you can stop the Cochran cycle of discord and give Chris the love and family he needs.''

"That's up to Chris, of course.''

Music wafted out onto the terrace from the ballroom located in one of the wings of the house. Kenneth glanced around. "Shall we go back inside? I think you may enjoy the band I hired to play tonight. As the host, I claim the right to ask you for the first dance.''

"Won't Bambi expect you to dance with her?''

He laughed, but it sounded a little forced. "Bambi? She doesn't even see me whenever Chris is around. That's not going to change.''

"Is that how you met her? Through Chris?''

"More or less. He never introduced us, but I'd seen them together at various functions around town. I made a point to find out more about her. Bambi's not a bad sort at all. She came from a big family in east Texas. Never had much but her looks and she's used them to her advantage. Did she tell you she used to model?''

"No.''

"Started young, got some breaks, but she hated the life. I called her one time, invited her to lunch. Told her I wanted to get to know her. It wasn't long until we were seeing each other, strictly platonic, mostly so she could complain about Chris's lack of commitment. One day, oh, I guess a year or more later, I told her that if she ever got tired of waiting for him to offer to marry her, that I would. She thought I was kidding at the time.''

''But you weren't.'' By now, they were circling the dance floor along with a roomful of people.

''Nope. You see, I liked Bambi. She is what she is. There's no pretense about her. I like that. That's what I like about you, as well. You may have re-styled your hair, found some more sophisticated clothes, but you don't pretend to be someone you're not.''

''I wouldn't know how.''

''Well, Bambi had the chance to go big in the modeling field, but she couldn't stand the phoniness, the backstabbing, the whole scene. So she stayed in Dallas and did quite well. Like I said, we became friends. I was tired of getting involved with women who saw me as a moneybags.''

''And Bambi doesn't?''

He laughed. ''Oh, I'm sure the money helped my cause a little. That and being Chris's father. She truly loves him, you know. And she wanted to be part of his life in some capacity. Of course I could have told her that marrying me was not the way to go about it, but I had my own agenda by that time. She found out soon enough.''

''How long have you been married?''

''About four months.''

''Oh! Somehow, I thought it had been longer.'' She was quiet for a moment, wondering if she dared to say what she was thinking. Finally she said, ''You really love her, don't you?''

"Oh, yes. I suppose that's why I can understand that you aren't going to have an easy time of it, being married to Chris. He's a tough man to love because he doesn't trust anyone. And how can there be love without a sense of trust?"

"Chris was helping me out of a really bad situation when he offered to marry me."

"Nonsense. Chris married you for only one reason. He wanted to marry you. You might ask yourself why, sometime. It's my guess that you've come closer to getting through his defenses than any of us. You deserve a medal for that."

"It's just that we've been friends for years."

"My point, exactly. Chris doesn't have many friends. At least he allowed you into that circle."

"We were children. He'd been living there for only a few months when my parents were killed. It was a bad time for me. He and Bobby helped me through a great deal of the pain by just being a part of my life."

"That's good."

"Excuse me, but may I have a dance with my wife or do you intend to monopolize her the whole evening?"

Maribeth looked around, startled by the grimness she heard in Chris's voice.

Kenneth stepped back, smiling. "By all means. We were just getting better acquainted, son, that's all. I like your wife, Chris. Very much."

"I've noticed," Chris replied, almost growling the words. He swept her into his arms and began to dance.

"I was beginning to think you'd left. I haven't seen you in some time," she said, her gaze on his clenched jaw.

"I hate these parties. I keep getting cornered by people." His gaze dropped to the scooped neck of her dress. "I can certainly see why my father enjoyed dancing with you. From this angle, I can almost see your belly button."

She grabbed the top of her dress. "You're kidding." She was horrified at the thought.

He circled the dance floor and she absently followed his lead.

"All that practice with my father seems to have you much more comfortable on the dance floor. Was it only a week ago when you were telling me that you didn't know how to dance?"

"I guess I wasn't paying that much attention. I was more interested in what he had to say."

"Another one of his fans, huh? Guess you and Bambi have a great deal in common."

"Actually, I had a chance to visit with her, as well."

"Oh?"

"She was reminiscing about how good you were in bed."

Chris stopped cold on the dance floor, causing another couple to bump into them. "She did what?"

"You heard me."

He took her hand and led her off the dance floor. They went through the French doors out onto the terrace. Most of the people were inside dancing. He led her to the edge of the terrace and followed a path that led to a gazebo.

He turned around and faced her. The lights from the terrace shown on his face. "I want to know exactly what Bambi said to you."

"Why?"

"Because I know her. I—"

"Yes, she did make that clear enough...in the Biblical sense, you mean."

"That's not what I meant. If she thought there was a chance to break us up, she'd do it."

"How could she? Whatever happened between the two of you happened before we married. Chris, don't you see? You and I have, at the most, ten days that we would need to account to each other. Anything prior to that happened before we made any commitment. From what I'm told, you aren't big on commitment."

He frowned. "What's that supposed to mean?"

"I have a much better understanding of the sacrifice you made when you offered to marry me."

"Damn it, Maribeth. I told you it wasn't a sacrifice to—"

"You gave up your privacy, Chris. I don't take that lightly. By the very nature of who you are, what you do for a living, everything about you makes it clear you don't want anyone to get close to you. Don't you realize how you've jeopardized all that by marrying me?"

He turned away from her, shoving his hands into his pockets. "I haven't jeopardized anything. I don't have anything to hide from you."

She smiled but of course he didn't see it.

"I really do like your father. I find that we have many things in common."

He spun around. "I doubt that very much. Of course he can be charming when he wants something, and it's obvious he wants your approval. Most women find him attractive. Why should you be different?"

"The most attractive thing I find about him is that he reminds me of you."

"We're nothing alike. Nothing."

"You look a great deal like him."

"I had no choice over that."

"Why do you dislike him so?"

"I have no feeling about him at all. I just prefer to live my own life. Not the one he mapped out for me."

"He chose where you lived?"

"No. My mother wanted to move back to Agua Verde. You know that."

"Then he chose the school you attended?"

"Are you kidding? He was determined I was going to go to SMU here in Dallas."

"But you chose Texas A & M so that you and Bobby and me went on to college together. I remember when we were planning that."

"So?"

"Nothing really. I'm just thinking about how your dad has ruled your life. You said he wanted you to work with him."

He sighed. "And that's what I'm doing."

"No, you aren't. You're working *for* him, strictly

as an employee, and whether he knows it or not you're there on temporary assignment for another job.''

''That's true.''

''What I'm sure he wanted was for you to learn the business so that he could turn it over to you someday.''

''He wants control over me. He wants to dangle the business in front of me as a carrot. I refuse to bite.''

''Have you ever wondered why he never had any more children?''

He turned and looked at her. ''I never had to wonder. I knew. If you'd ever seen his wives, you'd know that the last thing they wanted was motherhood.''

''How many times has your father been married?''

''Bambi is his third wife.''

''In other words, besides your mother and Bambi, he's had one other wife. What was she like?''

''I don't remember. She was only around a few years.''

''Which means your dad was single for several years before he and Bambi married.''

''He may have been single, but he always had someone around to fawn over him.''

Maribeth chuckled.

''What's so amusing?''

''This whole conversation, really. You didn't want to come here tonight. You want to have nothing to do with either your father or Bambi. And what I discover once I'm here are two people who love you very much.''

''Is that what Bambi told you?''

''Among other things. Are you upset that she married your father?''

''I didn't care who the hell she married. I used to see her occasionally. My hours at the agency don't leave me much spare time as you're beginning to find out for yourself. Whenever I had a free evening, I'd give her a call and we'd go out. It was never anything serious, we both knew that. And yes, dammit, I made love to her a few times, which is really sickening, now that you think about it. But who would ever have guessed that she would end up becoming my stepmother?''

''Maybe it wasn't serious to you, but I have a hunch it was more than that to her.''

''Nonsense. She was looking to get married. She didn't care who the fool was. My father's money was much more alluring than anything I had to offer.''

''Really. She told you that?''

''She didn't have to. Once I found out they were seeing each other, I knew.''

''How did you find out?''

''She told me. Of course she insisted they were just friends, which is absurd. She was just playing us one against the other.''

''But you saw through her.''

''That's right.''

''Nobody's going to hurt you.''

"You've got that right. So if you're through with all your questions, we can go home now."

"I wasn't the one who brought us out here, Chris."

"Well, I wasn't about to discuss Bambi in a roomful of people. You can rest assured that you have no reason to be jealous of her."

"I was trying to tell you that I'm not jealous of her."

He'd already started back to the house, but her words stopped him.

"Sorry, I forgot. Why should you be jealous? Your feelings for me are for a friend. There's no reason to be jealous in a friendship, is there?"

Eight

They had driven home in silence. Now Maribeth was in the bathroom removing her makeup and combing out her hair. She was getting used to her new hairstyle, and she rather liked it. It was actually just as easy to keep as the braid had been and a great deal more flattering.

Maybe she was becoming vain in her old age, but there was something energizing about knowing that she looked her best with just a few tips from experts on hair and complexion care.

If her plans worked out she would probably be too busy to worry with either in the coming months, but of course before she made definite plans, she needed to talk to Chris about them.

Chris. On the way home, he'd retreated into himself, becoming the aloof loner she'd known most of her life. She was coming to realize he used this response as a shield against hurt.

She'd never thought about how his parents' divorce had affected Chris. Would he have been a different person if his parents had stayed together? Obviously his mother had been unhappy or she would never have left his father. And his father had wanted him very, very much to have attempted to gain custody when he had no grounds.

What must all of that fighting have done to a young, sensitive child? How could he grow up with the two people he most closely identified with fighting each other without being scarred by it?

That was what she realized tonight. She'd learned a great deal about her new husband, seeing him in his father's home in Dallas, hearing about how his father felt about him, and meeting Bambi.

It was obvious that Kenneth and Bambi Cochran had an unusual relationship with each other, but no matter what the world thought, they were good for each other, and good to each other.

Granted, Maribeth had never met a woman like Bambi. If she had been Kenneth, she wouldn't have been quite so tolerant of the woman's obvious feelings for his son.

What Maribeth was beginning to understand was that there were all kinds of people in the world, each one with a specific upbringing that molded and shaped his or her personality. Wouldn't she be considerably different from who she was today if her parents had lived? She'd probably have another sister or two, possibly brothers as well. She was certain she wouldn't have been pampered as much as Megan and Mollie had pampered her.

Even Travis and Deke had made a definite impression on her perspective, especially regarding men. Whether she'd been aware of it or not, these past few years she had begun to compare Bobby with her brothers-in-law and found that his refusal to commit to their marriage was a bad sign.

When Megan agreed to marry Travis, he'd wanted to plan an immediate wedding, even though he was still following the rodeo circuit. It's true that he'd quit traveling the following year, but he'd made it clear that he wanted to stay home.

Bobby was such a child. Just as she had been. Just as she still was, in so many ways. Chris, on the other hand, had never had the chance to be a child. He'd acted like an adult as far back as she could remember.

Somehow, someway, she wanted to give him back his childhood. Was it even possible?

She opened the door into the bedroom and discovered that Chris wasn't in there. Maybe he'd gotten tired of waiting and used the bathroom down the hall. Peering into the hallway, she saw that a downstairs light was on.

She went downstairs and found him in the kitchen, eating a bowl of macaroni and cheese.

"Hi," she said, sitting across from him.

He glanced up, his eyes shadowed. "Hi, yourself."

"Didn't you eat at your father's?"

"I wasn't hungry then."

"Ah."

"I like your hair that way."

"I'm glad. So do I. The man who cut it said that it will have a tendency to wave more now that it's been layered. The weight of the length pulled out any natural curl I might have." She knew she was chattering, but she wanted to chase his dark mood away.

"I want you to be happy, Maribeth."

So much for chasing a mood away. "I am happy. Can't you see that? I couldn't be happier."

"I tricked you into marrying me."

She eyed him warily. "How did you do that? Were you lying when you said that Bobby called to say he'd gotten married?"

"No."

"Then what was the trick?"

"Offering to marry you when you were too emotional to make a rational decision."

"I was pretty emotional, all right."

"And I took advantage of that."

"I knew what I was doing."

"Not really."

"Let's put it another way, then. I would say that I'm rational at the moment, and I in no way regret having married you."

"You don't?"

"Not at all."

A glimmer of a smile appeared. "I'm glad to hear it."

"You mean you were actually worried about it?"

"Yeah. I feel like I stole you away from the life

you had and loved and brought you up here to a cast of characters that are too bizarre to be believed.''

Encouraged by his smile, she asked, ''What does your dad think you've been doing since you graduated from college?''

''As little as possible. I've had odd jobs on various covert assignments and he found out about them. Because he didn't know they were covers, he was irritated that I was wasting my education and talents.''

''You could have told him the truth.''

''Maybe, although too much talk can hurt you in this business.''

''But he's your father, for Pete's sake.''

''Yeah, so you've pointed out a time or two.''

''Do you really suspect him of being a part of this latest assignment?''

''I've already told you, I can't discuss the assignment with you. Not now. Not ever.''

''Fair enough. Just tell me this. How are you going to feel if you end up arresting your father?''

''If he's doing something illegal, he deserves whatever happens to him.''

''So you wouldn't care.''

''I didn't say that.''

''I can't tell you how relieved I am to hear you say that,'' she replied. Looking around the kitchen, she asked, ''Where did you get the macaroni and cheese?''

''Out of a package I cooked up. There's more on the stove if you want some.''

She hopped up and found a bowl and put a small

amount inside. "I need to make a grocery list and start planning some meals around here."

"Only if you want."

"I want. Don't you understand, Chris? I want to be a wife to you."

"You already are. You've got my ring on your finger to prove it."

She stuck her tongue out at him and he grinned. Then they both laughed.

Later, when they went upstairs, Chris made slow, exquisitely sensual love to her in ways she could never have imagined until he had her pleading for mercy from the onslaught. She forgot their conversations that evening in the heat of the moment, only to recall them in the days ahead when she worked at setting up a routine around his schedule.

She'd forgotten to tell him her idea about what she could do with her time now that she was living in Dallas. It was Friday before she'd decided how to bring up the subject. It was easy enough to plan his favorite dinner. She'd bought the T-bone steaks earlier that day. She intended to have him grill them over charcoals outside while she fried potatoes and made a big salad.

When the doorbell rang, she assumed it was a salesman of some sort and hurried to answer it. It was almost four o'clock. She was expecting Chris home before long.

She opened the door and then stood there in shock, thankful she had the solid door to hang on to. The man standing there looked just as shocked.

"Maribeth?"

"Bobby?"

"What are you doing here?" they both said at the same time.

Bobby looked ashen and she wondered if he was going to faint. Maribeth could certainly relate to the feeling.

"If you've come to see Chris, he isn't here, but I expect him soon. Would you like to come inside and wait for him?"

She looked past him and saw his truck sitting in the driveway. There was no one in it. She looked back at him and noticed that his face now looked flushed with embarrassment.

"You're the last person I ever expected to open that door," he drawled, his gaze not quite meeting hers.

"Why don't you come inside, Bobby? It's too hot to stand here with the door open."

"Oh, yeah. Sure." He walked inside, taking off his hat and turning it in his hands by the brim.

"Come on back to the kitchen. I'll fix you some tea if you'd like."

Bobby cleared his throat. "Yeah. Thanks. I could use something to drink. I've been driving for several hours."

She'd been cleaning house today and still wore her oldest clothes and a scarf around her hair. She could at least take the scarf off, she decided, tugging at it on the way to the kitchen.

"You cut your hair," he said, following her into the room.

"Yes."

He seemed to be studying everything about her without once meeting her gaze. Seeing how uncomfortable he was made her feel a little better. Actually a lot better. He looked tired.

She hadn't seen him in months. She wondered if she'd ever actually looked at him when he came home, or whether she saw the man she wanted to see. Looking at the man who had sat down on one of the bar stools, she was aware of a great many changes from the boy she'd grown up with.

Without the gauzy transparency of hero worship that she'd always wrapped around him, he was quite ordinary. He seemed shorter, but that was probably because she was used to being with Chris. His hair had darkened from blond to a light brown. His eyes were as blue as ever, startling in his deeply tanned face. She'd always loved his eyes.

She turned away and began to chop vegetables to go into the salad she'd planned.

"What are you doing here, Maribeth? You're the last person I ever expected to find here."

"Having a little trouble facing me, are you?"

"What's that supposed to mean?"

"Oh, there's the little matter of a wedding date that was set a couple of weeks ago."

"Hell. Didn't Chris tell you I wouldn't be there? Damn it, I specifically called him so that he'd let you know—"

"Why didn't *you* let me know, Bobby? You were the man I was going to marry. Why didn't you tell me you'd changed your mind?"

"Because I didn't change my mind! Hell, I've

been planning to marry you ever since we were in junior high. There was never anybody else and you know it.''

"I see." She continued to chop vegetables without looking up from the task. "I guess Chris must have gotten your message confused about being in Las Vegas and marrying somebody else."

Bobby stood and walked over to the sliding doors that led to the patio area. "No. He wasn't confused. I was just too ashamed to tell you."

"I can understand why. It was a shameful thing to pull, Bobby."

He turned and looked at her, his eyes haunted. "You think I don't know that? You think I haven't faced it every single day since then? You think I haven't remembered all the plans we made together, all the things we've done together, all the dreams we had? I went a little haywire, that's all. It was just a normal thing at first, getting jittery about finally getting hitched. And I've really been on a roll lately, winning my rounds, racking up the points. I guess I was scared that everything was going to change."

What could she say to that?

Bobby cleared his throat. In a gruff voice, he said, "If it makes you feel any better, I want you to know I'm sorry for hurting you. You never deserved that."

"I agree. I never did."

"Maribeth, you're still just as much a part of me as one of my arms or legs. I haven't felt the same since—"

"Well, hello, Bobby," Chris said from the doorway of the garage, "what a surprise to see you here."

Bobby spun around with a tremendous look of relief on his face. "Chris! There you are! I was passing through Dallas and was hoping I could crash here for the night. I didn't know you already had company. I guess you can imagine how surprised I was to find Maribeth here."

Maribeth could feel Chris's gaze on her, but she refused to look up. Instead she slipped the salad she'd just completed into the refrigerator and began to peel the potatoes for the French fries.

"Where's your wife, Bobby?" Chris asked, going to the refrigerator and reaching inside for two bottles of beer. He handed one to Bobby who looked grateful enough to cry.

"I, uh, well. That whole thing was just sort of a lark." He darted a glance at Maribeth. "I mean, hell, Chris, you know how it is. We'd all been drinking and—"

"That happens fairly often with you these days, doesn't it, Bobby? That's a way to get yourself killed on one of those bulls."

Bobby grinned, looking cocky. "I never drink before I'm going to ride. You know me better than that, Chris."

"I thought I did."

Bobby flushed. "Yeah. I was just telling Maribeth here how sorry I am for hurting her."

"I'm sure she appreciates hearing about your feelings on the matter."

"The thing is, Leona and I—well, neither one of

us was really thinking clearly. We knew after a couple of days that us being a couple would never work out. She's already talking about getting an annulment. She took off for Montana a week ago.''

Maribeth refused to look at Chris but she could feel his eyes on her.

''Sorry to hear that,'' he said. ''Why don't you come outside with me? I need to start some coals for the grill.'' He stepped outside and held the door open for Bobby. ''I've got some good-looking T-bones in there I plan to charcoal. Think you could wrap yourself around one of them?''

Bobby followed him out so quickly it was almost more than Maribeth could do not to laugh out loud. It was obvious the man couldn't get far enough away from her.

''Oh, no, that's all right,'' she heard Bobby say. ''You've already made plans and all. I don't want to butt into anything.''

''You aren't butting in, Bobby. It's good to see you again. You know you're always welcome to stay here whenever you're in town. It's just been a while, hasn't it?''

Maribeth recognized the subtle tone of amusement in Chris's voice. He was enjoying seeing how uncomfortable Bobby was as much as she had been. Not that Bobby didn't deserve a little squirming for the way he'd handled the matter.

And he wasn't even going to stay married!

What a narrow escape she'd had. It was almost scary to think about the fact that she could easily be married to Bobby right now and it could be Chris who had come to visit.

The thought sobered her. The suggestion that she would not be married to Chris Cochran was frightening. Tomorrow was their second-week anniversary. In fact, Bobby Metcalf was their very first guest.

How was that for being bizarre?

She'd expected to hate Bobby forever. She'd expected never to want to see him again, but that hadn't been the case at all. The truth was, seeing him again didn't matter to her one way or the other. Bobby was just somebody she'd known for ages. She had no feelings at seeing him...not anger, not pain, not even pleasure. She might have spent her life with a giant-size crush on him, but she'd never really seen him as a person, a friend.

Not like Chris, who had always been there for her.

Funny how things turn out.

She glanced at the time. She still had a few minutes before she needed to start the fries. Once the grease was hot, they would cook in minutes. Maribeth slipped upstairs to shower and change clothes for dinner. After all, they were entertaining for the first time and she wanted to look her best.

Chris noticed that Maribeth had left the kitchen when he came inside to get the steaks. He felt bad that he hadn't greeted her when he got home. Seeing Bobby Metcalf standing there in his kitchen talking to his wife had unnerved him considerably.

Until he'd looked at Maribeth. She was handling

Bobby's visit just fine, considering that his appearance must have been just as much a shock to her as it was to him.

She'd been wearing her old clothes, and from the looks of the house, she'd spent the day cleaning. He wasn't too surprised that she'd decided to get spruced up for their company.

He had a hunch that Bobby was going to have several shocks coming to him as the evening progressed. Chris couldn't think of anyone more deserving.

He waited until he saw that Maribeth was back in the kitchen before putting the steaks on the grill. A few minutes later she walked out holding a tray.

"I thought we could eat out here tonight, if you'd like." She brought dishes and silverware and a salad. He hurried over to help her with the tray.

She'd changed into one of her new dresses, a sundress with tiny straps across the shoulders and a full skirt that was short enough to show off those sexy legs of hers. She'd also done something to her hair, pulling it away from her face so that it fell in a cascade of waves and curls down her neck and shoulders.

She looked as sexy as hell and his body immediately responded. A quick glance at Bobby made it clear that Maribeth's new look had thrown him yet again.

"My God, Maribeth. Woman, you're dynamite in that outfit." Bobby swore softly. "Don't you agree, Chris?"

Chris took the tray from Maribeth and winked at her before turning back to Bobby. "Oh, Maribeth knows what I think about her."

Bobby was already up and trying to help her set the table. "Well, of course. We've all been friends for years but damn, honey, I've never seen you looking so...so..."

"You've probably never seen me in a dress."

Bobby laughed. "That could be it. I had no idea your legs were, I mean—"

"I think we know what you mean," Chris replied. "Ready for another beer?"

Obviously distracted, Bobby said, "Sure," while he tried to engage Maribeth in conversation. Chris went back into the house, deliberately leaving them alone.

So Bobby wasn't going to stay married and it was more than a little obvious that he was knocked off his feet by Maribeth's new image. The idiot hadn't noticed that he and Maribeth were wearing matching wedding bands. Chris wondered if he was going to have to say something to him, or whether Maribeth would.

Dinner was pleasant enough. Bobby was much more relaxed after the beers he'd had, and he was entertaining them with stories he'd seen and heard on the road. Without being totally conscious of it, the three of them had fallen into their old camaraderie. And why not? They'd been friends for most of their lives.

Chris was comfortable with the situation because he knew that Bobby had used up all of his chances with Maribeth. He could also see that she had come to grips with the kind of relationship she and Bobby had shared, and it was nothing like theirs.

He and Maribeth could talk. They understood each other. Maribeth understood him better than anyone in his life. He'd realized that at his father's party. He hadn't forgotten the questions she'd asked him and the way they pointed out his biased thinking toward his father and how he viewed what had happened to him in his youth.

Supposing, just supposing, that his father really loved him. If that were the case, then Chris had done and said some very hurtful things to the man over the years.

It was only because of his expanding relationship with Maribeth that he had the courage to reevaluate his relationship with his father and accept his own responsibility for the fact that it hadn't been a good one.

''Would you like a piece of pie?''

Maribeth interrupted his reverie. Chris raised his brows. ''Pie? On top of all of this? No, thanks.'' He eyed her with a grin. ''Thought you couldn't cook.''

''I'm not really good at it, but Mollie taught me how to bake a few things.''

Bobby was leaning back in his chair, looking relaxed. He gave Maribeth his killer smile and said, ''You never did tell me what you're doing visiting up here with Chris, honey. I'm surprised Megan would stand for it.''

Maribeth began to clear the table, carefully stacking the dishes on the tray she'd brought out earlier.

"I'm over twenty-one, Bobby. Megan doesn't have any say-so over me."

"Maybe not legally, but I bet she had a few things to say about your coming up here."

Maribeth looked at Chris and grinned. "Yeah, she did."

"But it didn't stop you."

"No."

"I should have had you go on the road with me. You'd love it, honey. Maybe one of these days you'd like to—"

"I don't think so," Chris said quietly.

Bobby glanced at Chris in surprise. "Come on, Chris. You know me better than to think I'd take advantage of her. Hell, in all these years I've never—"

"Yes, I know you've never, which is the only thing that saved our friendship."

Bobby straightened in his chair. "Hey, Chris. I know what I did was wrong, but I've apologized. Maribeth knows how I feel."

"Did you ever bother to ask her how she dealt with the fact that you disappeared on her three days before her wedding? Did you ever wonder how she was able to face everyone in Agua Verde and tell them what you had done?"

Bobby squirmed. "Well, I'm sure it wasn't easy. I figure I'm going to have to steer clear of the place for a while until something else happens for everybody to gossip about." He turned to Maribeth. "I guess I just figured you'd handle things like you always have."

"Actually, Chris was a big help."

"That's good. I guess that's what friends are for, to help out." He made a great show of stretching and yawning. "Look, I've really enjoyed visiting with y'all, but I've been on the road for hours and I'm really beat. I don't mind sacking out on the sofa. I've slept on harder surfaces before."

Chris said, "There's no reason to do that, Bobby. You know where the guest bedroom is. You're welcome to use it."

"Oh. Well, I just figured that...well...with Maribeth here and all, that she was sleeping in there."

Maribeth gave Bobby that friendly full-of-sunshine smile that always made Chris's heart soar with love for her and said, "Oh, no, Bobby. I'm sleeping with Chris."

Nine

Maribeth was already in bed when Chris finally came into the bedroom. He closed the door behind him, then leaned against it, looking at her.

"Well?" she asked.

"The guy's heartbroken."

She laughed. "Of course he is."

Chris pushed away from the door. "Actually there's every likelihood he is." He walked over to the bed and sat down, pulling his shoes and socks off. "The one constant in his life has always been you, Maribeth. Over the years you've accepted him without reservation, forgiven him time after time when he was thoughtless or self-absorbed. He took you for granted. He's probably never thought about a life without you in it somewhere. If the truth were known, I have a strong hunch that Bobby stopped by here tonight to get the lay of the land where you were concerned. Finding you here was a shock, it was true, but by the time dinner was over, he was already convinced that he'd gotten back into your good graces.''

''Surely even Bobby isn't that insensitive.''

He laughed at the disbelief in her voice. He stood long enough to take off the rest of his clothes, then slid into bed next to her. ''I don't think it ever occurred to him that you could look at another man.''

''Much less sleep with one.'' She curled up on his shoulder.

''Exactly.'' He trailed his fingers down her spine and was rewarded with her sigh of contentment.

''So the shock was pretty intense, huh?''

''Yeah.''

She brushed her lips across his. ''Tough.''

''My sentiments, exactly.''

She straightened so that she could see his face. ''We're no longer kids playing games, Chris. I would have thought he'd know that.''

''Bobby's beginning to get the picture now, anyway.'' He pulled her across him so that she straddled his body. From this position he had a full range of motion to sculpt and shape her breasts. He took full advantage of it. ''He had his chance and he blew it.''

She ran her hands over his chest. ''Oh, Chris,'' she whispered. ''It scares me to think how close I came to making a horrible mistake.''

''Then you don't consider our marriage a mistake?''

"Not at all."

"Even if I send you home tomorrow?"

Her hands stopped. "What do you mean, home? I am home."

"I want you to go to Agua Verde for a few days. This assignment I'm on is about ready to blow, which means I've got to make myself scarce for the next week or so. I want you to be unavailable as well."

"Couldn't I just go with you?"

"You're too distracting."

"I certainly hope so."

"You can take my car."

"Your beautiful baby? Are you sure you can live without it?"

"No. But I'm going to do my best."

"You trust me to drive it?"

"I trust you totally."

"When do I have to go?"

"In the morning. You may not have noticed, but I actually came home early tonight so we'd have this evening together, since this would be our last one for a while."

"It's going to be dangerous, isn't it, Chris?"

"C'mon, Maribeth. It's a job and I'm trained to do it. It's just that I don't want to worry about you."

"Why would you do that?"

"I don't know. Guess it's just a habit of mine I can't seem to break. So. Will you go visit your family?" He lifted her, positioning her over him, then smoothly entered her.

She wriggled with pleasure and sighed, gently

rocking on him. "Married two weeks and you're already trying to get rid of me."

He was having a little trouble breathing and more trouble concentrating. "But it was a great two weeks," he managed to say.

"Mmm," she agreed, moving more rapidly.

"And when, umm, this is…o-over…we'll have plenty…m-m-m-more."

"I'll remind you of that—" she whispered urgently "—as well as of this."

It was a long time later and they were almost asleep before Maribeth remembered to ask, "How long will I have to be gone?"

"Hopefully no more than a few days."

She curled into him a little closer. "At least I'll have some really good memories to take with me."

He held her for the longest time, staring into the dark. Would she want to have anything to do with him, once she found out what he'd been doing?

By the time Maribeth left the Dallas city limits she was in love with Chris's car. She couldn't believe how fun it was to drive. How responsive it was. It carried the faint scent of Chris's after-shave, which she savored.

She missed him already. He'd been gone when she woke up that morning, but he'd left her a note telling her that he would be in touch and for her not to worry. She didn't even know how he'd managed to leave, since she had the car. She had forgotten to ask so many things the night before. He must have had someone pick him up.

Telling her not to worry was like telling her not to think about the black horse. If he hadn't mentioned it, she might not have thought about it. Now she could think of nothing else.

She just kept feeling a sense of uneasiness, the farther south she drove. What was it? It didn't have anything to do with Bobby, she knew that. He, too, was gone. She'd heard his truck drive away before daylight.

What a sense of freedom there had been for her when she realized that although she may have loved Bobby, she really didn't like him. He'd fallen in with a rambunctious crowd that encouraged his wildness. What had been attractive to her in the young boy and rowdy teenager was much less attractive to her in the grown man.

She was at peace now. She had a husband who was attentive, attractive and adorable. What more could she possibly want?

Love?

Where had that come from? Of course she loved Chris. Why, she had loved him for years. Maybe she hadn't understood her feelings for him at the time. How could she, through that haze of hero worship around Bobby?

What she didn't understand, and could not help wondering about, was how Chris felt about her. If his actions were any indication, he was attracted to her, felt comfortable with her, enjoyed her company.

So why is he sending you away?

That has something to do with his job, and the fact that their marriage had come at an awkward time in his work. She tried to put the idea that he was finding his marriage inconvenient out of her mind.

She wanted to see her family again anyway. Chris had just offered her the opportunity to do so. Stop imagining problems where they don't exist, she muttered to herself, glad to see from a sign she'd just passed that she didn't have too much farther to go.

As soon as she parked the car in front of the ranch house, there was a clamor of children's voices. "It's Maribeth! Mama, look who's here. It's Maribeth!"

In addition to Megan's three, she also spotted Mollie's three racing around the yard. Good. Mollie must be over visiting. She'd timed her arrival perfectly.

"Hi, guys," she said, after carefully closing the gate behind her. "Looks like you've been having fun."

Each one of them had something to share with her, so it took her a while to reach the porch, climb the stairs and get inside the kitchen door.

"Y'all go on and play now," Megan said, when they tried to follow her into the house, "and let Maribeth rest for a minute. You can see her later." She turned to Maribeth and grinned. "Well, my goodness, honey. I don't have to ask how you like married life. It's obvious that it's agreeing with you. You look scrumptious."

She hugged her, then motioned to one of the kitchen chairs. "Sit down and let me get you something to drink. Tea, soda, lemonade, you name it."

"Iced tea sounds wonderful."

Then they both asked at the same time,

"Where's Chris?"

"Where's Mollie?"

Both tried to answer at the same time, then burst out laughing. Megan said, "You first. What did you do with your new husband?"

"He was really busy with work and suggested I might want to take some time to come visit. It sounded like a good idea to me. I've got so much to tell you and Mollie, about Chris's dad, our honeymoon in Atlanta and Miami, the new house and seeing Bobby." She paused for a breath. "But I don't want to have to tell it all twice." She looked around again. "Is Mollie upstairs?"

Megan set two glasses and a plate of cookies on the table. "She's not here. I offered to keep the children today, more for Deke's peace of mind than anything."

Maribeth straightened. "What's wrong? What's happened?"

Megan grinned. "Nothing much. Mollie fainted yesterday and scared Deke half to death. 'Course he rushes her to the doctor's office right away and they found out she's a few weeks pregnant."

"Mollie's pregnant again? I thought Deke absolutely swore she wasn't going through all that again."

"What he means is *he* can't go through all of it again, but it looks like he's going to have to, 'cause the doctor confirmed it. I guess there's no guarantee with any method short of doing without and Mollie made it clear she wasn't going to stand for that. Of course, she's thrilled to death. She'd have a dozen if she could.''

''Amy's four now. So she shouldn't have too much trouble with a new one to care for.''

''That's what I told Deke. The man's not rational where Mollie's concerned, especially not after losing his first wife shortly after she gave birth to Jolene.''

''I thought that given enough time, he'd get over his fear.''

''Not Deke. He demanded that Mollie stay in bed for a couple of days to rest. The doctor admitted she was probably pushing herself a little and bed rest wouldn't hurt.''

''Guess your hands are full, with all of them.''

''Travis helps to keep an eye on them. Plus I still have help several times a week. I don't mind.''

''I wonder if I could stay with Mollie for a few days and look after things for her?''

''A few days! I thought you just came for an overnight.''

''Chris talked as though he'd be tied up all week.''

''Oh.'' Megan studied her younger sister for a long while. ''Are you sure things are okay? You said you'd seen Bobby.''

''Oh, yes. As a matter of fact, he dropped by to see Chris yesterday. He had no idea I was there. And when he saw me he assumed I was up there visiting a friend. It never occurred to him that Chris and I were married.''

''I can understand that. You caught everyone by surprise with that one.''

"I have to admit that it was rather pleasing to be able to face Bobby in such a way. Even if he didn't want me, he found out that someone else did."

"I can understand how you feel, but getting married out of spite isn't the greatest basis on which to build a relationship."

"I know, Megan. But Chris and I have more than that together."

"I'm glad to hear it." She finished her tea and stood. "I've got to check on the children. You might give Mollie a call and let her know you're here."

"Better than that. I think I'll drive over and surprise her."

"Will you be back for supper?"

"Maybe not. I could stay over there and make something. Is Deke picking up his gang?"

"Yes. I tried to get him to let them stay overnight but he said he could handle them once he was through today. He planned his time so that he could stay close to home for the rest of the week."

"Then he can use some help feeding them." She gave her sister a quick hug. "I'll see you later."

She found Mollie in the kitchen when she arrived at her home. "Deke's going to tie you to that bed if he catches you up," she said by way of greeting through the screen door.

Mollie spun around and gave a little squeak. "Oh, Maribeth, I didn't hear you drive up." She chuckled. "And you're right. Deke would be hollering if he saw me up. But darn it, I'm always wanting something to snack on. So I snuck out of bed." She gave

Maribeth a big hug. "You're looking great, baby sister. I take it Megan filled you in on my news."

"Oh, yes. I'm so thrilled for you."

"I am, too. It was an accident. I swear it was, but I'm not sorry to be pregnant. I've just got to convince Deke that I'll be all right. However, after this one, I have a hunch he'll make sure I can't get pregnant again."

"Maybe you'll have another boy, so you'll have two pair."

"I don't care what it is, as long as it's healthy. I just look forward to having a baby in the house again." She grabbed a bowl of fruit and said, "Come on back and talk to me. Deke will be pleased you're here to keep me company and I want to hear about everything that's happened to you since you left."

Maribeth trailed behind her sister down the hallway and into the bedroom. Mollie looked pale. Knowing her, Maribeth could imagine that she was trying to do the work of three people around there.

"I'll talk for a little while, but then I want to start dinner so that it will be ready when Deke gets back with the children."

"Oh, you don't have to do that."

"I know, but I want to. I'm only beginning to realize how spoiled I was all these years, letting you and Megan do most of the work."

Mollie stretched out on the bed and folded her hands across her stomach, a tiny smile playing around her mouth. She listened while Maribeth described the plane, and Kenneth, the flights, the hotels, and Chris's home. Then she told her about Bobby's visit.

"What I don't understand is why Chris sent you down here. A lot of men work long hours, but that doesn't mean their wives have to leave home."

"I guess it's because I'm so new there and don't know anyone. Our marriage was so unexpected that he wasn't ready to have me there on a full-time basis. But it's only for a few days. We're both adjusting to being married to each other."

"Didn't you say he flew one of the company planes for his father?"

"Yes, but he also works for the government as one of the agents dealing with the drug problems we're having." Maribeth looked away for a moment. "I'm not supposed to tell anyone about that part, so please don't say anything to anybody. I have a hunch that what he does is really dangerous."

"Maribeth, what have you gotten yourself into?"

"I'm not sure, Mollie, and that's the truth."

"Your impulsiveness has always worried me, but I was hoping you were growing out of it."

"I'm really lucky that it was Chris who came to my rescue."

"But when are you going to get to the point in your life that you don't need to be rescued, that you don't need to be sent somewhere to be looked after?"

"Actually I'm hoping you'll let me look after you, at least for a few days."

"Of course you're welcome here. The children

adore you. We all do. I guess I still see you as a child.''

''Even though I'm only two years younger than you.''

''Yes. Even then.''

''Once Chris has more time to spend with me, I intend to tell him about my idea for something for me to do up there. His place is large enough to have a small horse barn and a couple of paddocks. I'm thinking about checking to see if I can work with a couple of horses at a time, maybe boarding or possibly training. That's what I love to do and I noticed that out where Chris lives there are several places with horses.''

''You haven't mentioned it to Chris yet?''

''No. We really haven't had much time with each other.''

''You're happy with him?''

''Oh, yes.''

''Then that's what counts, Maribeth. I want to see you happy.''

Hours later Maribeth sat at the dining room with the family laughing at the antics of the children as they told their mom and dad about their day. She enjoyed the children so much. That was something she and Chris hadn't talked about, but she hoped he wanted a family.

There were many things they hadn't talked about. Since their marriage they had been on a glamorous honeymoon and played house a few days. Now she was back in Agua Verde and having trouble not thinking her life with Chris had been a very pleasant dream.

They were eating dessert when she thought she heard the name "Cochran" mentioned on the television in the other room. The children had forgotten to turn it off when they were called to supper.

She hastily excused herself and went into the other room. The news had on-the-scene reporters discussing something that was going on in Dallas. Just as she reached the television, a shot of Kenneth Cochran was flashed on the screen. She listened in shock as the news anchor announced, "Kenneth Cochran, well-known businessman was one of several men arrested today on charges of being part of a widespread money-laundering system that spread from Florida to Texas. Mr. Cochran's attorney has refused all interviews on behalf of his client, other than to say that the charges are unfounded and will be easily disproved. Because of the amount of money involved in this case, and because federal investigators fear that he might try to leave the country if released on bail, Kenneth Cochran is being held without bail. We'll have the latest sports update after this word."

Maribeth stared blankly at the screen while an animated commercial flashed in front of her. Mollie spoke from behind her. "That was Chris's father, wasn't it?"

"Yes," she whispered.

"Do you think Chris knows about it?"

She turned and faced Mollie, her heart pounding. "Oh, Mollie, I think he's one of the investigators that helped to arrest him!"

Mollie looked horrified. "He had his own father arrested?"

"He really dislikes his father. I tried to get him to talk to me about his feelings, but you know Chris. He never lets anyone close to him."

"But do you think he's guilty?"

"How would I know? I just met the man. I know he has money. Lots of money. I never questioned where it came from. Oh, Mollie, I've got to call Chris. I need to talk to him."

"Use the phone in Deke's office. You'll have more privacy there."

Maribeth called their house but no one answered. When the machine came on, she said, "Chris, this is Maribeth. I'm at Mollie's. I'll be staying here." She gave the number. "Please call me as soon as you come home."

She hung up slowly, wondering if she could have said something more. Wondering what she could have said. What was Chris feeling now that all of this had happened?

She waited until almost midnight before getting ready for bed. He'd never returned her call. Before going to sleep, she decided to call him once again. This time the phone rang and rang but the machine didn't pick up. Had he been home and disconnected it? There was no way to know. She could only wait until he called her.

The next several days were like living in a nightmare to Maribeth. As more and more reporters dug into the story, it filled more and more news spots and newspapers. Three weekly magazines had lengthy articles on the money-laundering scheme.

It hadn't taken them long to discover a federal investigator by the name of Cochran had worked on the case and that he was the son of the man arrested. The media had a field day with that one.

They kept referring to Chris as the mysterious federal agent because no one had been able to locate him for an interview. They found a photograph of him that was shown with every news update. They'd even discovered that he had recently married, but so far hadn't been able to locate Maribeth. A few reporters had reached the two ranches but Travis and Deke quickly made it clear they wouldn't tolerate having their lives disrupted over the media's need to make news out of any and everything.

By far the worst thing was that Chris had never gotten back in touch with Maribeth. Not once since she'd left Dallas.

By Friday night, she was beginning to wonder if he had ever intended to stay in touch with her. She'd had six days to think about the two weeks she'd spent with Chris, to remember everything he had said and done, to remember all that he hadn't said and done. Never once had he talked about his feelings for her, other than to point out their friendship. He'd never talked about their future together.

He'd made love to her as though he cared for her, but then, she had no way of knowing or comparing what had happened between them with the way a man treated the woman he loved. But if Chris loved her, wouldn't he have said so? Had she been so naive as to take his feelings for her for granted without questioning him?

By Saturday she was numb. They'd been married for three weeks. She hadn't seen or spoken to him in a week, one-third the length of their marriage.

The phone rang sometime after eleven that night. Everyone in the family was in bed but Maribeth wasn't asleep. She hadn't been able to sleep much all week.

She heard a tap on the door. "Maribeth?" It was Deke. "Chris is on the phone."

She leaped out of the bed as though it were on fire, grabbed her robe and ran down the hall to Deke's office.

"Hello, Chris? Where are you?" she asked, out of breath.

His deep voice sounded tired. "That doesn't matter. I just wanted to see how you were."

"Upset that I haven't heard from you. What's going on? How is your dad? How are you? Why haven't you called?"

She heard him clear his throat. "I've been doing some serious thinking about us, and I really think it would be a good idea for you to talk to a lawyer."

"A lawyer! Why?"

"He can explain the law to you. He'll be able to tell you whether you can file for an annulment or whether you'll have to file for a divorce."

Maribeth's knees buckled and she sank to the floor beside the desk. "You're saying you want a divorce?"

There was a long pause. "I, uh, yeah, that's really

what I'm saying. I'm sorry the way things worked out for us. I don't think either one of us gave much thought to our future together. It would never have worked out. We should have seen that."

She clutched the phone so tightly her fingers ached. "I don't agree with you, Chris." She could feel her heart pounding like a drum and she wondered if he could hear it as well. "I think we were getting along fine. We weren't having any problems that I could see."

He didn't answer right away and she couldn't think of anything more to say. Finally he said, "The thing is, Maribeth, I'm not cut out for marriage. I've always known that. I thought I could help you out as a friend, but I...I can't follow through in the long haul. Besides, once Bobby's free maybe the two of you can—"

"Have you been drinking, Chris Cochran?" she demanded. "What's the matter with you? You were there. You saw what Bobby's like these days. He's still a teenager, and an immature one at that! Couldn't you see how relieved I was that I didn't marry him, how grateful I am that I married you?"

"Well, I'll accept your gratitude. I'm glad I could help out, but you need to be with someone like yourself. Someday you're going to meet the man who can give you everything you want and deserve."

"*You* gave me everything I could ever want, Chris, and much more than I ever deserved."

"Including a name that's been splashed across the United States."

"Is that what this is all about? Do you honestly

think I care what's being said about you, or about Kenneth?''

''If you don't, you should be. This whole thing has blown up in ways no one could have predicted. It may cost me my job. I may end up being indicted myself. There's been suggestions that I was part of the deal, playing both sides.''

''But that's not true.''

''How do you know, Maribeth? You don't know me or what I'm capable of. I could have been lying to you from the very beginning. Look, let's try to salvage the friendship, okay? I don't want to lose that. Go talk to a lawyer. Tell him I'll pay his fee, whatever it is. Let's put this behind us and get on with our lives.''

''You can't mean it, Chris. I thought that you—''

''That I what?''

''I thought that you loved me.''

''You were my childhood friend. Of course I loved you.''

She closed her eyes in an effort to stop the tears that were rolling down her cheeks.

''I never tried to be something I wasn't with you, Maribeth. I tried my damnedest to be straight with you.''

''I know.''

''Look, I've got to let you go. Keep the car if you want. I'm not going to need it. I'll send you money each month to—''

''For what?''

''You're my wife. I'll pay your bills until—''

''No, you won't. If you don't want to stay married

to me, fine. I'm not going to hang on to you if you want to be free. But I'm not going to take money from you. If this is what you want, then let's make it a clean break. I'm sorry you feel the way you do. But I'm not going to fight you.''

"Take care of yourself, okay? Let me hear from you. If you ever need anything, let me know.''

"Goodbye, Chris.''

She sat in the dark on the floor, cradling the phone in her arms. How strange. Within a few weeks both of the men in her life—the only men in her life other than her brothers-in-law—had made it clear they didn't want her as part of their lives.

What was the flaw in her that they could see so clearly that she'd never known was there? What was so wrong with her? How could she have reached this age and not understood that she had nothing that a man wanted?

Of course she wasn't going to keep his car. She wanted nothing that reminded her of him. Tomorrow she would drive it back to Dallas and leave it at his home. She still had a key to the house. She would drive back, pack the rest of her things, get a cab to the airport and fly back to Austin. She'd get Travis or Megan to meet her plane.

All right. She probably deserved this. She'd had too much pride to admit that Bobby had spurned her, so she had jumped into marriage with Chris. At least she still had enough pride not to beg him to reconsider.

If he didn't want her, she'd learn to accept it. Somehow. But not tonight. Tonight she could only feel the pain of losing the man she'd only recently discovered she loved with all her heart.

Ten

The weather appeared to be sympathizing with her mood. It had been raining on her steadily since she'd left Austin on Interstate 35 and headed north. By the time she reached Dallas she felt that the sky had been crying the tears she could no longer shed.

Because of the uncertainty of the weather, she'd decided not to say anything to the family when she left. She might not fly back right away. It would give her a little time to come to grips with what had happened.

Wherever Chris was, she was fairly certain he wasn't staying at home. Reporters would have staked out the place, waiting to talk to him about the situation. So she would stay at the house. Once she left his home, she would leave him the keys to the house and car he'd given her.

She slowed when she got to his driveway and noticed that he'd taken the name off his mailbox. No reason to advertise, she supposed, in case some enterprising soul hadn't as yet found him.

The place looked deserted. The grass needed trimming. The windows stared blankly, their draperies closed. She pulled around back and used the remote to open the garage door. There was no reason to advertise her presence, either.

Once inside, she looked around the kitchen. There were a couple of glasses sitting on the counter that hadn't been there when she left. So Chris had been here at one time.

She checked the refrigerator. She'd stocked it last week, thinking that she was setting up a routine for their marriage. Being back in the house was even more painful than she'd expected it to be. She'd hoped to be able to protect herself from hurt by holding on to her anger that Chris could so easily push her away, negating what they had together. Instead the pain seeped in when she remembered being here with him, his teasing her, his loving her.

Stop it! she admonished herself. *Haven't you already learned not to live in a fantasy world? The reality is that Chris doesn't want you.* There was no reason to think he ever did.

She went upstairs and when she reached the bedroom found the door shut. Opening it, she was surprised to find the room almost black. Drapes covered the windows. Chris must have come home to sleep during the day at one point, she decided.

She walked over and tugged on the draperies, opening them to the dreary light outside.

"Wha—? Who's there?" Chris's voice behind her caused her to jump in surprise. She spun around.

"Chris?"

From the light coming in through the window she saw him sprawled across the top of the bed, still dressed except for his shoes. His clothes were rumpled and he didn't look as though he'd shaved in a while.

"What are you doing here?" he asked, sitting up on the side of the bed and scrubbing his hand across his face.

"I was going to ask you the same thing."

He glanced up at her, his eyes bloodshot. "Well, hell, Maribeth. I live here. Where did you expect me to be?"

She was tempted to repeat his words back to him. Instead she said, "I thought you said you'd be working. Since you weren't answering your phone, I just thought—"

"I unplugged it days ago, not long after the story broke. Once the media found out the connection between me and my father, they wouldn't stop calling."

She walked over to the chest of drawers where she'd stored her things. Keeping her back to him, she asked, "Why didn't you return my calls that first night?"

He was quiet for a moment. Then he said, "It really doesn't matter at this point, does it?" He walked over to the bathroom and paused in the doorway. "You never said what you're doing here."

She turned and looked at him. He looked awful, as though he hadn't slept in days. Instead of answering him, she asked, "When was the last time you ate?"

"I don't remember."

"Why don't you get cleaned up and I'll have something ready for you to eat when you come down?"

"Why would you want to do anything for me? Didn't you hear anything I said last night?"

"Oh, yes. You said you'd like to hang on to the friendship. If that's all you want from me, I can accept that. I'm offering to feed you as a friend, not the woman you married."

For a moment she thought he'd flinched at the last word but when she continued to watch him, she decided she was mistaken. As usual, his expression gave nothing of his thoughts away.

She turned away and went downstairs, mentally running through what was there that she could quickly prepare for a hot meal.

Chris stood under the hard pressure of hot water beating down on him, wondering if he was ever going to wake up from the nightmare he'd found himself in.

When he'd first seen Maribeth standing there in the pale light from the window, he was certain he was hallucinating again. She'd been in his thoughts so much since the last time he'd seen her asleep in his bed that he assumed his mind had finally given way and conjured her here.

Why hadn't she had the sense to stay in Agua Verde where she belonged? She didn't deserve to be involved in this messy situation.

He'd once accused her of being naive. Hell, that was a laugh, wasn't it? Looking back, he could see that he'd been the one who'd been naive, blindly following orders, believing that he was working on the side of right and justice.

Wasn't he looking to stop the flow of drugs into the States? If he was assigned to work for his father, to follow his father's activities and report back, wasn't that part of it? Hadn't he felt self-righteous about what he was doing? If his father was doing something illegal, then he would be caught.

But what if his father wasn't doing something illegal? What if a few of his trusted executives had seen a way to make some money on the side and had carefully set it up to look as if it was the head of the company who was involved?

Chris was beginning to understand, much to his disgust at his own prejudices that had stopped him from seeing it sooner, how he had been used to help set up his father, to frame him. The first few days after the arrests had been made he'd begun to notice things he hadn't noticed before. He heard men he'd worked with deliberately lie about certain events that had taken place and he realized that he was in as deep trouble as his father.

All with a deliberate intent from someone within the agency.

He wasn't certain who was behind it, or how many agents had been in on the scheme. What he had to do was take responsibility for allowing himself to be used.

It was going to get much worse. He was going to be fighting a great many people on many different levels and issues. There was no way he could drag Maribeth into the mess. He had no guarantee that he would be able to prove anything. He refused to take her down with him.

She heard him on the stairs. By the time he reached the kitchen she had coffee and orange juice poured and was placing eggs, hash browns and bacon on a warmed plate.

"You look a little better," she observed judiciously. She nodded toward the table. "Eat."

"What about you?"

"I stopped a while ago and got something." She didn't want to admit that she hadn't been able to eat much since the last time she'd seen him. After their conversation last night, she could scarcely swallow anything.

Maribeth kept busy straightening the kitchen, wiping down the counters, anything so that she didn't have to look at Chris. The silence in the room seemed to develop its own weighty presence.

"Why did you come back, Maribeth?" he asked sometime later.

She glanced around and saw that he had eaten everything she'd put in front of him and was now drinking his third cup of coffee.

She sat down across from him and folded her hands on the table. "I could give you several reasons, all valid, but the truth of the matter is, I couldn't stay away. Those two weeks we were together may have meant nothing to you, Chris, but they changed my life in ways I'm only now beginning to understand. My home isn't in Agua Verde any longer. I can visit and I will because I love my sisters and their families but I can't go back there...not to live."

As though her answer would mean very little to him, he asked, "So what are you going to do?"

She looked away from him, staring sightlessly out the sliding glass door.

"I haven't gotten that far, yet. I wasn't here long enough to make any contacts. I'd had an idea of something I wanted to discuss with you the day Bobby showed up. I forgot to mention it then. And now? Well, I don't guess it would work for me."

"What was it?"

"I wanted to build a small horse barn back there—" she nodded toward the back of his property "—and maybe board or train horses, much like what I was doing with Travis, but on a much smaller scale."

"It wouldn't be a good idea to be anywhere around me at the moment. It's a good thing you haven't taken time to change your identification. The family name won't ever be quite so illustrious after all this."

"Do you think I care?"

"You should."

She studied him for a long time. "Is that why you said what you did last night? Are you under some misguided notion that you need to protect me from what has happened to your father?"

"It's not just that. I'm being pulled into it. No matter which way I go, I'm going to be made to look like I betrayed either the government investigation or my father."

"How?"

"It's complicated to explain and there's really no need. If you get out now, there's little damage done to your name or reputation."

"So you *are* trying to protect me! Just as you tried to protect me when Bobby got married. That's the reason you sent me back to Agua Verde, isn't it? Not because you were busy, but because of what was going to happen."

"I had no idea it was going to end up like this, believe me."

"Which gave you more reason to protect me. Chris, listen to me. I'm not a child any longer. Maybe it took me a while to grow up and understand how to be an adult, but that doesn't mean I'm not willing to take on the responsibility of being an adult."

"This isn't your fight."

"I know. But it's yours and you are my husband. Have you already forgotten those vows we took? Did you think they were just part of some meaningless ritual to go through? We committed our lives to each other, not just the good times or the fun times. We were fortunate to have those days for our honeymoon. It gave us a chance to forget about the world and discover each other, but we never pretended to each other that our life together would be spent in that way.''

He gave her a lopsided smile. ''I guess we did sort of blot out the world there for a while, despite everything going on around us.''

''Without a doubt. And we can do it again, from time to time, but I expected to face some downtimes as well. I don't want to run from what's happening now. I want this marriage to work and I think it can, if you'll give it a chance.

''I know you don't love me, at least as you would a wife, but I know you care about me as a friend. Let me give you that friendship in return. You were there for me when I desperately needed someone. Will you let me be here for you now?''

They sat across the table from each other, each intently watching the other. Maribeth knew she was fighting for the life she wanted, if she could only break through the wall he kept around him.

''You don't think I love you?'' he finally asked.

''Haven't you been listening to anything I've been saying?'' she replied with frustration.

He leaned back in his chair and stared up at the ceiling. In a quiet, musing voice, he said, ''I can't remember when I first realized that I loved you. I believe it was our junior year in high school when it finally occurred to me that what I felt for you was considerably more than friendship. But then, I always was a little slow where girls were concerned.''

She straightened in her chair. What was he saying? "Chris?" she murmured.

"Up until then I just thought it was perfectly natural that I wanted to be around you all the time, that regardless of the mood I was in, being around you made me feel better. I never asked myself why I hated summers away or why I resented my father so much for taking me away from what I really wanted...which was to be with you."

She couldn't believe what she was hearing. "But you never said anything back then. Nothing."

He lowered his gaze to meet hers. "It would never have done any good. I always knew that. You've probably forgotten the times when you'd come to me upset because of something Bobby had said or done to hurt your feelings, but those were the times when it was the hardest for me not to betray what I was feeling to you."

She stared at him in wonder. "You always took up for him and made his behavior sound perfectly natural and ordinary, as though all boys acted that way."

He grinned. "Well, mostly that was true. We're not all that sensitive to a young girl's feelings."

"But you were."

He shook his head. "Not with everyone. Just to you. I could almost sense your mood or how you felt by the expression on your face. I can't tell you how many times I just wanted to hold you in my arms and comfort you, instead of smoothing over whatever had happened."

The dull light was gradually fading but neither one of them turned on a lamp.

"So you weren't just doing me a favor by offering to marry me," she said softly.

"I thought I'd already made that clear."

"You love me." She felt the tension that she'd lived with for the past week dissolve within her.

"Yes."

She leaped up from her chair and lunged at him, almost knocking him out of his chair. "Then you're an even bigger idiot than I thought!" She shoved him away from the table, falling into his lap, and shook his shoulders. "How can you be so blind? Don't you know how much I love you and want to stay married to you? Can't you understand that you aren't the only one with deep feelings that go back into our shared past? I'll admit I was stupid not to understand that my feelings for Bobby were all mixed up with my feelings for our shared childhood and you and all that we had together. But it didn't take me long to figure out that what I was feeling for you had nothing to do with friendship."

He grinned at her ferocity and wrapped his arms around her. "Is this a proposal?"

She glared at him. "I don't have to propose to you, you big lug. I'm already married to you. I can't believe you can be so blind!"

"Maribeth?"

"What!"

"Kiss me."

That certainly took the wind out of her sails. "You're not going to send me away?"

"I should. It's the best thing I could do for you. But it took everything I could find inside me to force myself to tell you over the phone I didn't want to be married to you. There's no way in hell I can look you in the eye and say it."

She threw her arms around his neck and burst into tears. "Oh, Chris, I love you so much."

He stood, still holding her. "Before I have to go back to work, do you think you might be able to demonstrate some of that love for me?"

She kissed him and said, "I'll do my best, cowboy, I promise."

It was another five days before Chris could arrange to see his father. He'd had to pull in every favor he had with a lot of officials.

He no longer cared what visiting his father would look like. He didn't care about all the phrases being thrown around, such as "compromising the case against him," "hurting his image within the agency."

What he cared about was seeing his father again.

There were a few things he needed to tell him...things that he'd only come to understand since Maribeth had become a part of his life.

When his father was shown into the small room, Chris felt a lump form in his throat. He'd never seen his dad dressed in any way but the height of fashion. The orange coveralls were far from his usual attire.

There were lines on his face that hadn't been there before, but it was the pain in his eyes that hurt Chris the most.

"Thank you for seeing me," he said quietly once his father was seated. "I wouldn't have blamed you if you'd refused."

His father looked at him for a long moment, no doubt seeing the effect of the strain he'd been under, as well. "I've never refused you anything, son. Why would I start now?"

Chris almost lost his composure then. Why had he never seen that his father loved him? It had always been there. "I wanted to explain what I was doing working for you."

"You don't need to. I managed to figure that out on my own."

"I've worked for the agency since I first got out of school, Dad. It was something that I wanted to do, that I was good at."

"I wish I'd known. You have no idea how painful it was for me to see you taking those dead-end jobs rather than to work with me. If I'd ever needed proof of what you thought of me, that did it. But you were with the agency then, you say?"

"Yes." He took a deep breath and exhaled, trying to release some of the tension within him. "I have no excuse for my attitude toward you all these years, and no way to go back and undo what's been done between us. I couldn't see it, of course, not until Maribeth made me look at what I've been doing."

"How is she, by the way?"

"God, Dad, I don't know what I would do without her. I wake up at night sometimes afraid I dreamed it all and that she's actually married to someone else. The thing is, she's the one who made me look at how much I'm like you. We both want to be the one in control.''

''I can't argue with you there.''

''Neither of us seems to know how to compromise. I realize that I've been fighting you just for the sake of the fight. I used to accuse you and Mom of placing me in the middle of your power struggles. Only now I realize that I've been in a power struggle with you, myself.''

''Well, I would say any power struggle we've been engaged in has been settled to your satisfaction. You've got me behind bars now.''

''I don't believe you had anything to do with any of this,'' Chris said hoarsely.

''Oh? What makes you believe that?''

''I know you are determined to make it big in the business world. And you have. You did it all on your own, without anyone else's help.''

''You could be describing yourself, you know.''

''But you aren't greedy. You don't amass money for the sake of making money. The money part has always been the way you kept score…like Monopoly. You'd get no satisfaction in working to beat the system. You want to win using the system.''

Kenneth studied him for several minutes without saying anything, then he nodded, a small smile hovering. ''Yes, you definitely are my son. And you've reasoned it out without my help.''

''I want you to know that I'm going to do everything I can to prove this case and to bring the real perps in. Right now they think they've got us just where they want us. With all the publicity you've been mentally convicted all over this country. I'm going to show them all they made a big mistake coming after a Cochran.''

"Don't forget that I've got some good people in my corner, son. I always have. I don't care what it looks like, I know I'm going to be able to prove that I wasn't involved.''

"You've got to be worried, Dad. That's only natural.''

"Not about me. I worry about Bambi. This has been tough on her. She hasn't had anyone to turn to that she can trust not to go to the tabloids with her concerns.''

"Maribeth and I'll go over there this evening. It will do all three of us good to talk about it.''

"You'd do that for me?''

"Isn't it about time I started acting like an adult where you're concerned?''

"Thank you, son. Just watch your back out there, and be careful who you trust.''

"I've already figured that one out. I hope it isn't too late. They may end up throwing me in there with you, but somehow I don't think they'll push me that far. I happen to have a couple of friends who are helping me in the in-house investigation.''

His dad smiled. "Go get 'em, tiger.''

"We'll get Bambi to start planning the party we're going to have the day you walk out of here.''

"Sounds good to me.''

"I love you, Dad.'' It was the first time Chris had

ever said it. He was amazed at how easy those words were to say to this man.

His dad blinked rapidly a few times and a muscle in his jaw clenched. Finally he nodded, saying, "The feeling's mutual, son. The feeling's mutual."

Epilogue

"**T**he press is having another field day," Maribeth commented, handing Chris the paper as soon as he walked into the kitchen. He leaned over and kissed her before sitting down to breakfast. "Mmm," she said dreamily, "you smell good."

"It's the after-shave."

"And you. What a combination."

"What's the paper say?"

"Oh, it's full of stories about the new information that was uncovered regarding the government's investigation of the money laundering. Everyone is pointing the finger at everyone else. They're talking about a shake-up at the agency, a full investigation, and so forth and so on. There's very little mention that the charges against your dad have been dropped and that he was released."

"No. That doesn't make the news. Only scandals and crooked agents."

"It's nice to know your name was cleared."

He grinned. "Yeah, I'll agree with that." He glanced at his watch. "When do you want to leave?"

"Sometime after breakfast. If we get down there by midafternoon, I'll be able to help Mollie in the kitchen. She says Thanksgiving is her favorite holiday at mealtime. Megan's been helping her this week, as well. She's doing fine, according to the doctor, but everyone hovers because of Deke."

He pulled her onto his lap and nuzzled her neck. "Are you going to tell them our news?"

"I thought I might wait until Christmas. I want to savor the secret for a while longer."

"Then you'd better muzzle Bambi. I think she's already bought out every baby department in the city, announcing to one and all that she's finally going to be a grandmother, as though she's been waiting for years."

They both laughed. "I'm glad they're going to Agua Verde with us. I want your dad to meet my family."

"Be prepared for him to insist that everyone come to his place for Christmas. You know how he can be. He'll have it all organized with a fleet of limos to bring them up here."

"Actually that might be fun. Wouldn't the kids love it? I think he's going to enjoy them, as well."

"So do I. I suppose I should have checked with you first before I told him about the baby."

"No, you did exactly what your heart told you to do. Never doubt a prompting from your heart. It's never wrong."

"Ah, Maribeth, you are something else. Have I told you how pleased I am to be married to you?"

"Not since you woke me up this morning." She gave him a lingering kiss, then smiled. "Can you think of a better Christmas gift in all the world than to know we've got a baby on the way?"

"What's just as important to me is that he or she is going to get to know his grandfather without any influence."

"You know your mother isn't going to like the changes you're making in your life."

"I know. But she'll have to deal with it. My grandfather reminded me that he's leaving the ranch to me. He already wants me to take more of an active role in the place."

"And you told him that you don't want any part of something that is controlled by the weather and market prices, right?"

"Actually I told him that we'd probably spend part of our time down there, even though I'll be spending much of my time working here with Dad."

"Maybe you can build a runway on the ranch, so we can fly back and forth."

"That's certainly a possibility." He set her on her feet and stood. "C'mon, let's get these dishes out of the way and finish packing. I'm eager to get on the road."

"You always look forward to returning to Agua Verde, don't you?"

"It was always the best part of my life. Or so I thought as a kid. I didn't realize it wasn't the place, it was you. I want to be wherever you are, making certain that you are happy."

"Funny. I feel the same way about you."

"That's probably why we've been friends for so many years. We have so much in common."

He took her by the hand and they companionably went upstairs to find everything they intended to take to the families belonging to the O'Brien sisters of Agua Verde.

It was truly a time for thanksgiving.

* * * * *

...

...

From bestselling author
Annette Broadrick
Comes her most compelling novel yet...
CALLAWAY COUNTRY
On sale May 2000
An earth-shattering explosion...a mysterious
call to duty...the woman he'd
never forgotten. They all beckoned rugged Clay
Callaway—one of the last of
the family's bachelors—home to Texas!
Enjoy this sneak preview of Annette Broadrick's
brand-new
Sons of Texas love story.

Clay Callaway's attention was drawn to a woman dancing nearby. She was tall and held herself proudly. The high-neck, long-sleeve silver dress she wore was provocative in its simplicity, subtly drawing the eye to her sleek lines. She wore her blond hair drawn up in a classic style that emplasized the pure, aristocratic planes of her face.

She looked like a princess to Clay.

Only when the thought registered did he realize who the woman was.

Pamela McCall.

He stiffened. "What is Pamela McCall doing here?" he asked his mother, seated across the table from him.

"All of that happened years ago, Clay," Carina

said in a gentle voice. "Don't you think it's time you forgive her? You're both different people now."

The coltish girl he remembered had matured into a stunning woman. He could feel his heart pounding at the sudden shock of seeing her after all these years.

"You're right," he agreed smoothly, fighting to control his reaction to the unexpected sighting. "She means nothing to me."

Clay draped his arm around his date, movie star Melanie Montez. "Having fun?" he said, leaning over and playfully nipping at her ear.

She chuckled. "Actually, I am. This kind of party has all the ingredients that filled my childhood dreams. To be rubbing shoulders with all the rich and well-known families of Texas is something to be savored."

He straightened. "Ah, now I know why you were so interested when we first met."

She batted her lashes. "Absolutely. To meet one of the Callaways of Texas has always been a fantasy of mine."

He heard a slight rustle behind him and glanced up to see his mother smiling at someone behind him.

Carina held out her hand and said, "Pamela. Come join us and give us a chance to catch up."

Clay fought to maintain no expression at all as Pam eased by him and sat down in the empty chair between him and Carina. "Hello, Mama Cee," she said in a husky voice. A wisp of a floral scent wafted past him. "It's so good to see you again." She slowly turned her head and said, "Hello, Clay."

He noticed that she didn't add how she felt about seeing him again. At least she wasn't being a hypocrite.

Clay nodded. "Pam, I'd like you to meet Melanie Montez." He turned to Melanie and said, "This is Pamela McCall, the senator's daughter. She's been friends with our family for years."

Pam smiled at Melanie. "Hello. I feel a little tongue-tied at meeting you in person. I've really enjoyed your work."

Clay watched Melanie's face as she quickly took in the woman's appearance. He wasn't sure how Pam managed to look both classical as well as seductive, all without baring any part of her body.

Melanie smiled and said, "Thank you," without losing her poise.

Clay hadn't realized it until that moment, but there was a strong resemblance between the two women—both blondes, both tall, and both with eye-catching figures. He hated the thought that he might have been attracted to Melanie because of her resemblance to Pam. He turned to Melanie. "I haven't had a chance to dance with you in a while. Shall we?" he asked smoothly, standing.

Melanie took his hand and rose. She looked over at Pam and said, "It was nice meeting you," before following Clay out on the dance floor.

Once dancing, Melanie asked, "What was that all about?"

Clay pulled her closer so that their bodies touched from chest to knees. "I don't know what you're talking about."

She leaned back in his arms and looked into his eyes. "Now that's interesting. You've never been evasive with me before. One of the things I've most admired about you is how you are so direct with me."

He sighed. "I don't know what you want me to say."

"I want to know what's between you and Ms. McCall. The tension between the two of you was undeniable. If it's none of my business, just say so."

"You're right. I was avoiding answering you because she isn't one of my favorite people. My family thinks the world of her. She grew up in our household more than at her own home." He moved slowly across the dance floor before adding, "And the truth is, we used to date in high school until she made it clear she was no longer interested in a relationship with me."

"Ah. You must have been quite serious about her or it wouldn't still bother you today."

"I was just a kid back then and it doesn't bother me to see her today. Not really. I haven't thought about her in years." He knew that was a lie as soon as it came out of his mouth. He'd worked hard not to think about her and most of the time he'd succeeded. Determined to put his past where it belonged, he added, "I'm much more interested in the future than I am in the past." He knew that statement to be a hundred percent true.

Pam watched them dance together for a moment before turning to Carina. "He's changed, hasn't he?'' She knew the regret she felt was echoed in her voice.

Carina patted her hand. "First loves are always hard to get over. He managed, just as you did. It was a tough time for you both."

"But he's never forgiven me. That's obvious." Pam didn't know why it should bother her after all of these years that she had made an enemy of Clay, but the truth was that it did. She'd been so caught up in her own pain and turmoil that she'd hadn't faced what her decision had done to him.

Carina nodded her head toward Clay. "He's done very well, you know, and loves his career, working in the special forces unit of the army. I don't think he has any regrets. It was just an adjustment to see you here when he wasn't expecting it."

"I want him to be happy. I figured his ego might be bruised but that he would eventually realize I saved us both from a serious mistake."

"Waiting until the night before your wedding to tell a man that you no longer want to marry him takes its toll, honey. He dealt with it the best way he knew how." Carina studied her for a moment before briskly saying, "All of that happened years ago. What I want to hear from you now is what's been going on in your life and more about that delectable-looking young man you're with."

Pam began to talk and forced herself to ignore that fact that she and Clay Callaway had come face-to-face for the first time in twelve years without a bolt of lightning scorching the spot where they met.

If you enjoyed what you just read,
then we've got an offer you can't resist!

Take 2 bestselling love stories FREE!

Plus get a FREE surprise gift!

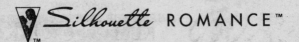